THE HIGH MOUNTAINS OF PORTUGAL

Lisbon, 1904: A man named Tomás discovers an old journal that hints of an extraordinary artefact which — if he can find it — would redefine history. Travelling in one of Europe's earliest automobiles, Tomás sets out in search of this strange treasure . . . Thirty-five years later, a Portuguese pathologist devoted to the murder mysteries of Agatha Christie finds himself at the centre of a murder mystery of his own, and is drawn into the consequences of Tomás's quest . . . Fifty years on, a Canadian senator seeks refuge in his ancestral village in northern Portugal, mourning the loss of his beloved wife. He arrives with an unusual companion: a chimpanzee. It is here that this centuries-old adventure comes to its conclusion . . .

THE HIGH MOUNTAINS OF PORTUGAL

YANN MARTEL

ISIS
LARGE
PRINT

First published in Great Britain 2016
by
Canongate Books Ltd.

First Isis Edition
published 2016
by arrangement with
Canongate Books Ltd.

A catalogue record for this book is available from the British Library.

ISBN 978–1–78541–270–7 (hb)
ISBN 978–1–78541–276–9 (pb)

Published by
F. A. Thorpe (Publishing)
Anstey, Leicestershire

Set by Words & Graphics Ltd.
Anstey, Leicestershire
Printed and bound in Great Britain by
T. J. International Ltd., Padstow, Cornwall

This book is printed on acid-free paper

To Alice, and to Theo, Lola, Felix, and Jasper:
the story of my life

Contents

PART ONE

Homeless

Tomás decides to walk.

From his modest flat on Rua São Miguel in the ill-famed Alfama district to his uncle's stately estate in leafy Lapa, it is a good walk across much of Lisbon. It will likely take him an hour. But the morning has broken bright and mild, and the walk will soothe him. And yesterday Sabio, one of his uncle's servants, came to fetch his suitcase and the wooden trunk that holds the documents he needs for his mission to the High Mountains of Portugal, so he has only himself to convey.

He feels the breast pocket of his jacket. Father Ulisses' diary is there, wrapped in a soft cloth. Foolish of him to bring it along like this, so casually. It would be a catastrophe if it were lost. If he had any sense he would have left it in the trunk. But he needs extra moral support this morning, as he does every time he visits his uncle.

Even in his excitement he remembers to forgo his regular cane and take the one his uncle gave him. The handle of this cane is made of elephant ivory and the shaft of African mahogany, but it is unusual mainly because of the round pocket mirror that juts out of its side just beneath the handle. This mirror is slightly convex, so the image it reflects is quite wide. Even so, it is entirely useless, a failed idea, because a walking cane in use is by its nature in constant motion, and the image the mirror reflects is therefore too shaky and fleeting to be helpful in any way. But this fancy cane is a custom-made gift from his uncle, and every time he pays a call Tomás brings it.

He heads off down Rua São Miguel onto Largo São Miguel and then Rua de São João da Praça before turning onto Arco de Jesus — the easy perambulation of a pedestrian walking through a city he has known his whole life, a city of beauty and bustle, of commerce and culture, of challenges and rewards. On Arco de Jesus he is ambushed by a memory of Dora, smiling and reaching out to touch him. For that, the cane is useful, because memories of her always throw him off balance.

"I got me a rich one," she said to him once, as they lay in bed in his flat.

"I'm afraid not," he replied. "It's my uncle who's rich. I'm the poor son of his poor brother. Papa has been as unsuccessful in business as my uncle Martim has been successful, in exact inverse proportion."

He had never said that to anyone, commented so flatly and truthfully about his father's checkered career, the business plans that collapsed one after the other, leaving him further beholden to the brother who rescued him each time. But to Dora he could reveal such things.

"Oh, you say that, but rich people always have troves of money hidden away."

He laughed. "Do they? I've never thought of my uncle as a man who was secretive about his wealth. And if that's so, if I'm rich, why won't you marry me?"

People stare at him as he walks. Some make a comment, a few in jest but most with helpful intent. "Be careful, you might trip!" calls a concerned woman. He is used to this public attention; beyond a smiling nod to those who mean well, he ignores it.

One step at a time he makes his way to Lapa, his stride free and easy, each foot lifted high, then dropped with aplomb. It is a graceful gait.

He steps on an orange peel but does not slip.

He does not notice a sleeping dog, but his heel lands just short of its tail.

He misses a step as he is going down some curving stairs, but he is holding on to the railing and he regains his footing easily.

And other such minor mishaps.

Dora's smile dropped at the mention of marriage. She was like that; she went from the lighthearted to the deeply serious in an instant.

"No, your family would banish you. Family is everything. You cannot turn your back on yours."

"You are my family," he replied, looking straight at her.

She shook her head. "No, I am not."

His eyes, for the most part relieved of the burden of directing him, relax in his skull like two passengers sitting on deck chairs at the rear of a ship. Rather than surveying the ground all the time, they glance about dreamily. They notice the shapes of clouds and of trees.

They dart after birds. They watch a horse snuffle as it pulls a cart. They come to rest on previously unnoticed architectural details in buildings. They observe the bustle of traffic on Rua Cais de Santarém. All in all, it should be a delightful morning stroll on this pleasant late-December day of the year 1904.

Dora, beautiful Dora. She worked as a servant in his uncle's household. Tomás noticed her right away the first time he visited his uncle after she was hired. He could hardly take his eyes off her or get her out of his mind. He made efforts to be especially courteous to her and to engage her in brief conversations over one minor matter after another. It allowed him to keep looking at her fine nose, her bright dark eyes, her small white teeth, the way she moved. Suddenly he became a frequent visitor. He could remember precisely the moment Dora realized that he was addressing her not as a servant but as a woman. Her eyes flitted up to his, their gazes locked for a moment, and then she turned away — but not before a quick complicit smile curled up a corner of her mouth.

Something great was released within him then, and the barrier of class, of status, of utter improbability and unacceptability vanished. Next visit, when he gave her his coat, their hands touched and both lingered on that touch. Matters proceeded swiftly from there. He had, until then, had experience of sexual intimacy only with a few prostitutes, occasions that had been terribly exciting and then terribly depressing. He had fled each time, ashamed of himself and vowing never to do it again. With Dora, it was terribly exciting and then terribly exciting. She played with the thick hairs of his chest as she rested her head on him. He had no desire to flee anywhere.

"Marry me, marry me, marry me," he pleaded. "We will be each other's wealth."

"No, we will only be poor and isolated. You don't know what that's like. I do, and I don't want you to go through it."

Into that amorous standstill was born their little Gaspar. If it were not for his strenuous pleading, she would have been dismissed from his uncle's household when it was discovered that she was with child. His father had been his sole supporter, telling him to live his love for Dora, in precise opposition to his uncle's silent opprobrium. Dora was relegated to invisible duties deep within the kitchen. Gaspar lived equally invisibly in the Lobo household, invisibly loved by his father, who invisibly loved his mother.

Tomás visited as often as he decently could. Dora and Gaspar came to see him in the Alfama on her days off. They would go to a park, sit on a bench, watch Gaspar play. On those days they were like any normal couple. He was in love and happy.

As he passes a tram stop, a tram rumbles up on its rails, a transportation newness hardly three years old, shiny yellow and electric. Commuters rush forward to get on it, commuters hurry to get off it. He avoids them all — except one, into whom he crashes. After a quick interaction in which mutual apologies are proffered and accepted, he moves on.

The sidewalk has several raised cobblestones but he glides over them easily.

His foot strikes the leg of a café chair. It is bumped, nothing more.

Death took Dora and Gaspar one unyielding step at a time, the doctor summoned by his uncle expending his skills to no avail. First a sore throat and fatigue, followed by fever, chills, aches, painful swallowing, difficulty breathing, convulsions, a wild-eyed, strangled losing of the mind — until they gave out, their bodies as grey, twisted, and still as the sheets they'd thrashed in. He was there with each of them. Gaspar was five years old, Dora was twenty-four.

He did not witness his father's death a few days later. He was in the music room of the Lobo house, sitting silently with one of his cousins, numb with grief, when his uncle entered, grim-faced. "Tomás," he said, "I have terrible news. Silvestro . . . your father, has died. I have lost my only brother." The words were only sounds but Tomás felt crushed physically, as if a great rock had fallen on him, and he keened like a wounded animal. His warm bear of a father! The man who had raised him, who had countenanced his dreams!

In the course of one week — Gaspar died on Monday, Dora on Thursday, his father on Sunday — his heart became undone like a bursting cocoon. Emerging from it came no butterfly but a grey moth that settled on the wall of his soul and stirred no farther.

There were two funerals, a paltry one for a servant girl from the provinces and her bastard son, and a rich one for a rich man's poor brother, whose lack of material success was discreetly not mentioned.

He does not see an approaching carriage as he steps off a curb, but the driver's cry alerts him and he scampers out of the way of the horse.

He brushes against a man standing with his back to him. He raises his hand and says, "My apologies." The man shrugs amiably and watches him go.

One step at a time, every few steps turning his head to glance over his shoulder at what lies onward, Tomás makes his way to Lapa walking backwards.

"Why? Why are you doing this? Why don't you walk like a normal person? Enough of this nonsense!" his uncle has cried on more than one occasion. In response Tomás has come up with good arguments in defence of his way of walking. Does it not make more sense to face the elements — the wind, the rain, the sun, the onslaught of insects, the glumness of strangers, the uncertainty of the future — with the shield that is the back of one's head, the back of one's jacket, the seat of one's pants? These are our protection, our armour. They are made to withstand the vagaries of fate. Meanwhile, when one is walking backwards, one's more delicate parts — the face, the chest, the attractive details of one's clothing — are sheltered from the cruel world ahead and displayed only when and to whom one wants with a simple voluntary turn that shatters one's anonymity. Not to mention arguments of a more athletic nature. What more natural way to walk downhill, he contends, than backwards? The forefeet touch down with nimble delicacy, and the calf muscles can calibrate their tensing and releasing with precision. Movement downwards is therefore elastic and without strain. And should one trip, what safer way to do so than backwards, the cushioned buttocks blunting one's fall? Better that than to break one's wrists in a forward tumble. And he's not excessively stubborn about it. He does make exceptions, when climbing the many long, winding stairs of the Alfama, for example, or when he has to run.

All of these justifications his uncle has waved aside impatiently. Martim Augusto Mendes Lobo is an impatient successful man. Yet he knows why Tomás walks backwards, despite his testy interrogations and his nephew's dissembling explanations. One day Tomás overheard him talking to a visiting friend. It was the very dropping of his uncle's voice that made him prick up his ears.

". . . the most ridiculous scene," his uncle was saying, sotto voce. "Imagine this: Ahead of him — that is, behind him — there is a streetlight. I call over my secretary, Benito, and we watch in silent fascination, our minds preoccupied with the same question: Will my nephew walk into the streetlight? At that moment, another pedestrian appears on the street, at the other end. This man sees Tomás walking towards him backwards. We can tell from his cocked head that my nephew's curious way of advancing has caught his attention. I know from experience that there will be an encounter of sorts — a comment made, a jest thrown out, at the very least a bewildered stare as he passes by. Sure enough, a few steps before Tomás reaches the streetlight, the other man quickens his pace and stops him with a tap on the shoulder. Tomás turns. Benito and I cannot hear what the two say to each other, but we can watch the pantomime. The stranger points to the streetlight. Tomás smiles, nods, and brings a hand to his chest to express his gratitude. The stranger smiles back. They shake hands. With a wave to each other they depart, each going his way, the stranger down the street, and Tomás — swivelling round, moving backwards once more — up the street. He circles the streetlight without the least trouble.

"Ah, but wait! It's not over. After a few steps the other pedestrian turns his head to glance back at Tomás, and clearly he is surprised to see that he is still walking backwards. Concern can be read on his face — *Careful, you'll have an accident if you don't watch out!* — but also a measure of embarrassment because Tomás is looking his way and has seen him turn to stare, and we all know it's rude to stare. The man quickly turns his head to face forward again, but it's too late: He collides with the next streetlight. He hits it like a clapper hits a bell. Both Benito and I wince instinctively in sympathy. Tottering, he grimaces as he brings his hands to his face and chest. Tomás runs to help him — he runs *forward*. You'd think it would look normal, his forward gait, but it doesn't. There is no bounce to his step. He advances with great, long strides, his torso moving smoothly in a straight line, as if on a conveyor belt.

"Another exchange takes place between the two men, Tomás expressing great concern, the other man

11

waving it aside while keeping a hand pressed to his face. Tomás retrieves the man's hat, which has fallen to the ground. With another handshake and a more muted wave, the poor man staggers off. Tomás — and Benito and I — watch him go. Only once the man has turned the corner of the street does Tomás, in his usual rearward manner, resume his course. But the incident has flustered him, evidently, because he now smartly bangs into the street-light he so artfully avoided a minute earlier. Rubbing the back of his head, he turns to glare at it.

"But still, Fausto, he persists. No matter how often he bangs his head, no matter how many times he falls over, he goes on walking backwards." Tomás heard his uncle laugh and the friend Fausto join in. Then his uncle continued more somberly. "It started the day his little boy, Gaspar, died of diphtheria. The boy was born out of wedlock to a servant here. She died of the sickness too. Then, as fate would have it, my brother, Silvestro, dropped dead a few days later, midday, mid-speech. Already Tomás's mother had died when he was young. Now his father. To be so assailed by tragedy! Some people never laugh again. Others take to drink. My nephew, in his case, chose to walk backwards. It's been a year. How long will this bizarre grieving last?"

What his uncle does not understand is that in walking backwards, his back to the world, his back to God, he is not grieving. He is *objecting*. Because when everything cherished by you in life has been taken away, what else is there to do but object?

He takes a roundabout route. He turns off Rua Nova de São Francisco and starts walking up Rua do Sacramento. He is nearly there. As he swivels his head to see over his shoulder — he remembers there's a streetlight ahead — he looks up at the rear of his uncle's grand residence, with its elaborate cornices and intricate mouldings and soaring windows. He feels eyes upon him and notices a figure at a window on the corner of the second floor. Given that is where his uncle's office is located, it is likely his uncle Martim, so he turns his head back and strives to walk confidently, carefully skirting the streetlight. He follows the wall surrounding his uncle's property until he comes up to the gate. He spins round to reach for the bell, but his hand pauses in midair. He pulls it back. Though he knows his uncle has seen him and is waiting for him, he tarries. Then he takes the old leather diary from the breast pocket of his jacket, slips it out of its cotton cloth, puts his back against the wall, and slides down to a sitting position on the sidewalk. He gazes at the book's cover.

Being the Life in Words
and the Instructions for the Gift
of Father Ulisses Manuel Rosario Pinto
humble Servant of God

He is well acquainted with Father Ulisses' diary. Whole sections he knows by heart. He opens it at random and reads.

As slave ships approach the island to deliver their cargo, they have much accounting & housecleaning to do. Within sight of the port, they throw body after body overboard, both port & starboard, some of them limp & pliant, others feebly gesticulating. These are the dead & the seriously sick, the first discarded because they are no longer of any value, the second for fear that whatever illness is afflicting them might spread & affect the value of the others. It happens that the wind carries to my ears the cries of the living slaves as they protest their expulsion from the ship, as it also carries the splash their bodies make upon hitting the water. They disappear into the crowded Limbo that is the bottom of the Bay of Ana Chaves.

His uncle's house is also a Limbo of unfinished, interrupted lives. He closes his eyes. Loneliness comes up to him like a sniffing dog. It circles him insistently. He waves it away, but it refuses to leave him alone.

He came upon Father Ulisses' diary mere weeks after his life was irretrievably blighted. The discovery was a happenstance related to his work at the National Museum of Ancient Art, where he works as assistant curator. The Cardinal-Patriarch of Lisbon, José Sebastião de Almeida Neto, had just made a donation to the museum of ecclesiastical and non-ecclesiastical objects accumulated over the centuries from across the Portuguese empire. With Cardinal Neto's permission, Tomás was sent by the museum to do research in the

Episcopal archives on Rua Serpa Pinto to establish the exact provenance of these beautiful artifacts, the story whereby an altar, chalice, crucifix or psalter, a painting or a book, had come into the hands of the Lisbon diocese.

What he found were not exemplary archives. Succeeding secretaries of the various archbishops of Lisbon clearly did not dwell overmuch on the earthly matter of organizing thousands of papers and documents. It was on one of the open shelves devoted to the patriarchate of Cardinal José Francisco de Mendoça Valdereis, Patriarch of Lisbon between 1788 and 1808, in a stuff-all section given the breezy title *Miudezas* — Odds and Ends — that he spotted the hand-stitched volume with the brown leather cover, the handwritten title legible despite the splotchy discolourations.

What life was this, what gift? he had wondered. What were the instructions? Who was this Father Ulisses? When he pried open the volume, the spine made the sound of small bones breaking. Handwriting burst out with startling freshness, the black ink standing in high contrast to the ivory paper. The italic, quill-penned script was from another age. The pages were faintly rimmed with sunny yellow, indicating that they had seen very little light since the day they were written upon. He doubted that Cardinal Valdereis had ever read the volume; in fact, given that there was no archival note attached to the cover or anywhere inside — no catalogue number, no date, no comment — and no reference to the book in the index, he had the distinct impression that *no one* had ever read it.

He studied the first page, noticing an entry with a date and a place name above it: *September 17, 1631, Luanda*. He turned the pages with care. Other dates appeared. The last year recorded, though without a day or month, was 1635. A diary, then. Here, there, he noted geographic references: "the mountains of Bailundu . . . the mountains of Pungo Ndongo . . . the old Benguela route," locales that all appeared to be in Portuguese Angola. On June 2, 1633, there was a new place name: São Tomé, the small island colony in the Gulf of Guinea, "that fleck of dandruff off the head of Africa, long days north along the damp coast of this pestilential continent." His eyes came upon a sentence written a few weeks later: *Isso é minha casa*. "This is home." But it wasn't written just once. The words covered the page. A whole page of the same short sentence, closely written, the repeated lines wavering up and down slightly: "This is home. This is home. This is home." Then they stopped, replaced by prose that was more normally discursive, only to appear again some pages later, covering half a page: "This is home. This is home. This is home." Then once more, further on, for a page and a quarter: "This is home. This is home. This is home."

What did it mean? Why the manic repetition? He eventually found a possible answer on a page where the reiteration was the same as in every other instance, covering nearly two pages this time, with one difference, a spillage at the end, a clue that the phrase on the page was an ellipsis that the author completed in his mind every time: "This is home. This is home. This is home where the Lord has put me until He takes me to His Breast." Father Ulisses evidently had been racked by acute homesickness.

On one page Tomás found a curious sketch, a drawing of a face. The features were hastily outlined except for the mournful eyes, which were meticulously drawn. He studied those eyes for many minutes. He plunged into their sadness. Memories of his recently lost son swirled in his mind. When he left the archives that day, he hid the diary among innocuous papers in his briefcase. He was honest to himself about his purpose. This was no informal loan — it was plain theft. The Episcopal archives of Lisbon, having neglected Father Ulisses' diary for over two hundred and fifty years, would not miss it now, and he wanted the leisure to examine it properly.

He began reading and transcribing the diary as soon as he found the time. He proceeded slowly. The penmanship went from the easily readable to skeins of calligraphy that required him to work out that this scribble represented that syllable, while that squiggle represented this syllable. What was striking was how the writing was poised in the early sections, then grew markedly worse. The final pages were barely decipherable. A number of words he could not make out, no matter how hard he tried.

What Father Ulisses wrote when he was in Angola was no more than a dutiful account and of modest interest. He was merely another minion of the Bishop of Luanda, who "sat in the shade on the pier upon his marble throne" while he worked himself to a listless stupor, running around baptizing batches of slaves. But on São Tomé a desperate force took hold of him. He began to work on an object, the gift of the title. Its making consumed his mind and took all his energy. He mentioned seeking the "most perfect wood" and "adequate tools" and recalled training in his uncle's shop when he was young. He describes oiling his gift several times to help in its preservation, "my glistening hands artisans of devoted love." Towards the end of the diary, Tomás found these odd words, extolling the imposing character of his creation:

> It shines, it shrieks, it barks, it roars. Truly the Son of God giving a loud cry & breathing his last as the curtain of the temple is torn from top to bottom. It is finished.

What did Father Ulisses train in, and what did his uncle's shop produce? What did he oil with his hands? What was shining and shrieking, barking and roaring? Tomás could not find a clear answer in Father Ulisses' diary, only hints. When did the Son of God give a loud cry and breathe his last? On the Cross. Could the object in question be a crucifix, then, Tomás wondered. It was certainly a sculpture of some sort. But there was more to it than that. It was, by Father Ulisses' account, a most peculiar work. The moth in Tomás's soul stirred. He remembered Dora's last hours. Once she was bedridden, she held on to a crucifix with both hands, and no matter how much she tossed and turned, no matter how much she cried out, she didn't let go of it.

It was a cheap brass effigy that glinted dully, smallish in size, the type that might hang on a wall. She died clasping it to her chest in her small, bare room, with only Tomás present, in a chair by her bed. When the final moment came, signaled to him by the dramatic stoppage of her loud, rasping breathing (whereas their son had departed so quietly, like the petals of a flower falling off), he felt like a sheet of ice being rushed along a river.

In the hours that followed, as the long night ended and the new day stretched on, as he waited for the undertaker, who kept failing to show up, he fled and returned to Dora's room repeatedly, pushed away by horror, drawn back by compulsion. "How will I survive without you?" he pleaded to her at one point. His attention fell on the crucifix. Until then he had floated along religiously, observant on the outside, indifferent on the inside. Now he realized that this matter of faith was either radically to be taken seriously or radically not to be taken seriously. He stared at the crucifix, balancing between utter belief and utter disbelief. Before he had cast his lot one way or the other, he thought to keep the crucifix as a memento. But Dora, or rather Dora's body, would not let go. Her hands and arms clutched the object with unyielding might, even as he practically lifted her body off the bed trying to wrench it from her. (Gaspar, by comparison, had been so soft in death, like a large stuffed doll.) In a sobbing rage, he gave up. At that moment, a resolution — more a threat — came to his mind. He glared at the crucifix and hissed, "You! You! I will deal with you, just you wait!"

The undertaker arrived at last and took Dora and her cursed crucifix away.

If the object that Father Ulisses had created was what Tomás inferred it was from the priest's wild scribblings, then it was a striking and unusual artifact, something quite extraordinary. It would do nothing less than turn Christianity upside down. It would make good his threat. *But did it survive?* That was the question that gripped Tomás from the moment he finished reading the diary in his flat after he had smuggled it out of the Episcopal archives. After all, the object might have been burned or hacked to pieces. But in a pre-industrial age, when goods were crafted one by one and distributed slowly, they shone with a value that has faded with the rise of modern industry. Even clothing was not thrown away. Christ's scanty clothing was shared by Roman soldiers who believed he was nothing more than a lowly Jewish rabble-rouser. If ordinary clothes were passed on, then surely a large sculpted object would be preserved, all the more so if it was religious in nature.

How to determine its fate? There were two options: Either the object had stayed on São Tomé, or it had left São Tomé. Since the island was poor and given over to commerce, he guessed that it had made its way off the island. He hoped it had gone to Portugal, to the mother country, but it could also have gone to one of the many trading posts and cities along the coast of Africa. In both cases, it would have travelled by ship.

After the death of his loved ones, Tomás spent months seeking evidence of Father Ulisses' creation. In the National Archives of Torre do Tombo, he searched and studied the logbooks of Portuguese ships that travelled the western coast of Africa in the few years after Father Ulisses' death. He worked on the assumption that the carving had left São Tomé on a Portuguese ship. If it had departed on a foreign ship, then God only knew where it had ended up.

Finally, he came upon the logbook of one Captain Rodolfo Pereira Pacheco, whose galleon had departed São Tomé on December 14, 1637, carrying, among other goods, "a rendition of Our Lord on the Cross, strange & marvellous." His pulse had quickened. This was the first and only reference to a religious object of any kind that he had seen in relation to the debased colony.

Written next to each item in the logbook was its point of disembarkation. A great number of goods were unloaded at one stop or another along the Slave and Gold coasts, sold or replaced by other goods for which they were traded. He read the word next to the cross in Captain Pacheco's logbook: Lisboa. It had reached the homeland! He whooped in a way unseemly for a study room in the National Archives.

He turned Torre do Tombo upside down trying to find where Father Ulisses' crucifix had gone once it reached Lisbon. He eventually found his answer not in the National Archives but back in the Episcopal archives, where he had started. The irony was more galling than that. The answer lay in the form of two letters on the very shelf of Cardinal Valdereis's archives where he had found the diary, right next to where it had rested before he filched it. If only a string had attached diary to letters, he would have been spared much work.

The first letter was from the Bishop of Bragança, António Luís Cabral e Câmara, dated April 9, 1804, asking if the good Cardinal Valdereis might have some gift for a parish in the High Mountains of Portugal whose church had lately suffered a fire that destroyed its chancel. It was "a fine old church," he said, though he did not name the church or give its location. In his reply, a copy of which was attached to Bishop Câmara's letter, Cardinal Valdereis stated: "It is my pleasure to send on to you an object of piety that has been with the Lisbon diocese for some time, a singular portrayal of our Lord on the Cross, from the African colonies." Next to a diary that came from the African colonies, could the reference be to any other portrayal of the Lord but Father Ulisses'? Amazing that despite having it right in front of his eyes, Cardinal Valdereis could not see the thing for what it was. But the cleric did not know — and so he could not see.

An exchange of letters with the diocese of Bragança revealed that there was no trace of an African object per se going through their office during Bishop Câmara's years. Tomás was vexed. A creation that was strange and marvellous at its point of origin had become singular in Lisbon and then, at the hands of provincials, mundane. That, or its nature had been deliberately ignored. Tomás had to take another tack. The crucifix

22

was meant to go to a church that had suffered a fire. Records showed that between 1793, when Câmara was consecrated bishop of Bragança, and 1804, when he wrote to Cardinal Valdereis, there had been fires of varying severity in a number of churches in the High Mountains of Portugal. Such are the dangers of illuminating churches with candles and torches and burning incense during high holidays. Câmara said the crucifix was destined for "a fine old church." What church would earn that favourable description from the bishop? Tomás surmised one that was Gothic or perhaps Romanesque. Which meant a church built in the fifteenth century or earlier. The secretary of the diocese of Bragança did not prove to be a keen ecclesiastical historian. Prodding on Tomás's part yielded the guess that five of the churches blighted by fires might be worthy recipients of Bishop Câmara's praise, namely the widely scattered churches of São Julião de Palácios, Santalha, Mofreita, Guadramil, and Espinhosela.

Tomás wrote to the priest of each church. Their replies were inconclusive. Each priest heaped praise upon his church, extolling its age and beauty. By the sounds of it, there were copies of Saint Peter's Basilica strewn across the High Mountains of Portugal. But none of the priests had much to say that was illuminating on the crucifix at the heart of his church. Each claimed that it was a stirring work of faith, but none knew when his church had acquired it or where it had come from. Finally Tomás decided that there was nothing to do but go and determine for himself if he was right about the true character of Father Ulisses' crucifix. It was a minor annoyance that it had ended up in the High Mountains of Portugal, that remote and isolated region to the very northeast of his country. Soon enough he would have the object before his eyes.

He is startled by a voice.

"Hello, Senhor Tomás. You are coming to see us, are you not?"

It is the old groundskeeper, Afonso. He has opened the gate and is looking down at Tomás. How did he open it so quietly?

"Yes, I am, Afonso."

"Are you not well?"

"I'm fine."

He works his way to his feet, slipping the book back into his pocket as he does so. The groundskeeper pulls the cord of the bell. As the bell jangles, so do Tomás's nerves. He must go in, it is so. It is not just this home, where Dora and Gaspar died, but every home that now has this effect on him. Love is a house with many rooms, this room to feed the love, this one to entertain it, this one to clean it, this one to dress it, this one to allow it to rest, and each of these rooms can also just as well be the room for laughing or the room for listening or the room for telling one's secrets or the room for sulking or the room for apologizing or the room for intimate togetherness, and, of course, there are the rooms for the new members of the household. Love is a house in which plumbing brings bubbly new emotions every morning, and sewers flush out disputes, and bright windows open up to admit the fresh air of renewed goodwill. Love is a house with an unshakable foundation and an indestructible roof. He had a house like that once, until it was demolished. Now he no longer has a home anywhere — his flat in the Alfama is as bare as a monk's cell — and to set foot in one is to be reminded of how homeless he is. He knows that is what drew him to Father Ulisses in the first place: their mutual homesickness. Tomás recalls the priest's words on the death of the governor of São Tomé's wife. She was the only European woman on the island. The next such woman lived in Lagos, some eight hundred kilometres across the waters. Father Ulisses had not actually met the governor's wife. He had seen her on only a few occasions.

> The death of a white man causes a greater
> breach on this pestilent island than it does in
> Lisbon. When it is a woman, then! Her demise is
> a weight that is most difficult to bear. I fear the
> sight of a woman of my own kind will never
> again comfort me. Never again beauty, gentility,
> grace. I do not know how much longer I can go
> on.

Tomás and Afonso cross the cobbled courtyard, the grounds-keeper a deferential step ahead of him. Since he is advancing backwards in his usual fashion, they walk in lockstep back to back. At the foot of the steps to the main entrance, Afonso moves aside and bows. As it's a matter of climbing only a few steps, Tomás climbs them backwards. Before he has even reached the door, it opens behind him and he enters the house backwards. Glancing over his shoulder, he sees Damião, his uncle's long-time butler who has known him since he was a child, waiting for him, his hands open, a smile upon his face. Tomás pivots to face him.

"Hello, Damião."

"Menino Tomás, what a pleasure to see you. You are well?"

"I am, thank you. How is my aunt Gabriela?"

"Splendid. She shines upon us like the sun."

Speaking of the sun, it shines through the high windows upon the bounty of objects in the entrance hall. His uncle has made his vast fortune trading in African goods, principally ivory and timber. Two enormous elephant tusks adorn one wall. Between them hangs a rich, glossy portrait of King Carlos I. His Majesty himself stood before this likeness when he honoured his uncle with his presence in the house. Other walls are decorated with zebra and lion hides, with mounted animal heads above them: lion and zebra, but also eland, hippopotamus, wildebeest, giraffe. Hides also provide the upholstery for the chairs and the couch. African handiworks are displayed in niches and on shelves: necklaces, rustic wooden busts, gris-gris, knives and spears, colourful fabrics, drums, and so on. Various paintings — landscapes, portraits of Portuguese land-owners and attending natives, but also a large map of Africa, with the Portuguese possessions highlighted — set the scene and evoke some of the characters. And on the right, artfully set amidst tall grass, the stalking stuffed lion.

The hall is a curatorial mess, a cultural mishmash, every artifact ripped out of the context that gave sense to it. But it lit up Dora's eyes. She marvelled at this colonial cornucopia. It made her proud of the Portuguese empire. She touched every object she could reach, except the lion.

"I'm glad to hear my aunt is well. Is my uncle in his office?" Tomás asks.

"He's waiting for you in the courtyard. If you would be so kind as to follow me."

Tomás does an about-face and follows Damião across the entrance hall and down a carpeted hallway lined with paintings and display cases. They turn in to another hallway. Ahead of Tomás, Damião opens two French windows and moves aside. Tomás steps out onto a semi-circular landing. He hears his uncle's loud, exuberant voice: "Tomás, behold the Iberian rhinoceros!"

Tomás looks over his right shoulder. Tackling the three steps down into the large courtyard, he hurries to him and spins round next to him. They shake hands.

"Uncle Martim, how good to see you. You are well?"

"How could I not be? I have the great pleasure of seeing my one and only nephew."

Tomás is about to inquire about his aunt again but his uncle waves these social niceties aside. "Enough, enough. Well, what do you think of my Iberian rhinoceros?" he asks, pointing. "It is the pride of my menagerie!"

The beast in question stands in the middle of the courtyard, not far from the lean and tall Sabio, its keeper. Tomás gazes at it. Though the light is soft and milky, wrapping it in a flattering gauze, it is in his eyes a farcical monstrosity. "It is . . . magnificent," he replies.

Despite its ungraceful appearance, he has always lamented the fate of the animal that once roamed the rural corners of his country. Was the Iberian rhinoceros's last bastion not, in fact, the High Mountains of Portugal? Curious, the hold the animal has had on the Portuguese imagination. Human advancement spelled its end. It was, in a sense, run over by modernity. It was hunted and hounded to extinction and vanished, as ridiculous as an old idea — only to be mourned and missed the moment it was gone. Now it is fodder for fado, a stock character in that peculiar form of Portuguese melancholy, *saudade*. Indeed, thinking of the long-gone creature, Tomás is overcome with *saudade*. He is, as the expression goes, *tão docemente triste quanto um rinoceronte*, as sweetly sad as a rhinoceros.

His uncle is pleased with his answer. Tomás observes him with a degree of apprehension. Upon a solid frame of bones his father's brother has padded his body with wealth, a layer of portliness he carries with jocular pride. He lives in Lapa, in the lap of luxury. He spends staggering sums of money on every new bauble. Some years ago his fancy was caught by the bicycle, a two-wheeled transportation device propelled by the rider's own legs. On the hilly, cobbled streets of Lisbon, a bicycle is not merely impractical but dangerous. It can be used safely only on the pathways of parks, a Sunday amusement in which the rider goes round and round in circles, annoying walkers and frightening their children and dogs. His uncle has a whole stable of French Peugeot bicycles. Then he went on to procure *motorized* bicycles that went even faster than pedal bicycles, besides making much noise. And here is a representative of the latest of his expensive curios, recently acquired. "But Uncle," he adds carefully, "I see only an *automobile*."

"*Only*, you say?" responds his uncle. "Well, this technical wonder is the eternal spirit of our nation brought to life again." He places a foot on the automobile's footboard, a narrow platform that runs along its edge between the front and back wheels. "I hesitated. Which should I lend you? My Darracq, my De Dion-Bouton, my Unic, my Peugeot, my Daimler, perhaps even my American Oldsmobile? The choice was difficult. Finally, because you are my dear nephew, in memory of my sorely missed brother, I settled on the champion of the lot. This is a brand new four-cylinder Renault, a masterpiece of engineering. Look at it! It is a creation that not only shines with the might of logic but sings with the allure of poetry. Let us be rid of the animal that so befouls our city! The automobile never needs to sleep — can the horse beat that? You can't compare their power output, either. This Renault is assessed to have a fourteen-horsepower engine, but that is a strict, conservative estimate. More likely it produces twenty horsepower of drive. And a mechanical horsepower is more powerful than an animal horsepower, so imagine a stagecoach with *thirty* horses tethered to it. Can you see that, the thirty horses lined up in rows of two, stamping and chafing at the bit?

29

Well, you don't have to imagine it: It's right here before your eyes. Those thirty horses have been compressed into a metal box fitted between these front wheels. The performance! The economy! Never has old fire been put to such brilliant new use. And where in the automobile is the offal that so offends with the horse? There is none, only a puff of smoke that vanishes in the air. An automobile is as harmless as a cigarette. Mark my words, Tomás: This century will be remembered as the century of the puff of smoke!"

His uncle beams, filled to the brim with pride and joy in his Gallic gewgaw. Tomás remains tight-lipped. He does not share his uncle's infatuation with automobiles. A few of these newfangled devices have lately found their way onto the streets of Lisbon. Amidst the bustling animal traffic of the city, all in all not so noisy, these automobiles now roar by like huge, buzzing insects, a nuisance offensive to the ears, painful to the eyes, and malodorous to the nose. He sees no beauty in them. His uncle's burgundy-coloured copy is no exception. It lacks in any elegance or symmetry. Its cabin appears to him absurdly oversized compared to the puny stable at the aft into which are stuffed the thirty horses. The metal of the thing, and there is much of it, glares shiny and hard — inhumanly, he would say.

He would happily be carted by a conventional beast of burden to the High Mountains of Portugal, but he is making the trip over the Christmas season, cumulating holiday time that is his due with the few days he begged, practically on his knees, from the chief curator at the museum. That gives him only ten days to accomplish his mission. The distance is too great, his time too limited. An animal won't do. And so he has to avail himself of his uncle's kindly offered but unsightly invention.

With a clattering of doors, Damião enters the courtyard bearing a tray with coffee and fig pastries. A stand for the tray is produced, as are two chairs. Tomás and his uncle sit down. Hot milk is poured, sugar is measured out. The moment is set for small talk, but instead he asks directly, "So how does it work, Uncle?"

He asks because he does not want to contemplate what is just beyond the automobile, fringing the wall of his uncle's estate, next to the path that leads to the servants' quarters: the row of orange trees. For it is there that his son used to wait for him, hiding behind a not-so-thick tree trunk. Gaspar would flee, shrieking, as soon as his father's eyes caught him. Tomás would run after the little clown, pretending that his aunt and uncle, or their many spies, did not see him go down the path, just as the servants pretended not to see him entering their quarters. Yes, better to talk about automobiles than to look at those orange trees.

"Ah, well you should ask! Let me show you the marvel within," replies his uncle, leaping up out of his seat. Tomás follows him to the front of the automobile as he unhooks the small, rounded metal hood and tips it forward on its hinges. Revealed are tangles of pipes and bulbous protuberances of shiny metal.

"Admire!" his uncle commands. "An in-line four-cylinder engine with a 3,054 cc capacity. A beauty and a feat. Notice the order of progress: engine, radiator, friction clutch, sliding-pinion gearbox, drive to the rear axle. Under this alignment, the future will take place. But first let me explain to you the wonder of the internal combustion engine."

He points with a finger that aims to make visible the magic that takes place within the opaque walls of the engine. "Here moto-naphtha vapour is sprayed by the carburetor into the explosion chambers. The magnet activates the sparking plugs; the vapour is thereby ignited and explodes. The pistons, here, are pushed down, which . . ."

Tomás understands nothing. He stares dumbly. At the end of the triumphant explanations, his uncle reaches in to pick up a thick booklet lying on the seat of the driving compartment. He places it in his nephew's hand. "This is the automobile manual. It will make clear what you might not have understood."

Tomás peers at the manual. "It's in French, Uncle."

"Yes. Renault Frères is a French company."

"But —"

"I've included a French-Portuguese dictionary in your kit. You must take utmost care to lubricate the automobile properly."

"*Lubricate* it?" His uncle might as well be *speaking* French.

Lobo ignores his quizzical expression. "Aren't the mudguards handsome? Guess what they're made of?" he says, slapping one. "Elephant ears! I had them custom-made as a souvenir from Angola. The same with the outside walls of the cabin: only the finest-grain elephant hide."

"What's this?" asks Tomás.

"The horn. To warn, to alert, to remind, to coax, to complain." His uncle squeezes the large rubber bulb affixed to the edge of the automobile, left of the steerage wheel. A tuba-like honk, with a little vibrato, erupts out of the trumpet attached to the bulb. It is loud and attention-getting. Tomás has a vision of a rider on a horse carrying a goose under his arm like a bagpipe, squeezing the bird whenever danger is nigh, and cannot repress a cough of laughter.

"Can I try it?"

He squeezes the bulb several times. Each honk makes him laugh. He stops when he sees that his uncle is less amused and endeavours to pay attention to the renewed motoring mumbo-jumbo. These are more venerations than clarifications. If his relative's smelly metallic toy could show feelings, it would surely turn pink with embarrassment.

They come to the steerage wheel, which is perfectly round and the size of a large dinner plate. Reaching into the driving compartment again, Lobo places a hand on it. "To turn the vehicle to the left, you turn the wheel to the left. To turn the vehicle to the right, you turn the wheel to the right. To drive straight, you hold the wheel straight. Perfectly logical."

Tomás peers closely. "But how can a stationary wheel be said to turn to the left or to the right?" he asks.

His uncle searches his face. "I'm not sure I understand what there is not to understand. Do you see the top of the wheel, next to my hand? You see it, yes? Well, imagine that there's a spot there, a little white spot. Now, if I turn the wheel *this* way" — and here he pulls on the wheel — "do you see how that little white spot moves to the *left?* Yes? Well then, the automobile will turn to the left. And do you see that if I turn the wheel *that* way" — and here he pushes the wheel — "do you see how the little white spot moves to the *right?* In that case, the automobile will turn to the right. Is the point obvious to you now?"

Tomás's expression darkens. "But look" — he points with a finger — "at the bottom of the steerage wheel! If there were a little white spot there, it would be moving in the opposite direction. You might be turning the wheel to the right, as you say, at the top, but at the bottom you're turning it to the left. And what about the sides of the wheel? As you're turning it both right and left, you're also turning one side up and the other side down. So either way, in whichever direction you spin the wheel, you're simultaneously turning it to the right, to the left, up, and down. Your claim to be turning the wheel in one particular direction sounds to me like one of those paradoxes devised by the Greek philosopher Zeno of Elea."

Lobo stares in consternation at the steerage wheel, the top of it, the bottom of it, the sides of it. He takes a long, deep breath. "Be that as it may, Tomás, you must drive this automobile the way it was designed. Keep your eyes on the *top* of the steerage wheel. Ignore all the other sides. Shall we move on? There are other details we must cover, the operation of the clutch and of the change-speed lever, for example . . ." He accompanies his talk with hand and foot gestures, but neither words nor mummery spark any comprehension in Tomás. For example, what is "torque"? Did the Iberian Peninsula not get enough torque with Grand Inquisitor Torquemada? And what sane person could make sense of "double declutch"?

"I have supplied you with a few items that you'll find useful."

His uncle pulls open the door of the cabin, which is located in its back half. Tomás leans forward to peer in. There is relative gloom within. He notes the features of the cabin. It has the elements of a domestic space, with a black sofa of the finest leather and walls and a ceiling of polished cedar strips. The front window and the side windows look like the windows of an elegant home, boasting clear, good-quality panes and gleaming metal sashes. And the back window above the sofa, so neatly framed, could well be a painting hanging on a wall. But the scale of it! The ceiling is so low. The sofa will accommodate no more than two people comfortably. Each side window is of a size that will allow only a single person to look out of it. As for the back window, if it were a painting, it would be a miniature. And to get into this confined space, one must bend down to get through the door. What happened to the opulent openness of the horse-drawn carriage? He pulls back and gazes at one of the automobile's side mirrors. It might plausibly belong in a washroom. And didn't his uncle mention something about a fire in the engine? He feels an inward sinking. This tiny habitation on wheels, with bit parts of the living room, the washroom, and the fireplace, is a pathetic admission that human life is no more than this: an attempt to feel at home while racing towards oblivion.

He has also noticed the multitude of objects in the cabin. There is his suitcase, with his few personal necessities. More important, there is his trunk of papers, which contains all sorts of essential items: his correspondence with the secretary of the Bishop of Bragança and with a number of parish priests across the High Mountains of Portugal; the transcription of Father Ulisses' diary; archival newspaper clippings on the occurrences of fires in village churches in that same region; excerpts from the logbook of a Portuguese ship returning to Lisbon in the mid-seventeenth century; as well as various monographs on the architectural history of northern Portugal. And usually, when he is not carrying it in his pocket — a folly, he reminds himself — the trunk would hold and protect Father Ulisses' invaluable diary. But suitcase and trunk are crowded alongside barrels, boxes, tin containers, and bags. The cabin is a cave of goods that would glut the Forty Thieves.

"Ali Baba, Uncle Martim! So many things? I'm not crossing Africa. I'm only going to the High Mountains of Portugal, some few days away."

"You're going farther than you think," his uncle replies. "You'll be venturing into lands that have never seen an automobile. You'll need the capacity to be autonomous. Which is why I've included a good canvas rain tarp and some blankets, although you might be better off sleeping in the cabin. That box there contains all the motoring tools you'll need. Next to it is the oiling can. This five-gallon metal barrel is full of water, for the radiator, and this one of moto-naphtha, the automobile's elixir of life. Resupply yourself as often as you can, because at some point you'll have to rely on your own stock. Along the way, look out for apothecaries, bicycle shops, blacksmiths, ironmongers. They'll have moto-naphtha, though they may give it another name: petroleum spirit, mineral spirit, something like that. Smell it before you buy it. I've also provided you with victuals. An automobile is best operated by a well-fed driver. Now, see if these fit."

From a bag on the floor of the cabin, his uncle pulls out a pair of pale leather gloves. Tomás tries them on, baffled. The fit is snug. The leather is pleasingly elastic and creaks when he makes a fist.

"Thank you," he says uncertainly.

"Take good care of them. They're from France too."

Next his uncle hands him goggles that are big and hideous. Tomás has hardly put them on when his uncle brings out a beige coat lined with fur that reaches well below his knees.

"Waxed cotton and mink. The finest quality," he says.

Tomás puts it on. The coat is heavy and bulky. Finally, Lobo slaps a hat on him that has straps that tie under the chin. Gloved, goggled, coated, and hatted, he feels like a giant mushroom. "Uncle, *what* is this costume for?"

"For motoring, of course. For the wind and the dust. For the rain and the cold. It *is* December. Have you not noticed the driving compartment?"

He looks. His uncle has a point. The back part of the automobile consists of the enclosed cubicle for the passengers. The driving compartment in front of it, however, is open to the elements but for the roof and a front window. There are no doors or windows on either side. Wind, dust, and rain will easily come in. He grouses internally. If his uncle hadn't cluttered the cabin with so much gear, making it impossible for him to sit within, he could take shelter there while Sabio drove the machine.

His uncle presses on. "I've included maps as good as they exist. When they're of no help, rely on the compass. You're heading north-northeast. The roads of Portugal are of the poorest quality, but the vehicle has a fine suspension system — leaf springs. They will handle any ruts. If the roads get to you, drink plenty of wine. There are two wineskins in the cabin. Avoid roadside inns and stagecoaches. They are not your friends. It's understandable. A degree of hostility is to be expected from those whose livelihood the automobile directly threatens. Right, as for the rest of the supplies, you'll figure out what's what. We should get going. Sabio, are you ready?"

"Yes, senhor," replies Sabio with military promptness.

"Let me get my jacket. I'll drive you to the edges of Lisbon, Tomás."

His uncle returns to the house. Tomás doffs the ludicrous motoring costume and returns it to the cabin. His uncle bounces back into the courtyard, a jacket on his back, gloves upon his hands, his cheeks flushed with excitement, exuding a nearly terrifying joviality.

"By the way, Tomás," he bellows, "I forgot to ask: Why on earth do you so badly want to go to the High Mountains of Portugal?"

"I'm looking for something," Tomás replies.

"What?"

Tomás hesitates. "It's in a church," he finally says, "only I'm not sure which one, in which village."

His uncle stands next to him and studies him. Tomás wonders whether he should say more. Whenever his uncle comes to the Museum of Ancient Art, he gazes at the exhibits with glazed eyes.

"Have you heard of Charles Darwin, Uncle?" Tomás asks.

"Yes, I've heard of Darwin," Lobo replies. "What, is he buried in a church in the High Mountains of Portugal?" He laughs. "You want to bring his body back and give it pride of place in the Museum of Ancient Art?"

"No. Through my work I came upon a diary written on São Tomé, in the Gulf of Guinea. The island has been a Portuguese colony since the late fifteenth century."

"A miserable one. I stopped there once on my way to Angola. I thought I might invest in some cocoa plantations there."

"It was an important place during the slave trade."

"Well, now it's a producer of bad chocolate. Beautiful plantations, though."

"No doubt. By a process of deduction involving three disparate elements — the diary I've just mentioned, the logbook of a ship returning to Lisbon, and a fire in a village church in the High Mountains of Portugal — I have discovered an unsuspected treasure and located it, approximately. I'm on the brink of a great find."

"Are you? And what is this treasure, exactly?" his uncle asks, his eyes steady on Tomás.

Tomás is sorely tempted. All these months he has told no one, especially not his colleagues, about his discovery, nor even about his research. He did it all on his own time, privately. But a secret yearns to be divulged. And in mere days the object will be found. So why not his uncle?

"It is . . . a religious statuary, a crucifix, I believe," he replies.

"Just what this Catholic country needs."

"No, you don't understand. It's a very odd crucifix. A wondrous crucifix."

"Is it? And what does it have to do with Darwin?"

"You'll see," Tomás replies, flushing with zeal. "This Christ on the Cross has something important to say. Of that, I am certain."

His uncle waits for more, but more does not come. "Well, I hope it makes your fortune. Off we go," he says. He climbs into the driver's seat. "Let me show you how to start the engine." He claps his hands and roars, "Sabio!"

Sabio steps forward, his gaze fixed on the automobile, his hands at the ready.

"Before starting the engine, the moto-naphtha tap has to be turned to open — good man, Sabio — the throttle handle, here under the steerage wheel, has to be placed at half-admission — so — and the change-speed lever set at the neutral point, like this. Next you flick the magneto switch — here on the dashboard — to ON. Then you open the lid of the hood — there's no need to open the whole hood, you see that small lid there at the front? — and you press down once or twice on the float of the carburetor to flood it. See how Sabio does it? You close the lid, and all that's left after that is turning the starting handle. Then you sit in the driver's seat, take the hand brake off, get into first gear, and away you go. It's child's play. Sabio, are you ready?"

Sabio faces the engine squarely and sets his legs apart, feet solidly planted on the ground. He bends down and grips the starting handle, a thin rod protruding from the front of the automobile. His arms straight, his back straight, he suddenly snaps the handle upward with great force, pulling himself upright, then, upon the handle completing a half-turn, he shoves down on it, using the full weight of his body, before working the upswing as he did the first time. He performs this circular action with enormous energy, with the result that not only does the whole automobile shake but the handle spins round two, maybe three times. Tomás is about to comment on Sabio's prowess but for the result attending this spinning of the handle: The automobile roars to life. It starts with a sputtering rumble from deep within its bowels, followed by a succession of piercing explosions. As it begins to judder and shudder, his uncle yells, "Come on, hop aboard. Let me show you what this remarkable invention can do!"

Tomás unwillingly but speedily clambers up to sit next to his uncle on the padded seat that stretches across the driving compartment. His uncle does a manoeuvre with his hands and feet, pulling this and pressing that. Tomás sees Sabio straddling a motorcycle that is standing next to a wall, then kick-starting it. He will be a good man to have along.

Then, with a jerk, *the machine moves.*

Quickly it gathers speed and swerves out of the courtyard, throwing itself over the threshold of the opened gates of the Lobo estate onto Rua do Pau de Bandeira, where it does a sharp right turn. Tomás slides across the smooth leather of the seat and slams into his uncle.

He cannot believe the bone-jarring, mind-unhinging quaking he is experiencing, directly related to the noise-making, because such trembling can come only from such noise. The machine will surely shake itself to pieces. He realizes he has misunderstood the point of the suspension springs his uncle mentioned. Clearly their purpose is not to protect the automobile from ruts, but ruts from the automobile.

Even more upsetting is the extremely fast and independent forward motion of the device. He sticks his head out the side and casts a look backwards, thinking — hoping — that he will see the Lobo household, every family member and employee, pushing the machine and laughing at the joke they are pulling on him. (Would that Dora were among those pushers!) But there are no pushers. It seems unreal to him that no animal should be pulling or pushing the device. It's an effect without a cause, and therefore disturbingly unnatural.

Oh, the alpine summits of Lapa! The automobile — coughing, sputtering, rattling, clattering, jouncing, bouncing, chuffing, puffing, whining, roaring — dashes down to the end of Rua do Pau de Bandeira, the cobblestones underfoot making their presence known with a ceaseless, explosive rat-a-tat, then violently lurches leftwards and falls off the street as if from a cliff, such is the steepness of Rua do Prior. Tomás's guts feel as if they are being squeezed into a funnel. The automobile reaches the bottom of the street with a flattening that sends him crashing to the floor of the driving compartment. The machine has barely stabilized itself — and he regained his seat, if not his composure — before it springs up the last upward part of Rua do Prior onto Rua da Santa Trindade, which in turn descends steeply. The automobile gaily starts to dance over the metallic jaws of Santa Trindade's tram tracks, sending him sliding to and fro across the seat, alternately smashing into his uncle, who does not seem to notice, or practically falling out of the automobile at the other end of the seat. From balconies that fleet by, he sees people scowling down at them.

His uncle takes the right turn at Rua de São João da Mata with ferocious conviction. Down the street they race. Tomás is blinded by the sun; his uncle seems unaffected. The automobile pounces across Rua de Santos-o-Velho and bolts down the curve of Calçada Ribeiro Santos. Upon reaching the Largo de Santos, he looks wistfully — and briefly — at the walkers indulging in the slow activities of its pleasant park. His uncle drives around it until, with a savage left turn, he flings the automobile onto the wide Avenida Vinte e Quatro de Julho. Lapa's lapping waters, the breathtaking Tagus, open up to the right in a burst of light, but Tomás does not have time to appreciate the sight as they hurtle through the urban density of Lisbon in a blur of wind and noise. They spin so fast around the busy roundabout of Praça do Duque da Terceira that the vehicle is projected, slingshot-like, down Rua do Arsenal. The hurly-burly of the Praça do Comércio is no impediment, merely an amusing challenge. Indistinctly Tomás sees the statue of the Marquis of Pombal standing in the middle of the square. Oh! If only the Marquis knew what horrors his streets were being subjected to, he might not have rebuilt them. On they go, onward and forward, in a roar of rush, in a smear of colour. Throughout, traffic of every kind — horses, carts, carriages, drays, trams, hordes of people and dogs — bumble around them blindly. Tomás expects a collision at any moment with an animal or a human, but his uncle saves them at the last second from every certain-death encounter with a sudden swerve or a harsh stoppage. A number of times Tomás feels the urge to scream, but his face is too stiff with fright. Instead, he presses his feet against the floorboards with all his might. If he thought his uncle would accept being treated like a life buoy, he would gladly hold on to him.

All along, his uncle — when he is not hurling insults at strangers — is lit up with joy, his red face radiating excitement, his mouth creased up in a smile, his eyes shining, and he laughs with insane abandon, or shouts a one-way conversation of acclamations and exclamations: "Amazing! . . . Glorious! . . . Fantastic! . . . Didn't I tell you? . . . Now, *that's* how you take a left turn! . . . Extraordinary, absolutely extraordinary! . . . Look, look: We must be hitting *fifty* kilometres an hour!"

Meanwhile, the Tagus flows, placid, unhurried, unperturbed, a gentle behemoth next to the outrageous flea that leaps along its bank.

Next to a field, upon a fledgling rural road without any cobblestone finery, his uncle at last stops the automobile. Behind them, at some distance, Lisbon's skyline stands, like the emerging teeth of a small child.

"See how far we've come — and so fast!" His uncle's voice booms in the refreshing silence. He is beaming like a boy on his birthday.

Tomás looks at him for a few seconds, incapable of speech, then practically falls to the ground getting out of the driving compartment. He staggers to a nearby tree and supports himself against it. He bends forward and a heaving gush of vomit spews from his mouth.

His uncle shows understanding. "Motion sickness," he diagnoses breezily as he removes his driving gloves. "It's a curious thing. Some passengers are subject to it, but never the driver. Must be something to do with controlling the vehicle, perhaps being able to anticipate the coming bumps and turns. That, or the mental effort of driving distracts the stomach from any malaise it might feel. You'll be fine once you're behind the wheel."

It takes a moment for Tomás to register the words. He cannot imagine holding the reins of this metallic stallion. "Sabio is coming with me, isn't he?" he asks breathlessly as he wipes the sides of his mouth with his handkerchief.

"I'm not lending you Sabio. Who will look after my other vehicles? Besides, he's made sure the Renault is in tip-top running order. You won't need him."

"But Sabio will drive the thing, Uncle."

"*Drive it?* Why would you want that? Why would anyone want to delegate to a servant the thrill of driving such an astonishing invention? Sabio is here to work, not to play."

Just then the servant in question appears, expertly directing the sputtering motorcycle off the road to stop it behind the automobile. Tomás turns to his uncle again. It's his blistering ill fortune to have a relative with the wealth to own several automobiles and the eccentricity to want to drive them himself.

"Sabio drives *you* around, dear Uncle."

"Only on formal occasions. It's mostly Gabriela he carts about. Silly mouse doesn't dare try it herself. You're young and smart. You'll do fine. Won't he, Sabio?"

Sabio, who is standing quietly next to them, nods in agreement, but the way his eyes linger on Tomás makes Tomás feel that he does not fully share his employer's sunny trust. Anxiety roils his stomach.

"Uncle Martim, please, I have no experience in —"

"Look here! You start in neutral, with the throttle at half. To get going, you put yourself in first gear, then release the clutch slowly as you press on the accelerator pedal. As you gather speed, you move up to second gear, then third. It's easy. Just start on flat ground. You'll get the knack in no time."

His uncle steps back and fondly contemplates the automobile. Tomás hopes that during this pause, kindness and solicitude will soften his uncle's heart. Instead, he delivers a last blast of peroration.

"Tomás, I hope you are aware that what you have before your eyes is a highly trained orchestra, and it plays the most lovely symphony. The pitch of the piece is pleasingly variable, the timbre dark but brilliant, the melody simple yet soaring, and the tempo lies between *vivace* and *presto*, although it does a fine *adagio*. When I am the conductor of this orchestra, what I hear is a glorious music: the music of the future. Now you are stepping up to the podium and I am passing you the baton. You must rise to the occasion." He pats the driver's seat in the automobile. "You sit here," he says.

Tomás's lungs are suddenly gasping for air. His uncle gestures to Sabio to start the engine. Once again the roar of the internal combustion engine fills the exterior countryside. He has no choice. He has waited too long, understood too late. He will have to get behind the steerage wheel of the monster.

He climbs aboard. His uncle again points, explains, nods, smiles.

"You'll be all right," he concludes. "Things will work out. I'll see you when you return, Tomás. Good luck. Sabio, stay and help him out."

With the finality of a door slamming, his uncle turns and disappears behind the automobile. Tomás cranes his head out the side to find him. "Uncle Martim!" he shouts. The motorcycle starts with a detonation, followed by a grinding sound as it moves off. His last view of his uncle is the sight of his ample girth overhanging both sides of the slender machine and his disappearance down the road in a thunder of mechanical flatulence.

Tomás turns his eyes to Sabio. It occurs to him that his uncle has departed on the motorcycle and that he is to leave with the automobile. How then will Sabio return from the outer north-east edge of Lisbon to his employer's house in western Lapa?

Sabio speaks quietly. "Driving the automobile is possible, senhor. It only needs a little practice."

"Of which I have none!" Tomás cries. "Neither practice nor knowledge, neither interest nor aptitude. Save my life and show me again how to use this blasted thing."

Sabio goes over the daunting details of piloting the manufactured animal. He instructs with untiring patience, spending much time over the proper order in which to press or release the pedals and pull or push the levers. He reminds Tomás about the left and right turning of the steerage wheel. He teaches him the use of the throttle handle, which is needed not only to start the engine but to stop it. And he speaks on matters

Uncle Martim said nothing about: the difference between pressing hard or lightly on the accelerator pedal; the usage of the brake pedal; the important hand brake, which he is to pull whenever the automobile is at rest; the use of the side mirrors. Sabio shows him how to turn the starting handle. When Tomás tries it, he feels something heavy turning inside the automobile, like a boar on a spit being rotated in a vat of thick sauce. On his third turn of the spit, the boar explodes.

He stalls the engine again and again. Each time Sabio gamely returns to the front of the machine, where he gets it to roar to life again. Then he proposes to put the machine into first gear. Tomás slides over to the passenger side of the driving compartment. Sabio does the necessary manoeuvres; the gears sigh consent and the machine inches forward. Sabio points to where he should put his hands and where he should press his foot. Tomás moves into place. Sabio works his way out of the driver's seat onto the footboard, nods gravely at him, and steps off the automobile.

Tomás feels cast off, thrown away, abandoned.

The road ahead is straight and the machine grunts along noisily in first gear. The steerage wheel is a hard, unfriendly thing. It shakes in his hands. He tugs it one way. Is it left? Is it right? He can't tell. He's barely able to make it move. How did his uncle do it so easily? And keeping the accelerator pedal pressed down is exceedingly tiresome; his foot is starting to cramp. At the first bend, a slight curve to the right, as the automobile starts to cross over the road and head towards a ditch, alarm pushes him to action and he lifts his foot and stamps on one pedal after another at random. The machine coughs and jolts to a halt. The clanging pandemonium mercifully stops.

Tomás looks about. His uncle is gone, Sabio is gone, there is no one else in sight — and his beloved Lisbon is gone too, scraped away like the leftovers of a meal off a plate. Into a silence that is more vacuum than repose, his little son vaults into his mind. Gaspar often ventured out to play in the courtyard of his uncle's house before being shooed away by one servant or another, like a stray cat. He also prowled about the garage, filled as it was with rows of bicycles and motorcycles and automobiles. His uncle would have found a kindred spirit in his son when it came to motoring. Gaspar stared at the automobiles like a hungry mouth eats. Then he died, and the courtyard now contains a silent parcel of emptiness. Other parts of his uncle's house similarly afflict Tomás with the absence of Dora or of his father, this door, that chair, this window. What are we without the ones we love? Would he ever get over the loss? When he looks in his eyes in the mirror when he shaves, he sees empty rooms. And the way he goes about his days, he is a ghost who haunts his own life.

Weeping is nothing new to him. He has wept many, many times since death dealt him a triple blow. A remembrance of Dora, Gaspar, or his father is often both the source and the focus of his grief, but there are times when he bursts into tears for no reason that he can discern, an occurrence as random as a sneeze. The situation now is clearly very different in nature. How can a noisy, uncontrollable machine and three coffins be compared in their effect? But strangely he feels upset in the same way, filled with that same acute sense of dread, aching loneliness, and helplessness. So he weeps and he pants, grief in competition with simmering panic. He pulls out the diary from his jacket pocket and presses it to his face. He smells its great age. He closes his eyes. He takes refuge in Africa, in the waters off its western equatorial coast, on the Portuguese island colony of São Tomé. His grief seeks the man who is leading him to the High Mountains of Portugal.

He tried to find information on Father Ulisses Manuel Rosario Pinto, but history seemed to have forgotten him nearly entirely. There was no trace of him but for two dates that gave his unfinished outlines: his birth on July 14, 1603, as attested by the São Tiago parish registry in Coimbra, and his ordination as a priest in that same city in the Cathedral of the Holy Cross on May 1, 1629. No other detail of his life, down to the date of his death, could Tomás find. All that remained of Father Ulisses in the river of time, pushed far downstream, was this floating leaf of a diary.

He pulls the diary away from his face. His tears have marred its cover. This does not please him. He is professionally annoyed. He dabs at the cover with his shirt. How strange, this habit of weeping. Do animals weep? Surely they feel sadness — but do they express it with tears? He doubts it. He has never heard of a weeping cat or dog, or of a weeping wild animal. It seems to be a uniquely human trait. He doesn't see what purpose it serves. He weeps hard, even violently, and at the end of it, what? Desolate tiredness. A handkerchief soaked in tears and mucus. Red eyes for everyone to notice. And weeping is undignified. It lies beyond the tutorials of etiquette and remains a personal idiom, individual in its expression. The twist of face, quantity of tears, quality of sob, pitch of voice, volume of clamour, effect on the complexion, the play of hands, the posture taken: One discovers weeping — one's weeping personality — only upon weeping. It is a strange discovery, not only to others but to oneself.

Resolve surges in him. There is a church in the High Mountains of Portugal waiting for him. He must get to it. This metal box on wheels will help him do that, and so sitting behind its controls is where he should be. *Isso é minha casa.* This is home. He looks down at the pedals. He looks at the levers.

It is a good hour before he heads off. The problem does not lie in starting the automobile. That, after seeing Sabio do it so many times, is manageable. Arms straight, back straight, legs doing the work, he turns the starting handle. The warm engine seems disposed to starting again. The problem lies in getting the machine *moving.* Whatever permutation of pedals and levers he uses, the end result is always the same: a grinding squeal or an angry barking, often quite violent, with no movement forward. He takes breaks. He sits in the driving compartment. He stands next to the automobile. He goes for short walks. Sitting on the footboard, he eats bread, ham, cheese, dried figs, and he drinks wine. It is a joyless meal. The automobile is always on his mind. It stands there, looking incongruous on the side of the road. The horse and ox traffic going by notice it — and notice him — but so close to Lisbon, either coming or going, the drivers hurry their animals on, only shouting or waving a greeting. He does not have to explain himself.

At last it happens. After countless fruitless efforts, he presses on the accelerator pedal and the machine advances. He mightily wrenches the steerage wheel in the direction he hopes is the correct one. It is.

The vehicle is now in the centre of the road and moving ahead. To avoid the ditch on either side, he has to hold his ship to a single fixed course: the narrow, shrunken horizon dead ahead. Maintaining a straight line towards that bottomless dot is exhausting. The machine constantly wants to veer off course, and there are bumps and holes in the road.

There are people too, who stare harder the farther he gets from Lisbon. Worse, though, are the large drays and carts heavily laden with goods and produce for the city. They appear ahead of him, plugging the horizon. As they get closer, they seem to take up an increasing share of the road. They clip-clop slowly, confidently, stupidly, while he races towards them. He has to calculate his course exactly so that he drives next to them and not *into* them. His eyes tire from the strain and his hands hurt from gripping the steerage wheel.

Suddenly, he has had enough. He presses on a pedal. The automobile coughs to a harsh stop, throwing him against the steerage wheel. He steps down, exhausted but relieved. He blinks in astonishment. The application of the brake pedal has unpacked the landscape and it billows out around him, trees, hills, and vineyards to his left, textured fields and the Tagus to his right. He saw none of these while he was driving. There was only the devouring road ahead. What luck to live in a land that so unceasingly agrees to be agreeable. No wonder wine is made here. The road is now empty and he is alone. In the dying light of the day, wispy and opal, he is soothed by the quiet of an early evening in the country. He remembers lines from Father Ulisses' diary, which he recites under his breath:

I come not to shepherd the free, but the unfree.
The first have their own church. My flock's
church has no walls & a ceiling that reaches up
to the Lord.

With his lungs and with his eyes, Tomás takes in the open church around him, the soft fecund appeal of Portugal. He doesn't know how far he has travelled, but surely more than he would have on foot. Enough for a first day. Tomorrow he will apply himself further.

Constructing a shelter from a rain tarp seems a great bother. He chooses instead to make a bedroom of the enclosed back cabin, as his uncle suggested, which leads him to inspect his uncle's contribution to the expedition. He finds: lightweight pots and pans; a small burner that works on white cubes of dried spirit; a bowl, a plate, a cup, utensils, all of metal; soup powder; rolls and loaves of bread; dried meats and fish; sausages; fresh vegetables; fresh and dried fruit; olives; cheese; milk powder; cocoa powder; coffee; honey;

cookies and biscuits; a bottle of cooking oil; spices and condiments; a large jug of water; the motoring coat with its attending items, the gloves, the hat, the hideous goggles; six automobile tires; rope; an axe; a sharp knife; matches and candles; a compass; a blank notebook; lead pencils; a set of maps; a French-Portuguese dictionary; the Renault manual; wool blankets; the box of tools and other motoring necessities; the barrel of moto-naphtha; the canvas rain tarp, with lanyards and pegs; and more.

So many things! His uncle's excessive solicitude means that he has difficulty making space for himself in the cabin. When he has cleared the sofa, he tries lying down on it. It's not very long — to sleep on it, he would have to lie with his knees tucked in. He peers through the wide front window of the cabin into the driving compartment. The seat there is a tad firm, but flat and level, more like a bench, and because it's not boxed in at either end by a door he will be able to stretch his feet out.

He picks out bread, dried cod, olives, a wineskin, his uncle's coat, as well as the automobile manual and the dictionary, and transfers back to the driving compartment. He lies on his back on the seat, feet sticking out of the compartment. Doing as he was told by his uncle, he settles down to some motoring study, his hands holding the automobile manual, the dictionary lying on his chest.

It turns out that lubrication is a serious affair. With dawning horror, he realizes that the gears, the clutch, the clutch cup, the back axle, the front and back joints of the transmission shaft, the bearings of all the wheels, the joints of the front axle, the spindle axle bearings, the connecting axles, the joints of the driving rod, the magneto shaft, the hinges of the doors, and the list goes on — essentially everything that moves in the machine — needs obsessive lubrication. Many of these need a little squirt every morning before the engine is started, some need it every two to three days, others once a week, while with still others it's a question of mileage. He sees the automobile in a different light: It is a hundred little chicks chirping frantically, their necks extended and their beaks opened wide, their whole beings trembling with need as they scream for their drops of oil. How will he keep track of all these begging mouths? How much simpler were the instructions for Father Ulisses' gift! These turned out to be no more than a plea that good Portuguese craftsmen back home, blessed with access to the highest-quality paint, should do a proper job of repainting his masterwork. In the meantime he had to do with poor local substitutes.

As the night freshens, Tomás is thankful for his uncle's coat. The mink is warm and soft. He falls asleep imagining that the coat is Dora. She too was warm and soft, and gentle and graceful, and beautiful and caring. But the ministrations of Dora are overcome by worry — all those begging mouths! — and he sleeps poorly.

The next morning, after breakfast, he finds the oiling can and he follows the manual's directives line by line, illustration by illustration, paragraph after paragraph, page after page. He lubricates the entire automobile, which involves not only lifting the hood up on its hinges and sticking his head in the machine's entrails, but removing the floor of the driving compartment to access parts of its anatomy there, and even crawling on the ground and sliding *under* the machine. It is a tiresome, finicky, dirty business. Then he gives it water. After that, he has to confront a pressing problem. The machine, which his uncle claimed was at the acme of technological perfection, fails to provide one of the more basic feats of technology: plumbing. He has to use the leaves of a nearby shrub.

The starting up of the cold engine is long and painful. If only his limbs were stronger. Then there is the maddening conundrum of getting the machine to giddy-up once it is huffing and rattling. From the moment of waking to the moment when the machine fortuitously jerks forward, four hours pass. He grips the wheel and focuses on the road. He approaches Póvoa de Santa Iria, a small town near Lisbon, the closest settlement to the northeast of the capital on this road, a place that until then has lain dormant in the atlas of his mind. His heart beats like a drum as he enters the town.

Men appear with napkins hanging from their shirt fronts, a chicken leg or other repast in their hands, and stare. Barbers holding foaming brushes, followed by men with shaving foam lathered on their faces, run out, and stare. A group of old women make the sign of the cross, and stare. Men stop their talking, and stare. Women stop their shopping, and stare. An old man makes a military salute, and stares. Two women laugh in fright, and stare. A bench of old men chew with their toothless jaws, and stare. Children shriek, run to hide, and stare. A horse neighs and makes to buck, startling its driver, and stares. Sheep in a pen off the main street bleat in despair, and stare. Cattle low, and stare. A donkey brays, and stares. Dogs bark, and stare.

In the midst of this excruciating visual autopsy, Tomás fails to press hard enough on the accelerator pedal. The machine coughs once, twice, then dies. He jabs at the pedal. Nothing happens. He closes his eyes to contain his frustration. After a moment he opens them and looks around. In front of him, to the sides of him, behind him, a thousand eyeballs, human and animal, are staring at him. Not a sound is to be heard.

The eyeballs blink, and the silence crumbles. Imperceptibly, shyly, the people of Póvoa de Santa Iria ooze forward, pressing the automobile on all sides until they are ten, fifteen thick.

Some are wreathed in smiles and pepper him with questions.

"Who are you?"

"Why have you stopped?"

"How does it work?"

"What does it cost?"

"Are you rich?"

"Are you married?"

A few glare and grumble.

"Have you no pity for our ears?"

"Why do you throw so much dust in our faces?"

Children shout silly questions.

"What's its name?"

"What does it eat?"

"Is the horse in the cabin?"

"What does its caca look like?"

Many people come forward to stroke the machine. Most simply stare in benign silence. The man of the military salute salutes every time Tomás happens to look his way. In the background, the sheep, horses, donkeys, and dogs start up again with their respective noises.

After an hour of idle talk with the townspeople, it becomes clear to Tomás that they will not go away until he has left their town. He has somewhere to go; they don't.

He must, at this moment, overcome his natural reticence. In a morass of self-consciousness, digging deep into his inner reserves, he climbs out of the driving compartment, stands on the footboard, and asks the people to move away from the front of the machine. The people do not seem to hear or understand. He exhorts them — but they only creep forward again and again, in ever greater numbers. There develops such a crush of people around the automobile that he has to squeeze himself between bodies to get to the starting handle, and he has to push them back to make space to turn it. Some gawkers stand on the footboards. Others even make to clamber into the driving compartment, though a stony glare dissuades them. Children, grins plastered upon their faces, keep squeezing the horn's rubber bulb with demented glee.

Fatefully, after several trips to the starting handle and yet another bout of plying pedals and levers, the vehicle leaps forward, then promptly dies. Cries erupt all round as the people in front of the machine shriek and clutch their chests in fright. Women scream, children wail, men mutter. The military man stops saluting.

Tomás shouts apologies, strikes the steerage wheel, reprimands the automobile in the strongest terms. He jumps out to help the affronted people. He kicks the vehicle's tires. He slaps its elephant-ear mudguards. He insults its ugly hood. He fiercely turns the starting handle, putting the machine in its place. All to no positive effect. The goodwill of the people of Póvoa de Santa Iria has evaporated in the wintry Portuguese sun.

He hurries back to the driving compartment. Miraculously, the automobile whines, shakes itself, and tiptoes ahead. The people of Póvoa de Santa Iria part fearfully before him and the road opens up. He urges the machine on.

He determinedly roars through the next town, Alverca do Ribatejo, keeping his foot firmly on the accelerator pedal. He ignores all the people and their stares. It is the same with the town of Alhandra. Past Alhandra he sees a sign saying Porto Alto, pointing to the right, off the main road, to the Tagus. Three bridges span two small islands. He peers across to the flat, desolate countryside beyond the river's eastern shore and brings the automobile to a halt.

He turns the engine off and fetches the maps of Portugal from the cabin. There are a number of these, neatly folded and labelled, a national map and regional ones of Estremadura, Ribatejo, Alto Alentejo, Beira Baixa, Beira Alta, Douro Litoral, and Alto Douro. There are even maps of the neighbouring Spanish provinces of Cáceres, Salamanca, and Zamora. It seems

60

his uncle has prepared him for every conceivable route to the High Mountains of Portugal, including the wayward and lost.

He examines the national map. Exactly as he thought. To the west and north of the Tagus, along or near Portugal's littoral, the land is crowded with towns and cities. By comparison, the backcountry beyond the river, to the east of the Tagus and in the lands bordering Spain, reassures him with the sparseness of its settlements. Only Castelo Branco, Covilhã, and Guarda glare with urban danger. Perhaps he can find ways to avoid them. Otherwise, what motorist would be afraid of settlements such as Rosmaninhal, Meimoa, or Zava? He has never heard of these obscure villages.

He starts the automobile and plies different pedals and pushes the change-speed lever into first gear. Fortune favours him. He turns to the right and works his way down the road to the bridges. On the cusp of the first bridge, he hesitates. It is a wooden bridge. He remembers about the thirty horses. But surely the engine does not *weigh* thirty horses? He is mindful of Father Ulisses' experience on water, sailing from Angola to his new mission on São Tomé:

Travelling over water is a form of hell, all the more so in a cramped & fetid slave ship holding five hundred & fifty-two slaves & their thirty-six European keepers. We are plagued by periods of dead calm, then rough seas. The slaves moan & cry at all hours of the day & night. The hot

61

stench of their quarters seeps through the whole ship.

Tomás presses on. He is not bedevilled by slaves, only ghosts. And his ship must only make three jumps over a river. The crossing of the bridges is a rumbling affair. He fears that he will drive the machine off them. When he has escaped the third bridge and reached the eastern shore of the river, he is too rattled to drive on. He decides that since he is motoring, perhaps he should properly learn *how* to motor. He stops and retrieves what he needs from the cabin. Sitting behind the steerage wheel, manual and dictionary at hand, he applies himself to learning the proper operation of the change-speed lever, the clutch pedal, and the accelerator pedal. The manual is illuminating, but the knowledge he gains from it is purely theoretical. Its application is the rub. He finds moving smoothly from neutral gear — as his uncle called it, though he finds nothing neutral about it — to first gear insuperably difficult. Over the course of the rest of the day, in jarring fits and starts, he advances perhaps five hundred metres, the machine roaring and coughing and shuddering and stopping the whole way. He curses until nightfall sends him to bed.

In the dimming light, as fingers of cold reach for him, he seeks calm in Father Ulisses' diary.

If the Empire be a man, then the hand that is holding up a solid gold bullion is Angola, while the other that is jingling pennies in the pocket — that is São Tomé.

So the priest quotes an aggrieved trader. Tomás has studied the history that Father Ulisses is fated to live: The priest set foot on São Tomé between sugar and chocolate, between the island's time as a leading exporter of sugar, in the late sixteenth century, and of the chocolate bean now, in the early twentieth century. He would live the rest of his short life at the start of a three-century-long trough of poverty, stagnation, despair, and decadence, a time when São Tomé was an island of half-abandoned plantations and feuding elites who made the better part of their meagre living off the living, that is, from the slave trade. The island supplied slave ships with provisions — water, wood, yams, maize flour, fruit — and exploited some slaves for its own needs — the ongoing marginal production of sugar, cotton, rice, ginger, and palm oil — but the white islanders mainly acted as slave brokers. They could not dream of rivalling Angola's vast and endless domestic supply, but the Bight of Benin was at their doorstep across the Gulf of Guinea and that coast was rich with slaves. The island was both an ideal way station for a ship about to cross the Atlantic, the hellish voyage that came to be called the Middle Passage — such an intestinal expression, Tomás thought — and an excellent back door into Portuguese Brazil and its ravenous hunger for slave labour. And so the slaves came, in their thousands. "This pocket jingles with dazed African souls," Father Ulisses comments.

That he travelled to São Tomé on a slave ship was not incidental. He had applied to be a slave priest, a priest assigned to the salvation of the souls of slaves. "I want to serve the humblest of the humble, those whose souls Man has forgot but God hasn't." He explains his urgent new mission on São Tomé:

A century & a half ago some Hebraic children, in ages from 2 to 8 yrs, were brought to the island. From these noxious seeds a wretched plant grew that spread its poison to all the soil, polluting the unwary. My mission is twice then — once more to bring the African soul to God & further to tear away from that soul the foul grappling roots of the Jew. I spend my days at the port, a sentinel of the Lord, waiting for slave ships to bring in their bounty. When one arrives, I board it and christen the Africans & read the Bible to them. You are all God's children, I repeat to them tirelessly. I also draw the odd sketch.

That is his duty, which he fulfils with unquestioning diligence: to welcome strangers to a faith they do not follow in a language they do not understand. At this stage in his diary, Father Ulisses appears to be a churchman typical of his time, steeped in the Lord, steeped in ignorance and contempt. That will change, Tomás knows.

He falls asleep in an unsettled frame of mind. He cannot find comfort in the automobile, neither in driving it nor in sleeping in it.

In the morning he would like to wash, but neither soap nor towel is to be found in the cabin. After the usual motoring difficulties he sets off. The road through a dull, flat landscape of tilled fields leads him to Porto Alto, which is a larger town than he expected. His skill in getting the automobile going has improved, but whatever composure this new ability gives him is seriously undermined by the surge of people who appear on all sides. People wave, people shout, people come close. A young man runs alongside the automobile. "Hello!" he shouts.

"Hello!" Tomás shouts back.

"What an incredible machine!"

"Thank you!"

"Won't you stop?"

"No!"

"Why not?"

"I still have far to go!" Tomás shouts.

The young man moves off. Another young man appears right away in his stead, eager to pursue his own hollered dialogue with Tomás. As he gives up, he is replaced by another. All the way through Porto Alto, Tomás is kept in constant, shouting conversation with eager strangers jogging next to the machine. When at last he reaches the far edge of the town, he would like to cry out in victory at having so adroitly controlled the machine, but his voice is too hoarse.

In the open country he eyes the change-speed lever. He has covered ground in the last three days, the machine has undeniable stamina — but so do snails. The manual is clear on the point, and his uncle proved it in practice in Lisbon: Real motoring results are to be achieved only in a higher gear. He rehearses in his mind. Finally it comes down to doing it or not. Pedals, buttons, levers — these are released or pressed, pushed or pulled, each according to its need. He performs all these actions without taking his eyes off the road — or letting air out of his lungs. The clutch pedal tingles, it seems, as if to signal to him that it has done its job and would be happy if he took his foot off its back, which he does. At the same moment, the accelerator pedal seems to fall forward ever so slightly, as if it, on the contrary, were hungry for the pressure of his foot. He pushes down harder.

The monster pounces forward in second gear. The road is disappearing under its wheels with such thunder that he feels it's no longer the machine that is moving forward on the landscape but the landscape that is being pulled from underneath it, like that hazardous trick in which a tablecloth is yanked off a fully set table. The landscape vanishes with the same menacing understanding that the trick will work only if done at lightning speed. Whereas earlier he was afraid of going too fast, now he's afraid of going too slowly, because if second gear malfunctions it won't be just he who meets his end smashing into a telegraph pole, but the entire porcelain landscape that will crash with him. In this madness, he is a teacup rattling on a saucer, his eyes glinting like bone china glaze.

As he careers through space, motionless while in headlong motion, furiously staring ahead, he yearns for still, thoughtful landscapes, a calm vineyard like he saw yesterday, or a shoreline like Father Ulisses frequents, where each small wave lands upon his feet in prayerful collapse like a pilgrim who has reached his destination. But the priest is jarred in his own way, is he not? As Tomás is shaking now in this infernal machine, so must Father Ulisses' hand shake at times as he commits his harrowed thoughts to the pages of his diary.

The priest quickly becomes disenchanted with São Tomé. He gets along no better with the natural world there than he did in Angola. There is the same strangle of vegetation, fed by the same incessant showers and coddled by the same unremitting heat. He is afflicted by the wet season, with its torrents of rain interspersed with gaps of stifling moist heat, and he is afflicted by the dry season, with its burning heat and ground-level clouds of dripping mist. He complains bitterly of this hothouse weather "that makes a green leaf sing & a man die." And then there are the supplementary, incidental miseries: the stench of a sugar mill, bad food, infestations of ants, ticks as large as cherry pips, a cut to his left thumb that becomes infected.

He speaks of a "mulatto silence," a miscegenation between the heat and humidity of the island and the unhappy people on it. This mulatto silence creeps into all the senses. The slaves are sullen, have to be pushed to do anything, which they do in silence. As for the Europeans who live out their lives on São Tomé, their words, usually curt and annoyed, are spoken, perhaps are heard, less likely are obeyed promptly, then are muffled by the silence. Work for the slaves on the plantations carries on from sunrise to sunset, with no singing or even conversation, with a one-hour break at noon to eat, rest, and become further aware of the silence. The working day ends with a speechless meal, solitude, and restless sleep. The nights are louder than the days on São Tomé, because of the lively insects. Then the sun rises and it all starts over, in silence.

Nourishing this silence are two emotions: despair and rage. Or, as Father Ulisses puts it, "the black pit & the red fire." (How well Tomás knows that pair!) His relations with the island clergy become fraught with tension. He never gives the precise nature of his grievances. Whatever the cause, the result is clear: He becomes increasingly cut off from everyone. As his diary progresses, there are fewer and fewer mentions of interactions with fellow Europeans. Who else is there? The barriers of social status, language, and culture preclude any amicable dealings between a white man, even a priest, and slaves. Slaves come and go, communicating with Europeans mostly with their wide-open eyes. As for the locals, freed slaves and mulattos, what they have to gain from Europeans is precarious. To trade with them, to work for them, to leave their sight — that is the best policy. Father Ulisses laments:

The shacks of natives disappear overnight & rings of emptiness form around isolated white men & I am that. I am an isolated white man in Africa.

Tomás stops the machine and decides, after poking his face up at the sky, that the afternoon has turned cool and cloudy, unsuited to further motoring. Better to settle down for the day under the mink coat.

The next day the road continues nearly villagelessly until Couço, where there is a bridge across the River Sorraia. Under the narrow bridge, alarmed egrets and herons, until then peaceably standing in the water, flutter away. He is pleased to see orange trees, the only splash of colour in an otherwise grey day. He wishes the sun would come out. It's the sun that makes a landscape, drawing out its colour, defining its contours, giving it its spirit.

On the outskirts of a town named Ponte de Sor, he halts the automobile. He sets out on foot for the town. It's good to walk. He kicks his feet back vigorously. He's practically skipping backwards. But what is this itch that is bothering him? He scratches his scalp, his face, and his chest. It is his body crying to be washed. His armpits are starting to smell, as are his nether regions.

He enters the town. People stare at him, at his manner of walking. He finds an apothecary to buy moto-naphtha, following his uncle's advice of resupplying himself as often as he can. He asks the man at the counter if he has the product. He has to use a few names before the implacably serious man nods and produces from a shelf a small glass bottle, barely half a litre.

"Do you have any more?" Tomás asks.

The apothecary turns and brings down another two bottles.

"I'll have still more, please."

"I don't have any more. That's my whole stock."

69

Tomás is disheartened. At this rate, he will have to ransack every apothecary between Ponte de Sor and the High Mountains of Portugal.

"I'll take these three bottles, then," he says.

The apothecary brings them to the till. The transaction is routine, but something in the man's manner is odd. He wraps the bottles in a sheet of newspaper, then, when two people enter the shop, he hastily slides the package over to him. Tomás notices that the man is staring at him fixedly. Self-consciousness overcomes him. He scratches the side of his head. "Is something wrong?" he asks.

"No, nothing," replies the apothecary.

Tomás is bewildered but says nothing. He leaves the shop and takes a walk around the town, memorizing the route he will take with the automobile.

When he returns to Ponte de Sor an hour later, it all goes wrong. He gets horribly lost. And the more he drives around the town, the more he attracts the attention of the population. Crowds assail him at every turn. At one sharp corner, as his hands frenetically wrestle with the steerage wheel, he stalls once again.

The multitude of the curious and the offended descends upon him.

He starts the automobile well enough, despite the crowd. He even feels that he can get it into first gear. Then he looks at the steerage wheel and has no idea in which direction he is supposed to turn it. In trying to satisfy the fiendish angle of the street he was attempting to get onto, he turned the wheel several times. before stalling. He tries to determine the matter logically —

this way? that way? — but he cannot come to any conclusion. He notices a plump man in his fifties standing on the sidewalk level with the automobile's headlights. He's better dressed than the others. Tomás leans out and calls to him above the din of the engine. "Excuse me, sir! I need your help, if you would be so kind. I'm having a mechanical problem. Something complicated I won't bore you with. But tell me, is the wheel there, the one right in front of you, is it turning?"

The man backs away and looks down at the wheel. Tomás grabs the steerage wheel and turns it. With the automobile completely at rest, it takes real effort.

"Well," Tomás puffs loudly, "is it turning?"

The man looks puzzled. "Turning? No. If it were turning, your carriage would be moving."

"I mean, is it turning the other way?"

The man looks to the rear of the automobile. "The other way? No, no, it's not moving that way, either. It's not moving at all."

Many in the crowd nod in agreement.

"I'm sorry, I'm not making myself clear. I'm not asking if the wheel turned on itself in a round way, like a cartwheel. Rather, did it" — he searches for the right words — "did it turn on the spot on its tiptoes, like a ballerina, so to speak?"

The man stares at the wheel doubtfully. He looks to his neighbours left and right, but they don't venture any opinion, either.

Tomás turns the steerage wheel again with brutal force. "Is there any movement at all from the wheel, any at all?" he shouts.

The man shouts in return, with many in the crowd joining in. "Yes! Yes! I see it. There is movement!"

A voice cries, "Your problem is solved!"

The crowd bursts into cheers and applause. Tomás wishes they would go away. His helper, the plump man, says it again, pleased with himself. "There was movement, more than the last time."

Tomás signals to him with his hand to come closer. The man sidles over only a little.

"That's good, that's good," says Tomás. "I'm most grateful for your help."

The man ventures no reaction beyond a single callisthenic blink and the vaguest nodding. If a broken egg were resting atop his bald head, the yolk might wobble a little.

"But tell me," Tomás pursues, leaning forward and speaking emphatically, "which *way* did the wheel turn?"

"Which way?" the man repeats.

"Yes. Did the wheel turn to the *left* or did it turn to the *right*?"

The man lowers his eyes and swallows visibly. A heavy silence spreads through the crowd as it waits for his response.

"Left or right?" Tomás asks again, leaning closer still, attempting to establish a manner of complicity with the man.

The egg yolk wobbles. There is a pause in which the whole town holds its breath.

"I don't know!" the plump man finally cries in a high-pitched voice, spilling the yolk. He pushes his way through the crowd and bolts. The sight of the ungainly, bandy-legged town notable racing down the street dumbfounds Tomás. He has lost his only ally.

A man speaks out. "It could have been left, it could have been right. Hard to tell."

Murmurs of agreement rise up. The crowd seems cooler now, its indulgence turning to edginess. He has lifted his foot off the pedal and the engine has died. He gets out and turns the starting handle. He pleads with the crowd in front of the machine. "Listen to me, please! This machine will move, it will jump! For the sake of your children, for your own sake, please move away! I beg you! This is a most dangerous device. Step back!"

A man next to him addresses him quietly. "Oh, here comes Demetrio and his mother. She's not one you want to cross."

"Who's Demetrio?" Tomás asks.

"He's the village idiot. But so nicely dressed by his mother."

Tomás looks up the street and sees the town notable returning. He's weeping, his face covered in glistening tears. Holding his hand, pulling him along, is a very small woman dressed in black. She's holding a club. Her eyes are fixed on Tomás. The way she's straining at the end of her son's arm, she looks like a tiny dog trying to hurry its leisurely owner along. Tomás returns to the driver's seat and grapples with the machine's controls.

He humours the machine into *not* pouncing forward. As he plies the pedals, it growls but only leans forward, like an enormous boulder that has lost the tiny pebble that holds it back but hasn't yet gone crashing down the slope to destroy the village below. The crowd gasps and instantly creates a space all around. He presses a touch harder on the accelerator pedal. He prepares to twist the steerage wheel with mania in whatever direction his instincts will choose, hoping it will be the correct direction, when he is confounded to see that the steerage wheel is turning on its own, of its own will. And it proves to be turning the right way: The vehicle creeps forward and finishes clearing the turn onto the cross street. He would continue to stare in wonderment if he didn't hear the clanging sound of a wooden club striking metal.

"YOU DARE TO MAKE FUN OF MY SON?" cries the mother of the broken egg. She has clocked one of the headlights with such force that it has cleanly broken off. He is horrified — his uncle's jewel! "I'M GOING TO SUFFOCATE YOU UP A SHEEP'S ASS!"

The machine has conveniently brought its hood level with the aggrieved mother. Up goes the club, down goes the club. With a mighty crash, a valley appears on the hood. Tomás would push harder on the accelerator pedal, but there are still many people close-by. "Please, I implore you, hold your club!" he calls out.

Now the sidelight is within her easy reach. Another swing. In a glass-shattering explosion it flies off. The madwoman, whose son persists with his inconsolable blubbering, is winding up her club again.

"I'LL FEED YOU TO A DOG AND THEN EAT THAT DOG!" she shrieks.

Tomás pushes hard on the accelerator pedal. The woman narrowly misses the side mirror; her club instead shatters the window of the door to the cabin. In a roar, he and the injured automobile leap forth and escape Ponte de Sor.

A few kilometres onward, next to a growth of bushes, he brings the machine to a standstill. He gets out and gazes at the automobile's amputations. He clears the glass shards from the cabin. His uncle will be livid at what has been done to the pride of his menagerie.

Just ahead is the village of Rosmaninhal. Is that not one of the villages he mocked for its obscurity? *Rosmaninhal, you can do me no harm*, he had boasted. Will the village now make him pay for his arrogance? He prepares for yet another night sleeping in the machine. This time he supplements his uncle's coat with a blanket. He extracts the precious diary from the trunk and opens it at random.

The sun brings no solace, nor does sleep. Food
no longer sates me, nor the company of men.
Merely to breathe is to display an optimism I do
not feel.

Tomás breathes deeply, finding optimism where Father Ulisses could not. Strange how this diary of misery brings him such joy. Poor Father Ulisses. He had such high hopes arriving on São Tomé. Before his energies were depleted by disease, solitary and without purpose, he spent much of his time wandering and watching. There seems to be no purpose to these

75

rambles other than the working off of despair — better
to be desperate and itinerant than desperate and sitting
in an overheated hut. And what he saw, he wrote down.

Today a slave asked me — signified to me — if
my leather shoes were made from the skin of an
African. They are of the same colour. Was the
man also eaten? Were his bones reduced to useful
powder? Some of the Africans believe that we
Europeans are cannibals. The notion is the result
of their incredulity at the use they are put to:
field labour. In their experience, the material part
of one's life, what we would call the earning of
it, demands no great effort. Tending a vegetable
garden in the tropics takes little time & occupies
few hands. Hunting is more demanding, but is a
group activity & source of some pleasure & the
effort is not begrudged. Why then would the
white man take so many of them if they didn't
have ulterior motives greater than gardening? I
reassured the slave that my shoes were not made
of his fellows' skin. I cannot say I convinced him.

Tomás knows what the slaves and Father Ulisses
cannot: the unending demands of the sugar cane fields
of Brazil and, later, of the cotton fields of America. A
man or a woman may not need to work so hard to live,
but a cog in a system must turn ceaselessly.

No matter their provenance — what territory,
what tribe — the slaves soon sink to the same

saturnine behaviour. They become lethargic, passive, indifferent. The more the overseers exert themselves to change this behaviour, freely using the whip, the more it becomes ingrained. Of the many signs of hopelessness the slaves manifest, the one that strikes me the most is geophagy. They paw the ground like dogs, gather a round ball, open their mouths, chew it & swallow it. I cannot decide if eating of the Lord's humus is unchristian.

Tomás turns his head and looks at the darkening fields around him. To be miserable upon the land — and then *to eat it*? Later, Father Ulisses records trying it himself.

A darkness blooms in me, a choking algae of the soul. I chew slowly. It does not taste bad, only is unpleasant on the teeth. How much longer, Lord, how much longer? I feel unwell & see in the eyes of others that I am worse. Walking to town exhausts me. I go to the bay instead and stare out at the waters.

Whatever it was that afflicted Father Ulisses — and Europeans in Africa had their unhappy choice of ailments: malaria, dysentery, respiratory illnesses, heart troubles, anemia, hepatitis, leprosy, and syphilis, among others, in addition to malnutrition — it was slowly and painfully killing him.

Tomás falls asleep thinking of his son and of how, sometimes at night, after an evening at his uncle's house, he would slip into Dora's room in the servants' quarters. She might be asleep already, after a long day of work. Then he would take sleeping Gaspar into his arms and hold him. Amazing how the two could sleep through any disturbance. He would hold his limp son and sing to him softly, nearly hoping he would wake so they could play.

He is woken the next morning by the itching of his head and chest. He rises and methodically scratches himself. His fingernails have rims of blackness under them. It has been five days since he has washed. He must find an inn soon, with a good bed and a hot bath. Then he remembers the next village he must cross, the one he scorned. It is fear of Rosmaninhal that pushes him to enter third gear that day, the automobile's mechanical pinnacle. He has barely started off when he works the machine into second gear. With the grimmest lack of hesitation, he repeats the hand-and-foot manoeuvre, pushing the change-speed lever farther than he has ever pushed it before. The dial on the instrument board blinks in disbelief. The automobile becomes pure velocity. Third gear is the fire of the internal combustion engine coming into itself and becoming an external combustion engine, thundering through the countryside like a meteorite. Yet, oddly, third gear is quieter than second gear, as if even sound cannot keep up with the machine. The wind howls around the driving compartment. Such is the swiftness of the machine that the telegraph poles along the road shift and begin to appear as close together as teeth in a comb. As for the landscape beyond the poles, none of it is to be seen. It flits by like a panic-stricken school of fish. In the blurry land of High Velocity, Tomás is aware of only two things: the roaring and rattling frame of the automobile, and the road straight ahead, so hypnotic in its allure that it's like a fishing line upon whose hook he is caught. Though he is in the open country, his mental focus is such that he might as well be driving through a tunnel. In a daze, barely cognizant in the ambient din, he worries about lubrication. He imagines a small engine part going dry, heating up, bursting into flames, then the whole machine exploding in an iridescent conflagration of moto-naphtha-fuelled blues, oranges, and reds.

Nothing bursts into flames. The automobile only clangs, bawls, and eats up the road with terrifying appetite. If there is evil resident in Rosmaninhal — indeed, if there is good resident in Rosmaninhal — he sees none of it. The village vanishes in a streak. He sees a figure — a man? a woman? — turn to look in his direction and fall over.

It is some kilometres past Rosmaninhal that he comes upon the stagecoach. His uncle warned him about these, did he not? Tomás slows down and thinks of holding back until an alternate route suggests itself or the coach turns off. But he grows impatient on the solitary country road. There is no comparison between the thirty horses galloping in his machine and the four horses cantering ahead of the coach.

He pushes down on the accelerator pedal. With a choke, a cough, and a shudder, the machine grips the road with greater determination. He feels his hands pulled forward while his head is pushed back. The distance between automobile and stagecoach begins to shrink. He sees a man's head appear from the top of the coach. The man waves at him. A moment later, the coach, which has been somewhat on the right side of the road, heaves to its centre. Is this the reason behind his uncle's warning about stagecoaches, their erratic weaving? He rather interprets the move as a courtesy, the stagecoach moving aside to let him go by, like a gentleman allowing a lady first passage through a doorway. The man's wave reinforces this interpretation in his mind. He urges the automobile on. He navigates into the space to the right of the stagecoach. Every part of the machine is shaking. The passengers in the stagecoach, which is wildly rocking to and fro and side to side, hold on to the edge of the windows and crane their necks to look at him, gawking with a number of expressions: curiosity, amazement, fear, disgust.

The two drivers of the stagecoach come into view, his colleagues in a way, and he eases off the accelerator pedal. The stagecoach drivers and he will greet each other like sea captains whose ships are crossing paths. He has read a great many captains' logbooks in the course of his investigations. The way stagecoach and automobile are pitching and rolling has something maritime to it. He lifts a hand, ready to wave, a smile building upon his face.

He looks up at the stagecoach drivers and is shocked at what he sees. If the passengers had a number of expressions on their faces, the drivers have only one: out-and-out loathing. The man who turned and waved at him earlier — or was he in fact shaking his fist? — is barking and growling at him like a dog and is making as if to leap from his seat down onto the roof of the machine. The man doing the driving looks even more incensed. His face is red with anger and his mouth is open in a continuous shout. He is brandishing a long whip, spurring his horses on. The whip rises and coils in the air like a serpent before coming down and flattening out with a sharp and piercing *snap* that goes off like a gun. Only then does Tomás realize that the steeds have been pushed to full thundering gallop. He can feel the ground beneath him shaking from their efforts. Despite the cushioning of the automobile's rubber wheels and the mediation of the suspension springs, the hard, marvellous work of the horses rattles his bones and awes his brain. In relative terms, he is slowly passing the stagecoach the way a man on a street might overtake an elderly walker, with such ease and comfort that he has the leisure to tip his hat and say a kind word. But from the point of view of someone standing by the side of the road, both he and the stagecoach are hurtling through space at a fantastic speed, as if the elderly walker and the man on the street were advancing on the roofs of two express trains racing on parallel tracks.

The silence that enveloped him as a result of his intense concentration suddenly explodes into the hammering of the galloping horses' hooves, the screaming creaking of the swaying stagecoach, the shouting of the drivers, the shrill distress of the frightened passengers, the cracking of the whip, and the roar of the automobile. He presses the accelerator pedal as hard as he can. The automobile surges ahead, but slowly.

A further noise, keen and metallic, stabs his ears. The driver has turned his whip off the horses and is now lashing the roof of the automobile. Tomás grimaces, as if the lashes were striking his own back. The driver's assistant has his arms raised. Above his head is a wooden chest with metal strappings. It looks heavy. The man hurls it at the automobile, and it hits the roof like a bomb, followed by scraping sounds as the chest and its contents slide off. The horses, less than a metre away from Tomás, are kicking up a storm of dirt and throwing off quantities of froth from their mouths. Their eyes bulge with terror. They veer closer. The driver is steering them into the automobile! *Death is upon me*, thinks Tomás.

The horses give out just as the automobile reaches its full speed. The machine moves ahead decisively and he is able to steady it and bring it back to the centre of the road, clipping the right lead horse so closely that he sees in the side mirror that it has to rear up its head to avoid hitting the back of the cabin.

The moment he is ahead, the exhausted horses falter to a halt. Behind him, the drivers continue to shout. In the side mirror he watches the passengers pour out of the stagecoach as they and the drivers direct their shouting and gesturing at each other.

He feels shattered by the encounter and wants to stop, but fear of the stagecoach catching up drives him on. As his unhappy ship forges ahead, he focuses on the road again. His stomach is as turbulent as a stormy sea. He squirms with itchiness.

He considers his situation. How many days has he been driving? He thinks and counts. One, two, three, four — four nights. Four nights and five days of his allotment of ten. Only ten days. And he is not even out of the province of Ribatejo, not a quarter of the way to his destination. How did he imagine that he could complete his mission in so few days? The notion is laughable. He was lured by the promise of his uncle's magic carpet. The chief curator of the Museum of Ancient Art will not tolerate him being late. If he misses even a single day of work, he will be fired, plain and simple. That is the work world he lives in, one where he is an insignificant, replaceable cog. His relations with the chief curator, the collections manager, and the other curators at the museum are no better than Father Ulisses' relations were with the Bishop and the island clergy. How happy is a work environment where colleagues never eat together but rather sit in sour isolation? Sometimes he feels he can match every misery that Father Ulisses experienced on São Tomé with one he has experienced at the museum. The same tedium. The same solitary nature of the work, broken by tense encounters with others. The same physical discomfort, in his case the unending days spent in damp and musty basement storage rooms or hot and dusty attics. The same choking misery. The same floundering attempt to make sense of things.

I find small shrines on the plantations, set up in remote locations. They are crudely made of wood or baked mud, with shells & rotting fruit lying about them. If they be destroyed — & it is not I who does so — they reappear somewhere else. I am pleased to come upon these shrines. The slaves, who in their native villages practice various crafts, do nothing here except the compulsory fieldwork. No metalwork, no woodwork, no basket weaving, no ornament-making, no tailoring, no body painting, no singing, nothing. On this green island of malefic riot, they are as productive as mules. Only in these shrines do I see a vestige of their former lives, a reach for pregnancy.

Tomás is assailed by doubt. Is his own quest "a reach for pregnancy"? He imagines that Gaspar would be taken by Father Ulisses' gift, given his childish sensibility, but he doubts Dora would approve. That has always tormented him, that in the service of frank truth, he would do something that would upset her. But the treasure exists! He is only bringing to light what is already there. He pleads with Dora in his mind, begs for her forgiveness. *It is an elevation of all creation, my love. No, no, there is no desecration.* But he knows Dora would not believe him, that he would lose the argument. He still does not dare to halt the machine, so he weeps and drives at the same time.

Outside the village of Atalaia, he finally stops. He climbs on a mudguard to assess the damage done to the roof of the machine. The sight is dispiriting. There is an enormous dent caused by the thrown chest. And the whip, expertly deployed, has done its own extensive damage. The bright burgundy paint of the roof is veined with cracks. Great chips of it are ready to come off. When he looks inside the cabin, he sees that the cedar panels of the ceiling have split and jut out, like broken bones.

He walks into Atalaia, looking for moto-naphtha. He finds a small shop that sells a bit of everything. After he lists the various sobriquets of the fuel, the shop owner nods her head and produces a small bottle. He asks for more. The shop owner is surprised. But what! An automobile doesn't run on mere cupfuls of sustenance. An automobile is an insatiable fiend. He gets all she has: two bottles.

Back at the automobile, as he is feeding the hungry beast the bottles of moto-naphtha he has gathered so far, he casually inspects an empty bottle's label. He starts. A lice and flea product! *Guaranteed to kill all vermin and their eggs in a pitiless fashion*, the label claims. *Apply liberally. Do not ingest. KEEP AWAY FROM FLAMES*.

Could the shop owners and apothecaries not have asked him why he needed so many bottles of the foul liquid? What he bought as fuel for the machine, they sold as a parasite killer. They thought he was a tornado of vermin, with a civilization of lice, fleas, and whatnot dancing upon his head. No wonder they looked at him askance. He holds still. But of course. Of course. There is no other explanation. The shop owners and apothecaries are right. He is itchy all over, in a manner that is absolutely maddening, precisely because he *is* a tornado of vermin, with a civilization of lice, fleas, and whatnot dancing upon his head.

He looks at his other hand. The bottle he is holding upside down has just gurgled itself empty. It was his last bottle. How many did he have? Fifteen or so. He's had bottles of the stuff practically since the beginning of his trip, clinking away in the cabin, besides a whole barrel of it. Now he has none of it, or none that he can get to. He grabs the tank's small round opening as if he could stretch it out. He can't. Between his suffering and its relief — a bathtub of it — there lies a narrow doorway that will not open.

He wonders, *Who touched me? Who touched my clothes? Who passed on the infestation?* The point of contact must have been either in Póvoa de Santa Iria or Ponte de Sor. In both places he rubbed shoulders — indeed, he rubbed against entire bodies — while rescuing the machine from the surrounding masses.

He expends himself in a frenzy of scratching.

The sky darkens. It begins to rain and he takes refuge in the automobile. The front window of the automobile becomes so streaked and marbled with drops of water that he has difficulty seeing through them to the road. As the rain grows to a steady downpour, he wonders: His uncle said nothing about the machine's ability to operate in the rain. He does not trust it to stay on the road. He will wait the rain out.

Dusk and then darkness come on like a miasma. In his sleep, stagecoaches are galloping down on him from all directions. He is cold. His feet protrude over the edge of the driving compartment and the rain soaks them. Itchiness periodically rouses him.

In the morning the rain is still coming down. He is too chilled to want to wash in it. He no more than wets a hand to wipe his face. His only comfort comes from remembering that Father Ulisses was plagued by rain on the island. There, it deluged with such insistence that minds became unhinged. By comparison, what is this mild European drizzle?

On this deserted road, only the odd peasant appears, inevitably stopping for an extended conversation. Some arrive along the road, alone or pulling a donkey, while others come off the land itself, peasant lords working their tiny fiefdoms. None of them seems to mind the rain.

From one peasant to the next, the reaction is the same. They inspect the vehicle's wheels, finding them dainty and small. They peer at the side mirrors, finding them ingenious. They gaze at the machine's controls, finding them intimidating. They stare at the machine's engine, finding it unfathomable. Each deems the whole a marvel.

Only one, a shepherd, seems to have no interest in the contraption. "Can I sit with you for a while?" he asks. "I am cold and wet."

Already his sheep are surrounding the vehicle, held hostage there by a small dog that races around and yips incessantly. The sheeps' bleating is constant and grating. Tomás nods to the man, who walks around to the other side of the vehicle and clambers in next to him in the driving compartment.

Tomás wishes that he would speak, but the crusty man says not a word, only gazes ahead. Minutes go by. The silence is framed by the steady hiss of the rain, the bleating of the sheep, and the yipping of the dog.

Finally it is Tomás who speaks. "Let me tell you why I'm travelling. It's been a difficult journey so far. I'm searching for a lost treasure. I've spent a year determining where it might be — and now I know. Or I nearly know. I'm close. When I find it, I'll take it to the National Museum of Ancient Art in Lisbon, but it would be worthy of a great museum in Paris or London. The thing in question, it's — well, I can't tell you what it is, but it's an impressive object. People will stare at it, their mouths open. It will cause an uproar. With this object I'll give God His comeuppance for what He did to the ones I love."

The old rube's sole response is to glance at him and nod. Otherwise, only the sheep seem to appreciate his momentous confession, with a blast of wavering *baahs*. The flock is no creamy billow of fluffy sheepdom. These creatures have bony faces, bulging eyes, ragged fleeces, and rear ends caked with excrement.

"Tell me," he asks the shepherd, "what do you think of animals?"

The shepherd once again glances at him, but this time he speaks. "What animals?"

"Well, these, for example," Tomás replies. "What do you think of your sheep?"

At length the man says, "They are my living."

Tomás thinks for a moment. "Yes, your living. You make a profound point there. Without your sheep, you would have no livelihood, you would die. This dependency creates a sort of equality, doesn't it? Not individually, but collectively. As a group, you and your sheep are at opposite ends of a seesaw, and somewhere in between there is a fulcrum. You must maintain the balance. In that sense, we are no better than they."

The man says not a word in response. At that moment Tomás is overcome by ravenous itchiness. It's all over his body now. "If you'll excuse me, I have business to attend to," he says to the shepherd. He makes his way back along the footboard to the cabin. From the cabin, through the wide window, the back of the shepherd's head is plainly visible. Thrashing and twisting on the sofa, Tomás battles itchiness, digging hard with his fingernails at his insect tormentors. The gratification is intense. The shepherd never turns around.

To block out the rain, Tomás covers the shattered door window with a blanket, securing the blanket to the frame by closing the door on it. The rain becomes a monotonous drumming on the roof. Amidst the scattered supplies he makes a space for himself on the leather sofa, covers himself with another blanket, and curls up tightly . . .

He wakes with a start. He has no idea if he has slept five or fifty-five minutes. The rain is still falling. But the shepherd is gone. Peering through the machine's rain-streaked windows, he can see a hazy grey shape up ahead on the road — it is the flock of sheep. He opens the cabin door and stands on the footboard. The shepherd is in the middle of his flock, looking as if he is walking on a cloud. The dog is flitting about as it did earlier, but Tomás can no longer hear it. The flock moves down the road, then flows off to one side of it, taking a path into the countryside.

Through the rain Tomás watches the flock get smaller and smaller. Just as it begins to disappear beyond a ridge, the shepherd, a black dot now, stops and turns. Is he checking for a lost sheep? Is he looking back at him? Tomás waves vigorously. He can't tell if the man has noticed his farewell. The black dot vanishes.

He returns to the driving compartment. There is a small package on the passenger seat. Wrapped in cloth are a piece of bread, a chunk of white cheese, and a tiny sealed earthen jar of honey. A Christmas gift? When is Christmas, exactly? Four days away? He realizes he's losing track of the days. At any rate, what a kindness on the part of the shepherd. He is touched. He eats. It tastes so good! He can't remember ever having eaten such savoury bread, such flavourful cheese, such delicious honey.

The rain stops and the sky clears. While waiting for the wintry sunshine to dry the road, he lubricates the machine with drops of oil. Then, impatiently, he sets off. When he reaches the edge of the small town of Arez, he enters it on foot. He is pleased to find a proper apothecary.

"I'll buy your whole stock. I have horses that are badly infested with lice," he informs the man behind the counter once he has produced the usual small bottle of moto-naphtha.

"You might want to try Hipolito, the blacksmith," the apothecary says.

"Why would he have any of the stuff?"

"Horses are his concern, including horses badly infested with lice, I would think. And what about your feet?"

"My feet?"

"Yes. What's wrong with them?"

"Nothing's wrong with my feet. Why would anything be wrong with them?"

"I saw the way you were walking."

"My feet are perfectly healthy."

Walking backwards through the village on his perfectly healthy feet, Tomás finds Hipolito's smithy down a lane. He is astonished to discover that the blacksmith has an enormous barrel of moto-naphtha. Tomás is dizzy with joy. The supply will not only glut the automobile with fuel but will also soothe his ravaged body.

"My good man, I'll buy lots of it. I have twelve horses that are badly infested with lice."

"Oh, you don't want to use this stuff on horses. That would be doing them a great disservice. It's very harsh on the skin. You need a powder that you'll mix with water."

"Why then do you have so much moto-naphtha? What's it for?"

"For automobiles. They're a new device."

"Perfect! I have one of those too, and as it happens it desperately needs to be fed."

"Why didn't you say so?" says the jovial rustic.

"My horses were on my mind. The poor beasts."

Hipolito the blacksmith is moved by the drama of Tomás's twelve afflicted horses and goes into tender, lengthy details about how the lice powder should be mixed with warm water, applied topically, allowed to dry, then carefully brushed and combed out, starting at the top of the head and working one's way back and down across the horse's body. It's a task that takes much time, but a horse deserves nothing less than the best treatment.

"Bring your horses and I'll help you do it," Hipolito adds in a burst of fellow equine love.

"I'm not from these parts. I only have my automobile here."

"Then you've come a long way searching for the wrong remedy for your horses. I have the powder right here. Twelve horses, you say? Six cans should do you, eight to be safe. And you'll need this comb-and-brush kit. The highest quality."

"Thank you. You can't imagine how relieved I am. Tell me, how long have you been selling moto-naphtha?"

"Oh, about six months."

"How's business?"

"You're my first customer! I've never seen an automobile in my life. But it's the carriage of the future, I'm told. And I'm a smart businessman, I am. I understand commerce. It's important to be up to date. No one wants to buy what's old. You want to be the first to spread the word and show off the product. That's how you corner the market."

"How did you get this enormous barrel all the way up here?"

"By stagecoach."

At the word Tomás's heart skips a beat.

"But you know," Hipolito adds, "I didn't tell them it was for automobiles. I told them it was to treat horses with lice. They're funny about automobiles, those stagecoach drivers."

"Are they? Any stagecoaches coming soon?"

"Oh, in the next hour or so."

Not only does Tomás run back to the automobile, he runs *forward* to it.

When he roars up to the smithy in his uncle's Renault with the alarm of a bank robber, Hipolito is surprised, stunned, aghast, and delighted at the throbbing, clanging invention Tomás has brought to his shop.

"So this is it? What a big, noisy thing! Quite ugly in a beautiful sort of way, I'd say. Reminds me of my wife," yells Hipolito.

Tomás turns the machine off. "I completely agree. I mean about the automobile. To be honest with you, I find it ugly in an ugly sort of way."

"Hmmm, you may be right," the blacksmith muses, perhaps pondering how the automobile will wreck his commerce and way of life. His forehead wrinkles. "Oh well, business is business. Where does the moto-naphtha go? Show me."

Tomás points eagerly. "Here, here, here, and here."

He has Hipolito fill the fuel tank, the barrel, and all the glass bottles of vermin lotion. He eyes the bottles hungrily. He sorely wants to empty one all over his body.

"Come again!" cries Hipolito after Tomás has paid for the fuel, the eight cans of lice powder for horses, and the comb-and-brush kit of the highest quality. "Remember, from back to front, starting at the top of the head and working your way back and down. Poor creatures!"

"Thank you, thank you!" shouts Tomás as he speeds away.

After Arez, he turns off the road onto a well-marked track. He trusts that his map, with its faint markings for secondary roads, will lead him back to the road beyond the larger town of Nisa, which he is hoping to circumvent by this deviation. From that track he turns onto another, then another. The quality of the tracks goes from bad to worse. There are rocks everywhere. He navigates the terrain as best he can. The land, meanwhile, rises and falls like heaving swells so that he can never see very far around him. Is this how Father Ulisses felt sailing to the island, closed in while in the wide open?

In the midst of his oceanic meanderings, the track simply vanishes. The directed smoothness of a pathway is replaced by a rockiness that is uniform and undefined, as if the track were a river that opened onto a delta, casting him adrift. He navigates on, but eventually he hears the voice of prudence and it urgently suggests he reverse his course.

He turns the machine around, but facing one way looks no different from facing another. He becomes confused. Surrounding him in all directions is the same countryside, rocky, dry, silent, with silver-green olive trees as far as the eye can see and bulbous white clouds boiling up high in the sky. He's lost, a castaway. And night is coming.

Finally it is not this predicament, of being lost, that leads him to drop anchor for the night. It is another, more personal one: Great armies of tiny vermin are rampaging over his body, and he cannot stand it any longer.

He reaches a rise in the land and halts the vehicle, tapping its front against a tree. The air, fragrant with the fertile labour of trees, is extraordinarily soft. There is not a sound around him, not from insects, not from birds, not from the wind. All that registers upon his ears are the few sounds he himself makes. In the absence of sound, he notices more with his eyes, in particular the delicate winter flowers that here and there brave the stony ground. Pink, light blue, red, white — he doesn't know what kind of flowers they are, only that they are beautiful. He breathes in deeply. He can well imagine that this land was once the last outpost of the storied Iberian rhinoceros, roaming free and wild.

In every direction he walks, he finds no trace of human presence. He wanted to wait until he reached a private spot to take care of his problem, and now he has found it. The moment has come. He returns to the automobile. No human being — no being of any kind — could stand such itchiness. But before slaying his enemies with his magic potions, he gives in one last time to the gratifying indulgence of scratching an itch.

He raises his ten fingers in the air. His blackened fingernails gleam. With a warlike cry, he throws himself into the fray. He rakes his fingernails over his head — the top, the sides, the nape — and over his bearded cheeks and neck. It is quick, hard, spirited work. Why do we make animal sounds in moments of pain or pleasure? He does not know, but he makes animal sounds and he makes animal faces. He goes *AAAAHHHHH!* and he goes *OOOOHHHHH!* He throws off his jacket, unbuttons and removes his shirt, tears off his undershirt. He attacks the enemies on his torso and in his armpits. His crotch is a cataclysm of itchiness. He unbuckles his belt and pulls his trousers and his underpants down to his ankles. He scratches his hairy sexual patch vigorously, his fingers like claws. Has he ever felt such relief? He pauses to bask in it. Then he starts over again. He moves down to his legs. There is blood under his fingernails. No matter. But the vandals have regrouped in the crack of his ass. Because there too he is hairy. He is hairy all over. It has always been a source of acute embarrassment to him, the forests of thick black hair that sprout from his pale white skin all over his body. That Dora liked to run her fingers through his chest hair always comforted him, because otherwise he finds his hairiness repulsive. He is an ape. Hence the care with which he has his hair cut, with which he shaves. He is normally a clean and neat man, and modest and reserved. But right now he is unhinged with itchiness. His ankles are constrained by his trousers. He kicks his shoes off, pulls his socks off, tears one pant leg off, then the other. That's better — now he can lift his legs. He attacks the crack of his ass with both hands. On he battles: His hands fly about and he hops from one foot to the other, he makes animal sounds and he makes animal faces, he goes *AAAAHHHHH!* and he goes *OOOHHHHH!*

It's as he's working his pubic patch, his hands vibrating like the wings of a hummingbird, his face displaying a particularly simian grin of satisfaction, that he sees the peasant. Just a short way off. Looking at him. Looking at the man hopping about naked, scratching himself madly, making animal sounds next to the strange horseless cart. Tomás freezes on the spot. How long has the man been watching him?

What is there to do at such a moment? What can he do to salvage his dignity, his very humanity? He removes the animal expression from his face. He stands upright. As solemnly as he can — with quick dips to gather his clothes — he walks to the automobile and disappears inside the cabin. Profound mortification brings on complete immobility.

When the sun has set and the sky is inky black, the darkness and the isolation begin to weigh on him. And full-out, unqualified, comprehensive humiliation is not a remedy against vermin. He is still covered in rioting insect life. He can practically hear them. He cautiously opens the automobile door. He peers out. He looks about. There is no one. The peasant has gone. Tomás lights a candle stub. He has nowhere to place the candle where it will not risk damaging the plush interior, so he unplugs one of the bottles of moto-naphtha and corks it with the lit candle. The effect is attractive. The cabin looks cosy, truly a very small living room.

Still fully naked, he steps out. He takes out the tin of horse lice powder and two bottles of moto-naphtha lotion. He will do better than what Hipolito suggested. He will mix the lice powder with moto-naphtha rather than with water, doubling the lethalness of the concoction. Besides, he has no water left. The water from the barrel in the cabin went into either him or the automobile. He has only a skin of wine left. He mixes moto-naphtha and horse lice powder in a pot until the paste is neither too runny nor too thick. It smells awful. He starts to apply it to his body, working it in with his fingers. He winces. His skin is tender from all the scratching. The paste burns. But he endures it because of the death blow it is striking against the vermin. *Apply liberally*, says the label on the bottle. He does, he does. After caking his head and face, he applies the mixture to his armpits and over his chest and stomach, on his legs and feet. He covers his pubic mound in a thick layer. Where the paste falls off his body, he applies double the quantity. For his rear, he places a great dollop on the footboard and sits in it. There. His head upright, his arms tight against his body, his hands spread out over his torso, he sits very still. Any movement, even breathing, not only loosens the paste but increases the burning.

This burning is infernal. He tries to get used to it, but he can't. It's as if the paste has consumed his skin and now is working through his flesh. He is being roasted alive. But so are the vermin. They and their eggs are dying by the thousands. He needs to endure the agony only a little longer, until they are all dead. After that, he will be well on the road to recovery. He continues to wait, slowly sizzling.

Then it happens: a shattering *BOOM!* He is projected from the footboard, as much by surprise and fright as by the force of the explosion. He turns and stares, the vermin and the pain all forgotten. The automobile is on fire! Where before there was only a single wavering flame atop the bottle of moto-naphtha, now there are great patches of fire all over the inside of the cabin. And upon feeling a prickling at the back of his head, he realizes that the fire has leapt from the cabin onto his head. In a moment it spreads to his beard, his chest, his entire body. *POUF!* goes his pubic mound, now an orange forest of flames. He screams. Luckily for him, the lice powder is not flammable. But there are stabs of pain coming from his head, from his chest, from his penis — wherever the moto-naphtha-fuelled fire has worked its way through lice powder and hair and reached bare skin. He hops about, slapping his hands all over his body, stamping the fires out. When he is done, he stands, smoke rising off him in a column.

The automobile is still burning. He runs to it. On the way he picks up off the ground the wet blanket that he used the previous day to cover the broken cabin window and keep the rain out. He dives into the cabin. Throwing the blanket around and flinging horse lice powder about, he manages to extinguish the fires.

He pulls the trunk out from the cabin and opens it. Father Ulisses' diary, for being inside it, is undamaged. He nearly cries with relief. But the cabin — the state of it! The leather of the sofa — charred and crispy. The side panels — scorched. The ceiling — black with soot. All the windows except the one in front of the driving compartment — blown out, shards of glass everywhere. The food, the motoring supplies, his clothes — all singed and burned. Everything covered in ashes and carbonized horse lice powder. And the reek!

He finishes the last of the red wine, clears the driving compartment seat of broken glass, then lies down naked on the blanket on the seat, covering himself with the mink coat. Pain racks his body, his uncle yells at him in his dreams. He is chilled by the night while yet burning from his sores.

In the morning light, he dresses gingerly. However carefully he puts his clothes on, they rake at his tender skin. He sweeps and cleans the cabin as best he can. He opens the trunk again to check the diary. He does not want to lose his connection to Father Ulisses. He has come to see in the priest a man perfected by his suffering. A man to be imitated. Because to suffer and do nothing is to be nothing, while to suffer and do something is to become someone. And that is what he is doing: He is doing something. He must strike onward to the High Mountains of Portugal and fulfil his quest.

But he is confronted with an unexpected problem: the tree right in front of the automobile. There's not enough space to drive around it. He has not encountered this situation until now. Always there has been space in front of the vehicle to make use of the steerage wheel and move forward. He exclaims and blames and curses. Finally he tries to think of a solution, and there is only one, clearly: to cut down the tree. There's an axe among the store of essential items in the cabin. He has just seen it, covered in soot. His ever considerate and farsighted uncle no doubt included it for this precise purpose. The grand march of progress apparently includes the unfortunate necessity of chopping down every obstacle in its way. But the tree is so large, the trunk so thick, his body so sore!

He dithers. Finally the sight of his trunk of papers in the breezy cabin focuses his scattered energies. He picks up the axe.

He stands, facing the side of the tree opposite where the automobile is held prisoner. He raises the axe and swings. He chops and chops and chops. The bark flies off well enough, but the pale flesh of the tree is rubbery and resistant. The axe, sharp though it is, bounces back, producing only the smallest indentation each time. Hitting the same spot repeatedly demands a skill that mostly eludes him. And every swing grinds tender flesh against harsh clothing.

Quickly he is bathing in perspiration. He rests, eats, goes at it again. The morning is spent in this fashion. Then the early afternoon slips by.

By late afternoon, he has hacked a large hollow into the side of the trunk. The hollow goes beyond the midway point, but the tree doesn't seem to feel any inclination to fall. His palms are shredded red and bleeding. The pain in his hands barely masks the pain he feels in his whole body. He is so exhausted he can barely stand.

He can chop no longer. The hindrance has to go away — now. He decides to use the weight of his body to make the tree topple. Placing one foot on the edge of the mudguard and another on the edge of the hood, he reaches for the first branch. It's torture to grip the bark with his hands, but he manages to hook a leg around another branch and heave himself up. After all his struggles with the axe, the comparative ease with which he climbs the tree cheers him.

He moves out along a bough. He holds on to two separate branches. Of course, when the tree falls, he will fall with it. But the height isn't great, and he will brace himself.

He begins to swing his body back and forth, ignoring the excruciating pain that is radiating from his palms. The head of the tree dances and dances. He expects to hear at any moment a sharp crack and feel himself drop through the air the short distance to the ground.

Instead, the tree gives up with quiet, rubbery elasticity. It tips over slowly. Tomás turns his head and sees the ground coming up. The landing is soft. But his feet slip off their bough, and where they come to rest on the ground is the precise spot where the tree chooses to press down with its heaviest limb. He yelps with pain.

He wrenches his feet free. He moves his toes. No bones are broken. He turns and looks at the automobile. He sees in an instant from the ground what he didn't during his long hours of toil standing up: The stump is too high. The automobile, its bottom, will never be able to reach over it. He should have chopped much lower. But even if he had, the tree is still attached to the stump. It has fallen over without breaking off. The point at which tree and stump cling to each other is twisted and will be even more resistant to the axe. And even if he did manage to chop through the rest of the trunk, and supposing the stump were shorter, *would he be able to pull the tree away?* It seems scarcely imaginable. It's no bush.

His efforts have been futile. The tree mocks him. Still entangled in the branches, he slumps. He begins to sob awkwardly. He closes his eyes and abandons himself to grief.

He hears the voice just before a hand touches his shoulder.

"My friend, you are hurt."

He looks up, startled. A peasant has materialized out of the air. Such a bright white shirt he is wearing.

Tomás chokes on his last sob and wipes his face with the back of his hand.

"You've been thrown so far!" says the man.

"Yes," replies Tomás.

The man is looking at the automobile and the tree. Tomás understood him to mean how far he was projected from the tree (which, in fact, he hasn't been at all; he's *in* the tree, like a bird in its nest). But the peasant meant from the *automobile*. He must think that Tomás crashed into the tree and was projected from the vehicle into its branches.

"My hands and feet hurt. And I'm so thirsty!" Tomás says.

The peasant wraps one of his arms around his waist. Though short, he's a powerful man and he lifts Tomás off the ground. He half-carries him to the automobile, setting him down on the footboard. Tomás massages his ankles.

"Anything broken?" the man asks.

"No. Just bruised."

"Have some water."

The man produces a gourd. Tomás drinks from it greedily.

"Thank you. For the water and for your help. I'm most grateful. My name is Tomás."

"My name is Simão."

Simão gazes at the fallen tree and the automobile's broken windows, burned-out cabin, and many dents and scratches. "What a terrible accident! Such a powerful machine!" he exclaims.

Tomás hopes Simão doesn't notice the axe on the ground.

"Pity about the tree," Simão adds.

"Is it yours?"

"No. This is Casimiro's grove."

For the first time Tomás looks at the tree not as an obstacle in his way but as a being in its own right. "How old was it?"

"By the looks of it, two to three hundred years old. A good one, producing plenty of olives."

Tomás is aghast. "I'm so sorry. Casimiro will be very angry."

"No, he'll understand. Accidents happen to all of us."

"Tell me, is Casimiro somewhat older, with a round face and greying hair?"

"Yes, that would describe Casimiro."

As it would the peasant from last night, the one who watched Tomás's vermin dance. Tomás suspects that Casimiro will see the events in his olive grove in a different, less forgiving light.

"Do you think the machine will still work?" asks Simão.

"I'm sure it will," replies Tomás. "It's a solid thing. But I need to move it backwards. That's my problem."

"Put it in neutral and we'll push it."

That word again. Tomás is not sure why the machine's neutrality will allow it to move backwards, but Simão seems to know what he's talking about.

"It's already in neutral. Only the hand brake needs to be released," Tomás says.

He puts his shoes back on and climbs into the driving compartment. With a sore hand, he releases the hand brake. Nothing happens. He doubts Simão's quick fix will yield anything more fruitful than his own tree-chopping solution.

"Come," says Simão.

Tomás joins him at the front of the automobile. This notion of pushing the automobile is preposterous. Still, to be polite to the man who has so obligingly helped him and is now ready beside him to push, he places a shoulder against the automobile.

"One — two — three!" cries Simão, and he pushes, and Tomás too, though not very hard.

To his amazement, the automobile moves. He's so amazed, in fact, that he forgets to move with it and he falls flat on his face. In a matter of seconds, the vehicle stands three lengths from the tree.

Simão is beaming. "What an astonishing machine!"

"Yes, it is," says Tomás, incredulous.

As he picks himself up off the ground, he discreetly takes hold of the axe. Placing it close to his leg, he returns it to the cabin. Simão is still gazing at the automobile with unbounded admiration.

Tomás would like nothing better than to stay where he is for the night, but the prospect of Casimiro arriving on the scene, and having to explain the attack on his quarter-millennium olive tree, strongly advises against the option. Besides, he's lost. If he stays the night, he will still be lost in the morning.

"Simão, I was wondering if you might help me find my way out of here. I seem to have got lost."

"Where do you want to go? To Nisa?"

"No, I've just come from there. I'm heading for Vila Velha de Ródão."

"Vila Velha? You have got very lost. But it's no problem. I know the way."

"That's wonderful. Might you help me start the automobile?"

With the condition his hands are in, the idea of having to turn the starting handle makes Tomás feel faint. He supposes Simão will take pleasure in it. He's right. The peasant's face breaks into a wide grin.

"Yes, of course. What do you want me to do?"

Tomás shows him the starting handle and the direction in which to turn it. As the machine explodes to life, Simão might as well be struck by lightning — the effect is the same. Tomás waves at him to get into the driving compartment and Simão scampers aboard. Tomás puts the vehicle into first gear, and as it moves forward he glances at his passenger. His face confirms what Tomás already suspected from watching his uncle: The machine turns grown men into little boys. Simão's weathered features are transformed by delight. If he shrieked and giggled, Tomás would not be surprised.

"Which way should I go?" he asks.

Simão points. Every few minutes Simão corrects his course and soon the trace of a track appears. Then a proper track, smoother and verged. The driving becomes easier and faster. Simão's delight continues undiminished.

After a good half hour of driving, they reach a true, blessed road. Tomás stops the automobile.

"I never thought I'd be so happy to see a road. So which way is Vila Velha de Ródão?" he asks.

Simão indicates to the right.

"Thank you very much, Simão. You've been of invaluable help. I must reward you." Tomás reaches into the pocket of his charred jacket.

Simão shakes his head. With a struggle, as if his tongue has been lost deep inside his body, he speaks. "My reward is having been in this amazing carriage. It is I who thank you."

"It's nothing. I'm sorry I've taken you so far out of your way."

"It's not so far on foot."

Simão reluctantly vacates the passenger seat, and Tomás prods the machine onward. "Thank you, thank you again," he shouts.

Simão waves until he disappears from view in the side mirror.

Shortly thereafter, with a dragging to one side and a *fluf-fluf-fluf-fluf* sound, Tomás realizes that something is wrong. He presses on one pedal, then another.

It takes a few walkabouts around the vehicle before he sees that the front right tire is — he searches for the word — *flat*. The roundness of the wheel is no longer so round. There were some pages in the manual about this eventuality. He skipped them when it became apparent that the wheels, in their roundness, at least, did not require lubrication. He retrieves the manual and finds the appropriate section. He blanches. This is serious engineering work. He can see that even before he has translated the details from the French.

Understanding the nature and operation of the jack; assembling it; finding where it must be placed under the automobile; jacking the automobile up; unbolting and removing the wheel; replacing it with the spare wheel from the footboard; tightly bolting the fresh wheel into place; returning everything to its proper place — an experienced motorist might do it in half an hour. It takes him, with his raw hands, two hours.

At last, his hands sullied and throbbing, his body sweaty and aching, the task is done. He should be pleased that he can proceed again, but all he feels is mortal exhaustion. He retreats to the driving compartment and stares out in front of him. His head is prickly, as is the unwanted beard that is growing on his face. "Enough! Enough!" he whispers. What does suffering do to a man? Does it open him up? Does he understand any more as a result of his suffering? In the case of Father Ulisses, for the longest time it seems the answer to these questions was no. Tomás remembers a telling incident:

Today I saw a fight on a plantation. Two slaves clashed. Others stood about, with stupefied expressions. A female slave, the object of contention, looked on, impassive, indifferent. Whoever won, she would lose. Continually shouting in their native gibberish, the two fought, at first with words & gestures, then their fists, then their tools. The matter proceeded swiftly, from injured prides to injured bodies, from bruising & bleeding to frenzied hacking, till the end was reached:

a dead slave with a torso cleft with deep cuts & a half-severed head. Whereupon the other slaves, the female included, turned & got back to their work lest the overseer arrive on the scene. The victor slave, his visage apathetic, threw some soil on the body, then returned to cutting cane. None of the slaves will come forward to acknowledge or explain, to accuse or defend. Just silence & the hoeing of sugar cane. The dead man's decay will be rapid, started by insects & predatory birds & beasts & accelerated by the sun & rain. Soon nothing but a lump will be left of him. Only if the overseer directly steps onto this lump will its gashed blackness reveal white bones & decaying red flesh. Then the overseer will know the whereabouts of the slave who went missing.

Of this appalling scene, Father Ulisses has only one significant comment to make:

Such were the Lord's wounds, like that dead slave's injuries. His hands, his feet, his forehead where the crown of thorns pierced his skin & especially the wound on his side from the soldier's spear — carmine red, very, very bright, a pull on the eyes.

Such was the suffering of Christ: "carmine red" and a "pull on the eyes". But the suffering of the two men who fought to death before his very eyes? They are not worth a word. No more than the spectator slaves would

Father Ulisses come forward to acknowledge or explain, to accuse or to defend. He seems to have been deaf and dumb to the suffering of the slaves. Or, to be more accurate, he seems to have seen nothing peculiar about it: *They suffer, but so do I — so what of it?*

The land begins to change as Tomás drives on. The Portugal that he knows is a land solemn in its beauty. A land that prizes the sound of work, both human and animal. A land devoted to duty. Now an element of wilderness begins to intrude. Great outcrops of round rocks. Dark green vegetation that is dry and scrubby. Wandering flocks of goats and sheep. He sees the High Mountains of Portugal foreshadowed in these extrusions of rocks, like the roots of a tree that break above ground, heralding the tree itself.

He is fretful. He is approaching Castelo Branco, which is a proper city, the largest on his deliberately rural route. An idea strikes him: He will drive through the city in the middle of the night. Thus will he avoid people, because it is people who are the problem. Streets, avenues, boulevards — these he can handle, if people aren't staring and shouting and congregating. If he crosses Castelo Branco at, say, two in the morning in full-throttle third gear, he will likely meet only the odd nightshift worker or drunkard.

When Castelo Branco is near, he leaves the automobile behind and makes his way into the city on foot, backwards as always. He hitches a ride with a man driving a cart, which is fortunate, as the distance to the city turns out to be considerable. The man asks if he saw the strange carriage down the road. He says that

111

he did, without mentioning that he is its driver. The man speaks of the machine in terms of wonder and worry. It's the quantity of metal that surprises him, he says. It reminds him of a safe.

In Castelo Branco Tomás determines the route he should take. He is pleased to discover that the road continuing to the north of the country mostly avoids the city, circling it on its northwest side. Only the junction with the road is tricky.

He tells three apothecaries his horses-afflicted-with-lice story, which gets him ten bottles of moto-naphtha and, as an unfortunate corollary, three tins of horse lice powder. He carries these in two bags, evenly balanced. He decides to check in to a hotel for the day to wash himself and rest, but the two hotels he finds refuse to admit him, as does the restaurant he seeks to eat in. The proprietors look him up and down, study his singed face and burned hair — one pinches his nose — and they all point to the door. He is too tired to protest. He buys food from a grocer and eats on a bench in a park. He drinks water from a fountain, gulping it avidly, splashing it over his face and head, scrubbing at the soot plastered to his scalp. He wishes he'd remembered to bring the two wineskins, which he could have filled with water. Then he walks in reverse back to the automobile, watching Castelo Branco recede into the distance.

He waits in the cabin for night to fall, idly leafing through the diary to pass the time.

The provenance of the slaves on São Tomé was at first a matter of concern and interest to Father Ulisses

— he named the newcomers' origins in his diary: "from the Mbundu tribe" or "the Chokwe tribe." But he was hazier on the origins of slaves who came from outside the Portuguese sphere of influence in Africa, and São Tomé, being usefully located, saw slave ships of every nationality — Dutch, English, French, Spanish — and soon he grew weary as a result of the slaves' too-great numbers. They received his weakening blessing in a state of increasing anonymity. "Does it matter," he wrote, "wherefrom a soul comes? The exiles of Eden are varied. A soul is a soul, to be blessed & brought to the love of God."

But one day there was a change. Father Ulisses wrote with uncharacteristic excitement:

I am at the port when a Dutch slaver is unloading its stock. Four captives catch my eye. I see them from afar as they shuffle down the gangplank in shackles & chains. What poor souls are these? They walk with a listless gait, their backs bent, their will broken. I know how they feel. My exhaustion & theirs is the same. The fever is upon me again. Jesus reached out to all, Romans, Samaritans, Syrophoenicians, and others. So must I. I want to get closer but am too weak, the sun too bright. A sailor from the ship is passing by. I beckon to him. I point & ask & he tells me that the captives come from deep within the Congo River basin & were captured in a raid, not traded by a tribe. Three females & a child. My Dutch is poor & I don't fully understand the sailor. I believe he uses the word "minstrel". They are to be entertainers of some sort. He gives no sense of impropriety to the term. What? I say to him. Straight from the jungles of the Congo to amusing the white man after his dinner in the New World? He laughs.

I have learned that the four are now jailed on García's plantation. The mother of the child attacked an overseer & was severely beaten for the offence. They were unwilling to put on clothes & it seemed they provided poor entertainment. Their fate will be decided shortly.

Though I am so feeble I cannot stay long on my feet, I went to García's today & slipped in to see his captives in their dark, hot cell. The rebellious female has died of her injuries. Her body was still there, her child at her side, listless, nearly unconscious. Fruit lay rotting on the ground. Are the two females that remain starving themselves to death? I spoke to them, knowing they would not understand me. They did not respond or even seem to hear me. I blessed them.

I have gone again. The stench! The child is most certainly dead. At first I had no greater success with the two survivors than yesterday. I read to them from the Gospel of Mark. I chose Mark because it is the most humble Gospel, revealing a messiah at his most human, racked by doubt & anxiety while still shining with loving kindness. I read until fatigue, the heat & the stench nearly overcame me. Thereafter I sat in silence. I was about to leave when one of the captives, the youngest, an adolescent female, stirred. She crawled & settled against the wall on the other side of the bars from me. I whispered to her, *"O senhor te ama, filha. Donde tu vens? Conte-me sobre o Jardim do Éden? Conta-me tua história. O que fizemos de errado?"* She did not react in any way. A time passed. Then she turned her head & looked me in the eyes. She looked only briefly before moving away. She guessed that she had nothing to gain from my nearness or inter-est. I said not a word. My tongue was stilled of any priestly cant. I am transformed. I saw. I have seen. I see. That short gaze made me see a wretchedness that until then had never echoed in my heart. I entered that cell thinking I was a Christian man. I walked out knowing I was a Roman soldier. We are no better than animals.

When I returned this day, they were dead, their bodies taken away and burned. They are free now, as they should have been all along.

The next entry in Father Ulisses' diary is fierce and accusatory, outlining the final rift between him and the island's civil and religious authorities. He made a scene at the cathedral, interrupting the Mass with his shouts and protests. The consequence was swift.

I was summoned by the Bishop today. I told him
that I had met the unequal & in meeting them
found them equal. We are no better than they, I
told him. In fact, we are worse. He yelled at me
that as there are hierarchies of angels in heaven
and of the damned in hell, so there are
hierarchies here on earth. The boundaries are not
to be blurred. I was sent off, struck by his harsh-
est thunderbolt, excommunication. In his eyes I
am no longer a man of the cloth. But I yet feel
the Lord's hand holding me up.

Tomás is amazed, as he is every time he reads this
passage. To exclude French and English pirates, or
Dutch sailors, little more than mercenaries, from the
communion of God is one thing — but an ordained
Portuguese priest? That seems an extreme measure,
even by the standards of São Tomé. But a place that
made its living off slavery would think poorly of a
fevered emancipator.

It is then that Father Ulisses mentioned the gift for
the first time. Tomás always reads the sentence with
trepidation.

I know my mission now. I will make this gift to
God before death takes me. I thank God that I
drew a sketch while I was at García's, visiting her
in her hellish confinement. Her eyes have opened
mine. I will bear witness to the wreckage we have
wrought. How great is our fall from the Garden!

Tomás turns the page and stares for the thousandth time at the sketch in question. It is this sketch, with its haunting eyes, that set him on his search.

Night has settled on the land and the time has come to drive through Castelo Branco. He lights the remaining sidelight and adjusts its broad wick. The flame that dances up sheds a circle of warm light. The brilliantly white flame of the surviving headlight hisses like an angry snake. Its illumination is focused forward by a crystal-glass encasement. If only the light cast by the headlight weren't so lopsided. His Cyclops looks rather sorry.

He reviews the route he will take. He has a series of markers in his head. At each point where a decision needs to be made, he has taken note of a detail — a house, a shop, a building, a tree. Because there will be no throngs of people at this time of night, he will have more leisure to guide himself correctly.

Whatever illusion he has that he's riding a firefly of sorts — and when he moves away from the vehicle's lit side, its radiance gives that image some credibility — is shattered when he starts up the machine. Its juddering roar rather brings to mind a dragon, although one with puny flames shooting from its mouth.

Not only puny: wholly ineffective. The lights, bright to his eyes close up, are mere pinpricks in the impenetrable night. All the headlight does, and poorly at that, is bring out the rough features of the road immediately under the automobile's nose. What lies beyond — every rut, every turn — comes as a frightening, ever-changing surprise.

117

His only recourse — wholly illogical, he knows, but he can't help himself and does it over and over — is to squeeze the horn, as if the night were a black cow obstructing the road that will jump out of the way with a few honks.

He does not move beyond first gear as he gropes his way towards Castelo Branco.

In Portugal the sunshine is often pearly, lambent, tickling, neighbourly. So too, in its own way, is the dark. There are dense, rich, and nourishing pockets of gloom to be found in the shadows of houses, in the courtyards of modest restaurants, on the hidden sides of large trees. During the night, these pockets spread, taking to the air like birds. The night, in Portugal, is a friend. These are the days and nights that he has mostly known. Only in his distant childhood was the night ever a breeder of terrors. Then he quaked and cried out. His father came to his rescue each time, stumbling half-asleep to his bed, where he would take him in his arms. He would fall asleep against his father's big, warm chest.

Castelo Branco does not have the streetlights that light up Lisbon's nights. Every marker on his route, so clear during the day, is now shrouded. Streets rear up like the tentacles of a giant squid. He never finds the road that skirts the city on its northwest. Instead, Castelo Branco is a breeder of terrors. He tries to hold a course in one direction until he reaches the city's edge, any edge, but every street he takes ends in a T-junction, either way plunging him back into the depths of the city. Worse are the people. Like the houses and buildings that surround him, they appear abruptly out of the darkness, their faces suddenly fixed by the white light of the one-eyed machine. Some shout in fright, spreading their fright to him, and stand frozen, while others turn and run. It's true that in the silence of the night the automobile is very loud, and he continues to honk the horn incessantly — but only to alert. At first there is hardly anyone about, but as he moves through the city like a blind creature scuttling at the bottom of the ocean, more and more people throw their shutters open, more and more people fling themselves into the streets, dishevelled but sharp-eyed. He moves into second gear and outpaces them. A short while later, on another circuit through the city, he encounters more groups. He sees them, they see him. They run towards him, he turns down another street. He moves into third gear.

If he cannot escape, then he must hide. After a series of turns, halfway down a deserted avenue, he abruptly stops the machine. He hurries to blow out the flames of the sidelight and headlight. Darkness and silence engulf him. He listens. Will the night hordes find him? He ventures out. He peers around corners and stares down streets. Nothing but benign darkness. It seems he has lost them.

He spends the rest of the night walking through Castelo Branco, establishing the route he will take at first light.

During his nocturnal exploration of the city, he comes upon a plain square, with its allotment of trees, benches, and a single statue veiled in darkness in its centre. He sees movement and he jumps, then realizes what it is. There has been a market that day in the square. The vendors' stalls still stand, and beneath the tables, strewn about, lies the bad produce that the vendors threw away, fruit, vegetables, perhaps even meat. Moving amidst this detritus are dogs. Under the great dome of the night, in the submarine quiet of a city returned to sleep after a brief disturbance, he gazes at these street dogs that are taking in what others have rejected. They go about their business with hopeful pokes and snuffles, occasionally finding and gratefully eating. A few of them look up and stare at him before returning to their rooting. They accept him, as he accepts them.

When he returns to the automobile, he feels the gratitude of a sea creature retreating into its sheltering shell. He lies down for a short nap in the cabin. Alas, the walking and the sleepless night have taxed him greatly. He oversleeps. At the honk of the machine's horn, pressed by some impertinent bystander, he wakes with a jerk to the sight of faces pressed through the window openings of the cabin, goggling eyes on him, noses sniffing the air. He has to push against the door of the cabin to move the people on the other side enough that he can squeeze out. He stands on the footboard and breathes in the fresh air of the new day. It is good to have escaped the night, but surrounding him now, sloshing and slapping against the automobile like the ocean's bright blue water, is seemingly the entire population of Castelo Branco, clamouring at him like breaking waves. His escape — involving the usual

120

shouted exhortations, the usual blinkered lack of understanding, the usual surprise when the automobile nudges forward, and the usual race ahead of the mob — drains him utterly. He drives until his nodding head hits the steerage wheel.

He wakes midafternoon and makes a groggy calculation. For each day established by a memory of it — the first day, the bridges, Ponte de Sor, the stagecoach, and so on — he raises a finger. Quickly the fingers of one hand stand erect. Then the fingers of the other, but for one. Nine, if his calculation is correct. Today is his ninth day on the road. His meagre ration of days is nearly expended. In two days, early in the morning, the chief curator at the museum will be expecting his return. He puts his head in his hands. Castelo Branco is not even halfway to his ultimate destination. Should he abandon his mission? But even if he does, he will not be back in Lisbon in time. To return now will be to fail twice, at his job and in his mission. To press on towards the High Mountains of Portugal will be to fail only at his job. And if his mission is crowned with success, he might perhaps get his job back. He will carry on, then, he will persevere. That is the only sensible course. But night is coming. He will persevere tomorrow.

With the changing land comes a changing climate. Winter in the Portuguese hinterland is cold and damp, and its bite is made worse by the metal cage that is the automobile's cabin and the drafts that blow through its broken windows. Tomás steps out. Beyond the faint gleam of the road, there is only blackness. He wonders:

Animals know boredom, but do they know loneliness? He doesn't think so. Not this kind of loneliness, of the body and the soul. He belongs to a lonely species. He returns to the sofa and wraps himself in the mink coat and three blankets. Perhaps he sleeps at odd moments, but if he does, he dreams that he is in the cabin of an automobile on a cold night, waiting, and so, awake or sleeping, he remains in the same state of misery. Through the hours, a question preoccupies him: When is Christmas? Did he miss it?

In the morning he is glad to get the machine going. The land continues to dry up, the cultivated weave plucked away, the sustaining frame of rock further exposed. The new landscape jumps out at him, luminous, the assertion of geology plain and direct.

He begins to lose his way regularly. Until now, thanks to the maps, to the forbearance of roads, to luck, he has never got lost for very long. This changes after Castelo Branco. After Castelo Branco, the days blur into a fog of time. He drives into a village in despair, finds a local, and asks him, "Please, I've been looking for Rapoula do Cãoa for three days. Where is it? In what direction does it lie?" The old villager looks in consternation at the smelly, distressed man in the smelly, distressing machine (whom he saw the previous day and the day before, roaring through the village) and responds shyly, "This *is* Rapoula do Cãa." Lost elsewhere Tomás begs to know where Almeida is, and the native smiles and cries out, "¿Almeida? No está aquí, hombre. Almeida está del otro lado de la frontera." Tomás stares at the man's mouth, aghast to hear the susurration of

Portuguese replaced by the growl of Spanish. He races back to Portugal, fearful that the border he did not even notice will now rear up like an impassable mountain range.

The compass is of no help. Always, no matter the road, it points away from the road into the wilderness, its needle trembling as he trembles.

How one gets lost can vary, but the state of being lost, the feeling of it, is always the same: paralysis, anger, lethargy, despair. A pack of wolf children somewhere past Macedo de Cavalerios pelt the machine with stones, gouging the elephant hide, denting the metal hood, and, worst of all, shattering the window of the driving compartment, so that he must now drive through howls of cold wind wearing the motoring coat, goggles, and hat, but not the fine gloves, which burned to a crisp in the cabin fire. He has another flat tire, and this time he must actually *repair* the tire, since the tire on the footboard is already punctured.

One afternoon he at last reaches his destination. Invisibly — but the map telling him so — he enters the High Mountains of Portugal. He can see it in the gentle lift in the land and in the increasing drop off the side of the road. He is jubilant. Soon, soon, he will find the church he's been seeking and his uncommon insight will be brilliantly demonstrated. His mission is nearly accomplished. What he has been saying with his backwards walking for a year, his outrage, his despair, he will now say with an unconventional crucifix. A broad smile illuminates his face.

The road soon settles into a steady flatness. He looks to his left and right, perplexed. He discovers that he is driving through an act of national vanity. Every country yearns to flaunt that glittering jewel called a mountain range, and so this barren wasteland, too low to be alpine but too high to be usefully fertile, has been bedecked with a grand title. But there are no mountains in the High Mountains of Portugal. There is nothing beyond mere hills, nothing *trás os montes*. It is an extensive, undulating, mostly treeless steppe, cool, dry, and bleached by a clear, dispassionate sunshine. Where he expected snow and rock, he finds a low, rampant golden-yellow grass that stretches as far as the eye can see, occasionally interrupted by patches of forest. And the only summits he sees are strange, pockmarked boulders, enormous in size, the detritus of some geologic bustle. Streams here and there flow with unexpected liveliness. The steppe is, as its homophone implies, a temporary place from which one proceeds elsewhere. Historically, generations of hardscrabble locals have hurried away from its poor soil, emigrating to more clement parts of the world, and he finds that he too wishes to hurry through it. The villages he encounters concentrate the loneliness he feels in the wide-open spaces between them. Every man and woman he encounters — he doesn't see any children — smells of time and radiates solitude. These people live in plain, square, solid stone houses with shale roofs, the habitable spaces built above the animal pens, so that the two groups live in joint dependency, the humans receiving warmth and sustenance, the animals food and safety. The land is not amenable to extensive economic use. There is nothing but small, hardy fields of rye, large vegetable gardens, chestnut trees, beehives, chickens in profusion, pens of pigs, and roaming flocks of goats and sheep.

The nights are of a coldness he didn't know existed in Portugal. He sleeps bundled up in blankets, wearing every item of clothing he can fit on. He cuts the canvas rain tarp into pieces and uses them to seal, more or less, the broken windows. This makes the cabin very dark. He burns candles inside it to heat it. One morning he awakes to a landscape of snow. It is midafternoon before it has melted enough for him to dare to drive on. Now that there is no front window, the driving is so cold that he must slow down.

There are moments in the days when he recognizes a formal beauty to the landscape. It often has less to do with geography and more to do with the weather and the play of light. He does not get as lost as he did farther south, because there are fewer villages and fewer roads. But the roads are rutty obscenities laid down by an enterprising government long ago and forgotten by every government since. In fact, the whole region has the feel of living in administrative amnesia. And yet churches were built in the High Mountains of Portugal, as they were everywhere else in the country. Geography clamours for history. He studies the map and locates the five villages of São Julião de Palácios, Santalha, Mofreita, Guadramil, and Espin-hosela. If his research delivers on its promise — and it must, it must — in one of these villages, washed up by the vagaries of history, he will find Father Ulisses' anguished creation.

He first heads for the village of São Julião de Palácios. The wooden crucifix in its church is ordinary and unremarkable. The same with the centrepiece of the church of Guadramil.

It is on the way to Espinhosela that it happens.

He awakes to a sharp dawn. The air is bright, odourless, dry, with none of the luxuriance of Portugal's coastal air. When he walks on the gravel at the side of the road, it crunches with parched crispness. A bird's cry startles him. He looks up. At that precise instant a falcon collides from above with a dove. There is a wobble in the air, a flutter of loosened feathers, then a smooth banking as the falcon resumes its controlled flight with the dove crushed in its talons. It flaps its wings and gains altitude. Tomás watches it vanish in the distance.

An hour or so later, the road he is driving along is open and flat, as is the land on either side. Just then, above the snout of the automobile's hood, the child appears — more precisely, its hand. The sight is so odd, so unexpected, that he cannot believe what he has seen. Was it a branch? No, it was most certainly a small hand. If a child were holding on to the front of the automobile and stood up, that's where its hand would appear. And if a child were holding on to the front of the automobile and slipped off, it would then fall under the moving machine. What is the sound of a body being run over by an automobile? Clearly it is what he has just heard: a sound soft, swift, and thumping.

His mind moves in that alternately slow and abrupt way of a mind that is jarred. He must check on the child. Perhaps it is hurt. Or at the very least frightened. If there even was a child. He sticks his head out of the driving compartment and looks back.

He sees behind him, receding, a lump, small and still.

He halts the machine and steps out. He removes his hat and goggles. He is breathless. The lump is far off. He walks backwards towards it. Every time he turns his head, it is closer and his chest feels tighter. He walks faster. His heart is jumping in his chest. He turns around and runs forward towards the lump.

It is indeed a child. A boy. Perhaps five or six years old. Dressed in overlarge clothes. A peasant boy with a large head, surprisingly blond hair, and a lovely, harmonious face marred only by streaks of dirt. And what Portuguese eyes are these — *blue*? Some atavism, some trace of the foreign. Their fixed gaze appalls him.

"Boy, are you all right? Boy?"

The last word he says louder, as if death were a hearing problem. The boy's eyes do not blink. His pale face remains frozen in a grave expression. Tomás kneels and touches the boy's chest. He feels only stillness. A small river of blood appears from under the body and flows along the ground in the usual way of rivers.

Tomás shudders. He lifts his head. A breeze is blowing. In whatever direction he looks, there is majestic normalcy: wild growth here, tilled fields over there, the road, the sky, the sun. Everything is in its place, and time is moving with its usual discretion. Then, in an instant, without any warning, a little boy tripped everything up. Surely the fields will notice; they will rise, dust themselves, and come closer to take a concerned look. The road will curl up like a snake and make sad pronouncements. The sun will darken with desolation. Gravity itself will be upset and objects will float in existential hesitation. But no. The fields remain still, the road continues to lie hard and fixed, and the morning sun does not stop shining with unblinking coolness.

Tomás thinks back to the last place he stopped. It was just a few kilometres earlier. He had a short nap, his forehead resting against the steerage wheel, the engine left running. Could the child have climbed onto the front of the automobile during that break, while his head was down, unnoticed by him?

Children will play.

This could well be something Gaspar would have done, climbed onto a warm, throbbing machine to see what it was like.

"I'm sorry, little one," he whispers.

He gets back to his feet. What is there to do but leave?

He walks away in his usual fashion, and so the child remains in his sight. He churns with horror. Then a hand seizes that horror and stuffs it in a box and closes the lid. If he leaves quickly enough, it will not have happened. For the moment this accident is in himself only, a private mark, a notch carved nowhere but upon his sensibility. Outside him, nothing cares. Look for yourself: The wind blows, time flows. Besides, it was an accident. It just *happened*, with no intent or knowledge on his part.

He turns and runs. Upon arriving at the front of the automobile to pull on the starting handle, he sees that the small lid of the hood is open. This lid is at the very front of the hood, out of sight of the driver in the driving compartment, and is designed to allow access to the engine without the hood having to be lifted. Did the child see it as a door into a little round dollhouse? Why must children be so curious? He notes how the boy would have held on, where his feet might have rested, what his hands must have gripped. The edge of the chassis, the base of the starting handle, the ends of the suspension springs, the thin rods that hold the headlights into place, the rim of the open lid — so many options for a little monkey. Comfortable enough a perch, perhaps even exhilarating when the warm noisy machine jerked into motion — but then fear and fatigue would have set in. So much speed and shaking, the ground disappearing beneath like a watery torrent.

He closes the lid and turns the starting handle. He hastens back to the driving compartment, puts the machine into first gear. He pauses. He considers what lies behind him and what lies ahead. With a shudder, the machine starts to move. He presses harder on the pedal. The automobile gains speed. He puts it into second gear, then third. He looks in the side mirror. The image is shaky, but he can still make out the lump. He turns his eyes to the road ahead.

He does not drive very far. The road snakes and ascends into a forest of pine trees. He stops, he turns the engine off, he sits. Then he lifts his gaze to look out the paneless window. Through the trees he sees the road he was on earlier. He is already far from that road, but nothing catches the eye like movement. He sees a tiny figure, just a speck. The figure is running. He recognizes that it's a man from the sparks of light that flash through the running legs. The man runs and then he stops. He falls forward. There is no movement for a long time. Then the man gets up, lifts the bundle off the road, and walks back the way he came.

Tomás's inner being plummets. To be the victim of a theft, and now to have committed a theft. In both cases, a child stolen. In both cases, his goodwill and grieving heart of no consequence. In both cases, mere chance. There is suffering and there is luck, and once again his luck has run out. He suddenly feels swallowed, as if he were a struggling insect floating on water and a great mouth gulped him in.

After a long time he looks away. He gets the automobile into gear and pushes on.

The church of Espinhosela yields no treasure; nor does the church of Mofreita. There is only the church of Santalha left. If Father Ulisses' crucifix is not there, what will he do next?

On the road to Santalha he begins to feel ill. The pain comes in waves, and at each wave it seems to him that he can feel the exact outline of his stomach. Within that outline he is gripped by cramps. Relief comes — only for another cramp to hit him. Nausea surges through him next. Its onset is violent. Saliva floods his mouth, and the taste of it, its very presence, increases the nausea. He halts the vehicle and hastily exits it, trembling and covered in a cold sweat. He falls to his knees. Vomit erupts out of his mouth, a white torrent that splatters the grass. It reeks of putrid cheese. He is left panting. The urge returns with unstoppable force and he retches again. At the end of it, bile is burning his throat.

He lurches back to the automobile. He examines himself in a side mirror. He is scruffy and wild-eyed. His hair is sticky and matted. His clothes are unrecognizably dirty. He looks like a skewer of roasted meat. He spends a grim, sleepless night haunted by a pair of blue eyes, by a sad solemn little face, his stomach clenching and unclenching. It dawns on him: He is sick because of the child. The child is pushing from within him.

That morning he enters a village named Tuizelo. The day is sunny but the village square is deserted. He gets down from the automobile and drinks from the fountain at the centre of the square. He should clean himself, but he cannot muster the will or the concern. Instead he goes searching for somewhere to buy a little food. In these small villages in the High Mountains of Portugal, where the inhabitants survive largely on a mix of self-sufficiency and barter, he has discovered that sometimes a private house acts as an informal shop — but even this is not to be found in Tuizelo, only large vegetable gardens and wandering animals. The village is in fact full of animals: cats, dogs, chickens, ducks, sheep, goats, cows, donkeys, songbirds. As he is returning to the automobile, another stomach cramp besets him.

As he pauses to steady himself, he catches sight of the village church. It is a squat building, plain and simple, though not unattractive for it. Its pale stone glows appealingly in the sunlight. He is of the opinion that architectural modesty best suits the religious sentiment. Only song needs to soar in a church; anything fancier is human arrogance disguised as faith. A church such as Tuizelo's, with no high pointed arches, no ribbed vaulting, no flying buttresses, more accurately reflects the true humble nature of the seeker who enters its walls. The church is not on his list — but visiting it might distract him from his aching stomach and guilty sorrow.

The two doors he tries are locked. As he steps away he catches sight of a woman. She is standing looking at him from a little way off.

"Father Abrahan has gone fishing for the day. I have the key, if you would like," she says.

He hesitates. There is more driving to be done. With great uncertainty ahead. But she is offering. And it doesn't escape his notice: The woman is beautiful. A peasant beauty. It lifts his spirits while dashing them at the same time. Once he had a beautiful woman in his life.

"That would be kind of you, senhora."

She tells him her name is Maria Dores Passos Castro and that he should wait. She disappears around a corner. While he waits for her return, he sits on the step of the church. It is a relief to be approached by a lone woman. He is grateful that no mob has descended on him in this lost village.

Senhora Castro returns. She produces an enormous iron key. "The custodian of the church is my husband, Rafael Miguel Santos Castro, but he is away for the week." With much clanging and grinding, she unlocks and opens the door to the church. She moves aside to let him in.

"Thank you," he says.

The interior is dim, because the windows are narrow and because he has just walked in from bright sunlight. He walks to the centre of the nave, to the single aisle between the rows of pews. He is preoccupied with his stomach. If only the child would stop pushing! He is afraid he will vomit inside the church. He hopes Senhora Castro will not follow him too closely. She doesn't; she stands back and leaves him in peace.

His eyes grow accustomed to the muted light. Stone pilasters connected by arched mouldings frame the white stucco walls around him. The capitals atop the pilasters are plain. Other than a commonplace pictorial Stations of the Cross, the walls are bare, and the windows have no stained glass. He makes his way in reverse along the nave. It is all sober and simple. He takes the church for what it aims to be: a shelter, a refuge, a harbour. He is so weary.

He notices the church's narrow windows, the thick walls, and the barrel-vaulted ceiling. The Romanesque style arrived late and died late in Portugal. This appears to be a typical small Romanesque church, unmarked by time and unmodified by later hands. A forgotten seven-centuries-old church.

"How old is the church?" he calls.

"Thirteenth century," the woman replies.

He is pleased to learn that he has identified it correctly. He backs up the aisle slowly, dropping his feet with care. The transepts appear, containing no surprises. He turns around to face the altar, lowering himself into a pew in the second row. He takes long, deep breaths. He glances at the altar and at the crucifix above it. The crucifix is not the standard-issue maudlin symbol he has found almost everywhere. It seems to be early Renaissance. Christ's long face, elongated arms, and foreshortened legs speak of an awkward attempt by the artist to correct the distortions caused by viewing an elevated figure from below. The extended arms and reduced legs make the body look normal to the viewer looking up at it. The work is no Mantegna or Michelangelo, but it's expressive, the face of Christ especially so, nearly Baroque in its emotional eloquence. It's a worthy attempt to express the humanity of Christ and juggle with perspective, circa the early fifteenth century.

He is going to throw up. He clamps his mouth shut. *Child, stop!* He stands and steadies himself. He makes his way backwards down the aisle and, as he is about to turn for the door, lets his eyes sweep through the church one last time. His eyes rest on the crucifix again. A point of stillness makes itself felt within him, a point that becalms not only the troubles of his body but also the rash workings of his brain.

To place one foot in front of the other feels unnatural, but he does not want to take his eyes off the crucifix. He walks forward. The crucifix is not Renaissance. It's more recent than that. In fact, he is

certain of its date: 1635. It is indeed Baroque, then —
what might be called African Baroque. Unmistakably,
what he is staring at is Father Ulisses' crucifix. There it
is, all the way from São Tomé. Oh, what a marvel! The
match between what Father Ulisses wrote in his diary
and fashioned with his hands is perfect. The arms, the
shoulders, the hanging body, the curled legs, and, above
all, the face! Now that he is properly taking in what his
eyes are seeing, the crucifix indeed shines and shrieks,
barks and roars. Truly this is the Son of God giving a
loud cry and breathing his last breath as the curtain of
the temple is torn in two from top to bottom.

"Excuse me," he cries out to Senhora Castro.

She takes a few steps.

He points with his arm and finger. He points to the
heart of the church and asks her, "What is that?"

The woman looks bemused. "It is Our Lord Jesus
Christ."

"Yes, but how is he represented?"

"Suffering on the Cross."

"But what *form* has he taken?"

"The form of a man. God so loved us that He gave
us His Son," she replies simply.

"No!" shouts Tomás, smiling though every muscle in
his midsection is twisting. "What you have here is a
chimpanzee! An ape. It's clear in his sketch — the facial
hair, the nose, the mouth. He's feathered away the hair,
but the features are unmistakable, once you know. And
those long arms and short legs, they're not stylized,
they're simian! Chimpanzees have limbs exactly like
that, long in the upper body and short in the lower. Do

135

you understand? You've been praying to a crucified chimpanzee all these years. Your Son of Man is not a god — *he's just an ape on a cross!"*

It is done. This Christ on the Cross, once it is displayed and widely known, will mock all the others. He whispers his private business: *There. You took my son, now I take yours.*

He wants his laughter to be light, but his victory is blighted by an onrushing emotion: a plummeting feeling of sadness. He fights it. Here is the truth about Jesus of Nazareth, the biological reality. All science points to the materiality of our condition. As an aside, the crucifix is breathtakingly beautiful, and to him will go the glory of discovering it and bringing it to the museum. Still, the feeling of sadness quickly deepens. He stares at Father Ulisses' crucified ape. *Not a god — only an animal.*

As he flees the church, a hand pressed to his mouth, a Gospel verse unexpectedly rings in his head. Jesus has just been arrested after the betrayal of Judas, the disciples have deserted him and fled, and then, from Mark: *A certain young man was following him, wearing nothing but a linen cloth. They caught hold of him, but he left the linen cloth and ran off naked.*

Is he not now similarly naked?

Senhora Castro watches him go, struck by his strange backwards gait; he looks as if a wind were sucking him out of the church. She does not follow him. Instead she approaches the altar and peers up at the crucifix. What was the man saying? *An ape?* The Jesus she sees has long arms because he's welcoming,

136

and a long face because he's doleful. She has never seen anything odd about the crucifix. The artist did his best. Besides, she pays more attention to Father Abrahan. And she prays with her eyes closed. It's just a crucifix. And if he's an ape, so be it — he's an ape. He's still the Son of God.

She decides she should check on the stranger.

Tomás is leaning against the automobile, retching violently. From his rectum to his throat he is a single constricting muscle at the mercy of the child who is wringing him like a wet rag. From the corner of his eye, he sees a priest appear in the square, holding a fishing rod in one hand and a line of three fish in the other.

Father Abrahan beholds Maria Passos Castro, who has a puzzled look on her face; he beholds one of those new, fashionable carriages he's heard about (but this one in very poor condition); and he beholds a bedraggled stranger next to it, dry-heaving with mighty roars.

Tomás climbs into the driving compartment. He wants to go. In a daze he looks at the steerage wheel. The machine needs to move to the right to avoid the wall next to it. What does that mean in terms of the rotation of the wheel in his hands? Grief surges through him ahead of his capacity to answer the question. The steerage wheel has finally and truly defeated him. He begins to weep. He weeps because he feels horribly sick. He weeps because he is soul-racked and bone-weary tired of driving the machine. He weeps because his ordeal is only half over; he still has to drive all the way back to Lisbon. He weeps because he is unwashed and unshaved. He weeps because he has spent days on end in foreign lands and nights on end sleeping in an automobile, cold and cramped. He weeps because he has lost his job, and what will he do next, how will he earn his living? He weeps because he has discovered a crucifix he no longer cares to have discovered. He weeps because he misses his father. He weeps because he misses his son and his lover. He weeps because he has killed a child. He weeps because, because, because.

He weeps like a child, catching his breath and hiccupping, his face drenched with tears. We are random animals. That is who we are, and we have only ourselves, nothing more — there is no greater relationship. Long before Darwin, a priest lucid in his madness encountered four chimpanzees on a forlorn island in Africa and hit upon a great truth: We are risen apes, not fallen angels. Tomás is strangled by loneliness.

"Father, I *need* you!" he cries out.

Father Abrahan throws his fishing gear to the ground and runs to help the piteous stranger.

PART TWO

Homeward

Eusebio Lozora says the Lord's Prayer three times slowly. After that he launches forth with unrehearsed praise and supplication. His thoughts wander but return, his sentences stop midway but eventually resume. He praises God, then he praises his wife to God. He asks God to bless her and their children. He asks for God's continued support and protection. Then, since he is a physician, a pathologist at that, rooted in the body, but also a believer, rooted in the promise of the Lord, he repeats, perhaps two dozen times, the words "The Body of Christ," after which he gets up off his knees and returns to his desk.

He considers himself a careful practitioner. He examines the paragraph he has been working on the way a farmer might look back at a freshly sowed furrow, checking to see that he has done a good job because he knows the furrow will yield a crop — in his case, a crop of understanding. Does the writing hold up to his high standards? Is it true, clear, concise, final?

He is catching up on his work. It is the last day of December of the year 1938, its final hours, in fact. A bleak Christmas has been dutifully celebrated, but otherwise he is in no mood for holiday festivities. His desk is covered with papers, some in clear view, others carefully, meaningfully eclipsed to varying degrees depending on their importance, and still others that are ready to be filed away.

His office is quiet, as is the hallway outside it. Bragança has a population of not thirty thousand people, but its Hospital São Francisco, in which he is head pathologist, is the largest in Alto Douro. Other parts of the hospital will be lit up and swollen with bustle and noise — the emergency wing, where people come in screaming and crying, the wards, where the patients ring bells and hold the nurses up in endless conversations — but the pathology wing, in the basement of the hospital, beneath all these lively floors, is typically hushed, like all pathology wings. He wishes it to stay that way.

With the adding of three words and the crossing out of one, he completes the paragraph. He reads it over one last time. It is his private opinion that pathologists are the only physicians who know how to write. All the other devotees of Hippocrates hold up as their triumph the restored patient, and the words they might write — a diagnosis, a prescription, instructions for a treatment — are of fleeting interest to them. These physicians of restoration, as soon as they see a patient standing on his or her feet, move on to a new case. And it is true that every day patients depart the hospital with quite a bounce to their step. Just an accident, or a little bout of this or that illness, they say to themselves. But Eusebio places greater store in those who were seriously sick. He notes in these patients leaving the hospital the tottering gait and the dishevelled hair, the desperately humbled look and the holy terror in their eyes. They know, with inescapable clarity, what is coming to them one day. There are many ways in which life's little candle can be snuffed out. A cold wind pursues us all. And when a stub of a candle is brought in, the wick blackened, the sides streaked with dripped wax, the attending physician — at the Hospital São Francisco, in Bragança, Portugal, at least — is either he or his colleague, Dr. José Otavio.

Every dead body is a book with a story to tell, each organ a chapter, the chapters united by a common narrative. It is Eusebio's professional duty to read these stories, turning every page with a scalpel, and at the end of each to write a book report. What he writes in a report must reflect exactly what he has read in the body. It makes for a hard-headed kind of poetry. Curiosity draws him on, like all readers. What happened to this body? How? Why? He searches for that crafty, enforced absence that overtakes us all. What is death? There is the corpse — but that is the result, not the thing itself. When he finds a grossly enlarged lymph node or tissue that is abnormally rugose, he knows that he's hot on death's trail. How curious, though: Death often comes disguised as life, a mass of exuberant, anomalous cells — or, like a murderer, it leaves a clue, a smoking gun, the sclerotic caking of an artery, before fleeing the scene. Always he comes upon death's handiwork just as death itself has turned the corner, its hem disappearing with a quiet swish.

He leans back in his chair to stretch. The chair creaks, like old bones. He notices a file on his workbench, along the wall, where his microscope stands. What is it doing there? And what is that on the floor beneath the bench — another file? And the glass on his desk — it's so dried out, it's collecting dust. He strongly believes in the importance of proper hydration. Life is moist. He should clean the glass and fill it with fresh, cool water. He shakes his head. Enough of these scattered thoughts. He has much that needs preserving, not only in solutions and slides but in words. In each case he must bring together the patient's clinical history, the findings from the autopsy, and the histological results into a smooth and coherent whole. He must apply himself. *Focus, man, focus. Find the words*. Besides, there are other reports that need finishing. There is the one he has been putting off. It has to be done tonight. A body that was crushed and left for several days half-exposed to the air, half-submerged in a river, inviting both rot and bloating.

A loud rap at the door startles him. He looks at his watch. It is half past ten at night.

"Come in," he calls out, exasperation escaping from his voice like steam from a kettle.

No one enters. But he senses a brooding presence on the other side of the solid wood door.

"I said come in," he calls out again.

Still no rattling of the doorknob. Pathology is not a medical art that is much subject to emergency. The sick, or rather their biopsied samples, can nearly always wait till the next morning, and the dead are even more patient, so it's unlikely to be a clerk with an urgent case. And pathologists' offices are not located so that the general public might find them easily. Who then, at such an hour, on New Year's Eve at that, would wend their way through the basement of the hospital to look for him?

He gets up, upsetting both himself and a number of papers. He walks around his desk, takes hold of the doorknob, and opens the door.

A woman in her fifties, with lovely features and large brown eyes, stands before him. In one hand she is holding a bag. He is surprised to see her. She eyes him. In a warm, deep voice, she starts up: "Why are you so far from helping me, from the words of my groaning? I cry by day, but you do not answer, and by night, but find no rest. I am poured out like water. My heart is like wax; it is melted within my breast. My mouth is dried up like a potsherd. Oh my darling, come quickly to my help!"

While a small part of Eusebio sighs, a larger part smiles. The woman at the door is his wife. She comes to his office to see him on occasion, though not usually at such a late hour. Her name is Maria Luisa Motaal Lozora, and he is familiar with the words of her lament. They are taken mostly from Psalm 22, her favourite psalm. She in fact has no cause for conventional suffering. She is in good mental and physical health, she lives in a nice house, she has no desire to leave him or the town where they live, she has good friends, she is never truly bored, they have three grown children who are happy and healthy — in short, she has all the elements that make for a good life. Only his wife, his dear wife, is an amateur theologian, a priest *manqué*, and she takes the parameters of life, her mortal coildom, her Jobdom, very seriously.

She is fond of quoting from Psalm 22, especially its first line: "My God, my God, why have you forsaken me?" His thought in response is that, nonetheless, there is "My God, my God" at the start of the plaint. It helps that there's someone listening, if not doing.

He has much listening to do, he does, with his wife, and not much doing. Her mouth might be dried up like a potsherd, but she never quotes the line that follows in Psalm 22 — "and my tongue sticks to my jaws" — because that would be an untruth. Her tongue is never stuck to her jaws. Maria ardently believes in the spoken word. To her, writing is making stock and reading is sipping broth, but only the spoken word is the full roasted chicken. And so she talks. She talks all the time. She talks to herself when she is alone at home and she talks to herself when she is alone in the street, and she has been talking to him incessantly since the day they met, thirty-eight years ago. His wife is an endlessly unfurling conversation, with never a true stop, only a pause. But she produces no drivel and has no patience for drivel. Sometimes she chafes at the inane talk she has to endure with her friends. She serves them coffee and cake, she listens to their prattle, and later she grouses, "Guinea pigs, I am surrounded by guinea pigs."

He surmises that his wife read about guinea pigs and something about them aroused her resentment: their smallness, their utter harmlessness and defencelessness, their fearfulness, their contentedness simply to chew on a grain or two and expect no more from life. As a pathologist he quite likes the guinea pig. It is indeed small in every way, especially when set against the stark and random cruelty of life. Every corpse he opens up whispers to him, "I am a guinea pig. Will you warm me to your breast?" Drivel, his wife would call that. She has no patience for death.

When they were young, Maria tolerated for a while the amorous cooing of which he was so fond. Despite the surface brutality of his profession, he is soft of heart. When he met her the first time — it was in the cafeteria of the university — she was the most alluring creature he'd ever seen, a serious girl with a beauty that lit him up. At the sight of her, song filled his ears and the world glowed with colour. His heart thumped with gratitude. But quickly she rolled her eyes and told him to stop twittering. It became clear to him that his mission was to listen to her and respond appropriately and not to annoy her with oral frivolity. She was the rich earth and the sun and the rain; he was merely the farmer who got the crop going. He was an essential but bit player. Which was fine with him. He loved her then and he loves her now. She is everything to him. She is still the rich earth and the sun and the rain and he is still happy to be the farmer who gets the crop going.

Only tonight he had hoped to get some work done. Clearly that is not to be the case. The Conversation is upon him.

"Hello, my angel," he says. "What a joyous surprise to see you! What's in the bag? You can't have been shopping. No shop would be open at this hour." He leans forward and kisses his wife.

Maria ignores the question. "Death is a difficult door," she says quietly. She steps into his office. "Eusebio, what's happened?" she exclaims. "Your office is an unholy mess. This is indecent. Where are your visitors supposed to sit?"

He surveys his office. He sees embarrassing disorder everywhere. Pathologists at work don't normally receive visitors who need to sit or who care for order. They usually lie flat and without complaint on a table across the hallway. He takes his workbench chair and places it in front of his desk. "I wasn't expecting you tonight, my angel. Here, sit here," he says.

"Thank you." She sits down and places the bag she brought with her on the floor.

He gathers up papers from his desk, which he stuffs in the nearest folder, which he stacks on other folders, which he then drops to the floor. He pushes the pile under his desk with a foot, out of sight. He crunches up stray bits of paper, sweeps up shameful accumulations of dust with the edge of his hand, using his other hand as a dustpan, which he empties into the wastepaper basket beside his desk. There, that's better. He sits down and looks across his desk at the woman sitting there. A man and his wife.

"I have found the solution at last, and I must tell you about it," she says.

The solution? Was there a problem?

148

"Why don't you do that, then," he replies.

She nods. "I first tried through laughter, because you like to laugh," she says without a trace of mirth. "You saw me, the books I was reading."

He thinks. Yes, that would explain the selection of books she ordered from her favourite Coimbra bookseller these last several months. Some plays of Aristophanes, Shakespeare, Lope de Vega, Molière, Georges Feydeau, some weightier tomes of Boccaccio, Rabelais, Cervantes, Swift, Voltaire. All of these she read wearing the grimmest expression. He himself is not such an accomplished reader. He was not sure why she was reading these books, but, as always, he let her be.

"Humour and religion do not mix well," she goes on. "Humour may point out the many mistakes of religion — any number of vilely immoral priests, or monsters who shed blood in the name of Jesus — but humour sheds no light on true religion. It is just humour unto itself. Worse, humour misunderstands religion, since there is little place for levity in religion — and let us not make the mistake of thinking that levity is the same thing as joy. Religion abounds in joy. Religion *is* joy. To laugh at religion with levity, then, is to miss the point, which is fine if one is in the mood to laugh, but not if one is in the mood to understand. Do you follow me?"

"Though it's late, I think I do," he replies.

"Next I tried children's books, Eusebio. Did Jesus not say that we must receive the Kingdom of God like a little child? So I reread the books we used to read to Renato, Luisa, and Antón."

Images of their three children when they were small appear in his mind. Those little ones lived with their mother's volubility like children live in a rainy climate: They just ran out to play in the puddles, shrieking and laughing, heedless of the downpour. She never took umbrage at these joyous interruptions. With difficulty, he returns his attention to his wife.

"These books brought back many happy memories — and some sadness that our children are all grown up — but they brought no religious illumination. I continued my search. Then the solution appeared right in front of me, with your favourite writer."

"Really? How interesting. When I saw your nose in those Agatha Christies, I thought you were taking a *break* from your arduous studies."

He and she are devoted to Agatha Christie. They have read all her books, starting with the very first, *The Mysterious Affair at Styles*. Thanks to the good works of the Círculo Português de Mistério, they receive her every new murder mystery the moment it is translated, and translation is prompt because Portuguese readers are eager. Husband and wife know better than to bother the other when one of them is absorbed in the latest arrival. Once they've both finished it, they go over the case together, discussing the clues they should have caught, and the avenues to the solution they ran down only to find they were dead ends. Agatha Christie's star detective is Hercule Poirot, a vain, odd-looking little Belgian man. But Poirot, inside his egg-shaped head, has the quickest, most observant mind. His "grey cells"

— as he calls his brain — work with order and method, and these cells perceive what no one else does.

"*Death on the Nile* was such a marvel of ingenuity! Her next book must be due soon," he says.

"It must."

"And what solution did you find in Agatha Christie?"

"Let me first explain the path I have taken," she replies. "This path twists and turns, so you must listen carefully. Let us start with the miracles of Jesus."

The miracles of Jesus. One of her favourite topics. He glances at the clock next to his microscope. The night is going to be long.

"Is something the matter with your microscope?" his wife asks.

"Not at all."

"Peering through it won't help you understand the miracles of Jesus."

"That is true."

"And staring at the clock won't save you from your future."

"True again. Are you thirsty? Can I offer you water before we start?"

"Water from *that* glass?" She peers critically at the filthy glass on his desk.

"I propose to clean it."

"That would be a good idea. I'm fine for the moment, though. But how appropriate that you should mention water — we shall come back to water. Now, pay attention. The miracles of Jesus — so many of them, are there not? And yet, if we look closely, we can see that they fall into two categories. Into one category fall those miracles that *benefit the human body*. There are many of these. Jesus makes the blind see, the deaf hear, the dumb speak, the lame walk. He cures fevers, treats epilepsy, exorcizes psychological maladies. He rids lepers of their disease. A woman suffering from haemorrhages for twelve years touches his cloak and her bleeding stops. And of course he raises the dead — Jairus's daughter and the widow of Nain's only son, both freshly dead, but also Lazarus, who has been dead for four days and whose body stinks of death. We might call these the *medical* miracles of Jesus, and they represent the overwhelming majority of his miraculous work."

Eusebio remembers the autopsy he performed earlier today, speaking of bodies that stink of death. The mushy, puffy body of a floater is an abhorrence to the eyes and to the nose, even when these are trained.

"But there are other miracles that benefit the human body besides the medical miracles," his wife continues. "Jesus makes the nets of fishermen bulge with catch. He multiplies fish and loaves of bread to feed thousands. At Cana he turns water into wine. In alleviating hunger and quenching thirst, Jesus again benefits the human body. So too when he stills a storm that is swamping the boat his disciples are travelling in and rescues them from drowning. And the same when he gets Peter to pay the temple tax with the coin from the fish's mouth; in doing that, he saves Peter from the beating he would have endured had he been arrested."

Maria has benefitted his body, Eusebio muses, as he has hers. To love and then to have a fun time of it — is there any greater joy? They were like birds in springtime. Their carnal relations settled over the years, but the satisfaction has remained — the comfort of a sturdy, warm nest. Renewed love for Maria flames within him. When they met, she never told him that her name was Legion, that teeming within her were all the prophets and apostles of the Bible, besides a good number of the Church Fathers. When she was giving birth to their children — with each one the ordeal began with something like a plate breaking inside her, she said — even then, as he sat in the waiting room listening to her panting and groaning and shrieking, she discoursed on religion. The doctor and the nurses came out with thoughtful expressions. He had to remind them to tell him about the new baby. Even as she suffered and they worked, she caused them to think. How did he end up with a wife who was both beautiful and profound? Did he deserve such luck? He smiles and winks at his wife.

"Eusebio, stop it. Time is short," she whispers. "Now, why does Jesus benefit the human body? Of course he does his miracle work to impress those around him — and they *are* impressed. They're amazed. But to show that he is the Messiah, why does Jesus cure infirmities and feed hungry stomachs? After all, he could also soar like a bird, as the devil asked him to do, or, as he himself mentioned, he could go about casting mountains into seas. These too would be miracles worthy of a Messiah. Why *body* miracles?"

Eusebio remains hushed. He's tired. Worse, he's hungry. He remembers the bag at his wife's feet.

Perhaps he should wash the glass in the small sink in his office and, when returning to his desk, try to glimpse inside the bag. She usually brings him something to eat when she visits.

His wife answers her question. "Jesus performs these miracles because they bring relief where we want it most. We all suffer in our bodies and die. It is our fate — as you well know, my dear, spending your days cutting up human carrion. In curing and feeding us, Jesus meets us at our weakest. He eases us of our heavy burden of mortality. And that impresses us more deeply than any other display of mighty power, be it flying in the air or throwing mountains into seas.

"Now to the *second* category of the miracles of Jesus, the category of the *miracle of interpretation*. This category contians only a single miracle. Do you know what that miracle is?"

"Tell me," Eusebio says softly.

"It is when Jesus walks on the water. There is no other miracle like it. Jesus tells his disciples to get into the boat and travel on ahead. They set out, while Jesus goes onto the mountain to pray. The day ends. The disciples strain at their oars against a strong wind — but there is no storm; their bodies are not in any danger. After a long night of toil, as the new day is starting, they see Jesus coming towards their boat, walking on the sea. They are terrified. Jesus reassures them: 'It is I; do not be afraid.' Matthew, in his version of the story, has Peter ask the Lord if he can join him. 'Come,' says Jesus. Peter gets out of the boat and walks on the water towards Jesus, but then the wind frightens him and he begins to sink. Jesus reaches out with his hand and brings Peter back to the boat. The adverse wind ceases.

"Why would Jesus walk on water? Did he do it to save a drowning soul, to benefit a human body? No — Peter got into trouble in the water *after* Jesus began walking on it. Was there some other impetus? Jesus started his miraculous walk very early in the morning from remote shores, alone, and at sea he was seen by no one but his disciples, who were out of sight of land. In other words, there was no *social* necessity to the miracle. Walking on water did no one any particular good, raised no specific hopes. It was neither asked for, nor expected, nor even *needed*. Why such an anomalous miracle in documents as spare and winnowed as the Gospels? And this unique miracle can't be hidden away. It appears in two of the synoptic Gospels — Matthew and Mark — *and* in John, one of the very few crossover miracles. What does it mean, Eusebio, *what does it mean?* In a moment of clarity, I saw."

He perks up. It always goes like this. She talks and talks and talks, and then suddenly he is hooked, like a fish in a biblical story. What did she see?

"I saw that the miracle of Jesus walking on the water means little when taken at face value. However, when it is taken as saying one thing but implying another — in other words, as *allegory* — then the miracle opens up. Swimming is a modern invention — people at the time of Jesus could not swim. If they fell into deep water, they sank and they drowned — that is the literal truth. But if we think of water as the experience of life, it is also the religious truth. Men and women are weak, and in their weakness they sink. Jesus does not sink. A man drowning in water naturally looks up. What does he see? While he is being engulfed by choking darkness, he sees above him the clear light and pure air of salvation. He sees Jesus, who stands above those struggling in weakness, offering them redemption. This explains Peter's hapless performance on the water: He is only human, and therefore he begins to sink. Read so, as an allegory about our weakness and Jesus' purity and the salvation that he offers, the miracle takes on a whole new meaning.

"Now, I asked myself, why would this miracle demand an allegorical reading but not the others? Would the miracles that benefit the human body gain from a similar reading? I had never thought of that. Poor stupid woman that I am, I had always taken the body miracles of Jesus as factual truth. In my mind Jesus really did cure leprosy, blindness, and other ailments and infirmities, and he really did feed the thousands. But is the Lord to be reduced to an itinerant doctor and a peddler of buns? I don't think so. The miracles that benefit the human body must also mean something greater."

"What?" Eusebio asks pliantly.

"Well, what else could they be but symbols of the Everlasting Kingdom? Each miraculous cure of Jesus is a glimpse of the ultimate place that is ours, *if we have faith*. Have faith, and you will be cured of your mortality, you will be fed forever. Do you understand the import of what I am saying?" Eusebio ventures a

156

nod. Maria's voice is warm, buttery, comforting. If only he could eat it. He peeks at the clock. "The miracle of Jesus walking on the water is a guide to how we must read Scripture as a whole. The Gospels are lesser, their message weakened, if we read them as though they are reports by four journalists. But if we understand them as written in a language of metaphors and symbols, then they open up with moral depth and truth. That is the language used by Jesus himself, is it not? How did he teach the people?"

"It says in the Gospels: 'He did not speak to them except in parables.'"

"That's right. The parable of the lost sheep, of the mustard seed, of the fig tree, of the yeast, of the sower, of the prodigal son, and so on. So many parables."

Mutton with mustard sauce, with stewed figs and a glass of wine — so many *edible* parables, thinks Eusebio.

"A parable is an allegory in the form of a simple story. It is a suitcase that we must open and unpack to see its contents. And the single key that unlocks these suitcases, that opens them wide, is allegory.

"Finally, only one miracle stands true and literal, the pillar of our faith: his resurrection. Once that is clear, we can start making sense of all the stories told by Jesus and told about him. That is Christianity at heart: a single miracle surrounded and sustained by stories, like an island surrounded by the sea."

Eusebio coughs a little. "You haven't been sharing these insights with Father Cecilio, have you?"

157

Father Cecilio is their local priest — and the subject of much eye-rolling on Maria's part. In her presence the poor man always looks like the chicken in the coop that hasn't laid enough eggs.

"What, and have us excommunicated? That dimwit is the very hammer of literalism that insults my faith. He's as dumb as an ox."

"But he means well," Eusebio suggests soothingly.

"As does an ox."

"That's all very interesting, what you've been saying."

"I'm not finished. I was searching, if you remember? There's a problem."

"Yes, and you found a solution."

"Oh, how my heart beats! I'll drink now, if you sanitize that glass."

Maria bends down and produces from the bag a bottle of red wine, which she places on the desk. Eusebio cracks a wide smile. "Maria, bless you!" He hurries to open the bottle. While it breathes, he washes the glass thoroughly.

"I don't have another glass," he says. "You drink from it and I'll drink from the bottle."

"That's unseemly. We'll share the glass."

"All right." He tips some of the elixir into the glass. It glows like a firefly. He licks his lips at the prospect of pouring it down his throat, but offers the glass to his wife. "You first, my angel."

Maria takes a small, thoughtful sip. She closes her eyes as she considers its distilled effect on her. She purrs and opens her eyes. "It's a good one."

She passes him the glass. He takes a larger sip, grunts with pleasure, empties the glass in one go. "Oh! Indeed. Just a little more." He half-fills the glass, perhaps a little more than half.

Maria has another sip. "That'll be enough for me," she says. "Happy New Year."

"Sorry?"

"What's the point of looking at a clock if you don't notice the time? Look at the two hands. It's midnight. We're now in 1939."

"You're right. Happy New Year to you, my angel. May this year be a good one."

He finishes off the glass and sits down again. Now it is his turn to glow like a firefly, and his mind flits about inconsequentially as his wife starts up again.

"Why would Jesus speak in parables? Why would he both tell stories and let himself be presented through stories? *Why would Truth use the tools of fiction?* Stories full of metaphors are by writers who play the language like a mandolin for our entertainment, novelists, poets, playwrights, and other crafters of *inventions.* Meanwhile, isn't it extraordinary that there are no significant *historical* accounts of Jesus of Nazareth? A minor government official from Lisbon comes to Bragança, a tight little man with nothing to say, and it's all over the papers, which end up in archives for the rest of time. Or you, your work, Eusebio. Someone does that ordinary thing of dying — and you write a report, you immortalize that ordinary mortal. Meanwhile, the Son of God comes to town, he travels around, he meets anyone and everyone, he impresses mightily, he is murdered — *and no one writes about it?* Of this great divine comet hitting the earth, the only impact is *a swirl of oral tales?*

"There are hundreds of documents from pagan authors from the first century of our Christian era. Jesus is not mentioned in a single one. No contemporary Roman figure — no official, no general, no administrator, no historian, no philosopher, no poet, no scientist, no merchant, no writer of any sort — mentions him. Not the least reference to him is to be found on any public inscription or in any surviving private correspondence. He left behind no birth record, no trial report, no death certificate. A century after his death — one hundred years! — there are only two pagan references to Jesus, one from Pliny the Younger, a Roman senator and writer, the other from Tacitus, a Roman historian. A letter and a few pages — that's all from the zealous bureaucrats and the proud administrators of an empire whose next religion was founded on Jesus, whose capital would become the capital of his cult. The pagans didn't notice the man who would transform them from Romans into Christians. That seems as unlikely as the French not noticing the French Revolution.

"If Jews of the day had more to say about Jesus, it's been lost. There is nothing from any of the Pharisees who conspired against him, nothing from the Sanhedrin, the religious council that condemned him. The historian Josephus makes two brief references to Jesus, but many decades after his crucifixion. The entire historical record on Jesus of Nazareth from non-Christian sources fits into a handful of pages, and it's all second hand. None of it tells us anything we don't already know from Christian sources.

"No, no, no. The historical record is of no help. Our knowledge of the flesh-and-blood Jesus all comes down to four *allegorists*. Even more astonishing, these word minstrels never met Jesus. Matthew, Mark, Luke, and John, whoever they were, weren't eyewitnesses. Like the Romans and Jews, they wrote about Jesus years after his passage on earth. They were inspired scribes who recorded and arranged oral tales that had been circulating for decades. Jesus has come to us, then, through old stories that survived mostly by word of mouth. What a casual, risky way of making one's mark on history.

"Stranger still, it's as if Jesus wanted it that way. Jews are obsessively literate. A Jew's every finger is a pen. God merely *speaks* to the rest of us, while Jews get handed inscribed stone tablets. Yet here was an important Jew who preferred the wind to the written word. Who chose the eddying of oral tales over the recorded facts. Why this approach? Why not impose himself like the great military Messiah Jews were hoping for? Why storytelling over history-making?"

His wife has led him down one grand corridor after another. Now, Eusebio senses, they are about to enter the ballroom, with its vast dancing floor and glittering chandeliers and high windows.

"I think it's because, once more, Jesus seeks to benefit us. A story is a wedding in which we listeners are the groom watching the bride coming up the aisle. It is together, in an act of imaginary consummation, that the story is born. This act wholly involves us, as any marriage would, and just as no marriage is exactly the same as another, so each of us interprets a story differently, feels for it differently. A story calls upon us as God calls upon us, as individuals — *and we like that*. Stories benefit the human mind. Jesus trod the earth with the calm assurance that he would stay with us and we would stay with him so long as he touched us through stories, so long as he left a fingerprint upon our startled imagination. And so he came not charging on a horse but quietly riding a story.

"Imagine, Eusebio, that you've been invited to a feast and a splendid table has been presented to you, with the finest wines and the most delicious food. You eat and you drink till you are full. Would you then turn to your host and ask about the barn animals you've eaten? You might, and you might get some information about these animals — but what does it compare to the feast you've just had? We must abandon this reductionist quest for the historical Jesus. He won't be found, because that's not where — that's not *how* — he chose to make his mark. Jesus told stories and lived through stories. Our faith is faith in his story, and there is very little beyond that story-faith. The holy word is story, and story is the holy word."

Maria breathes deeply. A smile lights up her face. "Well, stories are still with us. And so I come to the solution, to Agatha Christie."

She leans over and brings up from the bag at her feet handfuls of books with which Eusebio is familiar: *The Man in the Brown Suit, The Mystery of the Blue*

Train, *The Seven Dials Mystery*, *The Murder at the Vicarage*, *Why Didn't They Ask Evans?*, *Three Act Tragedy*, *Murder in Mesopotamia*, *Death on the Nile*, *The Mysterious Mr. Quin*, *The ABC Murders*, *Lord Edgware Dies*, *The Murder of Roger Ackroyd*, *The Mysterious Affair at Styles*, *The Thirteen Problems*, *The Hound of Death*, *The Sittaford Mystery*, *Murder on the Orient Express*, *Dumb Witness*, *Peril at End House*. They all end up on his desk, so many brightly jacketed hardcovers, except for a few that fall with a thud to the floor.

"The thought first struck me as I was rereading *Murder on the Orient Express*. I noticed how the train comes from the East. There are thirteen passengers at the heart of the story, one of whom is a monster, a Judas. I noticed how these passengers come from all walks of life and all nationalities. I noticed how one of the investigators, a helper of Hercule Poirot, is a Dr. Constantine. Isn't the story of Jesus an Eastern story made popular by another Constantine? Did Jesus not have twelve disciples, with a Judas among them? Was Palestine not a mixed Orient Express of nationalities? The foreignness of Hercule Poirot is often remarked upon. Time and again he saves the day. The foreigner whose intervention is salvific — isn't that one way of seeing Jesus? These observations led me to examine the murder mysteries of Agatha Christie in a new light.

"I began to notice things in a jumble. There is meaning in every small incident — Agatha Christie's stories are narratives of revelatory detail, hence the spare, direct language and the short, numerous paragraphs and chapters, as in the Gospels. Only the essential is recounted. Murder mysteries, like the Gospels, are distillations.

"I noticed the near total absence of children in Agatha Christie — because murder is a decidedly adult entertainment — just as they are largely absent from the Gospels, which also address an adult sensibility.

"I noticed how those who know the truth are always treated with suspicion and disdain. That was the case with Jesus, of course. But look at old Miss Marple. Always she knows, and everyone is surprised that she does. And the same with Hercule Poirot. How can that ridiculous little man know anything? But he does, he does. It is the triumph of the meek, in Agatha Christie as in the Gospels.

"The gravest sin — the taking of a life — is always at the core of an Agatha Christie story — as it is at the core of the story of Jesus. In both narratives numerous characters are briefly introduced and for the same purpose: the parading of all the suspects, so that the reader can see who gives in to the temptation of evil in contrast to who does not. Fortitude is set next to weakness, both in the Gospels and in Agatha Christie. And in both, the light of understanding comes in the same way: We are given facts, neutral in themselves, then we are given an interpretation that imprints meaning upon these facts. So proceed the parables of Jesus — exposition, then explanation — and so proceeds the Passion of Jesus; his death and resurrection were explained, given meaning to, by Paul, after the fact. And so proceed the denouements of the murder mysteries of Agatha Christie: Hercule Poirot summarizes all the facts before he tells us what they mean.

"Notice the vital role of the witness. Neither Jesus nor Hercule Poirot cared to pick up a pen. Both were content to live in the spoken word. The act of witness was therefore a necessity — how else would we know what they said and did? But it was also a *consequence*. Each man, in his own sphere, did such amazing things that people felt compelled to bear witness. Those who met Jesus spent the rest of their lives talking about him to family, friends, and strangers, until what they said reached the ears of Paul, and later of Matthew, Mark, Luke, and John. And the same with Arthur Hastings, the Watson-like narrator of many of the Hercule Poirot stories, a narrator no less loyal than the narrators of the Gospels.

"But every witness is to some degree unreliable. We see that clearly with Arthur Hastings, who is always a few steps behind Hercule Poirot until Poirot helps him catch up with lucid explanations. We realize then that it is not only Arthur Hastings who is obtuse. We too have missed clues, misunderstood import, failed to seize the meaning. We too need Hercule Poirot to help us catch up. And so with Jesus. He was surrounded by so many Arthur Hastingses who were perpetually missing clues, misunderstanding import, failing to seize the meaning. He too had to explain everything to his disciples so that they might catch up. And still the disciples got it wrong, still they couldn't agree on what Jesus said or did. Look at the Gospels: *four of them*, each a little different from the others, each *inconsistent* with the others, as always happens with the testimony of witnesses.

"In an Agatha Christie mystery, the murderer is nearly always a figure closer than we expected. Remember *The Man in the Brown Suit* and *The Seven Dials Mystery* and *Three Act Tragedy* and *The ABC Murders* and especially *The Murder of Roger Ackroyd*, to name just a few. Our vision of evil far away is acute, but the closer the evil, the greater the moral myopia. The edges become blurred, the centre hard to see. Thus the reaction when it is revealed who did it: 'Et tu, Brute?' The disciples must have reacted in this way when Judas, good Judas Iscariot, our dear friend and travelling companion, proved to be a traitor. How blind we are to evil close-by, how willing to look away.

"Speaking of blindness, there is this curious phenomenon. We read Agatha Christie in the grip of compulsion. We *must* keep on reading. We want to know who did it, and how, and why. Then we find out. We're amazed at the complexity of the crime's execution. Oh, the coolness of the murderer's mind, the steadiness of his or her hand. Our devouring curiosity satisfied, we put the book down — and instantly we forget who did it! Isn't that so? We don't forget the victim. Agatha Christie can title her novels *The Murder of Roger Ackroyd* or *Lord Edgware Dies* without any fear of losing her readers' interest. The victim is a given, and he or she stays with us. But how quickly the murderer vanishes from our mind. We pick up an Agatha Christie murder mystery — she's written so many — and we wonder, *Have I read this one? Let me* see. *She's the victim, yes, I remember that, but who did it? Oh, I can't remember.* We must reread a hundred pages before we recall who it was that took a human life.

"We apply the same amnesia to the Gospels. We remember the victim. Of course we do. But do we remember who killed him? If you went up to your average person on the street and said 'Quick — tell me — *who murdered Jesus?*' my guess is that the person would be at a loss for words. Who *did* murder Jesus of Nazareth? Who was responsible? Judas Iscariot? Bah! He was a tool, an accessory. He betrayed Jesus, he gave him up to people who sought him, but he did not kill him. Pontius Pilate, then, the Roman procurator who sentenced him to death? Hardly. He just went along. He found Jesus innocent of any wrongdoing, sought to have him released, preferred to have Barabbas crucified, and yielded only in the face of the angry crowd. Pilate chose to sacrifice an innocent man rather than have a riot on his hands. So he was a weak man, another accessory to murder, but he was not the actual murderer.

"Who, then, did the deed? The Romans, more generally? Jesus *was* strung up by Roman soldiers following Roman orders according to Roman law in a Roman province. But who's ever heard of such a nebulous murderer? Are we to accept theologically that the Son of God was murdered by the nameless servants of a long-vanished empire to appease a squabbling local tribe? If that's the case, no wonder no one can remember who did it.

"Ah! But of course: It was Jews who murdered Jesus! That's a familiar refrain, is it not? A group of manipulative Jewish elders, in collusion with the Roman authorities, conspired to get rid of a troublesome fellow Jew. (And we remembered to hate Jews but not Italians — how did that happen? The shame of it!) But if it was Jews who were responsible, which ones? What were their names? We have Caiaphas, the high priest. Any others? None who is named. And really, like Judas, like Pilate, Caiaphas was an accessory. Jews could not openly kill a Jew — remember the Ten Commandments? Caiaphas had to find others who would do it. So he and his fellow elders whipped up the crowd, and it's the crowd that decided matters against Jesus. With them lies the true, practical guilt. If the crowd had cried for Jesus' release and Barabbas's crucifixion, Pilate would have obliged, Caiaphas would have been stymied, and Judas would have had to return his blood money.

"There we seem to have it, then: It was *a crowd* that was responsible for the murder of Jesus of Nazareth. To put it in exact terms, a crowd framed by mostly anonymous officials, manipulated by mostly anonymous elders, wished him dead, and then anonymous soldiers actually killed him. But it started with a crowd, and is there anything more anonymous than a crowd? Is a crowd not, by definition, anonymous? From this assessment, it's clear: These guilty Jews, these guilty Romans — they are straw men, red herrings, in the best tradition of Agatha Christie. No wonder the common brutish mind thinks it's the Jew next door who murdered Jesus — that's more concrete. But in theological actuality, it was Anonymous who killed Jesus of Nazareth. And who is Anonymous?"

Maria stops. After some seconds of silence, Eusebio realizes with a start that his wife is waiting for him to answer the question.

"Oh! I'm not sure. I've never —"

"Anonymous is you, is me, is all of us. We murdered Jesus of Nazareth. We are the crowd. We are Anonymous. It is not the guilt of Jews that goes down through history, it is the guilt of all of us. But how quick we are to forget that. We don't like guilt, do we? We prefer to hide it, to forget it, to twist it and present it in a better light, to pass it on to others. And so, because of our aversion to guilt, we strain to remember who killed the victim in the Gospels, as we strain to remember who killed the victim in an Agatha Christie murder mystery.

"And at the end of it, is that not the plainest way to describe the life of Jesus, as a Murder Mystery? A life was taken, the victim completely innocent. Who did it? Who had the motive and the opportunity? What happened to the body? What did it all mean? An exceptional detective was needed to solve the crime, and he came along, some years after the murder, the Hercule Poirot of the first century: Paul of Tarsus. Christianity starts with Paul. The earliest Christian documents are his letters. With them we have the story of Jesus, years before the life of Jesus of the Gospels. Paul vowed to get to the bottom of the Jesus affair. Using his grey cells, he sleuthed about, listening to testimony, poring over the record of events, gathering clues, studying every detail. He had a big break in the case in the form of a vision on the road to Damascus.

And at the end of his investigation he drew the only conclusion possible. Then he preached and he wrote, and Jesus went from being a failed Messiah to the resurrected Son of God who takes on our burden of sins. Paul closed the case on Jesus of Nazareth. And just as the resolution of the crime in an Agatha Christie brings on a sort of glee, and the reader is struck by her amazing ingenuity, so the resurrection of Jesus and its meaning induces a powerful glee in the Christian — more: a lasting joy — and the Christian thanks God for His amazing ingenuity, as well as His boundless compassion. Because the resurrection of Jesus to wash away our sins is the only possible solution to the problem as understood by Paul, the problem of a loving God unexpectedly put to death who then resurrects. Hercule Poirot would heartily approve of the logic of Paul's solution.

"The world of the Gospels is stark. There is much suffering in it, suffering of the body, suffering of the soul. It is a world of moral extremes in which the good are purely good and the evil insistently evil. Agatha Christie's world is equally stark. Who among us lives a life so beset by murders as Hercule Poirot and Jane Marple? And behind these murders, so much conniving evil! Our world is not like that, is it? Most of us know neither so much good nor so much evil. We sail a tempered middle. And yet murders happen, sometimes on a large scale, do they not? The Great War ended not so long ago. Next door the Spaniards are killing each other with abandon. And now there are insistent rumours of another war across our continent. The

170

symbolic crime of our century is the murder, Eusebio. Anonymous is still very much with us. That tempered middle we sail is an illusion. Our world is stark too, but we hide in a shelter built of luck and closed eyes. What will you do when your luck runs out, when your eyes are ripped open?

"The sad fact is that there are no natural deaths, despite what doctors say. Every death is felt by someone as a murder, as the unjust taking of a loved being. And even the luckiest of us will encounter at least one murder in our lives: our own. It is our fate. We all live a murder mystery of which we are the victim.

"The only modern genre that plays on the same high moral register as the Gospels is the lowly regarded murder mystery. If we set the murder mysteries of Agatha Christie atop the Gospels and shine a light through, we see correspondence and congruence, agreement and equivalence. We find matching patterns and narrative similarities. They are maps of the same city, parables of the same existence. They glow with the same moral transparency. And so the explanation for why Agatha Christie is the most popular author in the history of the world. Her appeal is as wide and her dissemination as great as the Bible's, because she is a modern apostle, a female one — about time, after two thousand years of men blathering on. And this new apostle answers the same questions Jesus answered: What are we to do with death? Because murder mysteries are always resolved in the end, the mystery neatly dispelled. We must do the same with death in our

171

lives: resolve it, give it meaning, put it into context, however hard that might be.

"And yet Agatha Christie and the Gospels are different in a key way. We no longer live in an age of prophecy and miracle. We no longer have Jesus among us the way the people of the Gospels did. The Gospels of Matthew, Mark, Luke, and John are narratives of presence. Agatha Christie's are gospels of *absence*. They are modern gospels for a modern people, a people more suspicious, less willing to believe. And so Jesus is present only in fragments, in traces, cloaked and masked, obscured and hidden. But look — he's right there in her last name. Mainly, though, he hovers, he whispers."

A smile creeps across Maria Lozora's face as she watches for his reaction. He smiles back but stays silent. If he is honest, it is jarring to hear Jesus Christ and Agatha Christie, the apostle Paul and Hercule Poirot so closely matched. The Pope in Rome will not be pleased to hear that he has a serious rival in the form of a forty-eight-year-old woman from Torquay, England, the author of many highly engaging entertainments.

Maria speaks again, her gentle voice coming like an embrace. "That's the great, enduring challenge of our modern times, is it not, to marry faith and reason? So hard — so *unreasonable* — to root our lives upon a distant wisp of holiness. Faith is grand but impractical: How does one live an eternal idea in a daily way? It's so much easier to be reasonable. Reason is practical, its rewards are immediate, its workings are clear. But alas, reason is blind. Reason, on its own, leads us nowhere, especially in the face of adversity. How do we balance the two, how do we live with both faith and reason? In your case, Eusebio, I thought the solution would be stories that put reason on brilliant display while also keeping you close to Jesus of Nazareth. That way you can hold on to your faith, should it ever waver. And so I give to you: Agatha Christie."

She is radiant. Her two-word gift, wrapped in spools of speech, is now in his lap. From decades of experience he knows that his turn to intervene has come. But he is unexpectedly tongue-tied. *What*? The miracles of Jesus, Jesus benefitting the human body, Jesus walking on water, Jesus the allegorist saved by other allegorists, Jesus the victim in a murder mystery, Jesus a whispering background character in Agatha Christie — all that winding argumentation so that he might read his favourite writer *with greater religious comfort*? He stumbles his way to words. "Thank you, Maria. I've never thought of Agatha Christie in this way. It's a —"

"I love you," his wife interrupts him, "and I've done this for you. All you ever read is Agatha Christie. Next time you're at home sick with sadness pick up one of her books and imagine you're in a boat. Standing on the water alongside the boat is Jesus of Nazareth. He begins to read the Agatha Christie to you. The warm breath of God, who loves you, comes off the page and touches your face. How can you not smile, then?"

"Why, M-M-Maria —" he cries. What is this stammer that is suddenly afflicting him? He looks at her and is reminded of that for which he is grateful, the rich earth and the sun and the rain and the crops. "My angel, it's so kind of you! I'm truly thankful."

He stands and moves around the desk towards her. She also gets to her feet. He takes her in his arms. They kiss. She is cold. He holds her tighter to warm her with his body. He speaks into her shoulder. "It's a wonderful gift. I'm so lucky to have —"

She pulls back and pats his cheek. "You're welcome, my dear husband, you're welcome. You're a good man." She sighs. "I should be getting home. Can you help me put the books back in the bag, please?"

"Of course!" He bends down to pick up the volumes that fell to the floor. Together they fill the bag with all the Agatha Christies and walk the few steps to the door of his office. He opens the door.

"You left the milk out," she says on the threshold. "For three days. It's gone bad. It stinks. I didn't notice, since I never drink the stuff. If you're going to work all night, get some fresh milk on your way home. And buy bread. Make sure you don't get lentil bread. It gives you gas. And lastly I've brought you a little gift. Don't look now. I'm leaving."

But still he wants to hold her back, to thank her for the gift of her, his dear wife of thirty-eight years, still he wants to say things to her.

"Shall we pray?" he asks, typically a good way to stop his wife in her tracks.

"I'm too tired. But you pray. And you have work to do. What are you working on?"

He looks at his desk. His work? He'd forgotten all about his work. "I have a number of reports to write up.

One case is particularly unpleasant, a woman who was pushed off a bridge. A wicked murder."

He sighs. Only the autopsies of babies and children are worse — all those toy organs. Otherwise, there is no greater abomination than the decomposed human body. Two or three days after death, the putrefying body manifests a greenish patch on the abdomen, which spreads to the chest and to the upper thighs. This green tinge is the result of a gas produced by bacteria in the intestinal system. During life, these bacteria help digest food, but in death they help digest the body. Nature is full of such friends. This gas contains sulphur and it smells foul. Some of it escapes from the rectum — the decaying body is often smelled before it is seen. But there is shortly much to be seen. When the gas has finished discolouring the skin, it proceeds to bloat the body. The eyes — their eyelids puffed — bulge out. The tongue protrudes from the mouth. The vagina turns inside out and is pushed out, as are the intestines from the anus. The colour of the skin continues to change. After a mere week, a pale white body, if given over to thoroughgoing, wet gangrene decomposition, will go from pale green to purple to a dark green marbled with streaks of black along the veins. Seeping blisters grow and burst, leaving puddles of rot on the skin. Cadaver juices seep out of the nose, the mouth, and other body orifices. Two of the chemicals found in these fluids are called putrescine and cadaverine, nicely capturing their aroma. By the second week of death, the body is taut with swelling, especially the abdomen, scrotum, breasts, and tongue. The slimmest person becomes gross with

175

corpulence. The distended skin rips and starts to come off in sheets. Within another week, hair, nails, and teeth lose their grip. Most internal organs have ruptured and begun to liquefy, including the brain, which in its last solid phase is a dark green gelatin. All these organs become a stinking, gloppy river that flows off the bones.

Outdoors, other organisms besides bacteria play a role in uglifying the body. Any number of birds will peck at dead flesh, gashing the way in for hosts of smaller invaders, among them flies, principally flesh flies and blowflies, with their generous and abundant contribution of maggots, but also beetles, ants, spiders, mites, millipedes, centipedes, wasps, and others. Each mars the body in its own way. And there are still more disfigurers: shrews, voles, mice, rats, foxes, cats, dogs, wolves, lynxes. These eat the face, pull away chunks of flesh, remove entire limbs. All this is done to a body that was, until very recently, living, whole, and standing, walking, smiling, and laughing.

"How terrible," Maria says.

"Yes. I'm going to avoid that bridge from now on."

His wife nods. "Faith is the answer to death. Good-bye."

She tilts her face up and they kiss one last time. To have her lovely face so close to his! To feel her body against his! She pulls away. A little smile and a glance of farewell, and she leaves his office and starts moving down the hallway. He follows her out.

"Good-bye, my angel. Thank you for all your gifts. I love you."

She disappears around a bend. He gazes down the deserted hallway, then returns to his office and closes the door.

His office now feels empty and too quiet. Perhaps he should pray again, although he is not, as it happens, one who has seen many victories won through prayer, devoted though he is to Jesus of Nazareth. Nor is he of the age when throwing oneself upon one's knees comes easily. Genuflection proceeds with groaning and the slow working of parts, a precarious balancing act accompanied by moments of sudden giving way. And at the end of it, knees are painfully pressed against a marble floor that is hard and cold (though perfect for mopping up blood and cadaver juices). He begins to work his way down, using the desk for help. Then he remembers: Maria mentioned a gift. He looks at his desk. She must have placed her gift on it while he was bent down, gathering the Agatha Christies off the floor. Sure enough, some papers betray a bump that was not there earlier. He straightens himself and reaches over. A book. He takes it in his hands and turns it over.

Appointment with Death, by Agatha Christie. He searches his memory. The title does not seem familiar, nor does the cover. But there are so many titles, so many covers. He checks the copyright page: 1938, this very year — or this year until a few minutes ago. His heart leaps. *It's a new Agatha Christie! A* successor to *Death on the Nile*. It must have arrived that day from the Círculo Português de Mistério. Bless them. Bless his wife, who graced him with the further gift of letting him read it first.

The reports will wait. He settles in his chair. Or rather, as his wife suggested, he settles in a boat. A voice comes to his ears:

"*You do see, don't you, that she's got to be killed?*"

The question floated out into the still night air, seemed to hang there a moment and then drift away down into the darkness towards the Dead Sea.

Hercule Poirot paused a minute with his hand on the window catch. Frowning, he shut it decisively, thereby excluding any injurious night air! Hercule Poirot had been brought up to believe that all outside air was best left outside, and that night air was especially dangerous to the health.

As he pulled the curtains neatly over the window and walked to his bed, he smiled tolerantly to himself.

"*You do see, don't you, that she's got to be killed?*"

Curious words for one Hercule Poirot, detective, to overhear on his first night in Jerusalem.

"Decidedly, wherever I go, there is something to remind me of crime!" he murmured to himself.

Eusebio pauses. An Agatha Christie that starts in *Jerusalem*? The last one took place on the Nile, there was one set in Mesopotamia — circling around Palestine — but now Jerusalem itself. After all that

Maria was saying, the coincidence amazes him. She will take it as confirmation of her theory.

A rap at the door startles him. The book in his hands flies up like a bird. "Maria!" he cries. She has come back! He hurries to the door. He must tell her.

"Maria!" he calls again as he pulls the door open.

A woman stands before him. But it's not his wife. It is a different woman. This woman is older. A black-dressed widow. A stranger. She eyes him. There is a large beat-up suitcase at her feet. Surely the woman hasn't been travelling at this late hour? He notes something else. Hidden by wrinkles, blurred by time, hindered by black peasant dress, but shining through nonetheless: The woman is a great beauty. A luminous face, a striking figure, a graceful carriage. She must have been something to behold when she was young.

"How did you know I was coming?" the woman asks, startled.

"I'm sorry, I thought you were someone else."

"My name is Maria Dores Passos Castro."

Maria that she is, who is she? She's not his Maria, his wife, she's a different Maria. What does she want? What is she doing here?

"How can I be of assistance, Senhora Castro?" he asks stiffly.

Maria Castro answers with a question. "Are you the doctor who deals with bodies?"

That's one way of putting it. "Yes, I'm head of the department of pathology. My name is Dr. Eusebio Lozora."

"In that case, I need to talk to you, Senhor doctor, if you have a few minutes to spare."

He leans out to look down the hallway, searching for his wife. She isn't there. She and this woman must have crossed paths. He sighs inwardly. Another woman who wants to talk to him. Is she also concerned with his salvation? How many more biblical prophets lie waiting for him in the night? All he wants to do is get a little work done, get caught up. And since when do pathologists have consultations with the public, in the middle of the night at that? He's starving too. He should have brought something to eat if he was going to work all night.

He will turn this woman away. For whatever ails her, she should see a family doctor, she should go to the emergency room. His hand is set to close the door when he remembers: No men attended Jesus when he was buried. Only women came to his tomb, only women.

Perhaps one of the cases on his desk has to do with her? A relative, a loved one. It's highly unusual for him to deal with family members. He prides himself on his ability to determine what may cause grief, but grief itself, dealing with it, is neither his medical specialty nor a talent he happens to have. That is why he went into pathology. Pathology is medicine reduced to its pure science, without the draining contact with patients. But before training to track down death, he studied life, and here is a living woman who wants to consult with him. This, he remembers, is what the original calling of the medical arts is about: the alleviating of suffering.

In as gentle a voice as his weary frame can muster, he says, "Please come in, Senhora Castro."

The old woman picks up her suitcase and enters his office. "Much obliged, Senhor doctor."

"Here, sit here," he says, indicating the chair his wife has just vacated. His office is still a mess, his workbench still covered in papers — and what's that file on the floor in the corner? But it will have to do for now. He sits down in his chair, across the desk from his new visitor. A doctor and his patient. Except for the bottle of red wine standing on the desk and the Agatha Christie murder mystery lying on the floor.

"How can I help you?" he asks.

She hesitates, then makes up her mind. "I've come down from the village of Tuizelo, in the High Mountains of Portugal."

Ah yes. The few people who live in the High Mountains of Portugal trickle down to Bragança because there's not a hospital in the whole thankless plateau or, indeed, a commercial centre of any size.

"It's about my husband."

"Yes?" he encourages her.

She says nothing. He waits. He'll let her come round. Hers will be an emotional lament disguised as a question. He will need to wrap in kind words the explanation for her husband's death.

"I tried to write about it," she finally says. "But it's so vulgar on the page. And to speak about it is worse."

181

"It's all right," he responds in a soothing voice, though he finds her choice of words odd. *Vulgar?* "It's perfectly natural. And inevitable. It comes to all of us."

"Does it? Not in Tuizelo. I'd say it's quite rare there."

Eusebio's eyebrows knit. Does the woman live in a village of immortals where only a few are rudely visited by death? His wife often tells him that he spends so much time with the dead that he sometimes misses the social cues of the living. Did he not hear right? Did she not just ask him if he was the doctor who deals with bodies?

"Senhora Castro, death is universal. We must all go through it."

"Death? Who's talking about death? I'm talking about sex."

Now that the dreaded word has been said, Maria Castro moves forward comfortably. "Love came into my life in the disguise I least expected. That of a man. I was as surprised as a flower that sees for the first time a bee coming towards it. It was my mother who suggested I marry Rafael. She consulted with my father and they decided it was a good match. It wasn't an arranged marriage, then, not exactly, but I would have had to come up with a good, solid excuse not to want to marry Rafael. I couldn't think of one. All we had to do was get along, and how difficult could that be? I had known him my whole life. He was one of the boys in the village. He'd always been there, like a rock in a field. I must have first set eyes on him when I was a toddler, and he, being older, perhaps gazed at me when I was a baby. He was a slim, pleasant-faced boy, quieter and more retiring than the others in the village. I don't know if I had ever spent more than twenty minutes with him before it was suggested that we spend the rest of our lives together.

"We did have one moment, when I think back. It must have been a year or two earlier. I was running an errand and I came upon him on a path. He was fixing a gate. He asked me to hold something. I bent down and so brought my head close to his. Just then a gust of wind lifted a mass of my hair and threw it in his face. I felt it, the gentle lashing, and I pulled my head back, catching the last strands as they flowed off his face. He was smiling and looking straight at me.

"I remember too that he played the sweet flute, a little wooden thing. I liked the sound of it, its springtime bird-like tweeting.

"So the suggestion of marriage was made and I thought, *Why not?* I had to marry at some point. You don't want to live your whole life alone. He would no doubt be useful to me and I would try my best to be useful to him. I looked at him in a new light and the idea of being married to him pleased me.

"His father had died when he was young, so it was his mother who was consulted. She thought the same thing and he presumably thought the same thing. Everyone thought, *Why not?* So we married under the banner of *Why not?* Everything happened swiftly. The ceremony was businesslike. The priest went through his pieties. No money was wasted on any celebration. We were moved into a shack of a house that Rafael's uncle Valerio gave us until we found better.

"We were alone for the first time since the ceremony. The door had barely closed when Rafael turned to me and said, 'Take your clothes off.' I looked at him askance and said, 'No, you take yours off.' 'All right,' he replied, and he stripped down quickly and completely. It was impressive. I had never seen a naked man before. He came up to me and put his hand on my breast and squeezed. 'Is this nice?' he asked. I shrugged and said, 'It's all right.' 'How about this?' he asked, squeezing again in a softer way, pinching the nipple. 'It's all right,' I replied, but this time I didn't shrug.

"Next, he was very forward. He came round behind me and pressed me to him. I could feel his cucumber against me. He ran his hand under my dress, all the way under, until it rested *there*. I didn't fight him off. I guessed that this was what it meant to be married, that I had to put up with this.

" 'Is this nice?' he asked.

" 'I'm not sure,' I replied.

" 'And this?' he asked as he prodded around some more.

" 'I'm not sure,' I replied.

" 'And this?'

" 'Not . . . sure.'

" 'And this?'

"Suddenly I couldn't answer. A feeling began to overcome me. He had touched a spot that shrivelled my tongue. Oh, it was so good. What was it?

" 'And this?' he asked again.

"I nodded. He kept at it. I bent forward and he bent with me. I lost my balance and we stumbled around the room, overturning a chair, hitting a wall, shoving the table. Rafael held on to me firmly and brought us to the ground, onto the small carpet from his brother Batista. All the while he kept it up with his hand, and I stayed with the feeling. I had no idea what it was, but it rumbled through me like a train, and then there was an explosion of sorts, as if the train had suddenly come out of a tunnel into the light. I let it rumble through me. I was left breathless. I turned to Rafael. 'I'll take my clothes off now,' I said.

"He was twenty-one, I was seventeen. Desire was a discovery. Where would I have found it earlier? My parents expressed desire like a desert. I was the one hardy plant they had produced. Otherwise, theirs was a sour and hardworking life. Did the Church teach me desire? The thought would be worth a laugh, if I had time to waste. The Church taught me to shame something I didn't even know. As for those around me, young and old, perhaps there were innuendos, hints, slippages when I was growing up — but I missed their meaning.

"So there you have it: I had never desired. I had a body ready for it and a mind willing to learn, but it all lay asleep, unused, unsuspected. Then Rafael and I came together. Beneath plain clothing and shy manners we discovered our beautiful bodies, like gold hidden under the land. We were entirely ignorant in these matters. I didn't know what a cucumber was or what it was for. I didn't know what it could do for me or what I could do for it. And he was as ignorant about my nest. He stared at it, astonished. *What a strange thing*, his eyes said. *Have you seen your thing?* my eyes replied. *Yes, yes,* his eyes panted back, *it's all so very strange.*

"Strangest of all, we knew what to do. It all fell into place. We touched, we asked, we did, all in one go. What pleased him pleased me, what pleased me pleased him. It works out like that in life sometimes, doesn't it? A stamp takes pleasure in being licked and stuck to an envelope, and an envelope takes pleasure in the stick of that stamp. Each takes to the other without ever having suspected that the other existed. So Rafael and I were stamp and envelope.

"And to our astonishment, under the cover of marriage, our deportment was all good and proper. I had never imagined it could feel so good to be Portuguese.

"I used to hurry home along the crest of the hill from the neighbouring village, where I assisted the schoolteacher. There was no path to speak of, but it was the quickest route to get to our small house. I scrambled over large rocks, I plunged through hedges. There were stone walls, but they had gates. From the third-to-last gate, I often caught sight of him, down below in our second field, where the sheep grazed. It happened regularly that he noticed me too, just as I reached this particular gate. Every time I thought, *What an extraordinary coincidence! I have just crossed this gate and he has seen me.* He couldn't hear me — too far — but sensing the deepening colour of the sky, aware of the time of day, he knew I would be coming along soon, and constantly he turned and looked up, creating the conditions for the coincidence. He would see me and redouble his efforts in the field, hustling and pushing the sheep into their pen, to the yapping delight of the dog, who saw his master taking over his job.

"Often, before he had even properly finished the task, he started to run, as did I. He was ahead of me, but he had much to do. He charged into the yard and screamed after the chickens. As I got closer, I could hear their frantic clucking. They were hurled into the coop. Then there were the pigs, who needed their slop for the night. And more. The endless tasks of a farm. From the top of the hill, I raced down to the back of the house. I would laugh and shout, 'I'll get there first!' The front door would be the closest for him, the back door for me. When I was metres away, he would give up — to hell with the farm — and make a break for it. The doors would be torn open, sometimes his first, sometimes mine. Either way, they were slammed shut, shaking our hovel to its foundations, and we would be face to face, breathless, giddy, drunk with happiness. And why this rush? Why this unseemly race across the countryside? Why this neglect of farm duties? Because we were so eager to be naked with each other. We tore our clothes off as if they were on fire.

"One day my mother and I were working on preserves, a few months after my marriage. She asked me if Rafael and I had been 'intimate' yet. That was her language. She wasn't touched by her husband, my father, for eighteen months after they got married. I don't know what they did for those eighteen months. Lie in bed, back to back, waiting to fall asleep in dead silence, their eyes wide open? My mother's concern was grandchildren. Her lineage was not a richly reproductive lot. She herself was an only child, and fifty-four years of marriage resulted in a single daughter. She was worried that I would be afflicted with the family's barrenness. I told my mother that Rafael and I were intimate every night, and sometimes during the day too, if we happened both to be at home, on a Sunday, for example. Sometimes in the morning also, before we had to rush off to work. Sometimes we were intimate two times in a row.

"My mother looked at me. 'I mean the act, the *act*,' she whispered, though we were alone.

"Did my mother think I was referring to *naps*? That we went to bed early every night and that sometimes we napped during the day too? That sometimes in the morning we woke up and right away had a nap? That sometimes we had two naps in a row? Did she think we were as lazy and dozy as cats?

" 'Yes, yes, Mother,' I replied, 'we do the act all the time. Perhaps if I see him in the next half hour, we'll do it then.'

"My mother's eyes expressed surprise, consternation, horror. *Every night? On Sundays?* This was last century, mind you. Much has changed since. Everything is so modern these days. I could see in my mother's mind the pages of a Bible being speedily flipped. The preserving of fruit was done with. I could go now.

" 'He *is* my husband,' I told her, pushing the door open with a bump of my hip.

"She never brought up the subject again. At least now she hoped to be blessed with a dozen grandchildren. She would show them around the village like fine jewellery. And my answer was good for gossip. That was my mother, a prude who lived through gossip, like every prude. After that, the men in the village looked at me with lingering smiles — the older they were, the greater the twinkle in their eyes — while the women, the young ones and the old hens, were a muddled mix of envy, disdain, and curiosity. And from then onward my mother announced her arrival at our house a hundred metres away with a great fanfare of noise.

"On the count of grandchildren, her hopes were dashed. I proved to be as unreproductive as she was. Considering how often stamp was brought to envelope, it's surprising that there weren't more letters. But only one letter came, a delightful one, late, late, late, a darling boy who tore out of me not with a cry but with a burst of laughter. By the time I presented our little bear cub to my mother, her mind was gone. I could have been handing her a clucking chicken, the vacant smile would have been the same."

A vague smile comes to the old woman's lips, though not a vacant one.

"Now that I'm old, sleep has become a mystery to me. I can remember sleep, I just can't remember how to do it. Why has sleep betrayed me? Rafael and I used to give to it so generously when we were young. Despite our poverty, we had a comfortable bed, we had curtains, we obeyed the call of the night. Our sleep was

189

as deep as a well. Every morning we awoke and wondered at this refreshing event that so knocked us out. Now my nights are plagued by worries and sadness. I lie down tired, and nothing happens. I just lie there with my thoughts coiling around me like a snake."

Eusebio speaks quietly. "Ageing is not easy, Senhora Castro. It's a terrible, incurable pathology. And great love is another pathology. It starts well. It's a most desirable disease. One wouldn't want to do without it. It's like the yeast that corrupts the juice of grapes. One loves, one loves, one persists in loving — the incubation period can be very long — and then, with death, comes the heartbreak. Love must always meet its unwanted end."

But where's the body? That is the pressing question that he leaves unstated. And whose body? Perhaps it is not her husband's. She's wearing black, but so does every woman over forty in rural Portugal who has lost some relative somewhere. The apparel of mourning is a permanent dress for rural women. Perhaps she has come to inquire about someone younger. If that's the case, any one of the files at his feet under the desk might contain the information she wants. It could also be that hers is a case that Dr. Otavio, his colleague, dealt with. José has been gone now for close to three weeks, off on his month-long holiday to England to visit his daughter. Hence all of the extra work right now. But José signed off on all his cases, so if Maria Castro is inquiring about one of those, he will be able to find it in the filing cabinets next door.

At any rate, there needs to be a body, because he's a pathologist. Those who have sleep problems go elsewhere, to a family doctor who will prescribe a sleep potion, or to a priest who will absolve their sins. Those who are unhappy about getting old, who suffer from heartbreak, they too go elsewhere, to a priest again, or to a friend, or to a taverna, or even to a brothel. But not to a pathologist.

"I'm glad to hear about your joys and sad to hear about your troubles," he continues. "But why exactly have you come to see me? Are you here to inquire about a particular case?"

"I want to know how he lived."

How he *lived*? She means how he died. A slip-up due to age.

"Who?"

"Rafael, of course."

"What's his full name?"

"Rafael Miguel Santos Castro, from the village of Tuizelo."

"Your husband, then. Just a moment, please."

He bends over and pulls the files out from under his desk. Where is the master list? He finds the sheet of paper. He looks it over carefully. There is no Rafael Miguel Santos Castro among the cases pending.

"I don't see that name on my list. Your husband must have been dealt with by my colleague, Dr. Otavio. I must get his file. It will just take me a moment."

"What file?" asks Maria.

"Your husband's, of course. Every patient has a file."

"But you haven't even seen him yet."

191

"Oh. You didn't tell me that. In that case, you'll have to come back in a few days, after he's come through."

"But he's here."

"Where?"

He can't be in the cold room. Eusebio is well aware of the bodies currently stored there. Does she mean that her husband is here *in a spiritual sense*? He wonders about her state of mind from a medical point of view. A bit of delusional dementia?

Maria Castro looks at him with an expression of clear good sense and replies in a matter-of-fact tone, "Right here."

She leans over and undoes the clasps of the suitcase. The lid falls open and the sole content of the suitcase slips out like a baby being born: the dead and shoeless body of Rafael Castro.

Eusebio peers at the body. Bodies come to their deaths in many ways, but they always come to him in the hospital in the same way: on a gurney and properly prepared, with an accompanying clinical report. They don't tumble out of suitcases in their Sunday best. But peasants have their own customs, he knows. They live with death in ways that urban people left behind long ago. Sometimes in rural Portugal they bury their dead in old tree trunks, for example. In his long professional life he has examined a few such bodies for the purpose of determining that they died of natural causes and were buried, not murdered and disposed of. (In every instance it was a proper burial.) He has also worked on the bodies of peasants who had pins stuck under their fingernails. No cruelty, this; just a primitive method to

192

ensure that someone was actually dead. And here was another practical peasant way of dealing with death: doing one's own ambulance work. That must have been a lot of work for the old woman, hauling the suitcase down from the High Mountains of Portugal.

"How long has he been dead?" he asks.

"Three days," Maria replies.

That seems about right. The winter cold of the road has done a good job of preserving the body.

"How did he die?" he asks. "I mean, was he sick?"

"Not that he told me. He was having a cup of coffee in the kitchen. I went out. When I came back, he was on the floor and I couldn't wake him."

"I see." *Acute myocardial infarction, cerebral aneurysm, something like that*, he thinks. "And what do you want me to do with him, Senhora Castro?"

"Open him up, tell me how he lived."

That mistake again. Perhaps an aversion to the actual word. Although, come to think of it, her way of putting it is not inaccurate. In showing how a person died, an autopsy often indicates how that person lived. Still, it's odd. Perhaps a regional locution, born of superstition.

"You want me to perform an autopsy on your husband?"

"Yes. Isn't that what you do?"

"It is. But you don't order up an autopsy the way you order a meal in a restaurant."

"What's the problem?"

"There are procedures to follow."

"He's dead. What else is necessary?"

She has a point. Proper protocol or not, the body will be the same. Send her away with her suitcase, and Maria and Rafael Castro will be back the next day. In the meantime, an inn in Bragança will be displeased to find that one of its guests was a dead body. And overnight, in the warmth of a room, that body may reach the spillover point of decomposition, which will merely inconvenience him but will scandalize the innkeepers. If the couple even go to an inn. Since when have peasants had money to spend on paying accommodation? More likely she will spend the night at the train station, sitting on a bench, or, worse, outdoors in a park, sitting on her suitcase. Old Rafael Castro will not mind the cold, nor, for that matter, will his faithful wife — these ancient peasants are as rugged as the Iberian rhinoceros of yore. It's he, Eusebio, who will mind. A piece of paper is not worth such bodily ache, not after so much heartache. And better this fresh body than the body he will otherwise have to reckon with, the woman who was thrown off the bridge.

Maria Castro looks at him, waiting for his reply. Her patience weighs on him.

He is practical in his own way. How did she put it? She got married "under the banner of *Why not?*" Well, why not? This will be one to tell José about.

"All right, I'll perform an autopsy on your husband. You'll have to wait here."

"Why?"

"Autopsies are not a public spectacle."

Not true, of course. They have been a public spectacle throughout the history of medicine. But not for the *general* public. More for the specialized public. How else would doctors learn their trade?

"I'm not a spectator. I was his wife for sixty years. I will be there with him."

There is a forceful finality to her last sentence, the words of a woman who has so few wants left that the ones she still has are filled to the brim with her will.

It is unseemly to argue late at night, even more so with a grieving widow. Again his practicality suggests a solution. He will stand her next to a chair. At the first cut, the one that opens the chest, she will feel faint. He will assist her to the chair, and then, when she's recovered, bring her to his office, where he will leave her while he finishes his work.

"Very well. Have it your way, Senhora Castro. But I warn you, an autopsy, to the uninitiated, is not a pretty sight."

"I've slaughtered my share of pigs and chickens. A body is a body."

Except for the swirl of emotions, Eusebio observes to himself. We don't love our pigs and chickens. We don't mourn our pigs and chickens. We don't even remember our pigs and chickens. But let her see for herself. That is the very meaning of the word "autopsy", from the Greek, to see with one's own eyes. She will not last. Even the toughest old peasant, placed so close to death, will want to retreat back to life. Only she must not fall and hurt herself.

"Perhaps you could help me with the body," he says.

A few minutes later, Rafael Miguel Santos Castro is lying on his back on one of the two operating tables of

195

the pathology department. Without any fuss, Maria Castro helps him remove all her husband's clothes. She pats down his hair. She rights his penis, setting it straight over the scrotum. Then she surveys his body as she might her vegetable garden, pleased to see that everything is in good order.

Eusebio is unnerved. This is how he looked at a body when he was a medical student, interested, curious, game. Death was an impersonal sport. This here is her husband. He regrets his decision to allow Maria Castro to assist at the autopsy of her husband. What was he thinking? It's the fatigue. He will not face any problems with the hospital or the medical college. There are no rules about who can assist at an autopsy. He is captain of his ship. Only this is no sight for a loved one, the raw nakedness of the man, in a setting that is necessarily cold and sterile — and that's before he has even touched the peasant's body with his science. How will the man's wife react then?

He dons his apron and ties the knot. He could offer one to Maria Castro but thinks better of it. An apron will encourage her to get close.

He looks at his tray of tools. They are simple but effective: a few sharp scalpels and knives, some forceps and clamps, a pair of blunt-nosed curved scissors, a chisel, a wooden mallet, a good saw, a scale to weigh organs, a ruler clearly marked in centimetres and millimetres to measure them, a long, flat knife to slice them, sundry sponges, and needle and twine, to sew the body up afterwards. And the pail for slop, at the foot of the table. Of course his main tool is his microscope, with which he examines the slides of the biopsied and excisional specimens and the samples of body fluids. That is a key part of his work, the histological work. Under the pathologist's microscope, life and death fight in an illuminated circle in a sort of cellular bullfight. The pathologist's job is to find the bull among the matador cells.

He should have taken the body away and returned a few minutes later with some slides, claiming they were specimens from her husband's body. She wouldn't know better. Flying over these colourful landscapes using José's two-headed microscope, he would have spouted medical hocus-pocus. *Ah yes, it's absolutely clear to me, Senhora Castro. You see the pattern here and here. It's the classic architecture. No doubt about it. Your husband died of liver cancer.* Or, since she avoided the word, he would have said that her husband *lived* of liver cancer. Then she would have gone away, sad but satisfied, able to move on — and spared the butchery of her husband.

But it's too late for that. There she stands, next to the table, without the least interest in the chair he has brought in for her.

Perhaps he could get her to sit in Senhora Melo's alcove. What would he and José do without the indefatigable Senhora Melo? Her office, which is not much wider than the table on which rests her typewriter, abuts the wall shared by the two autopsy rooms. On either side of it, at the level of her head, is an opening fitted with a panel of straw weave that gives onto each room. The multiple tiny holes of the weave

197

allow her to hear with her ears but not see with her eyes. If it were otherwise, if she saw the dripping organs and the disembowelled bodies, she would shriek and faint, and she is there to record, not to react. She types with extraordinary speed and accuracy, and her Latin spelling is excellent. Senhora Melo's assistance allows him and José to observe and speak as they are doing, without having to stop to write. They have so many autopsies to do. As it is, while one doctor works and dictates, the other finishes up with a body, takes a break, then prepares for the next case. Alternating like this, the two doctors efficiently perform autopsy after autopsy.

Sometimes, after he has made his confession to Father Cecilio, it occurs to him that Senhora Melo might be a better confessor. To her, many more harsh truths have been revealed than to Father Cecilio.

He normally wears rubber gloves when he performs an autopsy — a fairly recent and welcome advance in technology. He treats his gloves with great care, washing them with soap and water every day and keeping them moist with mercury biniodide spirit. But he hesitates to pull them out now. Maria Castro might think that by wearing them he is expressing disdain for her husband's body. Better in this case to go back to the old bare-hands technique.

But first he will replace the strip of flypaper. Flies are a persistent problem in Portugal's climate. They thrive as peddlers of contagion. He makes it his regular business to replace the yellow coils that hang in the autopsy rooms.

198

"If you'll excuse me," he says to Maria Castro. "Hygiene, order, routine — all very important." He takes the chair intended for her and places it under the used strip, climbs onto it, removes the strip studded with the fat bodies of dead flies, and replaces it with a new, bright, gluey strip.

Maria Castro watches him silently.

From the chair he gazes down at the autopsy table. They never look very big on the table, the bodies. It's built to accommodate the largest frames, there's that. And they're naked. But it's something else. That parcel of the being called the soul — weighing twenty-one grams, according to the experiments of the American doctor Duncan MacDougall — takes up a surprising amount of space, like a loud voice. In its absence, the body seems to shrink. That is, before the bloat of decomposition.

Of which Rafael Castro seems to be free, likely the result of the cold, but also of the jumbling of his body while travelling in a suitcase. Eusebio is used to being greeted by the Mortis sisters when he comes to work. The oldest, Algor, chills the patient to the ambient temperature; Livor, the middle sister, neatly applies her favourite colour scheme — yellowish grey to the top half of the patient and purple red to the bottom half, where the blood has settled — and Rigor, the youngest, so stiffens the body that bones can be broken if limbs are forced. They are cheery ones, these sisters, eternal spinsters who ravish innumerable bodies.

Rafael Castro's ears are deep purple; there is only that touch of Livor Mortis. And his mouth is open. The agonal moment is the last knock of the body at the door of the eternal before that door swings open. The body convulses, the breath rattles in the chest, the mouth opens, and it's over. Perhaps the mouth opens to release the twenty-one grams. Or perhaps it's nothing more than a relaxing of the mandibular muscles. Whatever the case, the mouth is usually closed, because bodies always come to him washed and prepared, the jaw tied shut with a strip of cotton fabric, the knot resting on top of the head, the hands bound together in front of the body, and the rectum and, if the case be, the vagina packed with cotton batting. Cutting these ligatures and removing these stops are the first steps in opening the book of the body.

The teeth seem in good condition, a departure from the stock peasant with the healthy bones but the decayed teeth.

No identifying tag is attached to the big toe. Eusebio has to take it on faith that the dead man is indeed Rafael Miguel Santos Castro, from the village of Tuizelo. But he has no reason to doubt that Maria Castro is telling the truth.

Nor is there a clinical report. That report is like the jacket copy of a book, announcing what is to come. But just as jacket copy can stray from the actual content of a book, so can a clinical report. With no knowledge of the case at all, he will nonetheless find out what racked Rafael Castro, what pushed his body to give up.

He steps off the chair. He looks at the shelf of bottles along the wall near the table. He picks out the bottle of carbolic oil. Since he's not going to use his rubber gloves, he smears his hands with the oil to protect them. Then he finds the bar of Marseille soap and scratches it so that slivers of soap stick under his fingernails. This precaution, along with vigorous hand washing and the application of scented oils, means that he can reach for his wife in the evenings without her recoiling and beating him away.

He will start with words. Words will be the anaesthetic that will prepare Maria Castro for what he is about to do.

"Senhora Castro, let me explain a little what is going to happen. I will now perform an autopsy on your husband. The purpose of it will be to discover the physiological abnormality — that is, the disease or the injury — that led to his death. In some instances, when the clinical report is very clear, this object is determined fairly easily, as a result of examining a single organ, say the heart or the liver. The healthy body is a balancing act of a thousand parts, and the serious imbalance of a single part can, on its own, throw a life off its tightrope. But in other cases, where we have no clinical information, as is the case here, the dead body is, well, a murder mystery. Needless to say, I'm using this as a figure of speech. I don't mean a real murder. I mean the body becomes a house inhabited by a cast of characters, each of whom denies having anything to do with the death, but in a few rooms we will find clues. The pathologist is the detective who pays close attention and uses his grey cells to apply order and logic until the mask of one of the organs can be torn off and its true nature, its black guilt, proved beyond a doubt."

He smiles to himself. Maria, his Maria, would be pleased with his murder-mystery analogy. Maria Castro just stares at him steadily. He moves on.

"Where do we begin? With the surface. Before any incision is made, the body undergoes a surface examination. Does the body appear to have been nourished appropriately? Is it thin or emaciated or, on the contrary, obese? Is the chest barrel-shaped, indicative of bronchitis and emphysema, or is there a pigeon breast, a sign of rickets in early life? Is there unusual pallor to the skin or the opposite, any deepening of the colour or any sign of jaundice? Skin eruptions, scars and lesions, fresh wounds — all these must be noted, their extent, their severity.

"The orifices of the body — the mouth, the nose, the ears, the anus — must be checked for discharges or abnormalities, as must the external genitalia. Lastly, the teeth.

"In your husband's case, everything seems in order. I look here and here. Here. Here. He looks like a normal, externally healthy man of his age who died of an internal cause. I notice, here, an old scar."

"He slipped on a rock," Maria Castro says.

"It's a source of no concern. I am only noting it. This external part of the examination is usually cursory, since it adds little to my findings. Disease most often develops from the inside to the outside. So the liver fails before the skin turns yellow, for example. There are notable exceptions, of course: skin cancers, lesions and the like, and accidents. And death by crime often starts on the outside, but that is not an issue here. In this case, the skin has little to tell us.

"Now we must, well, we must *enter* the body, we must examine it on the inside. It is safe to say there's no reason to start an autopsy with an extremity, say, the patient's feet. In pathology, the equivalent of the king and the queen in chess are the thorax and the head. Each is vital to the game, so to speak, and one can start an autopsy with either one. The pathologist's standard opening gambit is the thorax."

Eusebio mentally curses himself. Why is he talking about chess? Enough of this prattle!

"I will start by cutting a Y-shaped incision in your husband's chest, using this scalpel, starting at the shoulders and meeting over the sternum, then heading down over the abdomen to the pubic mound. You will notice that subcutaneous fat is very yellow, and muscles look very much like raw beef, very red. That is normal. Already I'm looking for indicators. The appearance of the muscles, for example, which could signal a wasting disease or a toxic one, such as typhoid fever.

"Next the sternum and the anterior part of the ribs are removed. I will use these curved scissors to cut through the ribs" — his wife uses an identical pair in their garden and swears by them — "making sure not to damage underlying organs. Now the innards are exposed, lying in a colourful mass. I will look to see how they sit with each other. Organs are siblings that work in the same family business. Is there any obvious abnormality that has thrown the family into disarray?

Any swelling? Any unusual colouration? Normally, the surface of the viscera should be shiny and smooth.

"After this overview, I need to look at the organs individually. Since we don't know what brought on your husband's death, I am inclined to take out his thoracic contents altogether to examine them in continuity, before separating them and studying each component on its own.

"I will ask of each organ roughly the same questions. What is its general form? Is it shrunken or, on the contrary, swollen? The surface of the organ — is there any exudate, that is, any matter that has flowed out? Does the exudate crumble easily, or is it stringy and difficult to remove? Are there any areas that are pearly white, indicating chronic inflammation? Are there cicatrices — scars — or rugosity, wrinkles if you want, a sign of fibrosis? And so on. Next will come the internal examinations. I will incise each organ — I will use this knife — with the idea of assessing its inner condition. The heart is the locus of many pathological possibilities, and I will examine it with extra care."

He pauses. The woman says nothing. Perhaps she is overwhelmed. It is time to abridge and sum up.

"The abdominal viscera will be next, the small and large intestines, the stomach, the duodenum, the pancreas, the spleen, the kidneys — I will be thorough in my approach." He sweeps a hand over the torso. "The king is done. Now we can move on to the queen, that is, the head. Examining your husband's brain and stem will involve removing the scalp by means of an incision and sawing through the skull — but never mind that. Details, details. Lastly, I may examine peripheral nerves, bones, joints, vessels, et cetera, if I feel there is a need. Throughout, I will be excising samples — small bits of organs — which I'll fix in formalin, embed in paraffin, then slice, stain, and examine under the microscope. This lab work comes later.

"At this stage the essential work on your husband's body is over, Senhora Castro. I will return his organs to his body and fill any hollowness with newspaper. I will replace the sternum and sew the skin shut, the same with the top of his skull. There, the job is done. Once dressed, your husband will look as if nothing has happened to him and no one outside this room will know better — but science will. We will know with certainty how and why your husband died — or, as you put it, how he lived. Do you have any questions?"

The old woman sighs and shakes her head. Did she roll her eyes?

All right, then. Reluctantly, he picks up the scalpel. "This is the scalpel," he says.

The sharp blade hovers over Rafael Castro's chest. Eusebio's mind is racing. There's no way around it. He will have to open the thorax. But he will zero in quickly on an organ — the heart. *Oh, this explains it. We clearly have our answer right here. We need proceed no further.*

"Well, here we go . . ."

"Start with the foot," Maria Castro says.

He looks up. What did she say? Did she say *pé* or *fé* — foot or faith? And what does that mean, *Start with*

205

the faith? Does she want him to say a prayer before he starts? He's happy to oblige, not that he's ever done that in the autopsy room. The Body of Christ is elsewhere. Here is more simply the body of a man.

"I'm sorry. What did you say?" he asks.

Maria repeats herself. "Start with the foot."

This time she points. He looks at Rafael Castro's yellowed feet. They are as far away from the acute myocardial infarction he wants to diagnose as is physiologically possible.

"But Senhora Castro, as I just explained to you, in fact using that very example, it makes no sense to start an autopsy with a patient's foot. Feet are peripheral organs, both literally and pathologically. And as concerns your husband's feet, I see no sign of fractures or any other injury — no, nothing at all — nor any sign of a skin tumour or other disease, or any condition at all, bunions, ingrown toenails, anything. There's some slight peripheral oedema — swelling, that is — but that is normal for someone who has been dead three days. There is also a trace of livor mortis around the heel. Once again, that is normal."

Maria Castro says it a third time. "Start with the foot."

He is silent. What a disaster of a night. He should have stayed at home. Not only will he get no work done, but now he has an insane peasant woman in his autopsy room. This is precisely why he went into pathology, to avoid situations like this. He can deal with the clogging and liquefaction of bodies, but not the clogging and liquefaction of emotions. What is he to do? Say no and tell her to go slice her husband's feet on her kitchen table if she's so keen on it? That would mean stuffing the old man in the suitcase again, naked this time. And would the old battleaxe go quietly? He doubts it.

He gives up. She will have it her way. He feels like a hawker at a market, selling his wares. *Autopsy, autopsy, who wants an autopsy? Don't hesitate, step right up! Today's special: Pay for one eyeball, get the other free. You, senhor, how about a testicle, just one testicle for starters? Come on, get your autopsy!* Why not start with the feet? If she wants her husband's autopsy to start there, then let it start there. Whatever the customer wants. He sighs and moves to the distal extremity of the body, scalpel in hand. Maria Castro joins him.

"His foot, you say?"

"Yes," she replies.

"Do you care which one I start with?"

She shakes her head. He is closest to Rafael Castro's right foot. He looks at it. In his medical student days he dissected a foot, he vaguely remembers, but as a practicing pathologist, beyond the occasional surface excision, he has never worked on one. How many bones is it again? Twenty-six, and thirty-three joints in each foot? All bound together and operated by an array of muscles and ligaments and nerves. A very efficient arrangement that can both support and transport.

Where should he cut? *Better the plantar surface than the dorsal*, he thinks. Less bony. He takes hold of the ball of the foot and pushes. The foot flexes with little stiffness. He examines the sole. The callused skin will part, subcutaneous fat will show, some jellified blood might seep out — just a foot with a random cut in it. No indignity to the body, just an indignity to the attending pathologist.

He presses the blade of the scalpel into the head of the medial metatarsals. He lets the blade go in deeply — it doesn't matter what it cuts — and he pushes down, towards the heel. The scalpel easily slices through the ball of the foot and into the arch, along the long plantar ligament. He brings the blade out as it digs into the fat pad of the heel.

A thick substance pushes out of the cut. Blobs of it start to drop onto the autopsy table. It is whitish and lumpy, covered in a sheen of brightness, with a slight yellow runoff. It has a pungent smell.

"I thought so," Maria Castro says.

He stares in amazement. *What in God's name is this?* Though he has not uttered the question aloud, Maria Castro answers it.

"It's vomit," she says.

He examines the oozing mass closely. He sniffs it. The glutinous appearance, the bilious smell — yes, it is indeed vomit, fresh vomit. But how is that possible? *It's a foot.* He's seen necrosis and putrefaction in every form, but nothing like this, ever.

"Where else would it go?" she says. "Gravity pulls." He seems in need of further explanation. "The child died, you see," she adds. She pauses for a moment. Then she converts all the silence in her into words. "Let me tell you how a funeral goes in Tuizelo. First, you must have the excuse for one. A life must be given up. If you want it to be a good funeral, it must be a precious life, not some distant uncle or the friend of a friend. Make it your own son. That's the way to start a funeral, with a thunderbolt that hammers you right in the chest and cleaves your insides into pieces. Deaf, dumb, witless, you can now attend to the details. A ready-made ceremony is handed to you, old and worn. You go along because you don't know better. There is a hearse — just someone's cart dressed up — a stiff, unreal ceremony in the church, then a burial in the cemetery on a grey day, everyone dressed in their Sunday best and looking uncomfortable for it, all of it unbearable. Then it's over.

"People hang around for a while, but then they drift off. You're given an allotment of time, after which you're expected to return to the world, to your life of old. But why would anyone do that? After a funeral, a good funeral, everything loses its worth and there's no life of old to return to. You're left with nothing. You don't even have words, not right away. Right away, death is word-eating. Words for it come later, because how else can you think of him, since he's no longer with you?

"At the funeral Rafael said only one thing. He cried out, 'The size of the coffin, the size of it!' It's true, it wasn't very big.

"The day Rafael returned to Tuizelo, he didn't have to say anything to tell me. He couldn't, anyway. Distress had paralyzed his face and stunned his mouth. I knew right away. Nothing else would do that to him. I

209

knew just looking at him that our precious one had died. Already people in the village had assembled in front of our house, milling around silently. He lay him on the dining table. I fainted. I wish I had fainted forever, that I had followed behind him swiftly and protectively, the way a mother should. Instead I awoke surrounded by smelly old widows. Rafael kept away. Close-by but away. He was eaten up with guilt. Our son had died on his watch. He was the shepherd that day. He had let his flock stray.

"We loved our son like the sea loves an island, always surrounding him with our arms, always touching him and crashing upon his shore with our care and concern. When he was gone, the sea had only itself to contemplate. Our arms folded onto nothing until they met their frame. We wept all the time. If a job was left unfinished at the end of a day — the coop not repaired, a row of vegetables not weeded — we knew that one of us had sat down and wept. That's the nature of grief: It's a creature with many arms but few legs, and it staggers about, searching for support. Frayed chicken wire and a profusion of weeds became expressions of our loss. I can't look at chicken wire now without thinking of my lost son. There's something about the warp and weft of it, so thin yet strong, so porous yet solid, that reminds me of how we loved him. Later, because of our neglect, chickens died at the jaws of a fox that slipped into the coop, and the crop of vegetables was not so bountiful — but so it goes: A son dies and the earth becomes barren.

210

"When he wasn't well or couldn't fall asleep, he crept into our bed between us. After he was gone, that space in our bed became unbridgeable. We met, Rafael and I, only below it, where in the night our toenails jabbed at each other like loose knives in a drawer, or above it, where we stared at each other without saying a word. Rafael never wanted to close that space, because to do so would be to acknowledge that our bear cub was never coming back. Some nights I saw his hand reach into the space and stroke its emptiness. Then the hand retreated, like the limb of a tortoise deep into its shell, and every morning Rafael woke with the weary, wrinkled eyes of a tortoise that has lived too long. His eyes blinked slowly, as did mine.

"Grief is a disease. We were riddled with its pockmarks, tormented by its fevers, broken by its blows. It ate at us like maggots, attacked us like lice — we scratched ourselves to the edge of madness. In the process we became as withered as crickets, as tired as old dogs.

"Nothing fit right in our lives anymore. Drawers no longer closed cleanly, chairs and tables wobbled, plates became chipped, spoons appeared flecked with dried food, clothes started to stain and tear — and the outside world was just as ill-fitting.

"His death made little difference to the outside world. Isn't that so with all children? When a child dies, there is no land to be handed down, hardly any possessions to be divided up, no job or role left unfilled, no debts that need paying off. A child is a small sun that shines in the shadow of its parents, and when that sun goes out there is darkness only for the parents.

"What's the point of being a mother if you have no one to mother? It's like being a flower without a head. On the day our son died, I became a bald stem.

"If there's one thing I held against Rafael for the longest time, it's that he delayed coming home by a day. He dithered. But a mother has a right to know right away when her child has died. For her to imagine that he is alive and well even for a minute when he is not is a crime against motherhood.

"And then that thought that takes root in your mind: *And now, how do I dare love anything?*

"When you forget about him ever so briefly — then comes the stab. Rafael would shout, 'My beautiful boy!' and he would collapse. Mostly, though, we went about with quiet, reserved insanity. It's what you do. Rafael started walking backwards. The first times I noticed him doing it, along the road or in the fields, I thought nothing of it. I thought he was doing it for a moment, to keep his eye on something. Then one morning he did it as we were going to church. No one said anything. They let him be. I asked him that night why this, why the walking backwards. He said that on that day he returned to Tuizelo he saw a man, a stranger, leaving the village. Rafael was sitting off the end of the cart, holding our little cub in his arms, wrapped in a sheet. The stranger was on foot and he was moving quickly, nearly running, and he was doing so backwards. He had the saddest face, Rafael said, a face of grief and anguish. He forgot about him until he found he wanted

212

to do the same thing; it sat well with his emotions, he said. And so he started doing it when he left the house, going into the world. As often as not, he would turn around and start walking backwards.

"I knew who the man was. He had stopped to visit the church. A strange city man, quite filthy and sick. Father Abrahan spoke with him, then he ran off. He left behind the device he'd come on — an automobile, the first one we'd ever seen. It must have been an arduous journey back, all the way to wherever he came from. His automobile stayed in the square for weeks, we didn't know what to do with it. Then one day a different man — a tall, thin one — walked into the village and drove it away without a word of explanation. People talked about the device and its driver, back and forth, back and forth. Was he just a visitor — or an angel of death? Whatever he was, I didn't care. I had turned to remembering. We never had much use for memory before. Why remember him when you have him right there in front of your eyes? Memory was just an occasional pleasure. Then it's all you're left with. You try your best to live in your memories of him. You try to turn memories into real things. You pull the strings of a puppet and you say, 'There, there, you see — *he's alive!*'

"It was Rafael who started calling him our bear cub after he died. Rafael said he was hibernating. 'Eventually he'll stir and wake, he'll be ravenously hungry,' he would say with a smile, attaching a fact — our son's good appetite after a nap — to a fancy, that he was coming back. I played along: It was my comfort too.

"He *was* such a joy. Everyone said that. Unplanned, unexpected — I thought I was long past my child-bearing years, such as they had been — and suddenly he came along. We used to look at him and ask ourselves, 'What child is this? Where did he come from?' We both have dark eyes and dark hair — doesn't everyone in Portugal? Yet his hair was as fair as a wheat field, and such eyes he had — bright blue. How did those eyes get into his head? Did a puff of the Atlantic blow into Tuizelo on the day he was conceived and add itself to his making? My theory is that the supplies in the pantry of our family tree were so rarely dipped into that when they finally were, only the best ingredients were used. He invented laughter. His joy-making was endless and his goodwill without limits. The whole village loved him. Everyone sought his attention and his affection, the adults and the other children. So much love was poured into those blue eyes. He took that love and gave it back, as happy and generous as a cloud.

"Rafael had gone down to help a friend near Cova da Lua. A week's work, small money. He took him, our five-year-old boy. It would be an adventure for him. And he could help. Then it happened, while Rafael was sharpening the scythes on the whetstone. He paused and listened. It was too quiet. He called out. He searched around the farm. He searched in ever greater circles. Eventually he went along the road, calling out his name. That's where he found him. What about the other foot?"

The question comes unexpectedly. Eusebio looks at the body's left foot. He nicks it at the heel. Again vomit comes out.

"And higher up?" asks Maria Castro.

He does not hesitate now. With the scalpel he cuts into the right leg next to the tibia, midway up; into the left knee, between the patella and the medial condyle of the femur; into the thighs, a cut into each quadriceps. Each cut is about five or six centimetres long, and each time vomit oozes out, although he notes that it comes out with less pressure from the cuts on the thighs. He cuts across the pelvic girdle, just above the pubic mound, a long cut. He pulls the skin back. A bulk of vomit shows. Atop it, on its edge, the scalpel touches something hard but loose. He probes. There is a glimmer. He dislodges it and turns it with the blade. A coin — a five-escudo silver coin. There are other coins next to it, some escudos, the others centavos, each lying flat atop the vomit. A peasant's meagre wealth.

He pauses. He wonders whether he should leave the coins there or extract them.

Maria Castro interrupts his thoughts. "The penis," she says.

He takes hold of Rafael Castro's sizable penis. At a glance, the shaft and the glans appear perfectly normal. No signs of Peyronie's disease, no condylomata, no bowenoid papulosis. He decides to cut along a corpus cavernosum, one of the two spongy, elongated chambers that, when filled with blood, were the source of such pleasure for the couple. He slices the length of the penis, through the foreskin and into the glans.

Again the scalpel strikes something hard where there should be nothing hard. He puts the blade down. With his thumbs on either side of the cut, and pushing on the opposite side of the penis with his fingers, he easily pushes out the hardness. It comes out in two pieces: wooden, smooth, round, and with holes.

"Oh!" says Maria Castro. "His sweet flute."

The two other pieces of the peasant flute lie in the second corpus cavernosum. Because he is a man of order and method, Eusebio assembles the instrument. He passes it to the old woman, who brings it to her lips. A three-note trill floats in the air.

"He played it so nicely. It was like having a canary bird in the house," she says.

She places it on the autopsy table, next to the body.

With a word here, a shake of the head there, displaying a perfect knowledge of Rafael Castro's experiential anatomy, Maria Castro directs Eusebio's scalpel. It is the simplest autopsy he has ever performed, requiring only that single sharp instrument, even for the head. She avoids the thorax and abdomen until the very end, preferring the distal discoveries of the upper limbs and of the neck and head.

The ring finger of the left hand is lightly packed with down feathers, as is the right hand's middle finger, while in the index fingers of both hands he finds blood, fresh, red blood — the only trace of blood he finds anywhere in the body. All the other digits contain mud. The palm of the right hand holds an oyster shell, the palm of the left, pages from a small wall calendar. The arms are crowded. From them he extracts a hammer, a pair of tongs, a long knife; an apple; a clump of mud; a sheaf of wheat; three eggs; a salted cod; a knife and fork. Rafael Castro's head proves roomier. Inside it he finds a square of red cloth; a small handmade wooden toy of a horse and cart with wheels that turn; a pocket mirror; more down feathers; a small wooden painted object, ochre in colour, that Maria Castro cannot identify; a candle; a long lock of dark hair; and three playing cards. In each eye he discovers a die, and a dried flower petal in place of the retina. The neck contains three chicken feet and what looks like kindling: dried leaves and twigs. The tongue holds ash except at its tip, where there is honey.

Lastly comes the thorax and abdomen. The old wife nods, though with evident trepidation this time. Eusebio ends the autopsy with the cut with which he expected to start it, the Y-shaped incision from the shoulders to the sternum down over the abdomen. He sections the skin as lightly as he can, barely slicing through the subcutaneous fat. Since he made a cut along the pelvic girdle earlier, the thoracic and abdominal cavities open up plainly to view.

He hears her gasp.

Though he's no expert on the matter, he is quite certain that it is a chimpanzee, a kind of African primate. It takes him a little longer to identify the second, smaller creature, partly hidden as it is.

Filling Rafael Castro's chest and abdomen, lying compactly in peaceful repose, are a chimpanzee and, wrapped in this chimpanzee's protective arms, a bear cub, small and brown.

Maria Castro leans forward and presses her face to the bear cub. Is this then how her husband *lived*? Eusebio says nothing, only watches. He notices the chimpanzee's bright, clear face and thick, glossy coat. A young one, he concludes.

She speaks quietly. "The heart has two choices: to shut down or to open up. I haven't told you my story entirely truthfully. I was the one who protested about the size of the coffin. I was the one who wailed, 'My beautiful boy!' and collapsed. I was the one who didn't want to close the space in our bed. Cut me some of the black creature's fur, will you? And please get the suitcase."

He obeys. With the scalpel he cuts a tuft from the chimpanzee's coat, from its side. She rubs the hairs between her fingers and sniffs them and presses them to her lips. "Rafael always had more faith than I did," she says. "He often repeated something Father Abrahan said to him once, how faith is ever young, how faith, unlike the rest of us, does not age."

Eusebio retrieves the suitcase from his office. Maria Castro opens it, places it on the autopsy table, and begins to transfer to it the objects from Rafael Castro's body, one by one.

Then she starts to undress.

The shocking nudity of an aged woman. The flesh sapped by gravity, the skin ravaged by age, the proportions ruined by time — and yet glowing with long-lived life, like a parchment page covered in writing. He has seen a great number of such women, but dead, without personality, and rendered even more abstract by being opened up. Inner organs, unless touched by a pathology, are ageless.

Maria Castro strips until she has not a piece of clothing on her. She takes off her wedding ring, she pulls off a band that holds her hair. All of it she puts in the suitcase, which she closes when she is done.

Using the chair he brought in for her, she climbs onto the autopsy table. Leaning over Rafael Castro's body, nudging here and there, pushing and wiggling, making space where there seems to be none, filled as he is already with two creatures, Maria Castro carefully settles into her husband's body. All the while she repeats, "This is home, this is home, this is home." She places herself so that the chimpanzee's back is nestled against her front and her arms encircle both the chimpanzee and the bear cub, with her hands resting on the cub.

"Please," she says.

He knows what to do; he is much practiced in the matter. He picks up the needle. He pushes the twine through its eye. Then he begins to sew the body shut. It is quick work, as skin is soft, a simple crossing-over back-and-forth of the twine in a zigzag, though in this case he sews the stitches close together, creating a suture that is finer than usual. He works across Rafael Castro's pelvic girdle, then closes the skin over the abdomen and over the chest, up to each shoulder. He is careful with the tip of the needle not to prick Maria Castro or the two animals. He hears her only faintly as he finishes the torso: "Thank you, Senhor doctor."

Never has he worked on a body that ended up having so many incisions. Professional ethic compels him to close every single one: across the head, along the arms, in the neck, on the legs and hands, through the penis and the tongue. The fingers are painstaking labour. The eyes are unsatisfying in the final result — he spends much time contriving to shut the eyelids over his botched job. He finishes with the soles of the feet.

Finally only a body remains on the autopsy table, and a suitcase on the floor, loosely packed with random objects.

He looks on dumbly for a long while. When he turns away, he notices something on a side table: the tuft of chimpanzee hairs. Maria Castro forgot them — or did she leave them behind deliberately? He takes hold of them and does what she did: He sniffs them and touches them to his lips.

He is utterly spent. He goes back to his office, the chimpanzee hairs in one hand, the suitcase in the other. He sets the suitcase on his desk and settles heavily into his chair. He opens the suitcase and stares at its contents. He opens a drawer, finds an envelope, places the chimpanzee hairs in it, and drops the envelope into the suitcase. He notices on the floor the Agatha Christie novel. He picks it up.

Senhora Melo arrives early, as is her habit. She is surprised to find Dr. Lozora collapsed on his desk. Her heart flutters. Is he dead? A dead pathologist — the notion strikes her as professionally unbecoming. She steps in. He is only sleeping. She can hear his breathing and see the gentle rising and falling of his shoulders.

And his colour is good. He has drooled on his desk. She will not share with anyone this embarrassing detail, the shiny river from his mouth, the small puddle. Nor will she mention the empty bottle of red wine. She lifts it and quietly places it on the floor behind the desk, out of sight. There is a large scuffed suitcase on the desk. Is it the doctor's? Is he going somewhere? Would he have such a shabby suitcase?

He is sleeping on top of a file. It is mostly concealed by a hand, but she can still read the first line:

Rafael Miguel Santos Castro, 83 anos, da aldeia de Tuizelo, as Altas Montanhas de Portugal

Odd — she doesn't recall the name or the locality. She is the guardian of names, the one who links with certitude each person with his or her fatality. And it's written in the doctor's hand, transiently, rather than set for eternity with her typewriter. Could it be an emergency case that arrived after she left last night? That would be highly unusual. In passing she notes the patient's age. Eighty-three is a sound age to live to. That reassures her. In spite of the tragedies of life, the world can still be a good place.

She notices that the clasps of the suitcase are undone. Though she knows she shouldn't, she quietly opens it, to see if it belongs to the doctor. Such a strange assortment of things — a flute, a knife and a fork, a candle, a plain black dress, a book, a square of red cloth, an envelope, among other bits and pieces —

221

would not likely be Dr. Lozora's. She closes the suitcase.

She leaves the office quietly, not wanting to embarrass the doctor by being there when he wakes up. She walks to her tiny work alcove. She likes to be properly set up before the day's work starts. The typewriter ribbon needs to be checked, the carbon paper restocked, her water carafe filled. The door to the autopsy room is open, which it shouldn't be. She glances in. She catches her breath. There is a body on the table! A shudder goes through her. What is it doing there? How long has it been out of the cold room? This is most improper. Normally there is a good hour of dictation of final reports before the autopsies start. Normally the bodies come and go shrouded, invisible to everyone except the doctors.

She enters the room. It will be like a living body, she tells herself, only dead.

It isn't at all like a living body. The corpse is that of a man, an old man. Yellow and sagging. Bony. His hairy pubic mound and large penis exposed with unspeakable obscenity. But far worse are the crude seams all over his body, ragged sutures of red, grey, and yellow that make him look like a cloth doll. His hands look like the underside of a starfish. Even his penis is marred by ghastly stitching. Senhora Melo gulps, thinks she might faint, steadies herself. She forces herself to look at the man's face. But there is nothing to be read upon his face, only age. She is aghast at how a dead body is such a — she searches for the word — such a *relic*. When she leaves the autopsy room on tiptoes, as if the relic might

222

be disturbed by her presence, she wonders: *Where's the gurney? How did he get here?*

She closes the door of the autopsy room and takes a few deep breaths. Clearly the doctor needs help. He has not been well lately. Sometimes he arrives late for work, sometimes he doesn't show up at all, sometimes he works all night. Poor man. The death of his wife has been very hard on him. He waved away the concerns of the other doctors, of the director of the hospital himself. He would do it, he said, he would do it. But what a thing to do! Dr. Otavio, his colleague, was away on holiday, but even if he had been here he would have refused to work on her on account of having known her. That's standard procedure. In the normal course of things, her body should have gone to the hospital in Vila Real. But Dr. Lozora couldn't bear the thought of anyone else doing it. And she was decomposing; it needed to be done right away. And so he performed the autopsy of his own wife.

In a state of shock, her eyes sheltered by the panel of straw weave, Senhora Melo witnessed the whole thing from her alcove. She did her best to record the report that came intermittently from the autopsy room. Periods of silence were followed by periods of weeping, then bursts of resolve, which was when Dr. Lozora spoke. But how do you record pain, how do you record wreckage? They recorded themselves in her, while she dutifully typed his words.

She knew many people thought of Maria Lozora as an eccentric woman. Lately, for example, she had taken to walking around town carrying a bag full of books.

She could have a sharp tongue. Her silences were ominous. Father Cecilio was terrified of her. He submitted to her extemporaneous lectures on religion without a quibble, and didn't say a word when she started reading from her bag of books in plain sight of everyone during his sermons. But she was at heart a very kind woman, always willing to help at any time of day or night. She never seemed to sleep. How many times had she appeared during the night at her friends' houses when their children were sick, with a pot of soup and her good doctor husband at her side? Lives had been comforted, and in some cases even saved, by their intervention. They were an inseparable pair, those two. Quite odd. She didn't know any other couple who took such pleasure in each other's company.

And then that this should happen to her! She had gone out walking alone one evening, as was her wont. She was not home when Dr. Lozora returned from the hospital. Increasingly worried, he had reported her missing to the police later that night. He had no idea where she might be. She had a mind of her own, he said, and perhaps she had decided to visit someone without telling him. Yes, he had been working late that evening.

A few days later, a book was found on the shore under the bridge. It was a novel, *Peril at End House*, by the English writer Agatha Christie. There was a bloated book stamp. Dr. Lozora positively identified the book as belonging to him and his wife. The river and its rocky banks were searched. Other books by Agatha Christie were discovered downstream. Eventually

Maria Lozora's body was found. It had unfortunately become wedged among the rocks in a spot that made it very hard to detect.

Who but Maria Lozora would be wandering about in such foul weather? And how had she fallen off the bridge?

It was entirely inexplicable — in fact, every possible explanation seemed more unbelievable than the next. Suicide? She was a happy, fulfilled woman with a network of family and friends who gave no sign of any mental or moral distress. And would a woman who was so comfortable with words not leave a suicide note? Furthermore, she was a thoughtful, devout Christian; such Christians do not take their lives. No one — not her husband or children, not her priest, not the police — found the explanation of suicide convincing. An accident, then? She plummeted to her death from a bridge that was safeguarded by thick solid stone balustrades whose height precluded anyone slipping or toppling over them. One might plausibly climb atop one, but why would any sensible soul do that except with the intent of jumping off? And since suicide was ruled out as a likely explanation for her death, so was the idea that she had willingly climbed the balustrade. If both suicide and accident were excluded, what was left? Murder. But this seemed the most improbable of all explanations. Who would want to murder Maria Lozora? She had no enemies. She was liked — even loved — by all who knew her. And this was Bragança, not Chicago. Murders were unknown in these parts. This was not a town where innocent women were randomly hoisted up in the air and thrown off bridges. The idea was preposterous. So it had to be either suicide or an accident. Round and round it went. The police pleaded for witnesses to step forward, but no one had seen anything. Forensic experts came all the way from Lisbon; they brought nothing to light. People adopted the explanation that seemed most plausible to them. Dr. Lozora espoused the theory of murder, while having no idea who would do that to his wife.

It distressed Senhora Melo that Maria Lozora's death would not have the neat resolution of the murder mysteries of which Maria and the doctor were so fond.

Senhora Melo hears a gasp. Dr. Lozora is awake. She hears him begin to weep. He doesn't know that she's arrived, that he isn't alone. The volume increases. Great cracking sobs. The poor man, the poor man. What is she to do? If he realizes that she's there, he will be mortified. She doesn't want that. Perhaps she should make a noise to alert him to her presence. He continues to weep. She stands very still and quiet. Then Senhora Melo becomes annoyed with herself. Can it be any more plain that the man needs help? Didn't she just think that a moment ago?

She turns and heads for Dr. Lozora's office.

PART THREE

Home

When Peter Tovy is appointed to the Senate in the summer of 1981 from the House of Commons to make way in his safe Toronto riding for a star candidate, there is no longer any need for him to spend much time in his constituency. He and his wife, Clara, buy a larger, nicer apartment in Ottawa, with a lovely view of the river. They prefer the quieter pace of the capital, and they're happy to be near their son, daughter-in-law, and granddaughter, who live in the city.

Then one morning he enters the bedroom and finds Clara sitting on their bed, holding her left side with both hands, crying.

"What's wrong?" he asks.

Clara only shakes her head. Fear grips him. They go to the hospital. Clara is sick, seriously so.

At the same time that his wife is fighting for her life, their son's marriage falls apart. He paints the rosiest picture possible of the breakdown for his wife. "It's best for all of them," he says. "They never got along. Away from each other they'll blossom. It's what people do these days."

She smiles in agreement. Her horizons are shrinking. But it isn't best, or even good. It's terrible. He watches conjugal partners become bitter enemies, he sees a child become war loot. His son, Ben, spends inordinate amounts of time, money, and energy fighting with his former wife, Dina, who fights back just as hard, to the delight of their lawyers and to his stupefaction. He tries to talk to Dina and play the mediator, but however civil her tone and open her heart at the start of each conversation, inevitably she loses her cool and boils up in anger. Being the father of, he can only be an abettor and a co-conspirator. "You're *just* like your son," she spat out once. Except, he pointed out, that he has lived in loving harmony with his wife for over four decades. She hung up on him. His granddaughter, Rachel, a cheerful sprite when she was a small child, turns sour on both her parents and walls herself in a teenage tower of caustic resentment. On a few occasions he takes her out for a walk and a restaurant meal to cheer her up — and to cheer himself up, he hopes — but he can never get past her sullenness. Then she moves to Vancouver with her mother, who has "won" her in the custody battle. He drives them to the airport. When they walk through security, already bickering, he does not see an adult woman and her growing daughter but two black scorpions, their venomous stingers raised, goading each other on.

As for Ben, who remains in Ottawa, he is hopeless. As far as Peter can tell, his son is incredibly brightly stupid. A medical researcher, Ben at one point studied why people accidentally bite their tongue. This painful breakdown in the tongue's ability to work around teeth, like a sheet worker operating heavy machinery, has surprisingly complex roots. Now Peter sees his son as a tongue blindly throwing itself under gnashing teeth, coming out bloody, but throwing itself under again the very next day, over and over, without an ounce of self-understanding or any realization of the costs or consequences. Instead Ben is always chafing with exasperation. Conversations between them end in stony silence, with the son rolling his eyes and the father at a loss for words.

Amidst a swirl of medical terms, after the waxing and waning of hope over every treatment, after the twisting, groaning, and sobbing, after the incontinence and the vanishing of all flesh, his beautiful Clara lies in a hospital bed, wearing a horrible green hospital gown, her eyes glazed and half-shut, her mouth open. She convulses, a rattle comes from her chest, and she dies.

He becomes a spectre on Parliament Hill.

One day he's speaking in the Senate. A fellow senator has turned and is looking up at him with a scrutiny that is more intense than simple interest should warrant. *Why are you looking at me like that?* he thinks. *What's the matter with you?* If he leans forward and blows into his colleague's face, his breath will have the effect of a blowtorch and the skin of his face will peel off. It'll be a grinning skull that will be looking up at him. *That will deal with your stupid expression.*

His reverie is interrupted by the Speaker of the Senate, who says, "Will the honourable member continue on the topic at hand, or . . . ?"

The trailing off of the Speaker's voice is significant. Peter looks down at his papers and realizes that he has no idea what he's been talking about — no idea, and no interest in going on even if he did remember. He has nothing to say. He looks at the Speaker, shakes his head, and sits down. His colleague, after another second of staring, turns away.

The Whip comes round to his desk. They are friends. "How's it going, Peter?" he asks.

Peter shrugs.

"Maybe you should take a break. Bust loose for a while. You've been through a lot."

He sighs. Yes, he needs to get out. He can't take it anymore. The speeches, the endless posturing, the cynical scheming, the swollen egos, the arrogant aides, the merciless media, the stifling minutiae, the scientific bureaucracy, the microscopic betterment of humanity — all are hallmarks of democracy, he recognizes. Democracy is such a crazy, wonderful thing. But he's had enough.

"I'll see if I can't find something for you," the Whip says. He pats him on the shoulder. "Hang in there. You'll make it."

A few days later the Whip comes back to him with a proposal. A trip.

"To *Oklahoma*?" Peter responds.

"Hey, great things come from remote places. Who'd ever heard of Nazareth before Jesus showed up?"

"Or of Saskatchewan before Tommy Douglas."

The Whip smiles. He's from Saskatchewan. "And it's what came up. Someone bailed out at the last minute. The State Legislature down there has invited Canadian Members of Parliament to visit. You know, the knitting

232

and maintaining of relations, that sort of thing. You won't have much to do."

Peter isn't even sure where Oklahoma is, exactly. A marginal state of the American empire, somewhere in the middle of it.

"Just a change of air, Peter. A little four-day holiday. Why not?"

He agrees. Sure, why not. Two weeks later he flies to Oklahoma with three Members of Parliament.

Oklahoma City is warm and pleasant in May, and their hosts display gracious hospitality. The Canadian delegation meets the governor of the state, state legislators, and business-people. They are shown around the State Capitol, they visit a factory. Each day ends with a dinner. The hotel where they are lodged is grand. Throughout the visit, Peter talks about Canada and hears about Oklahoma in a relaxed fog. The change of scenery, the change of air, even — soft and moist — is soothing, as the Whip predicted.

On the eve of their last full day, a day that has been left open for the recreation of the Canadian guests, he notices a tourist brochure about the Oklahoma City Zoo. He has a fondness for zoos, not because he's particularly interested in animals, but because Clara was. She was on the Board of Management of the Toronto Zoo at one time. He expresses the wish to visit the Oklahoma City Zoo. The legislative assistant who is their go-to person at the State Capitol looks into it and comes back to him with profuse apologies.

"I'm so sorry," she says. "Usually the zoo is open every day, but it's closed at the moment because of major renovations. I could check to see if they'd let you in anyway, if you're interested."

"No, no, I don't want to be a bother."

"There is a chimpanzee sanctuary south of town, in Norman, at the university," she suggests.

"A chimpanzee sanctuary?"

"Yes, it's an institute for the study of — of monkeys, I guess. It's not normally open to the public, but I'm sure we can make that happen."

She does make it happen. The word "senator" works wonders on American ears.

The next morning a car is waiting for him in front of the hotel. No one else in his delegation is interested in joining him, so he goes alone. The car drives him to the Institute for Primate Research, as the place is called, an outpost of the University of Oklahoma in the middle of empty, brushy countryside ten or so kilometres east of Norman. The sky is blue, the land is green.

At the institute, at the end of a winding gravel driveway, he sees a large, vaguely menacing-looking man with a beard and a big belly. Next to him stands a lanky younger man with long hair and bulging eyes; clearly, from his body language, he is a subordinate.

"Senator Tovy?" says the larger man as he steps out of the car.

"Yes."

They shake hands. "I'm Dr. Bill Lemnon, director of the Institute for Primate Research." Lemnon looks beyond him into the car, whose door is still open. "You don't have much of a delegation."

"No, it's just me." Peter closes the door of the car.

234

"What state are you from again?"

"The province of Ontario, in Canada."

"That so?" His answer seems to give the director reason to pause. "Well, come with me and I'll explain to you briefly what we do here."

Lemnon turns and walks away without waiting for him to fall into step. The unintroduced subordinate scampers along behind.

They walk around a bungalow and a few sheds until they come to a sizable pond shaded by giant cottonwood trees. The pond has two islands, one with a cluster of trees. In the branches of one of these, he sees a number of tall, skinny monkeys swinging about with extraordinary grace and agility. The other island is larger, its tall grasses, bushes, and few scattered trees dominated by an imposing log structure. High poles support four platforms at different heights, connected by a web of ropes and cargo-net hammocks. A truck tire hangs from a chain. Next to the structure is a round hut made of cinder blocks.

The director turns and faces Peter. He seems bored with what he is about to say even before he has started.

"Here at the IPR, we are at the forefront of studying primate behaviour and communication. What can we learn from chimpanzees? More than the man on the street might think. Chimpanzees are our closest evolutionary relatives. We share a common primate ancestor. We and chimpanzees parted company only about six million years ago. As Robert Ardrey put it: We are risen apes, not fallen angels. We both have large brains, an extraordinary capacity for communication, an ability to use tools, and a complex social structure. Take communication. Some of our chimpanzees here can sign up to a hundred and fifty words, which they can string together to form sentences. That is *language*. And they can make tools to forage for ants and termites or to break open nuts. They can hunt cooperatively, taking on different roles to catch their prey. They have, in short, the rudiments of *culture*. So when we study chimpanzees, we are studying an ancestral reflection of ourselves. In their facial expressions . . ."

It is interesting enough, if delivered somewhat automatically, without any warmth. Lemnon looks annoyed. Peter listens with a distracted ear. He suspects the assistant at the legislature oversold him. She probably didn't mention that the visiting senator wasn't from the U.S. Some of the chimpanzees appear on the larger island. At that moment he hears a voice calling.

"Dr. Lemnon! Dr. Terrace is on the phone." He turns to see a young woman standing next to one of the buildings.

Lemnon is jolted to life. "I have to take that call. If you'll excuse me," he grunts as he walks off, without waiting for a response from his guest.

Peter breathes a sigh of relief at seeing the man go. He turns to the chimpanzees once more. There are five of them. They move slowly on all fours, their heads low, the bulk of their weight in their upper bodies, held up by their thick, strong arms, while their shorter legs follow along like the back wheels of a tricycle. In the sunlight, they are surprisingly black — roving patches of night. They amble a little distance and sit down. One of them climbs onto the lowest platform of the log structure.

Nothing much, but there's something satisfying about watching them. Each animal is like a piece of a puzzle, and wherever it settles, it belongs, clicking into place perfectly.

The subordinate is still with him.

"We weren't introduced. I'm Peter," Peter says, extending his hand.

"I'm Bob. Pleased to meet you, sir."

"Same here."

They shake hands. Bob has a prominent Adam's apple. It keeps bobbing up and down, which makes his name easy to remember.

"How many monkeys do you have here?" Peter asks.

Bob follows his eyes to the main island. "Those are apes, sir. Chimpanzees are apes."

"Oh." Peter points to the other island, where he saw the creatures swinging through the trees. "And those over there are monkeys?"

"Well, as a matter of fact, they're also apes. They're gibbons. They're members of the 'lesser' apes, as they're called. The rule of thumb is, monkeys have tails and apes don't, and generally monkeys live in trees and apes live on the ground."

As Bob finishes speaking, the chimpanzee sitting on the low platform climbs and swings with acrobatic ease to the top platform. At the same time, the other apes, the lesser gibbons, reappear in the tree on their island, dancing through the air from branch to branch.

"Of course, nature serves up lots of exceptions to keep us on our toes," Bob adds.

"So, how many chimpanzees do you have here?" Peter asks.

"Thirty-four right now. We breed them to sell or loan to other researchers, so the number varies. And we have five being reared by families around Norman."

"Reared by human families?"

"Yeah. Norman must be the cross-fostering capital of the world." Bobbing Bob laughs, until he notices Peter's nonplused expression. "Cross-fostering is where baby chimps are raised by human families as if they were human."

"What's the point of that?"

"Oh, lots. They're taught sign language. It's amazing: We communicate with them and see how their minds work. And there's lots of other behavioural research going on, here and elsewhere, on the social relations of chimpanzees, their forms of communication, how they structure their groups, patterns of dominance and submission, maternal and sexual behaviour, how they adapt to change, and so on. Professors and PhD students from the university come here every day. It's as Dr. Lemnon said: They're different from us, but weirdly similar too."

"And all the chimpanzees live on that island?" Peter asks.

"No. We bring them out here in small groups for experiments and sign-language lessons, and for a little rest and relaxation, as is the case with the group you see now."

238

"Don't they try to run away?"

"They can't swim. They'd sink like stones. And even if they did get away, they wouldn't wander far. This is home for them."

"Aren't they dangerous?"

"They can be. They're strong and they have a mouthful of knives. They need proper handling. But they're mostly incredibly sweet, especially if you're promising them candy."

"Where are the other ones?"

Bob points. "In the main compound, there."

Peter turns and starts walking towards the building, assuming it's the next stop on the tour.

Bob comes up behind him. "Oh! I'm not sure that's part of — of the visit, sir."

Peter stops. "But I'd like to see the other chimpanzees closer up."

"Well — um — we should maybe talk to — he didn't say —"

"He's busy." Peter starts off again. He likes the idea of irking the almighty Dr. Lemnon.

Bob hops along, making noises of hesitation. "All right, I guess," he finally decides, when he sees that Peter isn't going to change his mind. "We'll make it quick. This way."

They turn a corner and come to a door. They enter a small room with a desk and lockers. There is another metal door. Bob pulls out a key. He unlocks the door and opens it. They go through.

If the island in the pond gave the appearance of a sunlit idyll, here, inside this windowless building, there is the reality of a dark and dank underworld. The smell hits Peter first, an animal reek of piss and misery, the tang of it made fierce by the heat. They are at the entrance of a rounded, tunnel-like corridor of metal bars that shreds the space around them, as if the bars were a grater. On either side of this corridor hang two rows of cubic metal cages. Each cage measures about five feet on either side and hangs in the air from a chain, like a birdcage. The front rows are set off from the back rows so that every cage is easily visible from the corridor, one closer up, the next a little farther in. The cages are built with round steel bars and are perfectly see-through, offering not the least privacy. Underneath each is a large plastic tray littered with the refuse of its inmate: rotting food, excrement, pools of urine. Some cages are empty, but many are not, and those that are not contain one thing and one thing only: a large black chimpanzee.

An ear-splitting explosion of shrieking and screaming greets them. Raw fear grips Peter. His breathing is cut short and he stands rooted to the spot.

"Quite the effect, huh?" shouts Bob. "It's because you're new and 'invading' their territory." With his fingers Bob signals the ironic quotation marks around the word "invading".

Peter stares. Some of the chimpanzees have bounded up and are shaking their cages with fury. Restrained by horizontal chains, the cages swing only so much. It's the way the apes are suspended in the air, cut off from each other, from the very earth, that freaks him out. They have nothing to hide behind, hold on to, or play with, not a toy or blanket or the least bit of straw. They just hang there in their barren cages, the very image of incarceration. Hasn't he seen movies like that, where a new inmate walks into a penitentiary and all the inmates start to jeer and catcall? He swallows hard and breathes deeply, trying to master his fear.

Bob moves forward, occasionally hollering some comment or other, unconcerned by the mad ruckus. Peter follows him closely, walking in the exact middle of the corridor, well clear of the bars. Though he can see that the animals are securely confined — in cages and then behind bars — he's still afraid.

Every three or four cages there is a heavy-gauge chain-link fence that runs from the corridor bars to the wall and ceiling of the building, separating one set of cages from the next. Yet another layer to the confinement. Each of these fences has a door through it, at the back, next to the wall.

Peter points to a fence. "Aren't the cages enough?" he yells.

Bob shouts back, "It allows us to release some of the chimpanzees so they can be together in larger but separate spaces."

Indeed, in the relative darkness of the compound, Peter notices on one side of the corridor four chimpanzees lolling about the floor, near the back wall. At the sight of him, they get up and start acting out. One makes to rush the bars. But at least they look more natural like that — on the ground, in a group, lively and dynamic. Bob gestures that Peter should squat down.

"They like it when we're at their height," he says in Peter's ear.

They both crouch. Bob puts his hand through the bars and waves to the chimpanzee that seemed the most aggressive, the one that made to attack them. After a moment of hesitation, the animal runs up to the bars, touches Bob's hand, then scampers back to rejoin the others at the back wall. Bob smiles.

Peter starts to calm down. *They're just doing their thing*, he tells himself. He and Bob stand up and resume moving down the corridor. Peter is able to observe the chimpanzees more steadily. They display various levels of aggression or agitation; they shake, they growl, they shriek, they grimace, they make forceful body movements. All are in an uproar.

Except one. The last prisoner at the end of the corridor sits quietly in its cage, lost in its own thoughts and seemingly oblivious to its surroundings. When Peter reaches its cage, he stops, struck by the creature's singular behaviour.

The ape is sitting with its back to its venting primate neighbours, presenting its profile to Peter. A straight arm casually lies atop a bent knee. Peter notices the coat of sleek black hair that covers the animal's body. It's so thick it looks like a costume. From it emerges hands and feet that are hairless and clearly very nimble. Of the head, he observes the receding, nearly absent forehead; the big saucer-like ears; the massive, overhanging brows; the perfunctory nose; and the smooth, bulging, pleasingly rounded mouth, with the hairless upper lip and the slightly bearded lower one.

Because of their great size, these lips are highly expressive. Peter gazes at them. At the moment, with this particular specimen, they are in slight motion — fluttering, parting, closing, puckering — as if the ape were in conversation with itself.

The creature turns its head and looks him in the eyes.

"It's looking at me," Peter says.

"Yep, they do that," responds Bob.

"I mean, right into my eyes."

"Yep, yep. Usually a sign of dominance, but this one's a very chilled-out dude."

Still looking at Peter, the ape purses its lips, funnel-like. From them, making its way through the raucous noise of the compound to Peter's ears, comes a panted *hoo-hoo* sound.

"What does that mean?" he asks.

"It's a greeting. He's saying hello."

The ape does it again, this time mouthing it without actually making the sound, relying on Peter's intent gaze rather than his assaulted ears.

Peter can't take his eyes off the ape. What an attractive face, the expression so vivacious, the scrutiny so intense. The large head is as densely covered with black hair as the body, but the face, in its essential parts, the upside-down triangle of the eyes and nose and the circle of the mouth, is bare, showing off smooth dark skin. Aside from some faint vertical wrinkles on the upper lip, the only wrinkles on the ape's face are around the eyes, concentric ones beneath each orbit, and a few wavy lines over the flattened bridge of the nose and between the prominent brows. The effect of these circles within circles is to draw attention to their dual centres. What colour are those eyes? Peter can't tell exactly in the artificial light of the compound, but they seem to be a bright rusty brown, nearly red, but of the earth. The eyes are closely set, the gaze steady. That gaze bores into him and holds him in place.

The ape turns its body to face Peter fully. Its stare is charged, but its posture is relaxed. It seems to be enjoying swallowing him with its eyes.

"I want to get closer," Peter says. He is amazed that he has said this. Where has his fear gone? Just a minute ago he was quaking with terror.

"Oh, you can't do that, sir," says Bob with evident alarm.

At the end of the corridor is a heavy wire door. There were two like it midway down the corridor, on either side. Peter looks around; there are no chimpanzees on the floor beyond the door. He steps towards it and puts his hand on the handle. It turns fully.

Bob's eyes open wide. "Ah, man, who forgot to lock that door? You *really* shouldn't go in!" he pleads. "You'll — you'll have to talk to Dr. Lemnon, sir."

"Bring him on," Peter says as he swings the door open and goes through.

Bob follows him in. "Don't touch him. They can be very aggressive. He might bite your hand off."

Peter stands in front of the cage. He and the ape lock gazes again. Once more he feels a magnetic pull. *What do you want?*

The ape squeezes its hand through the criss-cross bars and reaches out. The hand opens in front of Peter, narrow palm up. Peter stares at it, at the black leathery skin, at the long fingers. There is no question, no hesitation. He lifts his own hand.

"Oh boy, oh boy!" Bob whimpers.

The two hands wrap around each other. A short but strong opposable thumb reaches over and pins his hand down. The gesture comes with no grasping or pulling; there is no menace to it. The ape is simply squeezing his hand into its own. It's a surprisingly warm hand. Peter takes hold of it with both of his, one hand cupping it in a handshake, the other holding on to its hairy back. It has the appearance of a politician's glad hand, but fixed and intense. The ape's grasp tightens. It could crush his hand, he realizes, but it doesn't and he feels no fear. It continues to stare into his eyes. Peter doesn't know why, but his throat tightens and he feels close to tears. Is it that no one since Clara has looked at him like that, fully and frankly, the eyes like open doors?

"Where is this one from?" he asks without averting his eyes. "Does he have a name?"

Peter notices the switch in his pronouns, from *it* to *he*. It comes naturally. This creature is no object.

"His name's Odo," Bob answers, rocking nervously from side to side. "He's a rolling stone. He was brought over by someone who was volunteering in Africa for the Peace Corps. Then he was with NASA, for testing in the space program. Then he went to Yerkes, then LEMSIP, before —"

A burst of shrieking comes from the other end of the corridor. The chimpanzees, who have mostly settled down, start up again. It's even more deafening than when he and Bob entered. Dr. Lemnon has returned. "BOB, YOU BETTER HAVE A DAMN GOOD EXPLANATION FOR THIS!" he bellows.

Peter and Odo let go of each other's hands. The consent is mutual. The ape turns and resumes his former position, his side to Peter, his gaze somewhat lifted.

Bob looks as if he'd rather climb into one of the hanging cages than return to the corridor. Peter goes out first. The full menace of Dr. Bill Lemnon becomes plain as he strides down the corridor, his angry features alternately illuminated and obscured by the spaced-out light bulbs, the din of the animals amplifying as he gets closer.

"*WHAT* ARE YOU DOING IN HERE?" he yells at Peter.

Any pretence at cordiality is gone. Lemnon is an ape asserting his dominance.

"I'll buy that one off you," Peter says calmly. He points to Odo.

"Will you, now?" replies Lemnon. "Should we throw in four elephants and a hippo? Maybe two lions and a herd of zebras? *This isn't a pet store!* GET THE FUCK OUT OF HERE!"

"I'll pay you fifteen thousand dollars." Oh, the terrible appeal of round numbers. Fifteen thousand dollars — that's considerably more than his car cost.

246

Lemnon stares in disbelief, as does Bob, who has crept back into the corridor. "Well, well, you must be a senator after all, if you're throwing that kind of money around. Which one?"

"That one there."

Lemnon looks. "Huh. Can't get more omega than that bozo. He lives in la-la land." He thinks. "Fifteen thousand dollars, you say?"

Peter nods.

Lemnon laughs. "I guess we are a pet store. Bob, you've got a great eye for customers. Mr. Tovy — I'm sorry, *Senator* Tovy — you can have your pet chimpanzee if you want. Only thing is, we don't have a money-back policy. You buy him, you get tired of him, you want to give him back to us — we'll take him, but it'll still cost you fifteen grand. You hear me?"

"It's a deal," says Peter. He extends his hand. Lemnon shakes it, looking like he's enjoying the greatest joke in the world.

Peter glances at Odo. As he begins to move off, he sees from the corner of his eyes that the ape is turning his head. Peter looks again. Odo is staring at him once more. A quiet thrill goes through him. *He's been aware of me all along.* To himself as much as to the ape, he whispers, "I'm coming back, I promise."

They walk down the corridor. A last observation forces itself upon him as he looks left and right, something he didn't notice on his way in: He's struck by the chimpanzees' great diversity. He assumed that one chimpanzee would pretty much look and be like the next. It is not so, not at all. Each ape has its own body shape and bearing, its own coat of hair with its own colour and pattern, its own face with its own tone, complexion, and expressions. Each, he sees, is something he hadn't expected: an individual with a unique personality.

Bob sidles up to Peter at the door of the compound, looking worried and discombobulated. "We sell them," he whispers, "but not for that —"

Lemnon waves him away. "Git, git!"

They return to the car. Peter comes to a quick agreement with Lemnon. He will be back in a week or two, as soon as he can; he needs time to make the necessary arrangements. He promises to mail a cheque for a thousand dollars as a deposit. Lemnon agrees to get all the papers ready.

As the car drives away, Peter turns and looks out the rear window. Lemnon still wears his triumphant smirk. Then he turns to Bob and his expression changes. Bob is evidently about to be fully dressed down. Peter feels bad for him.

"Had a good visit?" the driver asks.

Peter sits back in a daze. "It was interesting."

He can't believe what he has just done. What will he do with a chimpanzee in Ottawa? He lives in an apartment, five floors off the ground. Will the other residents accept having a large, unwieldy ape in their building? Is it even legal to own a chimpanzee in Canada? How will the ape take to Canadian winters?

He shakes his head. Clara has been dead for just over six months. Did he not read somewhere that people who are grieving a major loss should wait at least a year before making important changes in their lives? Has grief caused him to throw away all good sense?

He's a fool.

Back at the hotel he tells no one, neither the Oklahomans nor his fellow Canadians, about what he has done. Nor does he tell anyone in Ottawa upon his return the following morning. He spends that first day at home alternating between denial and disbelief, and completely forgetting about it. The next day he hits upon an excellent idea: He will buy the chimpanzee after all, and donate it to a zoo. He's quite certain the Toronto Zoo doesn't have chimpanzees, but another zoo — Calgary? — will surely take the animal. It will be a stupidly expensive gift, but he'll make it in Clara's name. That will make it worth every penny. There, the matter is settled.

He wakes up early on the third morning. He stares at the ceiling from his pillow. Odo looked right into him with his reddish-brown eyes, and Peter said to him, *I'm coming back, I promise.* That wasn't a promise to drop him off at a zoo; it was a promise to take care of him.

He has to go through with it. Dammit all, he doesn't know why, but he *wants* to go through with it.

Once the first, central decision is made, all the ones that follow are easy. He mails the deposit cheque for Odo to Lemnon.

It's obvious that they can't stay in Ottawa. In Oklahoma, science was the excuse to keep the ape in a cage. In Canada, it would be the weather. They need a warmer climate.

It's good to think in terms of "they" again. Is it pathetic? Instead of throwing himself at another woman right away, on the rebound, as the expression goes, as if he were a ball in a pinball machine, is he doing worse by throwing himself at a *pet*? It doesn't feel that way. Whatever term might be given to their relationship, Odo is no pet.

Peter never thought he would move again. He and Clara had never talked about it, but they didn't mind the cold weather, and the idea was that they would stay in Ottawa into their old age.

Where will they go?

Florida. A lot of Canadians retire there, precisely for the purpose of fleeing Canada's winters. But the place means nothing to him. He doesn't want to live between a strip mall, a golf course, and a sweltering beach.

Portugal. The word illuminates his mind. He's of Portuguese origin. His family emigrated to Canada when he was two years old. He and Clara visited Lisbon once. He loved the tiled houses, the luxuriant gardens, the hills, the streets of rundown European charm. The city felt like a late-summer evening, a mix of soft light, nostalgia, and slight boredom. Only Lisbon, like Ottawa, is no place for an ape. They need a quiet spot, with lots of space and few people.

He recalls that his parents came from a rural area — the High Mountains of Portugal. A return to his roots? He might even have distant relatives there.

The destination fixes itself in his mind. His next step is to deal with his attachments to Canada. He considers what these attachments are. At one time they were everything: his wife, his son, his granddaughter, his sister in Toronto, the members of his extended family, his friends, his career — in a word, his life. Now, other than his son, he is surrounded by material relics: an apartment with stuff in it, a car, a pied-à-terre in Toronto, an office in the West Block on Parliament Hill.

His heart beats with excitement at the idea of getting rid of it all. The apartment is now unbearable to him, imprinted as it is in every room with Clara's suffering. His car is just a car — the same with his studio apartment in Toronto. And his job as a senator is a sinecure.

Distance might improve his relations with Ben. He isn't going to spend the rest of his life waiting around Ottawa for his son to find more time for him. His younger sister, Teresa, has her own life in Toronto. They talk on the phone regularly, so no reason why that should stop. As for Rachel, his granddaughter, for all he now sees of her or hears from her, he might as well live on Mars. She might be tempted to visit him one day, lured by the appeal of Europe. That's a valid hope.

He takes a deep breath. It all has to go.

With alarming glee, he sets about throwing off the chains that hold him down, as he now thinks of them. Already, when he and Clara moved from Toronto to Ottawa, they rid themselves of many personal possessions. Now, in a frenzied week, the rest goes. Their apartment in Ottawa — "*Such* a good location!" the agent beams — finds a buyer quickly, as does his place in Toronto. Books are carted away to a used bookstore, furniture and appliances sold off, clothes given to charity, personal papers donated to the National Archives, and knick-knacks and baubles simply thrown away. He pays off all his bills, closes his utility and phone accounts, and cancels his newspaper subscription. He gets his visa for Portugal. He wires a Portuguese bank and makes arrangements for opening an account. Ben helps dutifully, all the while grousing about why on earth Peter would pick up from his ordered life and leave.

Peter walks away from it all carrying nothing but a suitcase of clothes, a family photo album, some camping gear, a guidebook to Portugal, and an English-Portuguese dictionary.

He books their flight. It appears that it would be easier if he and the ape fly directly from the United States to Portugal. Fewer borders to cross with an exotic animal. The airline tells him that, provided he has a cage and the animal is calm, they will carry it. He consults with a veterinarian on how to sedate a chimpanzee.

Through connections, he finds a buyer for his car where he wants one, in New York City. "I'll deliver it myself," he tells the man from Brooklyn on the phone.

He doesn't say that he will be taking a slight detour via Oklahoma on his way down.

He cancels all his future appointments — with Senate committees, with family and friends, with his doctor (his heart isn't so good, but he packs a supply of medication and a renewal for his prescription), with everyone. He writes letters to those to whom he doesn't speak in person or on the phone.

"You suggested I bust loose," he tells the Whip.

"You sure took my words to heart. Why Portugal?"

"Warm weather. My parents came from there."

The Whip looks at him steadily. "Peter, have you met another woman?"

"No, I haven't. Not even close."

"All right, if you say so."

"How could I have met a woman in Portugal while living in Ottawa?" he asks. But the more he denies a romantic connection, the less the Whip seems to believe him.

He doesn't tell anyone about Odo, neither his family nor his friends. The ape remains a luminous secret in his heart.

He happens to have a dental appointment coming up. He spends his last night in Canada sleeping in a motel, and the next morning he has his teeth cleaned. He says good-bye to his dentist and he drives away.

It's a long drive through Ontario, Michigan, Ohio, Indiana, Illinois, and Missouri to Oklahoma. He doesn't want to tire himself too much, so he does it over five days. Along the way — from a corner store in Lansing, Michigan, from a diner in Lebanon, Missouri — he calls the Institute for Primate Research to make sure they are aware of his imminent arrival. He speaks to the young woman who told Lemnon about the phone call, the one that distracted him and allowed Peter to visit the chimpanzee compound. She assures him that all is ready.

After a last night in Tulsa, Peter makes his way to the IPR, arriving mid-morning. He parks the car and wanders over to the pond. On the main island, two people are having what looks like a sign-language lesson with a chimpanzee. A group of three apes lazes about in the centre, on the ground. Sitting among them is Bob, attending to a chimpanzee, inspecting its shoulder. Peter calls out and waves. Bob waves back, gets up, and heads for a rowboat that's resting on the shore. The ape he's with follows him. It leaps with ease into the rowboat and perches on a bench. Bob pushes off and rows over.

Halfway across the pond, when the boat turns, the chimpanzee, whose view was blocked by Bob, sees him. It hoots loudly and pounds the bench with a fist. Peter blinks. *Is that . . . ?* — yes, it is. Odo is larger than he remembered. The size of a big dog, only wider.

Before the boat has reached the shore, Odo leaps out, bounces once off the ground, and sails through the air towards Peter. He has no time to react. The ape slams against his chest, wrapping his arms around him. Peter falls over, landing inelegantly on his backside and sprawling flat on his back. He feels large wet lips and the smooth hardness of teeth against the side of his face. He's being attacked!

Bob's laughter comes through to him. "My, my, he's certainly taken to you. Gentle, Odo, gentle. You all right?"

Peter can't answer the question. He's shaking from head to toe. But he feels no pain. Odo has not bitten him. The ape has instead moved off and settled right next to him, pressed against his shoulder. He starts playing with Peter's hair.

Bob kneels next to him. "You all right?" he asks again.

"Y-y-yes, I think so," Peter answers. He slowly sits up. He stares with wide eyes and breathless incredulity. The strange black face, the thick, hairy body, the whole, warm animal literally breathing down his neck — with no bars between them, no protection for him, no safety. He doesn't dare push the ape away. He just sits there, alert and paralyzed, his gaze hovering. "What's he doing?" he finally asks. The ape is still plucking at his head.

"He's grooming you," Bob replies. "That's a big part of chimpanzee social life. I groom you, you groom me. It's how they get along. And it gets rid of ticks and fleas. Keeps them clean."

"What should I do?"

"Nothing. Or you can groom him back, if you want."

A knee is right there. He brings a trembling hand to it and strokes a few hairs.

"Here, I'll show you how," says Bob.

Bob sits on the ground and much more assertively starts grooming Odo's back. With the edge of one hand, he pushes through the chimpanzee's coat against the natural lie of the hairs, exposing their roots and bare skin. After doing this two or three times, he finds a good patch and sets to work with the other hand, scratching and picking out skin flakes, bits of dirt, and other detritus. All in all, a fussy, involving activity. Bob seems to forget about Peter.

Peter begins to regain his composure. It's not disagreeable, what the creature is doing to his head. He can feel soft fingers against his skull.

255

He looks into Odo's face. In immediate response the ape shifts his gaze to look at him. Their faces are maybe eight inches apart, eyes fully staring into eyes. Odo hoots lightly, the panted breath bouncing off his face, then folds out his lower lip, revealing a row of large teeth. Peter tenses.

"He's smiling at you," says Bob.

It's only then that the young man, who is so good at reading the ape's emotions, understands Peter's. He puts a hand on his shoulder.

"He won't harm you, sir. He likes you. And if he didn't like you, he'd just leave you alone."

"I'm sorry I got you into trouble last time."

"Don't worry about that. It was worth it. This place is bad. Wherever you're going with Odo will be better than here."

"Is Lemnon around?"

"No. He'll be back after lunch."

A stroke of good luck. Over the next few hours, Bob gives Peter a mini-course on Odo. He teaches him the basics about chimpanzee sounds and facial expressions. Peter learns about hoots and grunts, about barks and screams, about the pouting, puckering, and smacking of lips, about the many roles played by panting. Odo can be as loud as Krakatoa or as quiet as sunlight. He has no command of American Sign Language but does understand some English. And as is the case with humans, tone, gesture, and body language do much to convey meaning. The ape's hands also speak, as does his posture and the lie of his hair, and Peter must listen to what they have to say. A kiss and a hug are just that, a kiss and a hug, to be enjoyed and appreciated and perhaps returned, at least the hug. The best face is one where Odo's mouth is slightly open, his demeanour relaxed; this may be followed by one of the delights of chimpanzee language, the laughter, a bright-eyed, nearly silent panting, the mirth fully expressed without the grating *HA HA HA* of human laughter.

"It's a complete language," says Bob of chimpanzee communication.

"I'm not very good with foreign languages," Peter muses aloud.

"Don't worry. You'll understand him. He'll make sure of that."

He's potty-trained, Bob tells Peter, only the potty has to be within sight. Chimpanzees don't tolerate continence for very long. Bob supplies four potties to distribute around Odo's territory.

The cage that is to be Odo's means of transportation and his nighttime nest doesn't fit in the car. They take it apart and put it in the trunk. Odo will travel in the front seat.

At one point Peter goes to the restroom. He sits down on the toilet lid and puts his head into his hands. Was early fatherhood like this? He doesn't remember feeling so overwhelmed. Bringing baby Ben home was a giddy experience. He and Clara didn't know what they were doing — do any young parents know? But it was all right. They raised Ben with love and attention. And they weren't afraid of him. He badly wishes Clara were with him now. *What am I doing here?* he says to himself. *This is crazy.*

Bob and he go for a walk with Odo, much to the ape's delight. Odo forages for berries, climbs trees, asks (with a grunt and his arms raised, like a child) to be carried by Peter, who obliges, lurching and stumbling about until he's ready to drop. The way Odo holds on to him with his arms and legs, he feels he has a hundred-pound octopus on his back.

"I can give you his collar and his twenty-foot leash if you want, but they're pointless," Bob says. "If he's in a tree, he'll just pull you up like you're a yo-yo. And if you happen to be on a horse, he'll pull your horse up too. Chimpanzees are unbelievably strong."

"So how do I restrain him?"

Bob thinks for a few seconds before answering. "I don't mean to get personal, sir, but are you married?"

"I was," Peter replies soberly.

"And how did you restrain your wife?"

Restrain Clara? "I didn't."

"Right. You got along. And when you didn't, you argued and you coped. It's the same here. There's very little you can do to control him. You'll just have to cope. Odo likes figs. Placate him with figs."

During this exchange, Odo has been poking around a bush. He comes out and sits right next to Peter, on his foot. Brazenly, he feels, Peter reaches down and pats Odo's head.

"You gotta get physical," Bob says. He squats in front of the chimpanzee. "Odo, tickle-fest, tickle-fest?" he says, his eyes open wide. He begins to tickle the ape's sides. Soon the two are wildly rolling about the ground,

Bob laughing and Odo hooting and shrieking with delight.

"Join in, join in!" Bob shouts. The next moment Peter and Odo are thrashing about. The ape does indeed possess Herculean strength. There are times when he lifts Peter clear off the ground with arms and legs before crashing him back down.

When their roughhousing is over, Peter staggers to his feet. He's dishevelled, one of his shoes has come off, his shirt has lost two buttons, the front pocket is torn, and he's covered in grass, twigs, and soil stains. It was an embarrassingly juvenile episode, unbecoming of a man of sixty-two years — and utterly thrilling. He can feel his fear of the ape draining away.

Bob looks at him. "You'll do fine," he says.

Peter smiles and nods. He declines the collar and leash.

When Lemnon appears, there is only the commercial transaction that needs to be completed. Peter hands over the bank draft, which Lemnon inspects carefully. In return, he gives Peter various papers. One form states that he, Peter Tovy, is the legal owner of the male chimpanzee, *Pan troglodytes*, Odo. It is notarized by a lawyer in Oklahoma City. Another form is from a wildlife veterinarian; it gives the ape a clean bill of health and guarantees that Odo is up to date on all vaccinations. Yet another is an export permit from the U.S. Fish and Wildlife Service. They all look properly official, with signatures and embossed stamps. "All right, I guess that's it," Peter says. Lemnon and he don't shake hands, and Peter walks away without saying another word.

Bob places a folded towel on the front passenger seat. He bends down and hugs Odo. Then he stands and motions to him to get into the car. Odo does so without hesitation, making himself comfortable in the seat.

Bob takes hold of the ape's hand and holds it to his face. "Good-bye, Odo," he says, his voice strained by sadness.

Peter gets in the driver's seat and starts the engine. "Should we put his seatbelt on?" he asks.

"Why not," Bob replies. He reaches over and works it across Odo's waist. He snaps the buckle in. The shoulder strap is too high, running across Odo's face. Bob puts it behind his head. Odo does not mind the arrangement.

Peter feels panic simmering within him. *I can't do this. I should just call the whole thing off.* He lowers his window and waves at Bob. "Good-bye, Bob. Thanks again. You've been a tremendous help."

The drive from Oklahoma City takes longer than the drive to it. He goes at a moderate speed so as not to alarm Odo. And whereas from Ottawa to Oklahoma City he jumped from human colony to human colony — Toronto, Detroit, Indianapolis, St. Louis, Tulsa — on the way to New York City he avoids as many urban centres as he can, once again to spare the ape.

He would like to sleep in a proper bed and enjoy a shower, but he is quite certain that no motel owner will rent a room to a half-simian couple. On the first night, he turns off the road and stops the car next to an abandoned farmhouse. He assembles the cage, but he isn't sure where to place it. On the roof of the car? Sticking out of the trunk? A little ways off, in the ape's "own" territory? Finally he puts the cage, its door ajar, next to the car and leaves the front passenger window rolled open. He gives Odo a blanket, then he lies down on the back seat. When night falls, the ape comes in and out, making considerable noise, leaping into the back seat a few times, practically landing on Peter, until he settles in the foot well of the back seat, next to him. Odo doesn't snore, but his breathing is powerful. Peter does not sleep well, not only because he is overtly disturbed by the ape but because of nagging worries. This is a large, powerful animal, unrestrained and uncontrollable. *What have I got myself into?*

Other nights they sleep on the edge of a field, at the end of a dead-end road, wherever it's quiet and isolated.

One evening he has a closer look at the papers Lemnon gave him. Included among them is a report that gives an overview of Odo's life. He was "wild-caught as a baby" in Africa. No mention is made of the Peace Corps volunteer, only that Odo next spent time with NASA, at a place called Holloman Aerospace Medical Center, in Alamogordo, New Mexico. Then he went to the Yerkes National Primate Research Center, in Atlanta, Georgia, then to the Laboratory for Experimental Medicine and Surgery in Primates, LEMSIP for short, in Tuxedo, New York, before being sent to Lemnon's Institute for Primate Research. What an odyssey. No wonder Bob said Odo was a rolling stone.

Peter lingers on certain words: "medical" ... "biology" ... "laboratory" ... "research" — and especially "experimental medicine and surgery." *Experimental?* Odo was shunted from one medical Auschwitz to another, and this after being taken from his mother as a baby. Peter wonders what happened to Odo's mother. Earlier in the day, while grooming the ape, he noticed a tattoo on his chest. Only in that area can the dark skin be made out beneath the thick coat, and there, in the upper-right-hand corner, he found two wrinkled digits — the number 65 — inscribed on unacceptable paper.

He turns to Odo. "What have they done to you?"

He moves over and grooms him.

One afternoon in lush Kentucky, after filling up, he drives to the far end of the recreation area behind the gas station so they can eat. Odo gets out of the car and climbs a tree. At first Peter is relieved; the ape is out of the way. But then he can't get him to come down. He's afraid that Odo will reach over into another tree and then another and be gone. But the ape stays put. He only gazes at the forest on whose edge he is hovering. He seems drunk with joy at being in such a leafy haven. A chimpanzee afloat in a sea of green.

Peter waits. Time goes by. He has nothing to read and he doesn't feel like listening to the radio. He has a nap in the back seat. He reflects on Clara, on his disenchanted son, on the life he is leaving behind. He walks to the gas station to get food and water. He sits in the car and contemplates the layout of the gas station, its main building that was once brightly coloured but is now faded, the expanse of asphalt, the coming and going of cars and trucks and people, the recreation area, the edge of the forest, the tree in which Odo has ensconced himself, and then he sits there and just watches Odo.

No one notices the chimpanzee in the tree except children. While grown-ups busy themselves with trips to the restrooms and with fuelling up their cars and their families, children look around. They grin. Some point and try to alert their parents. A random, blind gaze is all they get. The children wave at Odo as they drive off.

Five hours later, as the day is coming to an end, Peter is still looking up at the chimpanzee. Odo isn't ignoring him. In fact, when he's not distracted by activity in the gas station, Odo looks down at him with the same relaxed interest that Peter shows looking up at him.

When dusk comes, the air cools a little and still the ape does not come down. Peter opens the trunk of the car and pulls out his sleeping bag and Odo's blanket. The ape hoots. Peter gets close to the tree and lifts the blanket in the air. The creature reaches down to grab it. He climbs back into the tree and wraps himself up cosily.

Peter leaves fruit, slices of bread spread with peanut butter, and a jug of water at the foot of the tree. When it gets dark, he lies down for the night in the car. He is exhausted. He is worried that Odo will flee during the night or, worse, attack someone. But he falls asleep with a last, pleasing realization: It is likely the first time since his African childhood that Odo has slept under the stars.

In the early morning, the fruit and bread slices are gone and the jug is half empty. When Peter emerges from the car, Odo comes down from the tree. He raises his arms towards him. Peter sits on the ground and they embrace and groom each other. Peter gives Odo a breakfast of chocolate milk and egg salad sandwiches.

At two other gas stations along the way, the same tree-dwelling scenario is repeated. Peter twice has to call the airline to change their reservations, at a cost each time.

During the day, as they drive across America, he finds himself at regular intervals turning his head to glance at his passenger, astounded again and again that he's in a car with a chimpanzee. And he senses that Odo, who is otherwise much taken by the landscape going by, does the same thing, turns his head at regular intervals to glance at him, astounded again and again that he's in a car with a human being. And so, in a constant and mutual state of wonder and amazement (and a little fear), they make their way to New York City.

Peter grows nervous as they approach the metropolis. He worries that Lemnon has played a trick on him, that at Kennedy Airport he will be stopped and Odo taken away.

The ape stares at the city, his jaw slack, his eyes unblinking. On a side road on the way to Kennedy, Peter stops the car. Now comes the hard part. He must inject into the ape a powerful animal sedative called Sernalyn, prescribed by the veterinarian. Will Odo attack him in retaliation?

"Look!" he says, pointing away. Odo looks. Peter jabs him in the arm with the syringe. Odo hardly seems to notice the prick and in a few minutes falls unconscious. At the airport, because of the nature of his cargo, Peter is allowed to go to a special bay to unload the ape. He assembles the cage and with considerable effort heaves Odo's limp body onto a blanket on the floor of it. He lingers, his fingers hooked around the metal bars. What if Odo doesn't wake up? Where will that leave him?

The cage is put on a dolly and wheeled into the labyrinth of JFK. Peter is accompanied by a security guard. When the customs official has gone through all the papers and verified his flight ticket, Odo is taken away. Peter is told that, if the captain gives his permission, he will be able to go in the hold during the flight to check on him.

He races away. He goes to a car wash, cleans the car inside and out, drives to Brooklyn. The prospective buyer proves to be a difficult man who magnifies every fault in the car and dismisses every quality. But Peter didn't practice politics for nearly twenty years for nothing. He listens to the man without saying a word, then restates the agreed-upon price. When the man makes to argue further, Peter says, "That's fine. I'll sell it to the other buyer." He gets into the car and starts it.

The man comes up to the window. "What other buyer?" he asks.

"Just after I agreed to sell it to you, another buyer called. I said no, because I made a commitment to you. But it's better for me if you don't want it. I'll get more money that way." He gets the car into gear and starts reversing out of the driveway.

The man waves. "Wait, wait! I'll take it," he yells. He quickly pays up.

Peter flags down a taxi and returns to Kennedy. He pesters the airline with his worries about Odo. They assure him that, no, they won't forget to load the ape onto the plane, and that, yes, he will be loaded in the top hold, which is pressurized and heated, and that, no, there have been no reports of him stirring, and that, yes, he gives all signs of still being alive, and that, no, Peter can't see him just yet, and that, yes, as soon as the plane is at cruising altitude they will inquire about Peter going to see him.

An hour into the flight, the captain gives his permission and Peter goes to the back of the plane. Through a narrow door, he enters the top hold. The light is turned on. He spots the cage right away, tethered to the wall of the plane with straps. It's set apart from the first-class luggage. He hurries to it. He is relieved to see Odo's chest rising and falling evenly. He puts his hand through the bars and feels the warm body. He would go inside the cage to groom him, but the airline has added its own padlock to the door.

Except for the odd trip to the restroom or for a meal, Peter stays next to the cage the whole flight. The flight attendants don't seem to mind him being there. The veterinarian told him that a chimpanzee can't overdose on Sernalyn. Twice during the flight he gives Odo an extra jab. He hates doing it, but he doesn't want the ape to wake up in such a noisy, strange place. He might panic.

Enough of this, Peter thinks. He promises that he will never subject Odo to such egregious strains again. The ape deserves better.

A flight attendant enters the hold half an hour before the plane is due to land. He must return to his seat, she tells him. He does as he is told and promptly falls asleep.

When the plane bumps to a landing early in the morning at Lisbon's Portela Airport, he groggily looks out the window, and it is he who feels panic racing through him. His heart jumps about his chest. His breathing is laboured. *This is all a mistake. I'll just turn around*. But what about Odo? Lisbon surely has a zoo. He could abandon the ape in his cage at the entrance, an animal foundling.

An hour after all the other passengers have picked up their luggage and moved on, he is still waiting in the arrivals area. He spends most of that hour in a cubicle of a restroom near the luggage carousel, weeping quietly. If only Clara were with him! She would steady him. But if she were around, he wouldn't be in this ridiculous predicament.

Eventually a man in a uniform finds him. "O senhor é o homem com o macaco?" he asks.

Peter stares at him dumbly.

"Macaco?" the man says, making to scratch his armpits while going *oo, oo, oo, oo*.

"Yes, yes!" Peter nods.

As they walk through secured doors, the man chats amiably in Portuguese to him. Peter nods, though he doesn't understand a word. He remembers from long-ago conversations between his parents that this is what Portuguese sounds like, a slurred mournful whisper.

In the middle of a hangar, the cage is resting on a luggage cart. Some airport workers are standing around it. Again Peter's heart jumps in his chest, but this time with gladness. The men are chatting about the *macaco* with evident interest. Odo is still unconscious. The men ask questions, to which Peter can only shake his head apologetically.

"Ele não fala português," says the man who brought him in.

Sign language takes over.

"O que o senhor vai fazer com ele?" says another man, his hands waving in front of him, palms up.

"I'm going to the High Mountains of Portugal," Peter replies. He cuts a rectangle in the air with a finger, says, "Portugal," and points to the top right of the rectangle.

"Ah, as Altas Montanhas de Portugal. Lá em cima com os rinocerontes," responds the man.

The others laugh. Peter nods, though he doesn't know what has amused them. *Rinocerontes?*

Eventually their work duties call. His passport is examined and stamped; Odo's papers are signed, stamped, and separated, one set for Peter, one set for them. There. A man leans against the luggage cart. The foreigner and his *macaco* are good to go.

Peter blanches. In the frenzy of the last two weeks, there is one detail he has forgotten to address: how he and Odo will get from Lisbon to the High Mountains of Portugal. They need a car, but he has made no arrangements for buying one.

He puts his palms face out. *Stop*. "I need to buy a car." He shakes his fists up and down, mimicking hands on a steering wheel.

"Um carro?"

"Yes. Where can I buy one, where?" He rubs thumb and forefinger together.

"O senhor quer comprar um carro?"

Comprar — that sounds right.

"Yes, yes, comprar um carro, where?"

The man calls over another and they discuss. They write on a piece of paper, which they hand to Peter. *Citroën*, it says, with an address. He knows *citron* is French for lemon. He hopes this isn't an omen.

"Near, near?" he asks, cupping his fingers towards him.

"Sim, é muito perto. Táxi."

He points to himself, then away and back. "I'm going and then I'm coming back."

"Sim, sim." The men nod.

He hurries away. He has brought with him substantial Canadian and American cash, in addition to traveller's cheques. And he has his credit card, for extra surety. He changes all his money into escudos and hops into a taxi.

The Citroën dealership is not very far from the airport. The cars are strange, roly-poly things. One has lovely lines, but it's expensive and too big for his needs. Finally, he decides on a very basic model, a dorky grey contraption that looks like it was made from tuna cans. It has no frills at all, no radio, no air conditioning, no armrests, no automatic transmission. It doesn't even have roll-down windows. The windows are cut in two horizontally and the lower half hinges up to rest against the top half, like a flap, held up by a clip. Nor is there a hardtop roof, or a glass rear window, only a piece of sturdy fabric that can be detached and rolled back, flexible transparent plastic window included. He opens and closes a door. The car feels rickety and rudimentary, but the salesman expresses great enthusiasm for it, praising it to the sky with his hands. Peter wonders at the name, which isn't a name at all, only an alphanumeric code: 2CV. He would prefer an American car. But he needs a car right away, before Odo wakes up.

He interrupts the salesman with a nod — he will take it. The man breaks into smiles and directs him to his office. Peter's international driver's licence is inspected, papers are filled out, money is taken, calls are made to his credit card company.

An hour later he drives up to the airport, a temporary licence plate taped to the inside of the car's rear window. The transmission on the car is clunky, with the gear stick poking straight out of the dashboard, the engine is noisy, and the ride is bouncy. He parks the car and makes his way back to the hangar.

Odo is still sleeping. Peter and the airport employee wheel the cage out to the car. They transfer the ape to the back seat. Right then, a problem arises. The cage, even folded up, doesn't fit in the tiny trunk of the 2CV. There's no question of strapping it onto the soft roof. It has to be left behind. Peter is not bothered. The thing is a nuisance, and besides, Odo hasn't used it at all. The airport man is amenable to taking it.

Peter checks one last time that he hasn't forgotten anything. He has his passport and papers, he's pulled out the map of Portugal, his luggage is jammed into the trunk, the ape is in the back seat — he's ready to set off. Only he's exhausted and thirsty and hungry. He steadies himself.

"How far to the Altas Montanhas de Portugal?" he asks.

"Para as Altas Montanhas de Portugal? Cerca de dez horas," the man answers.

Peter uses his fingers to make sure he has understood. Ten fingers. Ten hours. The man nods. Peter sighs.

He consults the map. As he did in the United States, he decides to avoid large cities. That means turning away from the coast and driving through the interior. Past a town called Alhandra, there is a bridge across the Tagus. After that, the map promises settlements that are so small they receive the minimal cartographic designation, a tiny black circle with a blank centre.

A couple of hours later, after only a quick stop at a café in a place called Porto Alto to eat and drink and buy supplies, he can keep his eyes open no longer. They come upon Ponte de Sor. It's a pleasantly bustling town. He eyes a hotel longingly; he would happily stop there. Instead he drives on. Back in the countryside, he turns off onto a quiet side road and parks next to an

271

olive grove. The car looks like a grey bubble about to be blown across the landscape. He leaves food next to Odo. He thinks to lay his sleeping bag across the front seats, but the seats are too far apart. Nor do they recline to any extent. He looks at the ground next to the car. Too rocky. Finally he gets in the back and works Odo's heavy body onto the floor of the car. He lies across the back seat in a fetal position and promptly falls into a deep sleep.

When Peter awakes late that afternoon, Odo is sitting right next to his head, practically on it. He's looking around. No doubt he's wondering what new trick the humans have pulled on him. Where is he now? Where have the big buildings gone? Peter can feel the warmth of Odo's body against his head. He's still tired, but anxiety revives him. Will Odo be angry and aggressive? If he is, there's no way Peter can escape him. He lifts himself slowly.

Odo embraces him with both arms. Peter embraces the ape back. They remain interlocked for several seconds. He gives Odo some water to drink and feeds him apples, bread, cheese, ham, all of which disappear in quick, full mouthfuls.

Peter notices a group of men a ways off, walking in their direction along the road. They're carrying shovels and hoes on their shoulders. He moves to the driver's seat. Odo hops into the passenger seat next to him. He starts the car. Odo hoots at the rumble of the engine but otherwise stays put. He turns the car around and returns to the road.

272

Like most emigrants, his parents departed the High Mountains of Portugal in a state of want, and they were determined that their children would have different, better lives in Canada. As if stanching a wound, they turned their backs on their origins. In Toronto, they deliberately avoided fellow Portuguese immigrants. They forced themselves to learn English well and passed on neither their native language nor their native culture to their son and daughter. Instead, they encouraged them to move in wider circles and were delighted when each married a non-Portuguese.

Only in their last years, once their identity engineering had succeeded, did his parents relent a little and did he and his sister, Teresa, on occasion get a glimpse into their long-ago former lives. It came in the form of brief stories, supported by family photos. A few names were floated and a hazy geography was sketched, centred on one place name: Tuizelo. That was where his parents came from, and that is where he and Odo will settle.

But he knows nothing of the country. He is Canadian through and through. As they drive in the fading light of day, he notes how pretty the landscape is, how busy the rurality. Everywhere there are flocks and herds, beehives and grapevines, ploughed fields and tended groves. He sees people carrying firewood on their backs and donkeys carrying loaded baskets on theirs.

The night stops them and sends them to sleep. He moves to the cramped back seat. At a late hour, he is vaguely aware of Odo exiting the car through the door, but he is too knocked out by sleep to check on him.

In the morning he finds the ape sleeping on top of the car, on its fabric roof. Peter does not rouse him. Instead he reads the guidebook. He learns from it that the peculiar tree he keeps seeing — stocky, thick-limbed, the trunk dark brown except where the precious bark has been neatly removed — is the cork tree. The parts of the trees that have been stripped glow a rich reddish brown. He vows from then on to drink only from wine bottles that have been cork-stoppered.

Visigoths, Francs, Romans, Moors — all were here. Some did no more than kick over furniture before moving on. Others stayed long enough to build a bridge or a castle. Then, in a sidebar, he discovers that "faunal anomaly of northern Portugal": the Iberian rhinoceros. Was that what the man at the airport meant? This biological relic, descended from the woolly rhinoceros of earlier glacial ages, existed in Portugal in shrinking pockets right up into the modern era, with the confirmed death of the last known specimen taking place in 1641. Hardy and fierce-looking but mostly benign — a herbivore, after all, slow to anger and quick to forgive — it fell out of step with the times, unable to adapt to the shrinking space given it, and so it vanished, though with occasional claims of sightings to this day. In 1515 King Manuel I of Portugal offered an Iberian rhinoceros as a gift to Pope Leo X. The guidebook has a reproduction of the Dürer woodcut of that rhinoceros, "incorrectly single-horned." He peers at the image. The animal looks grand, ancient, unlikely, appealing.

Odo awakes as Peter is preparing breakfast on the camping stove. When Odo sits up, and even more so

274

when he stands on the roof of the car, taking in his surroundings, Peter is again struck by his situation. If he were in this foreign land alone, it would be unbearable; he would die of loneliness. But because of his strange companion, loneliness is pushed away. For that he is deeply grateful. Even so, he can't ignore the other feeling troubling him at the moment, which seems to liquefy his innards: fear. He can't explain the sudden onset of the emotion. He's never been subject to panic attacks, but perhaps this is what they feel like. Fear melts through him, opening his every pore, causing his breaths to shorten and quicken. Then Odo climbs down from the car, ambles over on all fours to sit and stare at the camping stove, amiably disposed, and the fear goes away.

After breakfast, they hit the road again. They cross villages with stone houses, cobbled streets, sleeping dogs, and observant donkeys. Places of stillness, with few men and the women dressed in black, all of them older. He senses that the future comes like the night in these settlements, quietly and without surprise, each generation much like the previous one and the next, only shrinking in numbers.

In the early afternoon they reach — according to the map — the High Mountains of Portugal. The air is cooler. He is puzzled. Where are the mountains? He wasn't expecting soaring, winter-clad Alps, but he didn't expect an undulating barren savannah either, its forests hidden away in valleys, without any peaks any- where. He and Odo cross plains of enormous grey boulders, each sitting on its own in the grassland. Some

275

of these rocks reach past what would be the second floor of a house. Perhaps to a man standing next to one, there is something mountain-like about them, but it's a stretch. Odo is as intrigued by the boulders as he is.

Tuizelo appears at the end of a winding road, on the edge of a forest, tucked in a valley. The narrow, sloping, cobbled streets wend their way to a small square with a humble, gurgling fountain at its centre. On one side of the square is a church, on the other, a café, which also appears to be a small grocery store and bakery. These two institutions, each plying its own wares, are set amidst modest stone houses with wooden balconies. Only the many vegetable gardens are large, as large as fields, and neat. Here, there, everywhere, chickens, goats, sheep, lazing dogs.

Right away he is taken by the tranquility and isolation of the village. And his parents came from here. In fact, he was born here. He can hardly believe it. The distance between this place and the house in the heart of Toronto, in Cabbagetown, where he grew up, seems immeasurable. He has no memories of Tuizelo. His parents left when he was a toddler. Nonetheless, he will give the place a try.

"We've arrived," he announces. Odo looks around with a blank expression.

They eat sandwiches and drink water. Peter notices a small group of people in a vegetable garden. He reaches for the dictionary. He practices a phrase a few times.

"Don't move. Stay in the car," he says to Odo. The ape sits so low in the car seat that he's barely visible from the outside.

Peter gets out of the car and waves to the group. They wave back. A man shouts a greeting. Peter goes through the small gate and joins them. Each villager steps forward to shake his hand, a smile on his or her face. "Olá," he says each time. When the ceremony is over, he self-consciously recites his phrase. "Eu quero uma casa, por favor," he says slowly. *I would like a house, please.*

"Uma casa? Por uma noite?" says one.

"Não," he replies as he flips through the dictionary, "uma casa por . . . viver." *No, a house to live in.*

"Aqui, em *Tuizelo?*" says another, his wrinkled features expanding in surprise.

"Sim," Peter replies, "uma casa aqui em Tuizelo por viver." *Yes, a house here in Tuizelo to live in.* Clearly, immigration is unknown in these parts.

"Meu Deus! O que é aquela coisa?" a woman gasps. He guesses that the horror in her tone has nothing to do with his request to live in the village. She is looking beyond him. He turns. Sure enough, Odo has climbed onto the roof of the car and is observing them.

The group makes various startled, fearful noises. One man grips his hoe and lifts it in the air somewhat.

"No, no, he's friendly," Peter says, his palms raised to appease them. He rifles through the dictionary. "Ele é . . . amigável! Amigável!"

He repeats the word a few times, trying to heed the tonic accent and get the pronunciation right. He retreats to the car. The group stays frozen. Already Odo has attracted further attention. Two men are staring from the café, as is a woman from her doorstep, and another from a balcony.

Peter had hoped to *ease* Odo into village life, but the notion is foolish. There are no degrees to amazement.

"Amigável, amigável!" he repeats to all.

He beckons to Odo, who clambers down from the car and knuckle-walks to the vegetable garden with him. The ape chooses not to go through the gate but to leap onto the stone wall. Peter stands next to him, stroking one of his legs.

"Um macaco," he says to the group, to help with what they are seeing. "Um macaco amigável." *A friendly ape.*

The people stare while he and Odo wait. The woman who first noticed Odo is the first to relax a little. "E ele mora com o senhor?" she asks. Her tone is open, touched by wonder.

"Sim," he replies, though he doesn't know what "mora" means.

One villager decides that he's had enough. He turns to move away. His neighbour reaches for him, but in doing so he stumbles. The result is that he pulls hard on the first man's sleeve as he seeks to regain his balance. The other man in turn loses his balance momentarily, cries out, flings his arm back to throw off the other man's hand, and walks off in a huff. Odo instantly feels the tension and lifts himself onto his legs, following the departing man with his eyes. Standing on the wall as he is, he now towers over the group in the garden. Peter senses their apprehension. "It's all right," he whispers to the ape, tugging on one of Odo's hands, "it's all right." He's anxious. Might this be enough to make the ape run amok?

Odo doesn't run amok. He sits back down, producing a few inquisitive *hoo, hoo, hoos* in a rising pitch. Some faces in the group smile at hearing the sound, perhaps reassured by the confirmation of a stereotype — apes really do go *hoo, hoo, hoo.*

"De onde é que ele vem? O que é que faz?" asks the same woman.

"Sim, sim," Peter replies, again not knowing to what. "Eu quero uma casa em Tuizelo por viver com macaco amigável."

By now, other villagers have turned up. They gather at a respectful distance. Odo is as curious about the villagers as they are about him. He pivots on the wall, looking, engaging, commenting with quiet *hoos* and *aarrrhhhs.*

"Uma casa . . . ?" Peter repeats as he strokes the ape.

The group in the garden at last begins to address his request. They talk to each other and he can hear the word "casa" being repeated along with what sounds like names. The conversation widens when one woman turns and calls out to another woman who is standing near his car. This villager responds and soon another conversation begins there. Occasional verbal volleys are tossed between the villagers around the car and the ones in the vegetable garden. The reason why they don't come together is plain: Between the two groups is the gate, and guarding the gate like a sentinel is an ape.

Peter thinks that he should perhaps refine his request. A house on the edge of the village would be best. He looks in the dictionary.

"Uma casa ... nas bordas de Tuizelo ... nas proximidades," he calls out, somewhat addressing his request to the woman who first spoke about Odo, but intending it for everyone to hear.

The discussion starts again, until the woman, who has willingly taken on her role as his main interlocutor, announces the result of it. "Temos uma casa que provavelmente vai servir para si e o seu macaco."

He understands nothing except "uma casa" and "seu macaco". *A house* and *your ape*. He nods.

The woman smiles and looks pointedly at the gate. He promptly goes through it and nudges Odo off the stone wall. Odo drops to the ground next to him. They walk a few steps towards the car. The group in the garden advances towards the gate, while the group around the car melts away. He turns to the woman and indicates in various directions. She points to the right, up towards the top of the village. He moves in that direction. Mercifully, Odo stays at his side. The woman trails along at a safe distance. Villagers ahead of them disperse, as do the chickens and dogs. Except for the chickens, all the villagers, human and animal, join in following the newcomers. He regularly turns to make sure they are going the right way. The woman, leading the villagers some fifteen paces behind, nods to confirm that he is, or redirects him with her hand. And so, leading the group while in fact following it, he and Odo walk through the village. Odo strolls along nicely on all fours next to him, despite being powerfully interested in the chickens and dogs.

They emerge from the village. The cobbled street becomes a dirt road. After a turn, they cross a shallow stream. The trees grow more sparse, the plateau starts to show. Shortly, the woman calls out and points. They have reached the house.

It is no different from many of the others in the village. It is a small two-storey stone structure, L-shaped, with a gated stone wall completing the other two sides of the L to create a house with an enclosed courtyard. The woman invites him into this courtyard, while staying outside the gate with her companions. She indicates that the second floor is reached by the external stone staircase. Then she points at Odo and to a door on the ground floor. Peter opens it; it has no lock, only a latch. He is not happy with what he sees. Besides being filled with quantities of stuff, the room is filthy, everything covered in dust. Then he sees a ring attached to a wall and notices that the door he just opened is divided in two horizontally, and he understands. This floor is a pen, a stable, an enclosure for livestock. He has seen any number of such houses on their drive but only now grasps their design. The animals — the sheep, goats, pigs, chickens, donkeys — live below their owners, who thus have them close-by and safe, and who profit in winter from the warmth their livestock generate. It also explains the outside staircase. He closes the door.

"Macaco," the woman says in a helpful tone from the other side of the low stone wall.

"Não," he replies, shaking his head. He points up the stairs.

The people nod. The foreigner's *macaco* wants to live upstairs, does it? It has a taste for luxury?

He and Odo climb the stone stairs. The landing, of wood with a roof, is large enough to qualify as a balcony. He opens the door. It doesn't have a lock, either. Burglary doesn't seem to be a problem in Tuizelo.

He is better pleased with this top floor. It is rustic, but it will do. It has a stone floor (easy to clean) and little furniture (less to break). The walls are very thick and covered in uneven whitewash, showing areas of rise and fall, but clean; they look like a plausible map of the High Mountains of Portugal. The layout of the flat is simple. The door opens onto a main room that has a wooden table with four chairs, some shelves built into the wall, and a cast-iron woodstove. To one side of this room, the top of the L, separated by a wall that goes only halfway across, is the kitchen, which is fitted with a large sink, a propane gas stove, a counter, and more shelves. At the other end of the living room, through a doorway without a door, he finds two rooms in a row, the bottom of the L. The first room contains a wardrobe whose door holds a large mirror speckled with age. The end room has a bed with a mattress long past its prime, a small bedside table, a chest of drawers, and a primitive bathroom with a sink and a dusty, dry toilet. There is no shower or bathtub.

He returns to the living room, scanning the bottoms of the walls. He examines the ceiling of each room. There are no electrical outlets or light fixtures anywhere. In the kitchen he confirms what he thought he did *not* see; indeed, there is no refrigerator. The place has no electricity. And no phone jack, either. He sighs. He turns the kitchen faucet on. No gush of water disturbs the silence. Two of the windows are broken. Everything is covered in dust and grime. A wave of fatigue washes over him. From the Senate of Canada, surrounded by all the amenities of the modern world in a capital city, to this cave-age dwelling on the fringes of nowhere. From the comfort of family and friends to a place where he is a stranger and does not speak the language.

He is saved from his impending emotional meltdown by Odo. The ape is evidently delighted with their new digs. He gives out excited hoots and bobs his head as he races from one end of the apartment to the other. It is, Peter realizes, the first habitation Odo has seen outside the cages he has lived in his whole adult life. So much bigger and airier than anything he has known. And better than the cars he has been dwelling in this last week. Perhaps Odo thought he had traded living in a hanging cage for living in a cage on wheels. By captive ape standards, this house is the Ritz.

With good light, come to think of it: There are windows in every wall. The sun will be their light bulb. And there's charm — and economy — in the idea of lighting the place in the evenings with candles and lanterns. And if there is plumbing, there must once have been running water, which can no doubt be restored.

Peter approaches one of the windows facing the courtyard. He opens it. The villagers are waiting patiently on the other side of the courtyard wall. He waves and smiles at them. What is "good" in Portuguese? He consults his dictionary. "A casa é boa — muito boa!" he cries.

The villagers smile and clap their hands.

Odo joins him at the window. In a state of high excitement, he says the same thing Peter has just said, only in his own language, which, to his ears and those of the people down below, comes as a terrific shriek. The villagers cower.

"Macaco . . . macaco" — he searches for the word — "macaco . . . é feliz!"

The villagers break into applause once more. Which increases Odo's happiness. He shrieks again with primate glee — and throws himself out the window. Peter bends forward in alarm, his hands outstretched. He looks down. He cannot see the ape. The villagers are going *ooh* and *ahh* in surprise and slight alarm. They are looking up.

He runs down the outside steps and joins them. Odo has grabbed the edge of the schist-tile roof and, pushing himself off the stones of the wall, has climbed on top of the house. He is now perched on its peak, looking about with unbounded delight at the humans below, at the village, at the trees nearby, at the wide world around him.

The moment is good to conclude matters with the villagers. Peter introduces himself to their leader. Her name is Amélia Duarte; he should call her Dona Amélia, she tells him. He makes her understand that he would be happy to live in the house. (*Whose house?* he wonders. *What happened to those who lived in it?*) In butchered Portuguese he inquires about the windows and the plumbing and about the place being cleaned. To all these, Dona Amélia nods vigorously. All will be taken care of, she makes clear. She turns her hand over and over. *Amanhã, amanhã.* And how much? The same: *Tomorrow, tomorrow.*

To one and all he says, "Obrigado, obrigado, obrigado." Odo's shrieks echo the same gratitude. Eventually, after he has shaken hands with each and every one, the villagers move off, their eyes fixed on the roof of the house.

Odo is sitting in what Peter already recognizes is a posture of relaxation: feet apart, forearms resting on the knees, hands dangling between the legs, alert head peering about. After the villagers have gone, and with the ape showing continuing pleasure at being where he is, Peter walks down to retrieve the car. "I'll be back," he shouts to Odo.

Back at the house, he unpacks their few belongings. Then he makes an early supper using the camping gear, which requires him to find a bucket and walk down to the village fountain to get water.

A little later he calls out to the ape again. When Odo fails to appear, he moves to the window. Just then, the ape's head pops into view, upside down. Odo is clinging to the outside wall of the house.

"Supper's ready," Peter says, showing Odo the pot in which he has boiled eggs and potatoes.

They eat in thoughtful silence. Then Odo leaps out the window again.

Leery of the old mattress, Peter sets his camping mat and sleeping bag on the table in the living room.

And then he has nothing to do. After three weeks — or is it a lifetime? — of ceaseless activity, he has nothing to do. A very long sentence, anchored in solid nouns, with countless subordinate clauses, scores of adjectives and adverbs, and bold conjunctions that launched the sentence in a new direction — besides unexpected interludes — has finally, with a surprisingly quiet full stop, come to an end. For an hour or so, sitting outside on the landing at the top of the stairs, nursing a coffee, tired, a little relieved, a little worried, he contemplates that full stop. What will the next sentence bring?

He settles in his sleeping bag on the table. Odo stays on the roof till it's dark, then returns through the window, his shape cut out by the moonlight. He grunts with pleasure at discovering that he has the mattress in the bedroom all to himself. Soon the house is quiet. Peter falls asleep imagining that Clara is lying next to him. "I wish you were here," he whispers to her. "I think you'd like this house. We'd set it up really nicely, with lots of plants and flowers. I love you. Good night."

In the morning, a delegation stands before the house, the *tomorrow* crew, led by Dona Amélia. Armed with buckets, mops, and rags, with hammers and wrenches, with determination, they have come to fix the place up. As they set to work, Peter tries to help, but they shake their heads and shoo him away. Besides, he has his ape to take care of. They are nervous about having him around.

He and Odo go for a walk. Every eye, human and animal, turns to them and stares. The gaze is not hostile, not at all; in every case it comes with a greeting. Peter again marvels at the vegetable gardens. Turnips, potatoes, zucchini, gourds, tomatoes, onions, cabbages, cauliflowers, kale, beets, lettuce, leeks, sweet peppers, green beans, carrots, small fields of rye and corn — this is cottage-industry gardening on a serious scale. In one garden, the ape pulls out a head of lettuce and eats it. Peter claps his hands and calls Odo to him. The ape is hungry. So is he.

They stand before the village café. Its patio is deserted. He does not want to risk entering the café — but surely it would be all right to be served outside? He consults the dictionary, then lingers beside a table. The man behind the counter comes out, eyes wide and alert, but with an amiable mien.

"Como posso servi-lo?" he asks.

"Dois sanduíches de queijo, por favor, e um café com leite," Peter pronounces.

"Claro que sim, imediatamente," the man replies. Though he moves warily, he wipes down the table nearest them, which Peter takes as an invitation to sit down.

"Muito obrigado," he says.

"Ao seu serviço," replies the man as he returns inside the café.

Peter sits down. He expects Odo to stay seated on the ground beside him, but the ape's eyes are fixed on his metal chair. Odo climbs onto the one next to him. From there, he peers at the ground, rocks the chair, slaps its arms, generally explores the uses and capabilities of the peculiar device. Peter glances into the café. The patrons within are looking at them. And outside, people are starting to gather in a wide circle. "Steady, steady," he mutters to Odo.

He moves closer to Odo and makes a few grooming gestures. But the ape seems in no way distressed or under strain. On the contrary, as attested by his bright expression and lively curiosity, he's in good spirits. It's the people around who seem in need of social grooming, so to speak.

"Olá, bom dia," Peter calls out.

Greetings come back.

"De onde o senhor é?" asks a man.

"I'm from Canada," he replies.

Murmurs of approval. Lots of Portuguese immigrants in Canada. It's a good country.

"E o que está a fazer com um macaco?" asks a woman.

What is he doing with an ape? It's a question for which he doesn't have an answer, neither in English nor in Portuguese.

"Eu vive com ele," he replies simply. *I live with him.* That's as much as he can say.

Their order arrives. With the alertness of a bullfighter, the man places the coffee and the two plates on the side of the table farthest from Odo.

The ape loudly grunts and reaches across to take hold of both cheese sandwiches, which he devours in an instant, to the amusement of the villagers. Peter smiles along. He looks at the server.

"Outro dois sanduíches, por favor," he asks. He remembers that the café is also a grocery store. "E, para o macaco, dez . . ." He makes a long shape with his hands, which he then peels.

"Dez bananas?" the man asks.

Ah, it's the same word. "Sim, dez bananas, por favor."

"Como desejar."

If the villagers were amused by Odo eating both sandwiches, they are even more mirthful at his reaction to the bananas. Peter thought he was buying a supply that would last a few days. Not so. The chimpanzee, upon seeing the bananas, grunts ecstatically and proceeds to eat every single one, peels flying off, and would have eaten the two new sandwiches if Peter had not quickly grabbed one of them. As a chaser, he downs Peter's cup of coffee, first dipping his finger into it to test the temperature. When he's licked the cup clean, he dangles it from his mouth, playing with it with his tongue and lips, as if it were a large mint.

The villagers smile and laugh. The foreigner's *macaco* is funny! Peter is pleased. Odo is winning them over.

At the height of the merriment, in an act that Peter senses is meant to show that he is fully participating in the general social relaxation, Odo takes the cup in his hand, stands high on his chair, shrieks, and throws the cup to the ground with terrific force. The cup shatters into small pieces.

The villagers freeze. Peter lifts a placating hand to the server. "Desculpe," he says.

"Não há problema."

And to a wider audience Peter adds, "Macaco amigável é feliz, muito feliz."

Amigável and *feliz* — but with an edge. He pays, adding a handsome tip, and they take their leave, the crowd carefully parting before them.

When they return to the house on the edge of the village, it is transformed. The windows are fixed; the plumbing works; the gas stove has a new tank; every surface has been thoroughly cleaned; pots, pans, dishes, and cutlery — used, chipped, mismatched, but perfectly functional — are stacked on the shelves of the kitchen; the bed has a new mattress, with clean sheets, two wool blankets, and towels lying folded on it; and Dona Amélia is setting a vase bursting with bright flowers on the living room table.

Peter puts his hand over his heart. "Muito obrigado," he says.

"De nada," says Dona Amélia.

The mutual awkwardness of dealing with the cost of things is swiftly dispatched. He rubs his thumb and forefinger together, then points at the gas tank and the kitchenware and towards the bedroom. Next he looks up the word "rent" — it's a strange one: *aluguel*. In each case Dona Amélia proposes a sum with evident nervousness, and in each case Peter is convinced she has made a mistake by a factor of three or four. He agrees right away. Dona Amélia makes him understand that she would be willing to do his laundry and come once a week to clean the house. He hesitates. There isn't much to clean — and what else will he do with his time? But he thinks again. She will be his link to the rest of the village. More importantly, she will be Odo's link, the ape's ambassador. And it occurs to him that the villagers of Tuizelo are probably not a wealthy lot. By employing her, he will pump a little more money into the local economy.

"Sim, sim," he says to her. "Quanto?"

"Amanhã, amanhã," says Dona Amélia, smiling.

Now the next order of business. He needs to get himself and Odo organized. There is the question of formally opening his bank account and arranging for regular wire transfers from Canada, of getting a permanent licence plate for the car. Where is the closest bank?

"Bragança," she replies.

"Telephone?" he asks her. "Aqui?"

"Café," she replies. "Senhor Álvaro."

She gives him the number.

Bragança is about an hour away. Which should he worry about more: bringing the ape to an urban centre or leaving him here alone? These administrative chores need doing. And either way, whether in the town or in the village, he has no real control over Odo. Whatever he does, he must rely on the ape's cooperation. He can only hope that Odo will not stray far from the house or get into trouble.

Dona Amélia and her group of helpers leave.

"Stay, stay. I'll be back soon," he says to Odo, who at the moment is playing with a crack in the stone floor.

He leaves the house, closing the door, though he knows Odo can easily open it. He gets in the car and

291

drives away. Looking in the rear-view mirror, he sees the ape climbing onto the roof.

In Bragança he buys supplies — candles, lanterns, kerosene; soap; groceries, including cartoned milk that doesn't need refrigeration; sundry household and personal items — and does his business at the bank. The licence plate he will receive in the mail, at the café.

At the post office in Bragança, he makes two phone calls to Canada. Ben says he's pleased that his father has arrived safely. "What's your number?" he asks.

"There's no phone," Peter replies, "but I can give you the number of the café in the village. You can leave a message there and I'll call you back."

"What do you mean, there's no phone?"

"I mean just that. There's no phone in the house. But there's one in the café. Take the number."

"Do you have running water?"

"Yep. It's cold, but it runs."

"Great. Do you have electricity?"

"Well, as a matter of fact, I don't."

"Are you serious?"

"I am."

There's a pause. He senses that Ben is waiting for explanations, justifications, defences. He offers none. His son therefore continues in the same vein. "How about the roads — are they paved?"

"Cobbled, actually. How's work? How's Rachel? How's good ol' Ottawa?"

"Why are you doing this, Dad? What are you doing there?"

"It's a nice place. Your grandparents came from here."

They end the call with the grace of people learning how to dance on stilts. They promise to talk again soon, a future conversation being a relief from the one they're having.

He has a bubblier conversation with his sister, Teresa.

"What's the village like?" she asks. "Does it feel like home?"

"No, not when I don't speak the language. But it's quiet, rural, old — pleasantly exotic."

"Have you discovered the family home?"

"Nope. I'm just settling in. And I wasn't even three years old when we left. I'm not sure it makes much difference to me whether I was born in this house or that house. It's just a house."

"Okay, Mr. Sentimentality — how about scores of long-lost cousins?"

"They're still hiding, waiting to pounce on me."

"I think it would help Ben if you built the place up a bit. You know, tell him you're watering the genealogical tree and tending its roots. He's totally perplexed by your sudden departure."

"I'll try harder."

"How are you feeling about Clara?" she asks in a soft voice.

"I talk to her in my head. That's where she lives now."

"And are you taking care of yourself? How's your ticker?"

"Ticking away."

"I'm glad to hear that."

When he returns to Tuizelo, Odo is still on the roof. He hoots loudly upon seeing the car and cascades down. After many hoots of greeting, he drags bags of supplies into the house, walking erect with a side-to-side swaying gait. This helpful intent results in the bags splitting and their contents scattering. Peter gathers everything and brings it into the house.

He sets up the kitchen. He moves the table in the living room to a more pleasing spot, does the same with the bed in the bedroom. Odo watches him the whole time without making a sound. Peter feels slightly nervous. He still has to get used to this, to the ape's gaze. It sweeps around like the beam from a lighthouse, dazzling him as he bobs in the waters. Odo's gaze is a threshold beyond which he cannot see. He wonders what the ape is thinking and in what terms. Perhaps Odo has similar questions about him. Perhaps the ape sees him as a threshold too. But he doubts it. More likely, to Odo, he is a curio, an oddity of the natural world, a dressed-up ape that circles around this natural one, hypnotically attracted.

There. Everything is in its place. He looks about. Again he feels that he has come to the end of a sentence. He frets. He stares out the window. It's late afternoon and the weather looks to be changing for the worse. No matter.

"Let's go exploring," he says to Odo. He grabs the backpack and they head out. He doesn't want to deal with the villagers' insistent attention, so they turn up the road, towards the plateau, until he finds a path that leads back down into the forest. Odo advances on all fours, his gait plodding but easy, his head slung so low that from behind he looks headless. Once they enter the forest, he becomes excited by the great oaks and chestnuts, the clusters of lindens, elms, and poplars, the pine trees, the many shrubs and bushes, the explosions of ferns. He races ahead.

Peter moves at a steady pace, often overtaking Odo as he dawdles. Then the ape canters up and hurtles past him. Each time he notes how Odo touches him as he goes by, a slap against the back of his leg, nothing hard or aggressive, more a verification. *Good, good, you're there*. Then he lingers again and Peter gains the lead once more. In other words, Peter walks through the forest while Odo swings through it.

Odo is foraging. Bob from the IPR told him about this, how, given a chance, the ape would raid the larder of nature for shoots, flowers, wild fruit, insects, basically anything edible.

It starts to rain. Peter finds a large pine tree and takes refuge under it. Its protection is imperfect, but he doesn't mind, as he has brought a waterproof poncho. He puts it on and sits on the layer of pine needles, his back against the trunk of the tree. He waits for Odo to catch up. When he sees the ape racing along the path, he calls out. Odo brakes and stares at him. The ape has never seen a poncho before, doesn't understand where his body has gone. "Come, come," he says. Odo settles on his haunches close-by. Though the ape doesn't seem to mind the rain, Peter takes out a second poncho from his backpack. In doing so, he lifts his own. Odo grins.

Oh, there's the rest of you! He scoots next to him. Peter places the poncho over the ape's head. They are now two disembodied faces looking out. Above them the tree rises in a cone shape, like a teepee, the space broken up and fractured by branches. The pine smell is strong. They sit and watch the falling rain and its many consequences: the drops of water that swell up at the end of pine needles before falling, as if thoughtfully; the forming of puddles, complete with connecting rivers; the dampening of all sound except the patter of the rain; the creation of a dim, damp world of green and brown. They are surprised when a solitary wild boar trots past. Mostly they just listen to the living, breathing silence of the forest.

They return to the house in the near darkness. Peter finds matches and lights a candle. Before going to bed he starts a fire in the woodstove. He sets it to a slow burn.

The next morning he wakes early. During the night Odo hovered around the now-occupied mattress in the bedroom before moving away; the ape prefers to sleep on his own, for which Peter is thankful. He goes looking for the ape and finds him atop the wardrobe, in the room next to his, soundly asleep in a nest made of a towel and some of Peter's clothes, one hand between his legs, the other resting under his head.

Peter makes his way to the kitchen. He puts on a big pot of water to boil. He discovered the previous day a square metal basin about three feet square with low edges and a pattern of channels on the bottom. The key to proper hygiene in a house with no bathtub. Once the water is warm, he shaves, then stands in the basin and washes himself. Water splashes onto the stone floor. He will need a little practice to get it right, sponge-bathing in this basin. He dries himself, dresses, cleans up. Now for breakfast. Water for coffee. Perhaps Odo will like oatmeal porridge? He pours milk and rolled oats in a pot and sets it on the stovetop.

He turns to fetch the ground coffee and is startled to see Odo at the entrance of the kitchen. How long has he been squatting there, watching him? The ape's movements are soundless. His bones don't creak, and he doesn't have claws or hooves that clatter. Peter will have to get used to this too, to Odo's ubiquity in the house. Not that he minds it, he realizes. He much prefers Odo's presence to his own privacy.

"Good morning," he says.

The ape climbs onto the kitchen counter and sits right next to the stove, unafraid of the flame. The water for the coffee arouses no interest. The focus of his attention is the pot of porridge. When it starts to boil, Peter turns the heat down and stirs the mixture with a wooden spoon. The ape's mouth tenses. He reaches and takes hold of the spoon. He begins to stir carefully, without spilling the porridge or tipping the pot. Round and round goes the spoon, the ingredients swirling and tumbling. Odo looks up at him. "You're doing well," Peter whispers, nodding. The oat flakes are large and uncooked. He and Odo spend the next fifteen minutes watching the porridge thicken, riveted by the workings of food chemistry. Actually, the next *sixteen* minutes. Being a plodding, uninspired cook, Peter follows instructions precisely and he times it. When he puts in chopped walnuts and raisins, Odo stares like an apprentice awed to see the wizard reveal the ingredients that go into the magic potion. Odo's stirring continues, patient and unstinting. Only when Peter turns the burner off and covers the pot with its lid to allow the porridge to cool does the ape show signs of impatience. The laws of thermodynamics are a nuisance to him.

Peter sets the table. One banana for him, eight bananas for Odo. Two cups of milky coffee, one sugar each. Two bowls of oatmeal porridge. One spoon for him, five fingers for Odo.

The meal goes down exceedingly well. A lip-smacking, finger-licking, grunting feastorama. Odo eyes Peter's bowl. Peter holds it tightly to his chest. Tomorrow he will measure out more oats in the pot. He washes up and puts the bowls and the pot away.

He fetches his watch from the bedroom. It's not even eight o'clock in the morning. He looks at the table in the living room. There are no reports to be read, no letters to be written, no paperwork of any kind. There are no meetings to be organized or attended, no priorities to be set, no details to be worked out. There are no phone calls to make or receive, no people to see. There is no schedule, no program, no plan. There is — for a workingman — nothing at all.

Why then keep the time? He unstraps his watch. Already yesterday he noticed how the world is a timepiece. Birds announce dawn and dusk. Insects chime in further — the shrill cries of cicadas, like a dentist's drill, the frog-like warbling of crickets, among others. The church's bell also portions up the day helpfully. And finally the earth itself is a spinning clock, to each quadrant of hours a quality of light. The concordance of these many hour hands is approximate, but what does he gain from the censorious tick-tock tut-tut of a minute hand? Senhor Álvaro, in the café, can be the guardian of his minutes, if he needs them. Peter places his watch on the table.

He looks at Odo. The ape comes to him. Peter sits on the floor and begins to groom him. In response Odo plucks at his hair, at the fuzz balls on his cardigan, at his shirt buttons, at whatever is pluckable. He remembers Bob's suggestion that he crush a dried leaf on his head to give the ape a grooming challenge.

Grooming confounds Peter. The ape is so proximately alien: in his image — but not. There's also the living heat of him, felt so close up, the beating of the ape's heart coming through to his fingertips. Peter is spellbound.

Nonetheless, as he picks seeds, burrs, dirt, specks of old skin off Odo's coat, his mind wanders into the past. But quickly the past bores him. With the exception of Clara and Ben and Rachel, his past is settled, concluded, not worth the sifting. His life was always a happenstance. Not that he didn't work hard at every lucky turn, but there was never any overarching goal. He was happy enough with his work as a lawyer in a legal firm, but jumped ship when presented with the opportunity of politics. He preferred people to paper. Electoral success was more accurately electoral luck, since he saw any number of good candidates fail and mediocre ones succeed, depending on the political winds of the day. His run was good — nineteen years in the House, eight election wins — and he attended well to the needs of his constituents. Then he was kicked upstairs to the Senate, where he worked in good faith on committees, unfazed by the headlines-driven turmoil of the lower chamber. When he was young, he never imagined that politics would be his life. But all that is swept away now. Now it doesn't matter what he did yesterday — other than be bold enough to ask Clara on a date so many years ago. As for tomorrow, beyond certain modest hopes, he has no plans for the future.

Well, then, if the past and the future hold no appeal, why shouldn't he sit on the floor and groom a chimpanzee and be groomed in return? His mind settles back into the present moment, to the task at hand, to the enigma at the tip of his fingers.

"So, yesterday at the café, why did you throw that cup to the ground?" he asks as he works on Odo's shoulder.

"Aaaoouuhhhhh," the ape replies, a rounded sound, the wide-open mouth closing slowly.

Now, what does *aaaoouuhhhhh* in the language spoken by a chimpanzee mean? Peter considers various possibilities:

I broke the cup to make the people laugh more.
I broke the cup to make the people stop laughing.
I broke the cup because I was happy and excited.
I broke the cup because I was anxious and unhappy.
I broke the cup because a man took his hat off.

I broke the cup because of the shape of a cloud in the sky.
I broke the cup because I wanted porridge.
I don't know why I broke the cup.
I broke the cup because quaquaquaqua.

Curious. They both have brains and eyes. They both have language and culture. Yet the ape does something as simple as throw a cup to the ground, and the man is baffled. His tools of understanding — the yoking of evident cause to effect, a bank of knowledge, the use of language, intuition — shed little light on the ape's behaviour. To explain why Odo does what he does, Peter can only rely on conjecture and speculation.

Does it bother him that the ape is essentially unknowable? No, it doesn't. There's reward in the mystery, an enduring amazement. Whether that's the ape's intent, that he be amazed, he doesn't know — can't know — but a reward is a reward. He accepts it with gratitude. These rewards come unexpectedly. A random selection:

Odo stares at him.
Odo lifts him off the ground.
Odo settles in the car seat.
Odo examines a green leaf.
Odo sits up from being asleep on top of the car.
Odo picks up a plate and places it on the table.
Odo turns the page of a magazine.
Odo rests against the courtyard wall, absolutely still.
Odo runs on all fours.
Odo cracks open a nut with a rock.
Odo turns his head.

Each time Peter's mind goes *click* like a camera and an indelible picture is recorded in his memory. Odo's motions are fluid and precise, of an amplitude and force exactly suited to his intentions. And these motions are done entirely unselfconsciously. Odo doesn't appear to think when he's doing, only to do, purely. How does that make sense? Why should thinking — that human hallmark — make us clumsy? But come to think of it, the ape's movements do have a human parallel: that of a great actor giving a great performance. The same economy of means, the same formidable impact. But acting is the result of rigorous training, a strenuously achieved artifice on a human's part. Meanwhile Odo does — *is* — easily and naturally.

I should imitate him, Peter muses.

Odo *feels* — that he knows for certain. On their first evening in the village, for instance, Peter was sitting outside on the landing. The ape was down in the courtyard, examining the stone wall. Peter went in to make himself a cup of coffee. It seems Odo missed his departure. Within seconds, he raced up the stairs and flew in through the door, eyes searching for Peter, an inquisitive *hoo* on his lips.

"I'm here, I'm here," Peter said.

Odo grunted with satisfaction — an emotional wave that rippled over to Peter.

And the same yesterday, during their walk in the forest, the way Odo raced along the path, looking for him, clearly driven by the need to find him.

There is that, then, the ape's emotional state. From this emotional state certain practical thoughts seem to follow: *Where are you? Where have you gone? How can I find you?*

Why Odo wants his presence, his in particular, he doesn't know. It's another of his mysteries.

I love your company because you make me laugh.

I love your company because you take me seriously.

I love your company because you make me happy.

I love your company because you relieve my anxiety.

I love your company because you don't wear a hat.

I love your company because of the shape of a cloud in the sky.

I love your company because you give me porridge.

I don't know why I love your company.

I love your company because quaquaquaqua.

Odo stirs, waking Peter from his grooming hypnosis. He shakes himself. How long have they been on the floor like this? Hard to tell, since he's not wearing his watch.

"Let's go see Senhor Álvaro."

They walk to the café. He not only wants a coffee, he also wants to organize regular deliveries of food. They sit on the patio. When Senhor Álvaro steps out, Peter orders two coffees. When these are brought out, he stands up and says to Senhor Álvaro, "Posso . . . falar . . . com você um momento?"

Of course you can speak with me for a moment, the café owner signals with a nod. To Peter's surprise, Senhor Álvaro pulls up a chair and sits at the table. Peter sits back down. There they are, the three of them. If Odo produced a deck of cards, they could play poker.

Though his language is halting, his message is easy to seize. He sets up with Senhor Álvaro weekly deliveries of oranges, nuts, raisins, and especially figs and bananas. The café owner makes him understand that, in season, he will have no problems getting apples, pears, cherries, berries, and chestnuts from fellow villagers, as well as all manner of vegetables. Eggs and chickens, if his *macaco* cares to eat these, are available year-round, as well as the local sausage. The small grocery store always has canned goods and salted cod, as well as bread, rice, potatoes, and cheeses, both regional and from farther south, and other dairy products.

"Vamos ver o que ele gosta?" says Senhor Álvaro. He gets up and returns from the café with a plate. It has a chunk of soft white cheese on it, drizzled with honey. He places it in front of the ape. A grunt, a quick grasp of the hairy hand — honeyed cheese all gone.

Next Senhor Álvaro brings out a large slice of rye bread on which he has dumped a can of tuna, oil and all.

Same thing. In an instant. With louder grunts.

Lastly Senhor Álvaro tries strawberry yoghurt on the ape. This takes a little longer to vanish, but only because of the gelatinous consistency of the delicacy and the hindrance of the plastic container. It is nonetheless scooped out, licked out, slurped up in no time.

"O seu macaco não vai morrer de fome," Senhor Álvaro concludes.

Peter checks the dictionary. No, indeed, his ape won't starve to death.

Voracious, then — but not selfish. He already knows this. The lovely cut flowers so graciously left on the table by Dona Amélia? Before devouring them, Odo extended a white lily to him.

They return home, but the day beckons. He stocks the backpack and they depart, for the plateau this time. Once they reach it, they turn off the road and strike out into the open. They enter an environment that is, technically, as wild as the jungles of the Amazon. But the soil is thin and impoverished and the air dry. Life treads carefully here. In the folds of the land that are too shallow to shelter forests, there is thicker, spinier vegetation — gorse, heather, and the like — and man and ape have to navigate the maze-like channels in the vegetation to cross it, but out on the savannah, amidst the High Mountains of Portugal proper, only a golden grass abounds, for miles and miles, and on this grass it is easy for them to walk.

It is a land more uniform than the sky. A land where the weather is met directly because it's the only thing happening.

Standing out, both literally and in their effect on them, are the strange boulders they noticed on their way to Tuizelo. They stretch as far as the eye can see. Each boulder reaches three to five times the height of an average person. To walk around one takes a good forty paces. They rise, as elongated as obelisks, or sit, as squat as balls of geologic dough. Each is on its own, with no smaller rocks around it, no cast-off intermediaries. There are only big boulders and short, rough grass. Peter wonders about the origin of these boulders. The

305

frozen ejecta of ancient volcanoes? But how strange the spread, as if a volcano flings chunks of lava like a farmer throws seeds on the ground, with a concern for an even distribution. These boulders are more likely the result of a grinding glacier, he surmises. Being rolled under a glacier might explain their rough surfaces.

He likes the plateau very much. Its openness is breathtaking, intoxicating, exciting. He thinks Clara would enjoy it. They would trek through it hardily. Many years ago, when Ben was small, they went camping in Algonquin Park every summer. The landscape there couldn't be more different from this one, but the effect was similar, a bathing in light, silence, and solitude.

A flock of sheep appears out of the ether, timid, yet as forward-charging as an invading army. At the sight of him, and even more so of Odo, the ovine battalion splits into two around them, giving them a wide berth. For a few minutes the sheep become an amateur orchestra playing the one instrument they know: the bell. Their distracted conductor strides up, delighted to come upon company. He starts on a long conversation, entirely unbothered by the fact that Peter does not speak his language and is accompanied by a large chimpanzee. After a good chewing of the fat, he leaves them to catch up with his flock, which has disappeared as earnestly as it appeared. The silence and the solitude return.

Then they come upon a stream, a noisy fluvial baby swaddled in grass and granite. The stream babbles and bubbles as if it has just woken up. Once crossed and left behind, it vanishes from their senses. Once again the silence and the solitude return.

Odo is taken by the boulders. He sniffs at them with great interest, then often looks around sharply. Has his nose told his eyes something?

Peter's preference is to walk between the boulders, midway, at a distance that allows for perspective. Such is not Odo's impulse. The ape walks from boulder to boulder in a straight line, as if connecting dots in a greater design. A boulder is sniffed, walked around, contemplated, then left behind for the next one, dead ahead. This next boulder might be nearby or far away, at an angle of deflection that is acute or wide. The ape decides with assurance. Peter is not averse to this manner of rambling about the plateau. Each boulder presents its own artistic shapeliness, its own texture, its own civilization of lichen. He wonders only at the lack of variety to the approach. Why not strike out for the open seas, between the shoals? The captain does not brook the suggestion. Unlike in the forest, where each enjoys his liberty, on the plateau the ape inveighs Peter to stay close, grunting and snorting with displeasure if he wanders off. He obediently falls into step.

After one particularly intense sniff at a boulder, Odo decides to conquer it. He scales up its side without effort. Peter is mystified.

"Hey, why this one? What's special about it?" he cries.

The boulder doesn't look any different from any other, or, rather, it looks as mundanely different as they all do from each other. Odo looks down at him. He calls out quietly. Peter decides to give climbing the boulder a try. The feat is trickier for him. He doesn't have the ape's strength. And though the height does not seem great from the ground, as soon as he has climbed a few feet he becomes afraid that he'll fall. But he doesn't fall. The many pockmarks and cracks in the boulder ensure his safety. When he is within reach, Odo grabs him by the shoulder and helps him up.

He scrambles to the middle of the boulder's crown. He sits and waits for his heart to stop knocking about his chest. Odo acts like a vigil on a ship, scanning the far horizon but also scrutinizing their closer surroundings. Peter can tell from his excited tension that he's enjoying the activity. Is it the height, with nothing around to block his view? Has some childhood memory of Africa been evoked? Or is he looking for something specific, a signal from the land, from the distance? Peter doesn't know. He settles down for the duration, remembering Odo's tree-dwelling escapades in Kentucky. He takes in the view, looks at the clouds, feels the wind, studies the varying light. He attends to simple, domestic tasks, since he brought the camping stove — the making of coffee, the preparing of a meal of macaroni and cheese. They spend a pleasant hour or so on top of the boulder.

The climb down is more harrowing than the climb up for him. For Odo, backpack dangling from his mouth, it is a casual amble down.

When they get back home, Peter is exhausted. Odo makes his nest. Nest-building is a quick, casual affair, whether for a nap or for the night. It involves no greater effort than the spinning of a towel or a blanket into a spiral, with a few items thrown in when it is a nighttime nest. Tonight Odo adds one of Peter's shirts and the boots he has worn all day. Odo also varies where he sleeps. So far he has slept on top of the wardrobe; on the floor next to Peter's bed; on top of the chest of drawers; on the living room table; on two chairs brought together; on the kitchen counter. Now he builds his nest on the living room table.

They both go to sleep early.

At dawn the next day Peter tiptoes to the kitchen to make himself a cup of coffee. He settles with the steaming cup in front of Odo, watching him sleep, waiting.

Time passes, like clouds in the sky. Weeks and months go by as if they were a single day. Summer fades to fall, winter yields to spring, different minutes of the same hour.

Contact with Canada lessens. One morning Peter enters the café and Senhor Álvaro hands him a piece of paper. The message is never more than a name, usually Ben's or Teresa's. This time it's the Whip's. Peter goes to the phone at the end of the counter and dials Canada.

"Finally," the Whip says. "I've left three messages in the past week."

"Have you? I'm sorry, they didn't get to me."

"Don't worry about it. How's Portugal?" His voice crackles with distance. A far-off fire on a dark night.

"Good. April is a lovely time here."

The line suddenly becomes terribly clear, like a hot, urgent whisper. "Well, as you know, we're not doing well in the polls."

"Is that so?"

"Yeah. Peter, I've got to be frank. A senator's most fruitful work may very well take place away from the upper chamber, but a senator is nonetheless expected to sit, at least occasionally, in that chamber."

"You're right."

"You haven't been here for over nine months."

"I haven't."

"And you haven't been doing any Senate work."

"Nope. Neither fruitful nor otherwise."

"You just vanished. Except your name is still on the Senate roster. And" — the Whip clears his throat — "you're living with — uh — a monkey."

"An ape, actually."

"The story's made the rounds. It's been in the papers. Listen, I know it was really hard with Clara. Believe me, I feel for what you went through. But at the same time, it's hard to justify to Canadian taxpayers paying your salary as a senator to run a zoo in northern Portugal."

"I completely agree. It's outrageous."

"It's become somewhat of an issue. The party leadership is none too happy."

"I formally resign from the Senate of Canada."

"It's the right thing to do — unless you want to come back, of course."

"I don't. And I'll return my salary since the time I left Ottawa. I haven't even touched it. Been living off my savings. And now I'll have my pension."

"Even better. Can I get all that in writing?"

Two days later there's a new message at the café: Teresa.

"You've resigned. I read it in the papers. Why don't you want to come back to Canada?" she asks him. "I miss you. Come back." The tone of her voice is warm, sisterly. He misses her too, their regular phone calls that were not so long-distance, their dinners together when he lived in Toronto.

But he has not seriously entertained the idea of returning to Canada since he and Odo moved to Tuizelo. The members of his own species now bring on a feeling of weariness in him. They are too noisy, too fractious, too arrogant, too unreliable. He much prefers the intense silence of Odo's presence, his pensive slowness in whatever he does, the profound simplicity of his means and aims. Even if that means that Peter's humanity is thrown back in his face every time he's with Odo, the thoughtless haste of his own actions, the convoluted mess of his own means and aims. And despite the fact that Odo, nearly every day, drags him out to meet fellow members of his species. Odo is insatiably sociable.

"Oh, I don't know."

"I have a friend who's single. She's attractive and really nice. Have you thought about that, about giving love and family another try?"

He hasn't. His heart is expended in that way, of loving the single, particular individual. He loved Clara with every fibre of his being, but now he has nothing left. Or rather, he has learned to live with her absence, and he has no wish to fill that absence; that would be like losing her a second time. Instead he would prefer to be kind to everyone, a less personal but broader love.

As for physical desire, his libido no longer tempts him. He thinks of his erections as being the last of his adolescent pimples; after years of prodding and squeezing, they have finally gone away, and he is unblemished by carnal desire. He can remember the how of sex but not the why.

"Since Clara died, I just haven't been in that space," he says. "I can't —"

"It's your ape, isn't it?"

He doesn't say anything.

"What do you do with it all day long?" she asks.

"We go for walks. Sometimes we wrestle. Mostly we just hang out."

"You *wrestle* with it? Like with a kid?"

"Oh, Ben was never that strong, thank goodness. I come out of it banged and bruised."

"But what's the point of it, Peter? Of the walking, the wrestling, and the hanging out?"

"I don't know. It's" — what is it? — "interesting."

"*Interesting?*"

"Yes. Consuming, actually."

"You're in love with it," his sister says. "You're in love with your ape and it's taken over your life." She is not criticizing, she is not attacking — but there is a slight edge to the observation.

He considers what she's just said. In love with Odo, is he? If love it is, it's an exacting love, one that always demands that he pay attention, that he be alert. Does he mind? Not for one minute. So perhaps it is love. A curious love, if so. One that strips him of any privilege.

He has language, he has cognition, he knows how to tie a shoelace — what of that? Mere tricks.

And a love tinged with fear, still and always. Because Odo is so much stronger. Because Odo is alien. Because Odo is unknowable. It's a tiny, inexpungible parcel of fear, yet not incapacitating nor even a source of much worry. He never feels dread or anxiety with Odo, never anything so *lingering*. It rather goes like this: The ape appears without the least sound, seemingly out of nowhere, and among the emotions Peter feels — the surprise, the wonder, the pleasure, the joy — there is a pulse of fear. He can do nothing about it except wait for the pulse to go away. That is a lesson he has learned, to treat fear as a powerful but topical emotion. He is afraid only when he needs to be. And Odo, despite his capacity to overwhelm, has never given him real cause to be afraid.

And if it is love, then that implies some sort of *meeting*. What strikes him isn't the blurring of the boundary between the animal and the human that this meeting implies. He long ago accepted that blurring. Nor is it the slight, limited movement *up* for Odo to his presumably superior status. That Odo learned to make porridge, that he enjoys going through a magazine, that he responds appropriately to something Peter says only confirms a well-known trope of the entertainment industry, that apes can ape — to our superficial amusement. No, what's come as a surprise is his movement *down* to Odo's so-called lower status. Because that's what has happened. While Odo has mastered the simple human trick of making porridge, Peter has learned the difficult animal skill of doing nothing. He's learned to unshackle himself from the race of time and contemplate time itself. As far as he can tell, that's what Odo spends most of his time doing: being in time, like one sits by a river, watching the water go by. It's a lesson hard learned, just to sit there and *be*. At first he yearned for distractions. He would absent himself in memories, replaying the same old movies in his head, fretting over regrets, yearning for lost happiness. But he's getting better at being in a state of illuminated, sitting-by-a-river repose. So that's the real surprise: not that Odo would seek to be like him but that he would seek to be like Odo.

Teresa is right. Odo *has* taken over his life. She means the cleaning up and the looking after. But it's much more than that. He's been touched by the grace of the ape, and there's no going back to being a plain human being. That is love, then.

"Teresa, I think we all look for moments when things make sense. Here, cut off, I find these moments all the time, every day."

"With your ape?"

"Yes. Sometimes I think Odo *breathes* time, in and out, in and out. I sit next to him and I watch him weave a blanket made of minutes and hours. And while we're on top of a boulder watching a sunset, he'll make a gesture with his hand, just something in the air, and I swear he's working an angle or smoothing a surface of a sculpture whose shape I can't see. But that doesn't bother me. I'm in the presence of a weaver of time and a maker of space. That's enough for me."

314

At the other end of the phone line there's a long silence. "I don't know what to say, big brother," Teresa says at last. "You're a grown man who spends his days hanging out with an ape. Maybe it's counselling you need, not a girlfriend."

With Ben it's not much easier. "When are you coming home?" he asks insistently.

Could it be that his son, beyond the annoyance, is expressing a need to have him home? "This is home," he replies. "This is home. Why don't you come and see me?"

"When I find the time."

Peter never brings up Odo. When Ben found out about Odo, he threw an ice-cold tantrum. After that, it was as if his dad had turned out gay, and it was best not to ask questions lest unsavoury details be revealed.

His granddaughter, Rachel, surprisingly, turns out to be the sweetest. They do well, antipodally. The distance allows her to pour her teenage secrets into his ear. To her, he *is* her gay grandfather, and in the same tone in which she gushes about boys she asks him breathlessly about Odo and their cohabitation. She wants to visit him to meet the short, hairy boyfriend, but she has school and camp, and Portugal is so far away from Vancouver, and, not really mentioned, there is her unwilling mother.

Except for Odo, he is alone.

He subscribes to book clubs and various magazines. He gets his sister to mail him boxes of used paperbacks — colourful, plot-driven stuff — and old magazines. Odo is as big a reader as he is. The arrival of a new

National Geographic is greeted with loud hoots and the slapping of the ground with hands. Odo leafs through the magazine slowly, considering each image. Foldouts and maps are a particular source of interest.

One of Odo's favourite books, discovered early on, is the family photo album. Peter humours Odo and goes through his childhood and early adult years with the ape, recounting to him the story of the Tovy family in Canada, their growing and ageing members, the new additions, their friends, the special occasions remembered by a snapshot. When Peter reaches a certain age, Odo recognizes him with a pant of surprise. He taps on the photo emphatically with a black finger and looks up at him. When Peter turns the pages, going back in time, and points at younger and younger guises of himself, slimmer, darker-haired, taut-skinned, captured in colour and then, earlier, in black-and-white, Odo peers with great intensity. One leap at a time they come to the oldest photo of Peter, taken in Lisbon, before his family's move to Canada, when he was a child of two. The portrait feels from another century to him. Odo stares at it with blinking incredulity.

The few other photos in those opening pages evoke people from his parents' earlier years in Portugal. The largest one, filling a whole page, is a group shot, the people in it stiffly standing in front of an exterior whitewashed wall. Most of these relatives Peter can't identify. His parents must have told him who they were, but he's forgotten. They are from so long ago and so far away that he finds it hard to imagine they were ever truly alive. Odo seems to share his same sense of disbelief, but with a greater desire to believe.

A week later Odo opens the album again. Peter expects him to recognize the Lisbon photo, but the ape looks at it with a blank expression. Only by retracing the journey backwards in time, photo by photo, does he once again come to recognize Peter as a toddler. Which he forgets once more when they look at the album later. Odo is a being of the present moment, Peter realizes. Of the river of time, he worries about neither its spring nor its delta.

It is a bittersweet activity for Peter, to revisit his life. It mires him in nostalgia. Some photos evoke stabs of memory that overwhelm him. One evening, at a shot of young Clara holding baby Ben, he begins to weep. Ben is tiny, red, wrinkled. Clara looks exhausted but ecstatic. The tiniest hand is holding on to her little finger. Odo looks at him, nonplused but concerned. The ape puts the album down and embraces him. After a moment Peter shakes himself. What is this weeping for? What purpose does it serve? None. It only gets in the way of clarity. He opens the album again and stares hard at the photo of Clara and Ben. He resists the easy appeal of sadness. Instead he focuses on the fact, huge and simple, of his love for them.

He starts to keep a diary. In it he records his attempts at understanding Odo, the ape's habits and quirks, the general mystery of the creature. He also notes new Portuguese phrases he's learned. Then there are reflections about his life in the village, the life he's led, the sum of it all.

He takes to sitting on the floor, his back to the wall, on one of the woolen blankets he buys. He reads on the floor, he writes, he grooms and is groomed, sometimes he naps, and sometimes he just sits there, doing nothing at all on the floor. Sitting down and getting up is tiresome, but he reminds himself that it's good exercise for a man his age. Nearly always Odo is right next to him, lightly pressed against him, minding his own ape business — or meddling with his.

Odo rearranges the house. On the kitchen counter, the cutlery is lined up in the open, knives with knives, forks with forks, and so on. Cups and bowls are set on the counter, upside down and against the wall. The same with other objects in the house: They do not belong high up on shelves or hidden in drawers, but closer at hand, lined up against the foot of the wall, in the case of books and magazines, or set here or there on the floor.

Peter puts things back where they belong — he is a neat man — but straightaway Odo sets things right, simian-style. Peter mulls over the situation. He returns his shoes to where he normally has them, next to the door, and the case for his reading glasses back into a drawer, then he moves a few magazines to a different location along the wall. Right behind him, Odo takes the shoes and places them on the same stone tile he placed them on earlier, and he returns the glasses case to its designated tile and the magazines to his chosen spot along the wall. *Aha*, thinks Peter. It's not a mess, then. It's an order of a different kind. Well, it makes the

318

floor interesting. He lets go of his sense of neatness. It's all part of life at a crouch.

He regularly has to return items to the rooms on the ground floor. Ostensibly a space for the keeping and caring of animals and the storage of implements needed for living off the land, it is now filled to the ceiling with the junk of the ages, the villagers being pathological hoarders from one generation to the next. Odo loves the animal pen. It is a treasure trove that endlessly exercises his curiosity.

And beyond, there is the village, a place of a thousand points of interest for Odo. The cobblestones, for example. The flower boxes. The many stone walls, each easily climbable. The trees. The connecting roofs, of which Odo is particularly fond. Peter worries that the villagers will mind having an ape puttering atop their houses, but most don't even notice, and those who do, stare and smile. And Odo moves with nimble sure-footedness — he doesn't clatter about, displacing tiles. His favourite roof is that of the old church, from which he has a fine view. When he's up there, Peter sometimes goes inside the church. It's a humble place of worship, with bare walls, a plain altar, an awkward crucifix blackened by time, and, at the other end of the aisle, beyond the last pew, a shelf bookended by vases of flowers, the requisite shrine to some dusty saint of Christendom. He has no interest in organized religion. On his first visit, a two-minute once-over satisfied him. But the small church is a quiet spot, and it offers the same advantage as the café: a place to properly sit. He usually parks himself at a pew near a window from which he can see the downspout pipe Odo will take to descend from the roof. He's never come into the church with Odo, not wanting to risk it.

Mostly, though, in the village, it is the people who interest Odo. They have lost their wariness. He is particularly well disposed towards women. Was the Peace Corps volunteer who brought him over from Africa a woman? Did a female lab technician make a positive impression on him in his early years? Or is it simple biology? Whatever the reason, he always reaches out to women. As a result, the village widows who at first shrank away from him, retreating into surliness, transform into the ones who are the most devoted to him. Odo responds amiably to all of them, making faces and sounds that comfort them and open them up further. It's a good fit, the short, stooped women dressed in black and the short, stooped animal with the black coat. From a distance, one might be forgiven for mistaking one for the other.

Likely as not, the women — indeed, all the villagers — engage Odo in spirited conversation first. Then, when they turn to him, they speak in the simplest, most childish language, their voices raised, their expressions and gestures exaggerated, as if he were the village idiot. After all, he doesn't *fala* Portuguese.

Dona Amélia becomes Odo's closest female disciple. Soon there is no longer any need for them to leave the house when she comes to clean. In fact, it is the opposite: Her weekly visit is a time when Odo happily stays in and Peter can go out and run errands. From the moment she arrives, the ape remains at her side as she moves about the house doing her light duties, which lengthen in time while costing him no more in escudos. He has the most immaculate, nearly barren house in Tuizelo, though peculiarly ordered, since Dona Amélia respects the ape's odd sense of tidiness. All the while she's working, she chatters away to Odo in mellifluous Portuguese.

She tells Peter that Odo is "um verdadeiro presente para a aldeia" — a true gift to the village.

He makes his own observations about the village. The richest villager is Senhor Álvaro; as a shopkeeper, he has the most disposable income. Then come the villagers who own and cultivate land. Next come the shepherds, who own their flocks. Last come the workers, who own nothing except perhaps their own houses and who work for those who have work to give them. They are the poorest in the village and have the most freedom. Peopling every level of this hierarchy are family members young and old, all of whom work to some degree, according to their capacity. The priest, an amiable man named Father Eloi, stands apart, since he owns nothing but has business with everyone. He moves across all levels. Overall, the villagers of Tuizelo are monetarily poor, though this is not immediately apparent. In many ways they are autarkic, growing their own food, both animal and vegetable, and making and mending their own clothes and furniture. Barter — of goods and services — is still a common practice.

He observes an odd local tradition he has seen nowhere else. He first notices it at a funeral, as the procession makes its way through the village to the church: A number of the mourners are walking in reverse. It appears to be an expression of grief. Along the street, across the square, up the stairs, backwards they move, their grave faces tilted down as they dwell on their sorrow. Regularly they turn their heads to look over their shoulders to direct themselves, but others also assist them by reaching out with a hand. He is intrigued by the custom and inquires about it. Neither Dona Amélia nor anyone else seems to know where it comes from or why exactly it is done.

The ape's preferred spot in the village is the café. The villagers become used to seeing them sitting at an outdoor table, enjoying *cafés com muito leite*.

One wet day he and Odo are standing in front of the café. They have just come back from a long walk. They're both cold. The outdoor tables and chairs are puddled with rain. He hesitates. Senhor Álvaro is at the counter. He sees them and raises his hand and gestures that they should come in.

They settle in a corner of the room. The establishment is typical of its sort. There is a counter with the saucers piled up, each with its small spoon and package of sugar, ready to receive a cup of coffee. Behind the counter, the shelves are lined with bottles of wine and liqueur. In front of the counter are the round tables with their complement of metal chairs. Lording over the room is a television, which is always on but thankfully with the volume turned quite low.

To Peter's surprise, Odo is not engrossed by the television. He watches the small men chasing after the tiny white ball or, preferably, the couples looking at each other with great intensity — the ape prefers soaps to sports — but only for a short time. Of greater interest is the warm room and the real live people in it. The television is dethroned while the patrons look at Odo and Odo looks at them. Meanwhile, Peter and Senhor Álvaro catch each other's eyes. They smile. Peter lifts two fingers to place their usual order. Senhor Álvaro nods. After that, they become habitués at the café, even down to where they sit.

He and Odo often go on long hikes. Odo never again asks to be carried, as he did once in Oklahoma. Now the ape's energy is unflagging. But he still regularly takes refuge in trees, perching himself high up on a branch. Peter can only wait patiently below. For being so quiet in the forest — except when they find clearings of spongy moss, perfect for merry tussles — they see badgers, otters, weasels, hedgehogs, genets, wild boar, hares and rabbits, partridges, owls, crows, ibis, jays, swallows, doves and pigeons, other birds, once a shy lynx, and another time a rare Iberian wolf. Each time Peter thinks that Odo will go after them, a crashing chase through the undergrowth, but instead he stands stock-still and stares. Despite the evident wealth of the forest, they both prefer to explore the open plateau.

One afternoon, returning from a walk, they come upon two dogs by a stream, just outside the village. The village is full of shy mutts. The two dogs are drinking. Odo observes them with keen interest, unafraid. The dogs do not look unhealthy, but they are lean. When they notice the man and the chimpanzee, they tense. Odo hoots quietly and approaches them. The dogs crouch and the hair goes up on their backs. Peter feels uneasy, but the dogs are not particularly big and he knows the ape's strength. Still, a violent confrontation would be ugly. Before anything can happen, the dogs turn and bolt.

A few days later he is sitting on a chair on the landing at the top of the stairs when he sees two snouts poke through the gate. It is the same two dogs. Odo is next to him, propped on top of the landing wall. He sees the dogs too. Immediately Odo descends to the courtyard to open the gate. The dogs move away. He hoots quietly and crouches low. They eventually advance into the courtyard. Odo is delighted. By fits and starts, with *hoos* and whines, the space between a chimpanzee and two dogs begins to lessen until Odo dips a hand onto the back of the larger of the two dogs, a black mongrel. The ape starts to groom it. Peter suspects there is much to groom on these dogs that spend their entire lives outdoors. The black dog is fully crouched, nervous but submissive, and Odo works its fur gingerly, starting at the base of the tail.

Peter goes inside. A few minutes later, when he looks out again from the kitchen window, the dog has rolled over, exposing its belly. Odo stands half-risen over it, his hair standing on end, his teeth bared, his hand hovering claw-like over the dog's belly. The dog is whimpering and its eyes are fixed on the hairy hand. Peter is alarmed. Odo looks terrifying. *What's happening?* Just a moment ago the nervous canine was being reassured by Odo in a friendly and assiduous manner. Now it has rolled over, exposing its soft

324

underside, in effect saying to the ape that it is so abjectly afraid that it will not defend its life. He moves to the living room window. *What should I do? What should I do?* He has visions of Odo gutting the howling dog. Aside from what the poor dog might feel, what about the villagers? It's one thing shrieking on occasion and breaking the odd cup and vagabonding about roofs — but disembowelling a dog is another. The village dogs are not coddled the way North American pets are, but they nonetheless have owners who feed them scraps and casually care for them. As he crosses the second living room window, he sees that the dog's raised rear legs are twitching and that the animal is convulsing on the ground. He reaches the door and leaps onto the landing, a cry in his throat. Something makes him look a moment longer. The picture changes. He lets his outstretched hand drop. Odo is tickling the dog. It is shaking with canine mirth while the ape laughs along.

After that, more dogs begin to show up. Finally, in all, a pack of about twelve. Peter never feeds them; still, every morning they creep into the courtyard and wait quietly, not a whine or a whimper coming from them. When Odo appears at a window or on the landing, they become both excited and settled, odd to say. Odo perhaps joins them, but he might also ignore them. Attention makes the dogs stay, lack of it eventually makes them go away, only to show up the next morning, with hopeful expressions on their faces.

The interactions between the ape and the dogs vary greatly. At times they bask on the warm courtyard stones, their eyes closed, the only motion the rise and fall of their breathing, the only sound the odd snuffle. Then Odo raises an arm and taps a dog, showing his lower teeth in a grin. Or stands up and puts on a display, swaggering about erect on his legs, slapping and stamping the ground, huffing, hooting, and grunting. Tap, grin, and display all signal the same thing: It's time to play! Play involves either Odo chasing the dogs, or the dogs chasing Odo, or, more often than not, everyone chasing everyone. It's a rough, joyous riot in which dogs run, turn, twist, roll, jump up, scamper off, while Odo dashes or dodges, pounces or brakes, bounces off walls or scrambles across them, the whole accompanied by a deafening uproar of canine barks and primate shrieks. The ape is exceptionally agile. There is no corner from which he can't escape, no dog that he can't knock off its feet. Watching him makes Peter realize how much Odo restrains himself when they wrestle together. If Odo played with him the way he plays with the dogs, Peter would be in the hospital. The fun lasts until Odo falls over, breathless. The dogs, panting and dripping slobber, do the same.

Peter notes with interest the arrangement of the animals when they are at rest. Every time it is a different pattern. Nearly always one dog lies asleep with its head on Odo, while the others are nearby, piled up on each other or laid out this way and that. Sometimes Odo looks up at him and funnels his lips in a soundless *hoo* shape, the way he did when they first met, to salute him without waking up the dogs.

But diversion though it is, this play with the dogs is at times hair-raising, literally. There is always a feel of edginess, of a disquiet easily summoned. Every dog's scamper starts with a cower. Peter wonders why the dogs always come back.

One day the animals are lying about in the mild Portuguese sun, seemingly without a care in the world, when an uproar erupts, with much whining and barking. Odo is at the centre of the turmoil. He displays, but not for play this time. With a terrifying, teeth-baring *wraaaa* cry, he throws himself upon a dog who has mysteriously offended. The poor canine becomes the recipient of a full-on thrashing. The harsh slaps and blows that land on its body echo in the courtyard. The dog whines pitifully in a high pitch. These pleas for mercy are mostly drowned out by Odo's roar and by the other dogs, who are watching in a fever of anxiety, whining and howling and twitching and jerking about in circles with their tails tightly coiled between their legs.

Peter watches from the landing, petrified. The thought occurs to him: What if one day Odo finds fault with him?

Then it passes. After one last terrific slap, Odo throws the dog aside and moves away, his back turned to the assaulted animal. The dog lies prostrate, visibly trembling. The other dogs fall silent, though they still stare with their hair standing straight up and their eyes bulging. Odo's breathing slows, and the dog's trembling becomes intermittent. Peter thinks the incident is over, that each animal will now move off to lick its real or imaginary wounds. But a curious thing happens. The offending dog painfully rights itself.

Stomach resting flat against the ground, it crawls over to Odo and begins a very low whine. It does not let up until Odo, without turning his head, brings out a hand and touches it. When he takes his hand back, the dog resumes its whining. Odo returns his hand to the dog's body. After a while, the ape turns and moves closer and starts to groom the dog. The dog rolls onto its side and whines in a quieter tone. Odo's hands work across its body. When one side is done, he lifts the dog and gently turns it over to groom its other side. When he is done, he lies right next to it and they both fall asleep.

The next morning, that very dog, limping, looking frazzled and bedraggled, drags itself into the courtyard. Even more surprising, when Odo joins the dogs, he flops himself down beside it, as if nothing untoward had happened the previous day. And for the next ten days, they are together all the time, in play as well as in rest.

Peter realizes that every conflict between Odo and the dogs ends in this way, with all tensions revealed and expelled, after which nothing remains, nothing lingers. The animals live in a sort of emotional amnesia centered in the present moment. Turmoil and upheaval are like storm clouds, bursting dramatically but exhausting themselves quickly, then making way once more for the blue sky, the permanent blue sky.

The dogs cower yet come back every day. Is he any different? He's no longer palpably frightened of Odo. All the same, the ape does fill a room. He can't be ignored. Peter's heart at times still quickens upon seeing him. But it's not fear, that's not what he would call it anymore. It's more a kind of nerve-racking awareness that doesn't make him want to flee the ape's presence but, on the contrary, to address it, because Odo always addresses *his* presence. After all, as far as he can tell, Odo invariably appears in a room because Peter is in it to start with. And whatever he might be doing before Odo walks in does not fill his consciousness the way dealing with Odo does. Always there is that gaze that swallows him. Always, without diminishment, there is that sense of wonder.

There, has he not answered the question about why the dogs return every day? Is there anything else that so captivates their minds, their being? No, there isn't. So every morning they make their way back to the house — and every morning he is glad to wake not far from Odo.

The dogs carry lice, which they pass on to Odo. Peter uses a fine comb to get the vermin and their eggs out. And Odo finally gets the grooming challenge he yearns for when Peter too gets lice.

A few weeks later they're returning from a walk in the fields of boulders. The weather is lovely, the land discreetly exuberant in its springtime greening, but Peter is tired and he's looking forward to resting. A coffee would be nice. They head for the café. He sits down wearily. When his coffee arrives, he nurses it. Odo sits quietly.

Peter gazes outside — and it's as if a pane of frosted glass has shattered and he sees with clarity what is out there. He can't believe his eyes. Ben, his son Ben, is standing in the square, having just stepped out of a car.

THE HIGH MOUNTAINS OF PORTUGAL

Emotions congest him. Astonishment, worry — is something wrong? — but mainly pure, simple parental delight. His son, his son has come! It's been nearly two years since he's seen him.

He gets up and rushes out. "Ben!" he calls.

Ben turns and sees his father. "Surprise!" he says, embracing him. He too is quite clearly glad. "I got two weeks off — decided to see what you're up to in this godforsaken place."

"I've missed you so much," Peter says, smiling. His son looks so dazzlingly young and vigorous.

"Jesus Christ!" Ben pulls back, a look of panic on his face.

Peter turns. It is Odo, who is rapidly knuckle-walking up to them, his face alight with curiosity. Ben looks like he might turn and run.

"It's all right. He won't hurt you. He's just coming to say hi. Odo, this is my son, Ben."

Odo comes up and sniffs at Ben and pats his leg. Ben is evidently apprehensive.

"Welcome to Tuizelo," Peter says.

"They bite your face off," Ben says. "I read about it."

"This one won't," Peter replies.

Over the next ten days, Peter shares his life with his son. They talk, they walk. They obliquely mend relations, atoning for previous distance by acts of attentive proximity. The whole time Ben worries about Odo, about being attacked by him. He catches Peter wrestling with Odo once, a vaulting, turbulent circus. Peter hopes his son will join in, but he doesn't — he holds back, his expression tense.

One morning, as they are cleaning up after breakfast, Odo appears beside them in the kitchen holding a book.

"What have you got there?" Peter asks.

Odo hands it to him. It's an old Portuguese hardcover of an Agatha Christie murder mystery, the cover garish, the pages limp and yellow. The title is *Encontro com a morte*.

"Would that be *A Meeting with a Dead Man?*" asks Ben.

"Or *A Meeting with Death?* I'm not sure," Peter replies. He checks the copyright page, which gives the correct title in English. "Ah. It's *Appointment with Death*. Maybe we should improve our Portuguese by reading it."

"Why not?" Ben says. "You first."

Peter fetches the dictionary and the three of them settle on the floor, the father and the ape easily and comfortably, the son less so, and more warily. Peter reads aloud the first paragraphs, practicing not only his comprehension but his pronunciation:

'Compreendes que ela tem de ser morta, não compreendes?'

A pergunta flutuou no ar tranquilo da noite, parecendo pairar por um momento até se afastar na escuridão, na direção do Mar Morto.

Hercule Poirot deteve-se um minuto com a mão no fecho da janela. Franziu o sobrolho e fechou-a num gesto decidido, impedindo assim a entrada do nocivo ar noturno. Hercule Poirot crescera a acreditar que o melhor era deixar o ar exterior lá fora, e que o ar noturno era especialmente perigoso para a saúde.

Odo is enthralled. He stares at the page, at Peter's lips. What is it that the ape likes? The sound of his strong accent? The novelty of extended speech pronounced in a modulated voice, rather than the monosyllables of regular talk? Whatever it is, while Peter reads aloud, Odo sits still, listening intently, tucked up against him. Peter senses that Ben is also intrigued, perhaps by the Portuguese too, but more likely by his father's interaction with the ape.

Peter reads three pages before he gives up.

"So, how is it?" Ben asks.

"I understand it in the main, but it comes through a fog." Peter turns to Odo. "Where did you find this book?" he asks.

Odo points to the window. Peering out, Peter sees an open suitcase in the courtyard. He guesses its provenance: the junk-filled animal pen. He and Ben walk down, Odo in tow. Odo has a special fondness for suitcases he has unearthed, the mystery of them, what they open to reveal — which, most often, is bedsheets and old clothes. This one, however, at a glance, proves to hold an odd mix of things. Peter and Ben return one by one the contents that Odo has strewn about: a square of red cloth, some old coins, a knife and a fork, a few tools, a wooden toy, a pocket mirror, two dice, a candle, three playing cards, a black dress, a flute, and an oyster shell. There is an envelope that is closed but not sealed. It seems empty, but Peter opens it, just to check. He is puzzled to find some coarse black hairs. He touches them — they are stiff and dry. He would swear they were Odo's. "What game are you playing?" he asks the ape.

Peter is about to close the suitcase when Ben says, "Wait, you missed this."

He hands him a single sheet of paper. The sheet is sparsely covered, only four lines of a squarish black handwriting:

Rafael Miguel Santos Castro, 83 anos, da aldeia de Tuizelo, as Altas Montanhas de Portugal

Peter stares. Memory is nudged, facts are tentatively recalled, connections made, until a remembrance bursts into focus: Rafael Miguel Santos Castro — *Grandpa Batista's brother?* Above, to the right, appears a date. *1 Janeiro, 1939.* That timeline seems about right, his death then at age eighty-three. The letterhead announces *Departamento de Patologia, Hospital São Francisco, Bragança.* He is chilled. After Clara, he wants nothing more to do with pathology ever again. Nonetheless, his eyes can't help but read the two lines written beneath Rafael Castro's basic information:

Encontrei nele, com meus próprios olhos, um chimpanzé e um pequeno filhote de urso.

The words are unmistakable: *I found in him, with my own eyes, a chimpanzee and a small bear cub.* Beneath

333

are a semilegible signature and an official stamp that states the pathologist's name clearly: Dr. Eusebio Lozora.

"What's it say?" Ben asks.

"It says . . ." Peter's voice trails off as he opens the envelope again and rubs the black hairs between his fingers. He glances at the contents of the suitcase. What story is this suitcase trying to tell? What is his maternal great-uncle Rafael's pathology report — if that is what it is — doing in this house? He has made no inquiries about the family home. The discovery of his tenuous link to the village will generate noise and attention, which he doesn't care for. He does not feel like a returning native. More pertinently, like Odo, he is happy to live in the present moment, and the present moment has no past address. But now he wonders: Could this be the house? Could that be the explanation for its dereliction and its availability?

"Well?" his son prompts.

"Sorry. It seems to be some sort of pathology report. This doctor claims — how shall I put it? — that he found a chimpanzee and a bear cub in a man's body. It's what it says. Look, it's the same word: *um chimpanzé.*"

"*What?*" Ben shoots Odo an incredulous glance.

"Clearly, there is a metaphor here, a Portuguese idiom, that I'm not understanding."

"Clearly."

"What's also strange is the name of the deceased. This is a puzzle for Dona Amélia perhaps. Here, let's bring the suitcase upstairs."

"I'll do it. Don't strain yourself."

They head for Dona Amélia's. Peter brings along the family photo album, which Odo is happy to carry. Dona Amélia is at home. She greets the two men with gracious calm, smiles at the ape.

"Minha casa — a casa de quem?" Peter asks her.

"Batista Reinaldo Santos Castro," she answers. "Mas ele morreu há muito tempo. E a sua família" — she makes a sweeping motion with the back of her hand, accompanied by a quick blowing motion — "mudou-se para longe. As pessoas vão-se embora e nunca mais voltam."

Batista Santos Castro — it is so, then. Unexpectedly, without any effort, the transient renter has found the house where he was born.

"What'd she say?" Ben whispers.

"She said that the man who lived in the house died a long time ago and his family — I didn't understand her exact words, but her gesture was pretty clear — his family left, went away, abandoned the village, something like that. People leave and they never come back." He turns to Dona Amélia again. "E seu irmão?" he adds. *And his brother?*

"O seu irmão?" Dona Amélia suddenly seems more interested. "O seu irmão Rafael Miguel era o pai do anjo na igreja. O papá! O papá!" she emphasizes. *His brother is the father of the angel in the church. The daddy! The daddy!*

The angel in the church? Peter hasn't a notion what she's talking about, but at the moment he's interested only in the family connection. He takes the photo

335

album from Odo and opens it, prepared to throw away his anonymity.

"Batista Santos Castro — sim?" he says, pointing at a man in the first photo in the album, the group shot.

Dona Amélia seems astounded that he should have a photo of Batista in his possession. "Sim!" she says, her eyes opening wide. She grabs the album and devours the photo with her eyes. "Rafael!" she exclaims, pointing at another man. She points again. "E sua esposa, Maria." Then her breath is cut short. "É ele! A criança dourada! Outra foto dele!" she cries. *It's him! The Golden Child! Another photo of him!* She is pointing at a small child, a mottled speck of sepia peeking from behind his mother. Peter has never seen Dona Amélia so excited.

"Batista — meu . . . avô," he confesses. He points to Ben, but he doesn't know the Portuguese word for "great-grandfather".

"A criança dourada!" Dona Amélia practically shouts. She couldn't care less that Batista was his grandfather and his son's great-grandfather. She takes hold of his sleeve and drags him along. They head for the church. *The angel in the church*, she said. As they go, her excitement is contagious. Other villagers, mainly women, join them. They arrive at the church as a gaggle, in a flurry of rapid Portuguese. Odo seems pleased with the commotion, adds to it by hooting happily.

"What's happening?" Ben asks.

"I'm not sure," replies Peter.

They enter and take a left down the aisle, away from the altar. Dona Amélia stops them at the shrine set up at the back of the church, on the north wall. In front of the shelf book-ended by its vases of flowers stands a long three-tiered flower box filled with sand. The sand is studded with thin candles, some burning, most burned out. Any neatness in the arrangement is disturbed by the dozens and dozens of bits of paper that cover the shelf and the floor, some rolled up into scrolls, others neatly folded into squares. Peter never came close enough on his previous visits to see this scattered litter. A framed photo is fixed to the wall just above the middle of the shelf, a black-and-white head shot of a little boy. A handsome little boy. Staring straight out with a serious expression. His eyes are unusual, of such a pallor that, amidst the chiaroscuro of the photo, they match the white wall that is the background. The photo looks very old. A young child from a long time ago.

Dona Amélia opens the photo album. "É ele! É ele!" she repeats. She points to the child on the wall and to the child in the album. Peter looks and examines, tallying eyes with eyes, chin with chin, expression with expression. Yes, she's right; they are one and the same. "Sim," he says, nodding, bemused. Mutters of amazement come from the crowd. The album is taken from his hands and is passed around, everyone seeking personal confirmation. Dona Amélia is aglow with rapture — while keeping a sharp eye on the photo album.

After a few minutes she takes firm hold of it again. "Pronto, já chega! Tenho que ir buscar o Padre Eloi." *Okay, that's enough. I must get Father Eloi.* She rushes off.

337

Peter squeezes between people to get closer to the photo on the wall. The Golden Child. Again his memory is stirred. Some story his parents told. He searches his mind, but it is like the last leaves of autumn, blown away, dispersed. There is nothing he can seize, only the vague memory of a lost memory.

He suddenly wonders: *Where's Odo?* He sees his son on the edge of the group of villagers and the ape at the other end of the church. He extricates himself and he and his son make their way over to Odo. Odo is looking up and grunting. Peter follows with his eyes. Odo is staring at the wooden crucifix looming above and behind the altar. He appears to want to climb onto the altar, exactly the sort of scene Peter has feared would happen in the church. Mercifully, at that moment, Dona Amélia bustles back in with Father Eloi and hurries towards them. Her excitement distracts Odo.

The priest invites them to adjourn to the vestry. He places a thick folder on a round table and indicates that they should sit. Peter has had only cordial relations with the man, without ever feeling that the priest was trying to draw him into the flock. He takes a seat, as does Ben. Odo sets himself on a window ledge, watching them. He is silhouetted by daylight and Peter cannot read his expression.

Father Eloi opens the folder and spreads quantities of papers across the table — documents handwritten and typed, and a great number of letters. "Bragança, Lisboa, Roma," the priest says, pointing to some of the letterheads. The explanations come patiently, as Peter's consultations of the dictionary are frequent. Dona

Amélia at times gets emotional, with tears brimming in her eyes, then she smiles and laughs. The priest is more steady in his intensity. Ben stays as still and silent as a statue.

When they leave the church, they go straight to the café.

"Gosh, and I thought Portuguese village life would be dull," Ben says, nursing his espresso. "What was that all about?"

Peter is unsettled. "Well, for starters, we've found the family home."

"You're kidding? Where is it?"

"It happens to be the house I'm already living in."

"*Really?*"

"They had to put me in an empty one, and the house has been empty since our family left. They never sold it."

"Still, there are other empty houses. What an amazing coincidence."

"But listen — Father Eloi and Dona Amélia also told me a story."

"Something about a little boy a long time ago, I got that."

"Yes, it happened in 1904. The boy was five years old and he was Grandpa Batista's nephew, your great-grandfather's nephew. He was away from the village with his father — my great-uncle Rafael — who was helping out on a friend's farm. And then the next moment the boy was miles away, by the side of a road, dead. The villagers say his injuries matched exactly the injuries of Christ on the Cross: broken wrists, broken ankles, a deep gash in his side, bruises and lacerations. The story spread that an angel had plucked him from the field to bring him up to God, but the angel dropped him by accident, which explains his injuries."

"You say he was found by the side of a road?"

"Yes."

"Sounds to me like he was run over."

"As a matter of fact, two days later a car appeared in Tuizelo, the first ever in the whole region."

"There you go."

"Some villagers right away believed there was a link between the car and the boy's death. It quickly became such a story in the region that it was all documented. But there was no proof. And how did the boy, who was next to his father one moment, end up in front of a car miles away the next?"

"There must be some explanation."

"Well, they took it as an act of God. Whether it was by God's direct hand or by means of this strange new transportation device, God was behind it. And there's more to the story. O que é dourado deve ser substituído pelo que é dourado."

"What's that?"

"It's a local saying. *What is gilded should be replaced by what is gilded*. They say God was sorry about the angel dropping the boy and so He gave him special powers. Apparently any number of infertile women have prayed to the boy and shortly afterwards become pregnant. Dona Amélia swears it happened to her. It's a legend in these parts. More than that. There's a process afoot to have him declared *venerable* by Rome, and because of all the fertility stories attributed to him, they say he has a good chance."

"Is that so? We have an uncle who's a saint and you live with an ape — that's quite the extended-family situation we've got going."

"No, venerable, two notches down."

"Sorry, I can't seem to tell my venerables from my saints."

"Apparently, the little boy's death turned the whole village upside down. Poverty is a native plant here. Everyone grows it, everyone eats it. Then this child appeared and he was like living wealth. Everyone loved him. They call him the Golden Child. When he died, Father Eloi told me, they say days turned to grey and all colour drained from the village."

"Well, sure. It would be incredibly upsetting, a little boy's death."

"At the same time, they talk about him as if he's still alive. He *still* makes them happy. You saw Dona Amélia — and she never even met him."

"And how is this boy related to us again, exactly?"

"He was my mother's cousin — and therefore my second cousin, or maybe my first cousin once removed, I'm not sure. At any rate, he's family. Rafael and his wife, Maria, had their son very late, which means my mother was older than her cousin. She'd have been a teenager when he was born — as was Dad. So my parents both knew him. That's what got Dona Amélia so excited. And I vaguely remember a story my parents told me when I was young, about the death of a child in the family. They would start it but never finish it — like a terrible war story. They always shut up at a particular point. I think they left the village before he was revived, so to speak. I suspect they never knew about that."

"Or they didn't care to believe it."

"Could be that. Like the boy's mother. It seems the boy's father and mother stood on different sides of the story, the father believing in the boy's powers, the mother not."

"That's a sad story," Ben says. "And what was the deal about the chimpanzee in the body?"

"I don't know. They didn't bring that up."

Odo is sitting on a chair next to them, holding a coffee in his hands, looking out the window.

"Well, there's yours, sipping his cappuccino like a real European."

When they return to the house, Peter goes from room to room, wondering if he feels differently about it. Will the walls now exude memories? Will he hear the pitter-patter of small bare feet on the floor? Will young parents appear, holding a small child in their arms, his future still shrouded in mystery?

No. This isn't home. Home is his story with Odo.

That evening, over a simple meal, he and Ben go through the photo album again together and try to make sense of Dr. Lozora's curious autopsy report on Rafael Miguel Santos Castro. Ben shakes his head in confusion.

The next afternoon they walk across the cobbled square to the little church. The day is as soft as a caress. They return to the candlelit shrine and the picture of the clear-eyed child. Ben mutters something about being related to "religious royalty". They move to a pew near the front of the church to sit together.

Suddenly Ben looks startled. "Dad!" he says, pointing to the crucifix.

"What?"

"The cross there — it looks like a chimpanzee! I'm not kidding. Look at the face, the arms, the legs."

Peter studies the crucifix. "You're right. It does look like one."

"This is crazy. *What's with all the apes?*" Ben looks around nervously. "Where's yours, by the way?"

"Over there," Peter replies. "Stop fretting about him."

As they leave the church Peter turns to his son. "Ben, you asked me a question. I don't know what's with all the apes. All I know is that Odo fills my life. He brings me joy."

Odo grins and then lifts his hands and claps a few times, producing a muffled sound, as if quietly calling them to attention. Father and son both watch, transfixed.

"That's a hell of a state of grace," Ben says.

They wander home but right away Odo makes to strike out on a walk. Ben decides not to come. "I'll wander around the village, continue reconnecting with my ancestors," he says. It takes Peter a moment to realize that there is no irony in Ben's statement. He would gladly join his son, but he is loyal to Odo, so he waves at Ben, grabs the backpack, and follows Odo out.

Odo sets off for the boulders. They walk silently, as usual, across the savannah. Peter trails behind without paying much attention. Abruptly Odo stops in his tracks. He rises on his legs and sniffs, his eyes trained on a boulder just ahead. A bird is standing on top of it, eyeing them. The hairs on Odo's body rise till they are straight up on end. He sways from side to side. When he returns to all fours, he jerks himself up and down on his arms with great excitement, though he is strangely quiet. The next moment he takes off at a full run for the boulder. In the blink of an eye he has skipped to the top of it. The bird has long since fluttered away. Peter is perplexed. What was it about the bird that so excited him?

He thinks of staying put and letting Odo have his play on the boulder. He would like nothing more than to lie down and have a nap. But Odo turns and waves at him from his high perch. Clearly Peter is expected to follow. He makes his way to the boulder. At its base, he composes himself for the climb, taking a few deep breaths. When he feels ready, he looks up.

He is startled to see Odo directly above him, clinging to the rock fully upside down. Odo is staring at him furiously with his reddish-brown eyes while he beckons him with a hand, the long dark fingers curling and uncurling rhythmically in a manner that Peter finds mesmerizing. At the same time, Odo's funnel-shaped lips are putting out a silent but urgent *hoo, hoo, hoo.* Odo has never done anything like this, neither in the boulder fields nor anywhere else. To be so imperatively summoned by the ape, and therefore so forcefully acknowledged — he is shocked. He feels as if he's just been birthed out of nonexistence. He is an individual being, a unique being, one who has been asked *to climb*. Energized, he reaches for the first handhold. Though riddled with holes and bulges, the side of the boulder is quite vertical and he strains to pull his weary body up. As he climbs, the ape retreats. When they reach the top, Peter sits down heavily, panting and sweating. He doesn't feel well. His heart is jumping about his chest.

He and Odo are side by side, their bodies touching. He looks at the way he has come. It is a sheer drop. He looks the other way, in the direction Odo is facing. The view is the same as always, though losing nothing for its familiarity: a great sweep of savannah all the way to the horizon, covered in golden-yellow grass, punctuated by dark boulders, a vista of spare beauty except for the sky, which is in full late-afternoon bloom. The volume of air above them is tremendous. Within it, the sun and the white clouds are playing off each other. The abundant light is unspeakably gorgeous.

He turns to Odo. The ape will be gazing up and away, he thinks. He is not. Odo is looking down and close-by. He is in a frenzy of excitement, but oddly contained, with no riotous pant-hooting or wild gestures, only a bobbing up and down of the head. Odo leans forward to look at the foot of the boulder. Peter cannot see what he is looking at. He nearly cannot be bothered to find out — he needs to rest. Nonetheless he lies on his front and inches forward, making sure his hands have a good grip. A fall from such a height would cause grievous injury. He peeks over the edge of the boulder's summit to see what is drawing Odo's attention down below.

What he sees does not make him gasp, because he doesn't dare make a sound. But his eyes stay fixed and unblinking and his breath is stilled. He now understands Odo's strategy in navigating the boulder fields, why the ape goes from boulder to boulder in a straight line rather than wandering in the open, why he climbs and observes, why he asks his clumsy human companion to stay close.

Odo has been seeking, and now Odo has found.

Peter stares at the Iberian rhinoceros standing at the foot of the boulder. He feels he is looking at a galleon from the air, the body massive and curved, the two horns rising like masts, the tail fluttering like a flag. The animal is not aware that it is being observed.

Peter and Odo look at each other. They acknowledge their mutual amazement, he with a stunned smile, Odo with a funnelling of the lips, then a wide grin of the lower teeth.

The rhinoceros flicks its tail and occasionally gives its head a little roll.

Peter tries to estimate its size. It is perhaps ten feet in length. A well-built, big-boned beast. The hide grey and tough-looking. The head large, with a long, sloping fore-head. The horns as unmistakable as a shark's fin. The moist eyes surprisingly delicate, with long eyelashes.

The rhinoceros scratches itself against the rock. It lowers its head and sniffs at the grass but does not eat. It twitches its ears. Then, with a grunt, it sets off. The ground shakes. Despite its heft, the animal moves

346

swiftly, heading straight for another boulder, then another, then another, until it has disappeared.

Peter and Odo don't move for the longest time, not for fear of the rhinoceros, but because they don't want to lose anything of what they've just seen, and to move might bring on forgetfulness. The sky is a blaze of blues and reds and oranges. Peter finds himself weeping silently.

Finally he pushes himself back onto the top of the boulder. It is an effort to sit up. His heart is battering within him. He sits with his eyes closed, his head hung low, trying to breathe evenly. It's the worst heartburn he's ever had. He groans.

Odo, to his hazy surprise, turns and hugs him, one long arm wrapping around his back, supporting him, the other enveloping his raised knees, on which his arms are resting. It's a firm full-circle embrace. Peter finds it comforting and relaxes into it. The ape's body is warm. He places a trembling hand on Odo's hairy forearm. He feels Odo's breathing against the side of his face. He raises his head and opens his eyes to cast a sideways glance at his friend. Odo is looking straight at him. *Puff, puff, puff*, softly, go the ape's breaths against his face. Peter struggles a little, but not to get away, more an involuntary action.

He stops moving, lifeless, his heart clogged to stillness. Odo does nothing for several minutes, then moves back, gently laying him flat on the boulder. Odo stares at Peter's body and coughs mournfully. He stays next to him for a half hour or so.

The ape rises and drops off the rock, barely breaking his fall with his hands and feet. On the ground he moves out into the open. He stops and looks back at the boulder.

Then he turns and runs off in the direction of the Iberian rhinoceros.

Other titles published by Ulverscroft:

ABLE SEACAT SIMON

Lynne Barrett-Lee

Simon is discovered in the Hong Kong docks in 1948 and smuggled on board the HMS *Amethyst* by a British sailor who takes pity on the malnourished kitten. The young cat quickly establishes himself as the chief rat-catcher in residence, while also winning the hearts of the entire crew. Then the *Amethyst* is ordered to sail up the Yangtse, and tragedy strikes as it comes under fire from communist guns. Many of the crew are killed, and Simon is among those who are seriously wounded. With the help of the ship's doctor, the brave cat makes a full recovery and is soon spending time with the injured men in the sick bay, purring and keeping their spirits up. Soon, news of Simon's heroism spreads worldwide — but it is still a long journey back to England . . .

HOW TO MEASURE A COW

Margaret Forster

Tara Fraser leaves London to start a new life in a Cumbrian town selected at random. She plans to obliterate her past, which contains a shocking event that had serious consequences, by becoming a completely different personality from her previous volatile self. She is going to be quiet — even dull, and very private. But one of her new neighbours, Nancy, is intrigued by her, and wants to become her friend. Equally determined not to be discarded are three old friends who Tara feels let her down when she most needed them. Tara fights to keep herself to herself; but can she do it? And does she really want to? Slowly, reluctantly, she discovers that her attempts to suppress the past and reject other people are downright dangerous . . .

EXPOSURE

Helen Dunmore

London, November, 1960: The Cold War is at its height. Spy fever fills the newspapers, and the political establishment knows how and where to buy its secrets. When a highly sensitive file goes missing, Simon Callington is accused of passing information to the Soviets, and arrested. His wife, Lily, suspects that his imprisonment is part of a cover-up, and that more powerful men than Simon will do anything to prevent their own downfall. She knows that she too is in danger, and must fight to protect her children. But what she does not realise is that Simon has hidden vital truths about his past, and may be found guilty of another crime that carries with it an even greater penalty . . .

THE STORY OF LAND AND SEA

Katy Simpson Smith

August, 1793: On the hot, humid coast of North Carolina, nine-year-old Tabitha sits with her father John, to hear stories of her mother Helen, who died in childbirth. John longs to sail the sea as he did before the war, knowing he must instead stay on steady land for his daughter. But when Tab catches yellow fever, her life hanging in the balance, he turns to what he knows and steals her onto a boat bound for Bermuda . . . On the same coast twenty years earlier, Helen is given a slave girl for her tenth birthday, and soon the girls are confidantes. It's an enduring friendship until the arrival of John, a pirate-turned-soldier. Helen finds she must decide between a life of security on the family plantation, and a sea adventure with the man she loves . . .